G...
STORIES
FROM THE
PRAIRIES

GREAT STORIES FROM THE PRAIRIES

Edited by Birk Sproxton

Red Deer Press

Copyright © 2000 Birk Sproxton
Published in the United States in 2001
3rd printing 2003
All rights reserved. No part of this publication may be reproduced, stored in a retrieval system or transmitted, in any form or by any means, without the prior written permission of Red Deer Press or, in case of photocopying or other reprographic copying, a licence from CANCOPY (Canadian Copyright Licensing Agency), 1 Yonge Street, Suite 1900, Toronto, ON M5E 1E5, fax (416) 868-1621.

The Publishers
Red Deer Press
813, MacKimmie Library Tower
2500 University Drive N.W.
Calgary Alberta Canada T2N 1N4

Credits
Edited for the Press by Birk Sproxton
Cover and text design by Duncan Campbell
Cover photograph courtesy of Masterfile
Printed and bound in Canada by AGMV/Marquis for Red Deer Press

Acknowledgments
Financial support provided by the Canada Council, the Department of Canadian Heritage, the Alberta Foundation for the Arts, a beneficiary of the Lottery Fund of the Government of Alberta, and the University of Calgary.

THE CANADA COUNCIL | LE CONSEIL DES ARTS
FOR THE ARTS | DU CANADA
SINCE 1957 | DEPUIS 1957

Canadian Cataloguing in Publication Data
Main entry under title:
Great stories from the Prairies
ISBN 0-88995-223-X
1. Short stories, Canadian (English)—Prairie Provinces.* 2. Canadian fiction (English)—20th century.* 1. Sproxton, Birk.
PS8329.5.P7G73 2000   C813'.01089712   C00-9110600-7
PR9198.2.P682G73 2000

5 4 3 1

Contents

BIRK SPROXTON, *Introduction: Energy and Delight* 11

FREDERICK PHILIP GROVE, *Snow* 21

W.O. MITCHELL, *Melvin Arbuckle's First Course in Shock Therapy* 47

SINCLAIR ROSS, *One's a Heifer* 57

MARGARET LAURENCE, *Horses of the Night* 73

KEN MITCHELL, *The Great Electrical Revolution* 94

JACK LUDWIG, *Requiem for Bibul* 104

MERNA SUMMERS, *The Skating Party* 117

SANDRA BIRDSELL, *The Flood* 135

FRED WAH, *Diamond Grill* 148

SHARON BUTALA, *Eden* 155

RUDY WIEBE, *Where Is the Voice Coming From?* 168

GREG HOLLINGSHEAD, *In the Sixties* 178

EDNA ALFORD, *Head* 190

KRISTJANA GUNNARS, *Kolla, Ticks* 193

W.D. VALGARDSON, *God Is Not a Fish Inspector* 200

Guy Vanderhaeghe, *Man Descending* 213

Aritha van Herk, *Waiting for the Rodeo* 227

Armin Wiebe, *Boss in the House* 240

Meeka Walsh, *Light Reading* 250

Joan Crate, *Betwixt and Between* 258

David Bergen, *Hey* 265

Claire Harris, *It is a matter of fact* 271

David Arnason, *A Girl's Story* 287

Carol Shields, *Mrs. Turner Cutting the Grass* 295

Bonnie Burnard, *Ten Men Respond to an Air-Brushed Photograph of a Nude Woman Chained to a Bull* 305

Alford, Edna. "Head." From *The Garden of Eloise Loon*. Oolichan Books, 1986. Reprinted by permission of the publisher.

Arnason, David. "A Girl's Story." From *The Circus Performers' Bar*. Talonbooks, 1984. Reprinted by permission of the publisher.

Bergen, David. "Hey." From *Sitting Opposite My Brother*. Turnstone Press, 1993. Reprinted by permission of the publisher.

Birdsell, Sandra. "The Flood." From *Agassiz: A Novel in Stories*. Turnstone Press, 1991. Reprinted by permission of the publisher.

Burnard, Bonnie. "Ten Men Respond to an Air-Brushed Photograph of a Nude Woman Chained to a Bull." From *Casino & Other Stories*. A Phyllis Bruce Book, published by HarperPerennialCanada. Copyright 1994. All rights reserved. Reprinted by permission of the publisher.

Butala, Sharon. "Eden." From *Queen of the Headaches*. Coteau Books, 1985. Reprinted by permission of the publisher.

Crate, Joan. "Betwixt and Between." From *Boundless Alberta,* edited by Aritha van Herk. NeWest Press, 1993. Reprinted by permission of the author.

Grove, Frederick Philip. "Snow." From *Over Prairie Trails*. First published in 1922. Reprinted by McClelland and Stewart Limited in 1957 as Number 1 in the New Canadian Library Series. Malcolm Ross, General Editor.

Gunnars, Kristjana. "Kolla, Ticks." From *Sundogs: Stories from Saskatchewan,* edited by Robert Kroetsch. Coteau Books, 1980. A later version appeared in Kristjana Gunnars, *The Axe's Edge*. Press Porcépic, 1983. Reprinted by permission of the author.

Harris, Claire. "It is a matter of fact." From *Drawing Down a Daughter*. Goose Lane Editions, 1992. Reprinted by permission of the publisher.

Hollingshead, Greg. "In the Sixties." From *White Buick*. Oolichan Books, 1992. Reprinted by permission of the publisher.

Laurence, Margaret. "Horses of the Night." From *A Bird in the House* © 1989. Used by permission, McClelland & Stewart, Inc. *The Canadian Publishers*.

Ludwig, Jack. "Requiem for Bibul." Reprinted by permission of the author.

Mitchell, Ken. "The Great Electrical Revolution." Copyright © Ken Mitchell; first published in *Prism International,* 1970; reprinted by arrangement with Bella Pomer Agency Inc.

Mitchell, W.O. "Melvin Arbuckle's First Course in Shock Therapy." From *An Evening With W.O. Mitchell,* selected and edited by Barbara and Ormond Mitchell. Copyright © 1997. Used by permission, McClelland & Stewart, Inc. *The Canadian Publishers.*

Ross, Sinclair. "One's a Heifer." From *The Lamp at Noon and Other Stories.* Copyright © 1989. Used by permission, McClelland & Stewart, Inc. *The Canadian Publishers.*

Shields, Carol. "Mrs. Turner Cutting the Grass." From *Various Miracles.* Copyright © 1985. Reprinted by permission of Random House Canada.

Summers, Merna. "The Skating Party." From *North of the Battle.* Douglas & McIntyre, copyright © 1988. Reprinted by permission of the author.

Valgardson, W.D. "God Is Not a Fish Inspector." From *God Is Not a Fish Inspector,* Oberon, 1975. Reprinted by permission of the publisher.

van Herk, Aritha. "Waiting for the Rodeo." From *Alberta Bound: Thirty Stories by Alberta Writers,* edited by Fred Stenson. NeWest Press, 1986. Reprinted by permission of the author.

Vanderhaeghe, Guy. "Man Descending." From *Man Descending*, copyright © 2000. Used by permission, McClelland & Stewart, Inc. *The Canadian Publishers.*

Wah, Fred. "Diamond Grill." From *Diamond Grill.* NeWest Press, 1996. Reprinted by permission of the publisher.

Walsh, Meeka. "Light Reading." From *Prairie Fire* Volume 20 no. 2 (Summer 1999). Reprinted by permission of the author.

Wiebe, Armin. "Boss in the House." From *Made in Manitoba,* edited by Wayne Tefs, Turnstone Press, 1990, and *The Salvation of Yasch Siemans*, Turnstone Press, 1984. Reprinted by permission of the publisher.

Wiebe, Rudy. "Where Is the Voice Coming From?" From *River of Stone.* Copyright © 1995. Reprinted by permission of Vintage Canada.

Editor's Acknowledgment

The editor thanks the writers and publishers represented here for their kind support and cooperation, and the staff of Red Deer Press for their generous support throughout the development of this project. Special thanks, as well, to Maria Haubrich for her diligent and enthusiastic work as research assistant.

Editor's Note

To acknowledge the significance of the writing styles reproduced in this collection, all originally published spellings, punctuation and grammar have been preserved.

Introduction

ENERGY AND DELIGHT

BIRK SPROXTON

THE STORIES PRESENTED HERE SPAN THE LAST ONE HUNDRED years, cross the three Prairie provinces and display the formal variety and vitality of short fiction. They offer, by turn, charm and insight, weight and lightness, humour and reflection. Above all, they are engaging and rereadable.

While all of the stories in this collection are *from* the Prairies, many are also *of* the Prairies. You will find traditional images of the Prairie landscape—swirling wind and dust and snow, vast expanses of land and sky. Nestled against these is the rich circuitry of city life, small towns, the parklands, boreal forests and the great inland sea of Lake Winnipeg. You will get to know a Chinese café from the inside and contend with the urgencies of a massive flood. These stories also represent the formal variety of short fiction written in the last one hundred years, from conventional realism to magic realism, from short short stories to metafictions and fabulations. The great riches in these stories shine with Prairie experiences, events, people, places and icons.

Not surprisingly, the writers here have been much celebrated for their work and have won a special place among Canadians and others around the world. Nearly half are Governor General's Literary Award winners or nominees, not to mention the other provincial, national and international honours they have earned. As a group, they give special insight into Prairie and Canadian culture. Constraints of resources, space, authors' wishes and publishing contracts mean that deserving stories have been left aside for other times and anthologies. But what you have in hand are twenty-five excellent short stories that offer much to enjoy.

Whether you have a favourite Prairie writer or theme, or you simply want to know more about the Prairies, you will travel your own path through this book. Whatever path you choose, you will hear these voices resonate with that extraordinary body of stories that make up the Prairie archive.

Historical Span

The stories are arranged according to the approximate time of setting rather than to the time of composition, birthdate of the author or publication date. This grouping yields three clusters, recognizing that the boundary lines are not clean and fast.

The stories by Frederick Philip Grove, Sinclair Ross, W.O. Mitchell, Jack Ludwig, Ken Mitchell and Margaret Laurence give insight into the period between the turn of the century and World War II. Interestingly, each piece also works largely within the set of conventions we describe as realism. Allowing for the exaggerations of the comic stories, they all deal with recognizable characters caught in plausible circumstances with the story delivered in a language that mimics everyday life. Many deal with the Great Depression. The charming wit of Ludwig's urban tale "Requiem for Bibul" and the broad humour of Mitchell's "The Great Electrical Revolution" suggest that the Depression was not always depressing, no more than Prairie life is an unending battle with dust and snow among the gophers and grain elevators.

A second group, speaking of the immediate post-World War II period, includes greater formal variety. Here, for example, we find Merna Summers' "The Skating Party" (which also engages an earlier time since the skating party took place in a time before the telling of the story), Sandra Birdsell's "The Flood" and Fred Wah's biographical fiction from *Diamond Grill*.

In a series of amazing turns, "The Skating Party" reveals itself to be a story not so much about a farm family north of the Battle River in Alberta as about making choices and the internal battles that having made choices continues to entail. Sandra Birdsell's story reminds us that much of the Prairie was once the bottom of Glacial Lake Agassiz and that the lake lurks just beneath the surface, waiting for an opportunity to spring forth again. Fred Wah's story foregrounds the dynamics of Chinese–Canadian life. Wah makes us aware of the continual pull between these two cultures as the story moves forward not in a traditional time-bound line, but through the colour and suggestion of the moment. In formal terms Wah's text borders on the prose poem (just as Frederick Philip Grove's "Snow" borders on the personal reflective essay), and it speaks of the richness of experimental writing from the Prairies.

A third cluster includes the 1960s and beyond. The decade of the 1960s marked a turning point in the twentieth century. The world became a global village, to echo Marshal McLuhan, and new alliances emerged as people moved more readily, electronically or by jet plane, from one place to another. New relationships were fashioned between men and women, and among families and cultures. There was renewed feminism, new directions in moral and social inquiry and recharged realism in fiction. Greg Hollingshead's story, in the details of sex and drugs, and in the manner and language of narration, captures the ethos of the period. The decade also marked a great expansion in Canadian Prairie cities and corresponding growth in universities. On the literary front, expansion continued through the next decade. The 1970s saw the emergence of small literary publishing houses, new magazines and new interest among readers in writing rooted in the local.

Pastoral themes persisted during the period, even in the face of continued urbanization, though such themes are often touched with irony, as in the ending of Sharon Butala's "Eden." This turn to rural life renewed and reinvigorated Prairie writing.

Kristjana Gunnars' "Kolla, Ticks" represents a changing literary landscape that was beginning to reach northward, recognizing new and old voices and dramatizing city life. Gunnars' narrator finds herself in the boreal forest north of the Prairies reflecting on the ways that stories grow out of particular places. Most importantly for this collection, the Prairies from the 1960s forward saw the emergence of many new and brilliant writers such as Aritha van Herk, Guy Vanderhaeghe, David Arnason, Carol Shields and David Bergen to name only a handful. They take short fiction in new directions.

Apart from these historical clusters, the stories here talk among themselves to create the larger story of time and place that good anthologies always generate.

House and Horse

Frederick Philip Grove's "Snow," a chapter from *Over Prairie Trails,* presents the adventures of a narrator who heads across the Prairie sea in winter to visit his wife and daughter at "home," many miles distant from where he teaches during the week. He plays Odysseus to his wife's Penelope. He drives horses to her house, an instance of the horse–house dichotomy that Robert Kroetsch describes as generating the energy lines of Prairie fiction. The horse enables travel; the house gives motivation and purpose.

Later in the century the male hero undergoes a dramatic revision. The vision of the lonely male testing his strength against natural forces is given a delightful turn in Armin Wiebe's "Boss in the House." Poor bumbling Yasch Siemens finds himself in charge of the kitchen as his wife, Oata, takes over the care, feeding and operation of her huge self-propelled combine. She goes to town for parts, she greases and oils the combine and she works the fields while Yasch reluctantly learns to wash dishes. Not even his mother will help him with the challenges of the kitchen.

Father and daughter contend for possession of a house in W.D. Valgardson's "God Is Not a Fish Inspector." Fusie Bergman violates fishing laws so he may make small gifts of fresh fish to the people in the Old Folk's Home, a place he dreads. But his daughter, Emma, has designs on the house they share, and she attempts to steer him into the "home" he does not want.

This is a story that bristles with images of doorways and thresholds and with questions about authority and houses.

W.O. Mitchell's comic performance piece "Melvin Arbuckle's First Course in Shock Therapy" works another variation on the horse–house energy line. The boys in this story find energy in dynamite "borrowed" from the railroad (highway of the iron horse) while the house becomes an outhouse, a building subject to what Mitchell calls "Newton's Law of Falling Backhouses." The results are nothing less than hilarious. But the story reads more seriously along its historical dimensions as it reaches back to the Riel Rebellion— Grandfather in his aged confusion believes himself to be pursued by the ghost of Gabriel Dumont. Or is it, for him, Dumont in the flesh?

The story illustrates Mitchell's prowess as storyteller in the oral tradition, a tradition that includes his years on radio, especially in the 1950s, and the years of performances delivered in the last decades of the twentieth century. Mitchell had a canny sense of history as well as impeccable timing in his performances, and those delights can be savoured in the Melvin Arbuckle story.

Sinclair Ross's "One's a Heifer" speaks of coming of age during dark times, and once again the horse–house motif is a significant narrative thread. The barn and the house clearly take on symbolic force for the young man in quest of the heifer. He has discovered something on that isolated farm, but he does not know what to call it. As readers we are carried with him into a darkness and confusion that becomes a glimmering light only at the end.

Margaret Laurence's "Horses of the Night" is set primarily in the Depression, and Laurence's narrator, Vanessa Macleod, looks both ways in time, back to World War I and ahead to the horrors of World War II. And since the story is told in the past tense, the narrative dramatically implicates the time of the telling, sometime in the mid-1960s, when the fictional Vanessa is in her 40s. But the great beauty of the story lies in Vanessa's self-discovery as she learns to read her world, herself and her family with depth and sensitivity. To undertake these readings, she must unravel the meaning of various horses and houses, including the house of the body that her cousin, Chris, in his madness, vacates so as to fool the officers who would send him into battle.

City and Country

In looking at the world, Prairie people often assume the sky; they assume a great dome of light overhead. They tend to have what Margaret Laurence calls "horizon-accustomed eyes." This theme arises in the warm quirkiness of Edna Alford's "Head," a story that addresses issues of seeing and not seeing, a dilemma we find explored in other fiction (notably, Laurence's novel *The Stone Angel*). Alford's narrator returns to Saskatchewan from a British Columbia city only to discover that the head he had left behind (on a rock in the sun) has been picked clean and now wears wire-rimmed spectacles with no glass in them, an eyeless head with no corrective lenses. The puzzling head prompts us to compare visions of country and city. Alford's short short story, like the Greg Hollingshead story, can be read as a *character,* an ancient form that presents an incisive version, like an image on a coin, of a single quality or trait or habit (the quality of seeing or the quality of a decade). So, too, Jack Ludwig's story gives us Bibul, a character immersed in the multicultural milieu of northend Winnipeg. Ludwig insists this is not a pastoral tale, though his careful detailing of Bibul's city life establishes a sense of innocence that we often associate with a country existence.

Other urban stories refer extensively to space and light, and link Prairie cities into a larger fabric of distant cultures. In "Light Reading," Meeka Walsh brilliantly teases out the narrative of an artist drawn to light as inexorably as she is drawn to compose herself. The story traces the intersection of city streets, light and self, and we participate in that process of her making. Her character, composed by and of light, crosses country borders in finding herself. Joan Crate's story "Betwixt and Between" explores the magic of fantasy and the imagination even as she takes us from one country to another, one world to another. Crate stitches us into a domestic Prairie world with a family playing in the snow and prompts us to reimagine the landscape, the generally peaceful interactions among neighbours and even traditional religious values in the blend of cultures she projects. Crate's story, too, gives us striking insight into the character of her narrator.

Introduction: Energy and Delight 17

The Making of Fiction

Rudy Wiebe, Claire Harris and Sandra Birdsell bring a special urgency to questions about the connections between history and fiction, quotidian facts and legend. "Where is the Voice Coming From?" asks Wiebe in a story we might now describe as historiographical metafiction. Harris powerfully shows how autobiographical, historical and legendary stories overlap and intersect. Her conclusion is compelling. You have to think that what she has given us is *story.* Carol Shields discovers stories in the small rituals of domestic life. "Mrs Turner Cutting the Grass" reveals a world of stories swirling with the mower blades on an ordinary afternoon. David Arnason's "A Girl's Story" plays with the notion that setting determines character, and with other conventions of storytelling. His narrator gets a bit cranky, but in the face of his overall geniality and generosity, we forgive him.

Aritha van Herk's "Waiting for the Rodeo" and Guy Vanderhaeghe's "Man Descending" foreground the tangled negotiations among men and women that mark the 1970s and the years since. Van Herk takes us into magic and carnival and the construction of the self, issues explored in different ways by David Arnason and Carol Shields. Vanderhaeghe's story shows the persistent strengths of the realist mode of fiction: sharp dialogue, clearly constructed scenes, recognizable characters. David Bergen, too, in "Hey" works within the conventions of realism, and readers will sense a moral urgency in his story that calls to mind the stories by Rudy Wiebe and Frederick Philip Grove in this collection. From another angle, Bergen's focus on the woman's body contrasts with the virtuoso costuming and peeling of the self we find in van Herk or in Arnason and Shields.

The last story in this collection was published in the last years of the twentieth century. Bonnie Burnard's "Ten Men Respond to an Air-Brushed Photo of a Nude Woman Chained to a Bull" invites you to look many times (ten times at least) at a single (faked) artifact. Burnard also encourages us to consider the interactions of men and women, to look at our looking habits and the moral issues they provoke. She delightfully contrasts the habits of mind of her characters. Her story therefore brings to the fore questions of reading itself and invites us to look and to read again and again—an invitation that this book also makes to you.

IN MAKING A PATHWAY through this book, you will experience many pleasures—surprise in meeting new stories, assurance in old favourites, delight in the many tales of city and country, house and horse, and women and men. While this collection looks back to stories past, I hope it also piques your desire to seek out future stories from the everchanging Prairie anthology.

GREAT STORIES FROM THE PRAIRIES

SNOW

Frederick Philip Grove

THE BLIZZARD STARTED ON WEDNESDAY MORNING. It was that rather common, truly western combination of a heavy snowstorm with a blinding northern gale—such as piles the snow in hills and mountains and makes walking next to impossible.

I cannot exactly say that I viewed it with unmingled joy. There were special reasons for that. It was the second week in January; when I had left "home" the Sunday before, I had been feeling rather bad; so my wife would worry a good deal, especially if I did not come at all. I knew there was such a thing as its becoming quite impossible to make the drive. I had been lost in a blizzard once or twice before in my lifetime. And yet, so long as there was the least chance that horse-power and human willpower combined might pull me through at all, I was determined to make or anyway to try it.

At noon I heard the first dismal warning. For some reason or other I had to go down into the basement of the school. The janitor, a highly efficient but exceedingly bad-humoured cockney, who was dissatisfied with all things Canadian because "in the old country we do things differently"—whose sharp tongue was feared by many, and who once remarked to a lady teacher in the most casual way, "If you was a lidy, I'd wipe my boots on you!"—this selfsame janitor, standing by the furnace, turned slowly around, showed his pale and hollow-eyed face, and smiled a withering and commiserating smile. "Ye won't go north this week," he remarked—not without sympathy, for somehow he had taken a liking to me, which even prompted him off and on to favor me with caustic expressions of what he thought of the school board and the leading citizens of the town. I, of course, never encouraged him in his communicativeness which seemed to be just what he would expect, and no rebuff ever goaded him into the slightest show of resentment. "We'll see," I said briefly. "Well, Sir," he repeated apodeictically, "ye won't." I smiled and went out.

But in my classroom I looked from the window across the street. Not even in broad daylight could you see the opposite houses or trees. And I knew that, once a storm like that sets in, it is apt to continue for days at a stretch. It was one of those orgies in which Titan Wind indulges ever so often on our western prairies. I certainly needed something to encourage me, and so, before leaving the building, I went upstairs to the third story and looked through a window which faced north. But, though I was now above the drifting layer, I could not see very far here either; the snowflakes were small and like little round granules, hitting the panes of the windows with little sounds of "ping–ping"; and they came, driven by a relentless gale, in such numbers that they blotted out whatever was more than two or three hundred yards away.

The inhabitant of the middle latitudes of this continent has no data to picture to himself what a snowstorm in the north may be. To him snow is something benign that comes soft-footedly over night, and on the most silent wings like an owl, something that suggests the sleep of Nature rather than its battles. The further south you go, the more, of course, snow loses of its aggressive character.

At the dinner table in the hotel I heard a few more disheartening words. But after four I defiantly got my tarpaulin out and carried it to the stable. If I had to run the risk of getting lost, at least I was going to prepare for it. I had once stayed out, snow-bound, for a day and a half, nearly without food and altogether without shelter; and I was not going to get thus caught again. I also carefully overhauled my cutter. Not a bolt but I tested it with a wrench; and before the stores were closed, I bought myself enough canned goods to feed me for a week should through any untoward accident the need arise. I always carried a little alcohol stove, and with my tarpaulin I could convert my cutter within three minutes into a windproof tent. Cramped quarters, to be sure, but better than being given over to the wind at thirty below!

More than any remark on the part of friends or acquaintances one fact depressed me when I went home. There was not a team in town which had come in from the country. The streets were deserted: the stores were empty. The north wind and the snow had the town to themselves.

On Thursday the weather was unchanged. On the way to the school I had to scale a snowdrift thrown up to a height of nearly six feet, and, though it was beginning to harden, from its own weight and the pressure of the wind, I still broke in at every step and found the task tiring in the extreme. I did my work, of course, as if nothing oppressed me, but in my heart I was beginning to face the possibility that, even if I tried, I might fail to reach my goal. The day passed by. At noon the school-children, the teachers, and a few people hurrying to the post-office for their mail lent a fleeting appearance of life to the streets. It nearly cheered me; but soon after four the whole town again took on that deserted look which reminded me of an abandoned mining camp. The lights in the store windows had something artificial about them, as if they were merely painted on the canvas-wings of a stage-setting. Not a team came in all day.

On Friday morning the same. Burroughs would have said that the weather had gone into a rut. Still the wind whistled and howled through the bleak, dark, hollow dawn; the snow kept coming down and piling up, as if it could not be any otherwise. And as if to give notice of its intentions, the drift had completely closed up my front door. I fought my way to the school and thought things over. My wife and I had agreed, if ever the weather should be so bad that there was danger in going at night, I was to wait till Saturday morning and go by daylight. Neither one of us ever mentioned the possibility of giving the attempt up altogether. My wife probably understood that I would not bind myself by any such promise. Now even on this Friday I should have liked to go by night, if for no other reason, then for the experience's sake; but I reflected that I might get lost and not reach home at all. The horses knew the road—so long as there was any road; but there was none now. I felt it would not be fair to wife and child. So, reluctantly and with much hesitation, but definitely at last, I made up my mind that I was going to wait till morning. My cutter was ready—I had seen to that on Wednesday. As soon as the storm had set in, I had instinctively started to work in order to frustrate its designs.

At noon I met in front of the post-office a charming lady who with her husband and a young Anglican curate constituted about the only circle of real friends I had in town. "Why!" I exclaimed, "what takes you out into this storm, Mrs. ——?" "The desire," she gasped against the wind and yet in her inimitable way, as if she were asking a favour, "to have you come to our house for tea, my friend. You surely are not going this week?" "I am going to go tomorrow morning at seven," I said. "But I shall be delighted to have tea with you and Mr. ——." I read her at a glance. She knew that in not going out at night I should suffer—she wished to help me over the evening, so I should not feel too much thwarted, too helpless, and too lonesome. She smiled. "You really want to go? But I must not keep you. At six, if you please." And we went our ways without a salute, for none was possible at this gale-swept corner.

After four o'clock I took word to the stable to have my horses fed and harnessed by seven in the morning. The hostler had a tale to tell. "You going out north?" he enquired although he knew perfectly well I was. "Of course," I replied. "Well," he went on, "a man came in from ten miles out; he was half dead; come, look at his horses! He says, in places the snow is over the telephone posts." "I'll try it anyway," I said. "Just have the team ready. I know what I can ask my horses to do. If it cannot be done, I shall turn back, that is all."

When I stepped outside again, the wind seemed bent upon shaking the strongest faith. I went home to my house across the bridge and dressed. As soon as I was ready, I allowed myself to be swept past stable, past hotel and post-office till I reached the side street which led to the house where I was to be the guest.

How sheltered, homelike and protected everything looked inside. The hostess, as usual, was radiantly amiable. The host settled back after supper to talk old country. The Channel Islands, the French Coast, Kent and London—those were from common knowledge our most frequently recurring topics. Both host and hostess, that was easy to see, were bent upon beguiling the hours of their rather dark-humoured guest. But the howling gale outside was stronger than their good intentions. It was not very long before the conversation got around—reverted, so it seemed—to stories of storms, of being lost, of nearly freezing. The boys were sitting with wide and eager eyes, afraid they might be sent to bed before the feast of yarns was over. I told one or two of my most thrilling escapes, the host contributed a few more, and even the hostess had had an experience, driving on top of a railroad track for several miles, I believe, with a train, snowbound, behind her. I leaned over. "Mrs. ——," I said, "do not try to dissuade me. I am sorry to say it, but it is useless. I am bound to go." "Well," she said, "I wish you would not." "Thanks," I replied and looked at my watch. It was two o'clock. "There is only one thing wrong with coming to have tea in this home," I continued and smiled; "it is so hard to say good-bye."

I carefully lighted my lantern and got into my wraps. The wind was howling dismally outside. For a moment we stood in the hall, shaking hands and paying the usual compliments; then one of the boys opened the door for me; and in stepping out I had one of the greatest surprises. Not far from the western edge of the world there stood the setting half-moon in a cloudless sky; myriads of stars were dusted over the vast, dark blue expanse, twinkling and blazing at their liveliest. And though the wind still whistled and shrieked and rattled, no snow came down, and not much seemed to drift. I pointed to the sky, smiled, nodded and closed the door. As far as the drifting of the snow went, I was mistaken, as I found out when I turned to the north, into the less sheltered street, past the post-office, hotel and stable. In front of a store I stopped to read a thermometer which I had found halfways reliable the year before. It read minus thirty-two degrees. . . .

It was still dark, of course, when I left the house on Saturday morning to be on my way. Also, it was cold, bitterly cold, but there was very little wind. In crossing the bridge which was swept nearly clean of snow I noticed a small, but somehow ominous-looking drift at the southern end. It had such a disturbed, lashed-up appearance. The snow was still loose, yet packed just hard enough to have a certain degree of toughness. You could no longer swing your foot through it: had you run into it at any great speed, you would have fallen; but as yet it was not hard enough to carry you. I knew that kind of a drift; it is treacherous. On a later drive one just like it, only built on a vastly larger scale, was to lead to the first of a series of little accidents which finally shattered my nerve. That was the only time that my temerity failed me. I shall tell you about that drive later on.

At the stable I went about my preparations in a leisurely way. I knew that a supreme test was ahead of myself and the horses, and I meant to have daylight for tackling it. Once more I went over the most important bolts; once more I felt and pulled at every strap in the harness. I had a Clark foot-warmer and made sure that it functioned properly. I pulled the flaps of my military fur cap down over neck, ears and cheeks. I tucked a pillow under the sweater over my chest and made sure that my leggings clasped my furlined moccasins well. Then, to prevent my coat from opening even under the stress of motion, just before I got into the cutter, I tied a rope around my waist.

The hostler brought the horses into the shed. They pawed the floor and snorted with impatience. While I rolled my robes about my legs and drew the canvas curtain over the front part of the box, I weighed Dan with my eyes. I had no fear for Peter, but Dan would have to show to-day that he deserved the way I had fed and nursed him. Like a chain, the strength of which is measured by the strength of its weakest link, my team was measured by Dan's pulling power and endurance. But he looked good to me as he danced across the pole and threw his head, biting back at Peter who was teasing him.

The hostler was morose and in a biting mood. Every motion of his seemed to say, "What is the use of all this? No teamster would go out on a long drive in this weather, till the snow has settled down; and here a schoolmaster wants to try it."

At last he pushed the slide doors aside, and we swung out. I held the horses tight and drove them into that little drift at the bridge to slow them down right from the start.

The dawn was white, but with a strictly localised angry glow where the sun was still hidden below the horizon. In a very few minutes he would be up, and I counted on making that first mile just before he appeared.

This mile is a wide, well levelled road, but ever so often, at intervals of maybe fifty to sixty yards, steep and long promontories of snow had been flung across—some of them five to six feet high. They started at the edge of the field to the left where a rank growth of shrubby weeds gave shelter for the snow to pile in. Their base, alongside the fence, was broad, and they tapered across the road, with a perfectly flat top, and with concave sides of a most delicate, smooth, and finished looking curve, till at last they ran out into a sharp point, mostly beyond the road on the field to the right.

The wind plays strange pranks with snow; snow is the most plastic medium it has to mould into images and symbols of its moods. Here one of these promontories would slope down, and the very next one would slope upward as it advanced across the open space. In every case there had been two walls, as it were, of furious blow, and between the two a lane of comparative calm, caused by the shelter of a clump of brush or weeds, in which the snow had taken refuge from the wind's rough and savage play. Between these capes of snow there was an occasional bare patch of clean swept ground. Altogether there was an impression of barren, wild, bitter-cold windiness about the aspect that did not fail to awe my mind; it looked inhospitable, merciless, and cruelly playful.

As yet the horses seemed to take only delight in dashing through the drifts, so that the powdery crystals flew aloft and dusted me all over. I peered across the field to the left, and a curious sight struck me. There was apparently no steady wind at all, but here and there, and every now and then a little whirl of snow would rise and fall again. Every one of them looked for all the world like a rabbit reconnoitering in deep grass. It jumps up on its hindlegs, while running, peers out, and settles down again. It was as if the snow meant to have a look at me, the interloper at such an early morning hour. The snow was so utterly dry that it obeyed the lightest breath; and whatever there was of motion in the air, could not amount to more than a cat's-paw's sudden reach.

At the exact moment when the snow where it stood up highest became suffused with a rose-red tint from the rising sun, I arrived at the turn to the correction line. Had I been a novice at the work I was engaged in, the sight that met my eye might well have daunted me. Such drifts as I saw here should be broken by drivers who have short hauls to make before the long distance traveller attempts them. From the fence on the north side of the road a smoothly curved expanse covered the whole of the road allowance and gently sloped down into the field at my left. Its north edge stood like a cliff, the exact height of the fence, four feet I should say. In the centre it rose to probably six feet and then fell very gradually, whaleback fashion, to the south. Not one of the fence posts to the left was visible. The slow emergence of the tops of these fence posts became during the following week, when I drove out here daily, a measure for me of the settling down of the drift. I believe I can say from my observations that if no new snow falls or drifts in, and if no very considerable evaporation takes place, a newly piled snowdrift, undisturbed except by wind-pressure, will finally settle down to about from one third to one half of its original height, according to the pressure of the wind that was behind the snow when it first was thrown down. After it has, in this contracting process, reached two thirds of its first height, it can usually be relied upon to carry horse and man.

The surface of this drift, which covered a ditch besides the grade and its grassy flanks, showed that curious appearance that we also find in the glaciated surfaces of granite rock and which, in them, geologists call exfoliation. In the case of rock it is the consequence of extreme changes in temperature. The surface sheet in expanding under sudden heat detaches itself in large, leaflike layers. In front of my wife's cottage up north there lay an exfoliated rock in which I watched the process for a number of years. In snow, of course, the origin of this appearance is entirely different; snow is laid down in layers by the waves in the wind. "Adfoliation" would be a more nearly correct appellation of the process. But from the analogy of the appearance I shall retain the more common word and call it exfoliation. Layers upon layers of paperlike sheets are superimposed upon each other, their edges often "cropping out" on sloping surfaces; and since these edges, according to the curvatures of the surfaces, run in wavy lines, the total aspect is very often that of "moiré" silk.

I knew the road as well as I had ever known a road. In summer there was a grassy expanse some thirty feet wide to the north; then followed the grade, flanked to the south by a ditch; and the tangle of weeds and small brush beyond reached right up to the other fence. I had to stay on or rather above the grade; so I stood up and selected the exact spot where to tackle it. Later, I knew, this drift would be harmless enough; there was sufficient local traffic here to establish a well-packed trail. At present, however, it still seemed a formidable task for a team that was to pull me over thirty-three miles more. Besides it was a first test for my horses; I did not know yet how they would behave in snow.

But we went at it. For a moment things happened too fast for me to watch details. The horses plunged wildly and reared on their hind feet in a panic, straining against each other, pulling apart, going down underneath the pole, trying to turn and retrace their steps. And meanwhile the cutter went sharply up at first, as if on the crest of a wave, then toppled over into a hole made by Dan, and altogether behaved like a boat tossed on a stormy sea. Then order returned into the chaos. I had the lines short, wrapped double and treble around my wrists; my feet stood braced in the corner of the box, knees touching the dashboard; my robes slipped down. I spoke to the horses in a soft, quiet, purring voice; and at last I pulled in. Peter hated to stand. I held him. Then I looked back. This first wild plunge had taken us a matter of two hundred yards into the drift. Peter pulled and champed at the bit; the horses were sinking nearly out of sight. But I knew that many and many a time in the future I should have to go through just this and that from the beginning I must train the horses to tackle it right. So, in spite of my aching wrists I kept them standing till I thought that they were fully breathed. Then I relaxed my pull the slightest bit and clicked my tongue. "Good," I thought, "they are pulling together!" And I managed to hold them in line. They reared and plunged again like drowning things in their last agony, but they no longer clashed against nor pulled away from each other. I measured the distance with my eye. Another two hundred yards or thereabout, and I pulled them in again. Thus we stopped altogether four times. The horses were steaming when we got through this drift which was exactly half a mile long; my cutter was packed level full with slabs and clods of snow; and I was pretty well exhausted myself.

"If there is very much of this," I thought for the moment, "I may not be able to make it." But then I knew that a north-south road will drift in badly only under exceptional circumstances. It is the east-west grades that are most apt to give trouble. Not that I minded my part of it, but I did not mean to kill my horses. I had sized them up in their behaviour towards snow. Peter, as I had expected, was excitable. It was hard to recognize in him just now, as he walked quietly along, the uproar of playing muscle and rearing limbs that he had been when we first struck the snow. That was well and good for a short, supreme effort; but not even for Peter would it do in the long, endless drifts which I had to expect. Dan was quieter, but he did not have Peter's staying power; in fact, he was not really a horse for the road. Strange, in spite of his usual keenness on the level road, he seemed to show more snow sense in the drift. This was to be amply confirmed in the future. Whenever an accident happened, it was Peter's fault. As you will see if you read on, Dan once lay quiet when Peter stood right on top of him.

On this road north I found the same "promontories" that had been such a feature of the first one, flung across from the northwest to the southeast. Since the clumps of shrubs to the left were larger here, and more numerous, too, the drifts occasionally also were larger and higher; but not one of them was such that the horses could not clear it with one or two leaps. The sun was climbing, the air was winter-clear and still. None of the farms which I passed showed the slightest sign of life. I had wrapped up again and sat in comparative comfort and at ease, enjoying the clear sparkle and glitter of the virgin snow. It was not till considerably later that the real significance of the landscape dawned upon my consciousness. Still there was even now in my thoughts a speculative undertone. Subconsciously I wondered what might be ahead of me.

We made Bell's corner in good time. The mile to the west proved easy. There were drifts, it is true, and the going was heavy, but at no place did the snow for any length of time reach higher than the horses' hocks. We turned to the north again, and here, for a while, the road was very good indeed; the underbrush to the left, on those expanses of wild land, had fettered, as it were, the feet of the wind. The snow was held everywhere, and very little it had drifted. Only one spot I remember where a clump of Russian willow close to the trail had offered shelter enough to allow the wind to fill in the narrow road-gap to a depth of maybe eight or nine feet; but here it was easy to go around to the west. Without any further incident we reached the point where the useless, supernumerary fence post had caught my eye on my first trip out. I had made nearly eight miles now.

But right here I was to get my first inkling of sights that might shatter my nerve. You may remember that a grove of tall poplars ran to the east, skirted along its southern edge by a road and a long line of telephone posts. Now here, in this shelter of the poplars, the snow from the more or less level and unsheltered spaces to the northwest had piled in indeed. It sloped up to the east; and never shall I forget what I beheld.

The first of the posts stood a foot in snow; at the second one the drift reached six or seven feet up; the next one looked only half as long as the first one, and you might have imagined, standing as it did on a sloping hillside, that it had intentionally been made so much shorter than the others; but at the bottom of the visible part the wind, in sweeping around the pole, had scooped out a funnel-shaped crater which seemed to open into the very earth like a sinkhole. The next pole stood like a giant buried up to his chest and looked singularly helpless and footbound; and the last one I saw showed just its crossbar with three glassy, green insulators above the mountain of snow. The whole surface of this gigantic drift showed again that "exfoliated" appearance which I have described. Strange to say, this very exfoliation gave it something of a quite peculiarly desolate aspect. It looked so harsh, so millennial-old, so antediluvian and pre-adamic! I still remember with particular distinctness the slight dizziness that overcame me, the sinking feeling in my heart, the awe, and the foreboding that I had challenged a force in Nature which might defy all tireless effort and the most fearless heart.

So the hostler had not been fibbing after all!

But not for a moment did I think of turning back. I am fatalistic in temperament. What is to be, is to be, that is not my outlook. If at last we should get bound up in a drift, well and good, I should then see what the next move would have to be. While the wind blows, snow drifts; while my horses could walk and I was not disabled, my road led north, not south. Like the snow I obeyed the laws of my nature. So far the road was good, and we swung along.

Somewhere around here a field presented a curious view. Its crop had not been harvested; it still stood in stooks. But from my side I saw nothing of the sheaves—it seemed to be flax, for here and there a flag of loose heads showed at the top. The snow had been blown up from all directions, so it looked, by the counter-currents that set up in the lee of every obstacle. These mounds presented one and all the appearance of cones or pyramids of butter patted into shape by upward strokes made with a spoon. There were the sharp ridges, irregular and erratic, and there were the hollows running up their flanks—exactly as such a cone of butter will show them. And the whole field was dotted with them, as if there were so many fresh graves.

I made the twelve-mile bridge—passing through the cottonwood gate—reached the "hovel," and dropped into the wilderness again. Here the bigger trees stood strangely bare. Winter reveals the bark and the "habit" of trees. All ornaments and unessentials have been dropped. The naked skeletons show. I remember how I was more than ever struck by that dappled appearance of the bark of the balm: an olive-green, yellowish hue, ridged and spotted with the black of ancient, overgrown leaf-scars; there was actually something gay about it; these poplars are certainly beautiful winter trees. The aspens were different. Although their stems stood white on white in the snow, that greenish tinge in their white gave them a curious look. From the picture that I carry about in my memory of this morning I cannot help the impression that they looked as if their white were not natural at all; they looked white-washed! I have often since confirmed this impression when there was snow on the ground.

In the copses of saplings the zigzagging of the boles from twig to twig showed very distinctly, more so, I believe, than to me it had ever done before. How slender and straight they look in their summer garb—now they were stripped, and bone and sinew appeared.

We came to the "half way farms," and the marsh lay ahead. I watered the horses, and I do not know what made me rest them for a little while, but I did. On the yard of the farm where I had turned in there was not a soul to be seen. Barns and stables were closed—and I noticed that the back door of the dwelling was buried tight by the snow. No doubt everybody preferred the neighbourhood of the fire to the cold outside. While stopping, I faced for the first time the sun. He was high in the sky by now—it was half-past ten—and it suddenly came home to me that there was something relentless, inexorable, cruel, yes, something of a sneer in the pitiless way in which he looked down on the infertile waste around. Unaccountably two Greek words formed on my lips: Homer's Pontos atrygetos—the barren sea. Half an hour later I was to realize the significance of it.

I turned back to the road and north again. For another half mile the fields continued on either side; but somehow they seemed to take on a sinister look. There was more snow on them than I had found on the level land further south; the snow lay more smoothly, again under those "exfoliated" surface sheets which here, too, gave it an inhuman, primeval look; in the higher sun the vast expanse looked, I suppose, more blindingly white; and nowhere did buildings or thickets seem to emerge. Yet, so long as the grade continued, the going was fair enough.

Then I came to the corner which marked half the distance, and there I stopped. Right in front, where the trail had been and where a ditch had divided off the marsh, a fortress of snow lay now: a seemingly impregnable bulwark, six or seven feet high, with rounded top, fitting descriptions which I had read of the underground bombproofs around Belgian strongholds—those forts which were hammered to pieces by the Germans in their first, heart-breaking forward surge in 1914. There was not a wrinkle in this inverted bowl. There it lay, smooth and slick—curled up in security, as it were, some twenty, thirty feet across; and behind it others, and more of them to the right and to the left. This had been a stretch, covered with brush and bush, willow and poplar thickets; but my eye saw nothing except a mammiferous waste, cruelly white, glittering in the heatless, chuckling sun, and scoffing at me, the intruder. I stood up again and peered out. To the east it seemed as if these buttes of snow were a trifle lower; but maybe the ground underneath also sloped down. I wished I had travelled here more often by daytime, so I might know. As it was, there was nothing to it; I had to tackle the task. And we plunged in.

I had learned something from my first experience in the drift one mile north of town, and I kept my horses well under control. Still, it was a wild enough dash. Peter lost his footing two or three times and worked himself into a mild panic. But Dan—I could not help admiring the way in which, buried over his back in snow, he would slowly and deliberately rear on his hindfeet and take his bound. For fully five minutes I never saw anything of the horses except their heads. I inferred their motions from the dusting snowcloud that rose above their bodies and settled on myself. And then somehow we emerged. We reached a stretch of ground where the snow was just high enough to cover the hocks of the horses. It was a hollow scooped out by some freak of the wind. I pulled in, and the horses stood panting. Peter no longer showed any desire to fret and to jump. Both horses apparently felt the wisdom of sparing their strength. They were all white with the frost of their sweat and the spray of the snow. . . .

While I gave them their time, I looked around, and here a lesson came home to me. In the hollow where we stood, snow did not lie smoothly. A huge obstacle to the northwest, probably a buried clump of brush, had made the wind turn back upon itself, first downward, then, at the bottom of the pit, in a direction opposite to that of the main current above, and finally slantways upward again to the summit of the obstacle, where it rejoined the parent blow. The floor of the hollow was cleanly scooped out and chiselled in low ridges; and these ridges came from the southeast, running their points to the northwest. I learned to look out for this sign, and I verily believe that, had I not learned that lesson right now, I should never have reached the creek which was still four or five miles distant.

The huge mound in the lee of which I was stopping was a matter of two hundred yards away; nearer to it the snow was considerably deeper; and since it presented an appearance very characteristic of Prairie bush-drifts, I shall describe it in some detail. Apparently the winds had first bent over all the stems of the clump; for whenever I saw one of them from the north, it showed a smooth, clean upward sweep. On the south side the snow first fell in a sheer cliff; then there was a hollow which was partly filled by a talus-shaped drift thrown in by the counter currents from the southern pit in which we were stopping; the sides of this talus again showed the marks that reminded of those left by the spoon when butter is roughly stroked into the shape of a pyramid. The interesting parts of the structure consisted in the beetling brow of the cliff and the roof of the cavity underneath. The brow had a honeycombed appearance; the snow had been laid down in layers of varying density (I shall discuss this more fully in the next chapter when we are going to look in on the snow while it is actually at work); and the counter currents that here swept upward in a slanting direction had bitten out the softer layers, leaving a fine network of little ridges which reminded strangely of the delicate fretwork-tracery in wind-sculptured rock—as I had seen it in the Black Hills in South Dakota. This piece of work of the wind is exceedingly short-lived in snow, and it must not be confounded with the honeycombed appearance of those faces of snow cliffs which are "rotting" by reason of their exposure to the heat of the noonday sun. These latter are coarse, often dirty, and nearly always have something bristling about them which is entirely absent in the sculptures of the wind. The under side of the roof in the cavity looked very much as a very stiff or viscid treacle would look when spread over a meshy surface, as, for instance, over a closely woven netting of wire. The stems and the branches of the brush took the place of the wire, and in their meshes the snow had been pressed through by its own weight, but held together by its curious ductility or tensile strength of which I was to find further evidence soon enough. It thus formed innumerable, blunted little stalactites, but without the corresponding stalagmites which you find in limestone caves or on the north side of buildings when the snow from the roof thaws and forms icicles and slender cones of ice growing up to meet them from the ground where the trickling drops fall and freeze again.

By the help of these various tokens I had picked my next resting place before we started up again. It was on this second dash that I understood why those Homeric words had come to my lips a while ago. This was indeed like nothing so much as like being out on rough waters and in a troubled sea, with nothing to brace the storm with but a wind-tossed nutshell of a one-man sailing craft. I knew that experience for having outridden many a gale in the mouth of the mighty St. Lawrence River. When the snow reached its extreme in depth, it gave you the feeling which a drowning man may have when fighting his desperate fight with the salty waves. But more impressive than that was the frequent outer resemblance. The waves of the ocean rise up and reach out and batter against the rocks and battlements of the shore, retreating again and ever returning to the assault, covering the obstacles thrown in the way of their progress with thin sheets of licking tongues at least. And if such a high crest wave had suddenly been frozen into solidity, its outline would have mimicked to perfection many a one of the snow shapes that I saw around.

Once the horses had really learned to pull exactly together—and they learned it thoroughly here—our progress was not too bad. Of course, it was not like going on a grade, be it ever so badly drifted in. Here the ground underneath, too, was uneven and overgrown with a veritable entanglement of brush in which often the horses' feet would get caught. As for the road, there was none left, nothing that even by the boldest stretch of imagination could have been considered even as the slightest indication of one. And worst of all, I knew positively that there would be no trail at any time during the winter. I was well aware of the fact that, after it once snowed up, nobody ever crossed this waste between the "half way farms" and the "White Range Line House." This morning it took me two and a half solid hours to make four miles.

But the ordeal had its reward. Here where the fact that there was snow on the ground, and plenty of it, did no longer need to be sunk into my brain—as soon as it had lost its value as a piece of news and a lesson, I began to enjoy it just as the hunter in India will enjoy the battle of wits when he is pitted against a yellow-black tiger. I began to catch on to the ways of this snow; I began, as it were, to study the mentality of my enemy. Though I never kill, I am after all something of a sportsman. And still another thing gave me back that mental equilibrium which you need in order to see things and to reason calmly about them. Every dash of two hundred yards or so brought me that much nearer to my goal. Up to the "half way farms" I had, as it were, been working uphill: there was more ahead than behind. This was now reversed: there was more behind than ahead, and as yet I did not worry about the return trip.

Now I have already said that snow is the only really plastic element in which the wind can carve the vagaries of its mood and leave a record of at least some permanency. The surface of the sea is a wonderful book to be read with a lightning-quick eye; I do not know anything better to do as a cure for ragged nerves—provided you are a good sailor. But the forms are too fleeting, they change too quickly—so quickly, indeed, that I have never succeeded in so fixing their record upon my memory as to be able to develop one form from the other in descriptive notes. It is that very fact, I believe, upon which hinges the curative value of the sight: you are so completely absorbed by the moment, and all other things fall away. Many and many a day have I lain in my deck chair on board a liner and watched the play of the waves; but the pleasure, which was very great indeed, was momentary; and sometimes, when in an unsympathetic mood, I have since impatiently wondered in what that fascination may have consisted. It was different here. Snow is very nearly as yielding as water and, once it fully responds in its surface to the carving forces of the wind, it stays—as if frozen into the glittering marble image of its motion. I know few things that are as truly fascinating as the sculptures of the wind in snow; for here you have time and opportunity a-plenty to probe not only into the what, but also into the why. Maybe that one day I shall write down a fuller account of my observations. In this report I shall have to restrict myself to a few indications, for this is not the record of the whims of the wind, but merely the narrative of my drives.

In places, for instance, the rounded, "bomb-proof" aspect of the expanses would be changed into the distinct contour of gigantic waves with a very fine, very sharp crest-line. The upsweep from the northwest would be ever so slightly convex, and the downward sweep into the trough was always very distinctly concave. This was not the ripple which we find in beach sand. That ripple was there, too, and in places it covered the wide backs of these huge waves all over; but never was it found on the concave side. Occasionally, but rarely, one of these great waves would resemble a large breaker with a curly crest. Here the onward sweep from the northwest had built the snow out, beyond the supporting base, into a thick overhanging ledge which here and there had sagged; but by virtue of that tensile strength and cohesion in snow which I have mentioned already, it still held together and now looked convoluted and ruffled in the most deceiving way. I believe I actually listened for the muffled roar which the breaker makes when its subaqueous part begins to sweep the upward sloping beach. To make this illusion complete, or to break it by the very absurdity and exaggeration of a comparison drawn out too far—I do not know which—there would, every now and then, from the crest of one of these waves, jut out something which closely resembled the wide back of a large fish diving down into the concave side towards the trough. This looked very much like porpoises or dolphins jumping in a heaving sea; only that in my memory picture the real dolphins always jump in the opposite direction, against the run of the waves, bridging the trough.

In other places a fine, exceedingly delicate crest-line would spring up from the high point of some buried obstacle and sweep along in the most graceful curve as far as the eye would carry. I particularly remember one of them, and I could discover no earthly reason for the curvature in it.

Again there would be a triangular—or should I say "tetrahedral"?—upsweep from the direction of the wind, ending in a sharp, perfectly plane down-sweep on the south side; and the point of this three-sided but oblique pyramid would hang over like the flap of a tam. There was something of the consistency of very thick cloth about this overhanging flap.

Or an up-slope from the north would end in a long, nearly perpendicular cliff-line facing south. And the talus formation which I have mentioned would be perfectly smooth; but it did not reach quite to the top of the cliff, maybe to within a foot of it. The upsloping layer from the north would hang out again, with an even brow; but between this smooth cornice and the upper edge of the talus the snow looked as if it had been squeezed out by tremendous pressure from above, like an exceedingly viscid liquid—cooling glue, for instance, which is being squeezed out from between the core and the veneer in a veneering press.

Once I passed close to and south of, two thickets which were completely buried by the snow. Between them a ditch had been scooped out in a very curious fashion. It resembled exactly a winding river bed with its water drained off; it was two or three feet deep, and wherever it turned, its banks were undermined on the "throw" side by the "wash" of the furious blow. The analogy between the work of the wind and the work of flowing water constantly obtrudes, especially where this work is one of "erosion."

But as flowing water will swing up and down in the most surprising forms where the bed of the river is rough with rocks and throws it into choppy waves which do not seem to move, so the snow was thrown up into the most curious forms where the frozen swamp ground underneath had bubbled, as it were, into phantastic shapes. I remember several places where a perfect circle was formed by a sharp crestline that bounded an hemispherical, crater-like hollow. When steam bubbles up through thick porridge, in its leisurely and impeded way, and the bubble bursts with a clucking sound, then for a moment a crater is formed just like these circular holes; only here in the snow they were on a much larger scale, of course, some of them six to ten feet in diameter.

And again the snow was thrown up into a bulwark, twenty and more feet high, with that always repeating cliff-face to the south, resembling a miniature Gibraltar, with many smaller ones of most curiously similar form on its back: bulwarks upon bulwarks, all lowering to the south. In these the aggressive nature of storm-flung snow was most apparent. They were formidable structures; formidable and intimidating, more through the suggestiveness of their shape than through mere size.

I came to places where the wind had had its moments of frolicksome humour, where it had made grim fun of its own massive and cumbersome and yet so pliable and elastic majesty. It had turned around and around, running with breathless speed, with its tongue lolling out, as it were, and probably yapping and snapping in mocking mimicry of a pup trying to catch its tail; and it had scooped out a spiral trough with overhanging rim. I felt sorry that I had not been there to watch it, because after all, what I saw, was only the dead record of something that had been very much alive and vociferatingly noisy. And in another place it had reared and raised its head like a boa constrictor, ready to strike at its prey; up to the flashing, forked tongue it was there. But one spot I remember, where it looked exactly as if quite consciously it had attempted the outright ludicrous: it had thrown up the snow into the semblance of some formidable animal—more like a gorilla than anything else it looked, a gorilla that stands on its four hands and raises every hair on its back and snarls in order to frighten that which it is afraid of itself—a leopard maybe.

And then I reached the "White Range Line House." Curiously enough, there it stood, sheltered by its majestic bluff to the north, as peaceful looking as if there were no such a thing as that record, which I had crossed, of the uproar and fury of one of the forces of Nature engaged in an orgy. And it looked so empty, too, and so deserted, with never a wisp of smoke curling from its flue-pipe, that for a moment I was tempted to turn in and see whether maybe the lonely dweller was ill. But then I felt as if I could not be burdened with any stranger's worries that day.

The effective shelter of the poplar forest along the creek made itself felt. The last mile to the northeast was peaceful driving. I felt quite cheered, though I walked the horses over the whole of the mile since both began to show signs of wear. The last four miles had been a test to try any living creature's mettle. To me it had been one of the culminating points in that glorious winter, but the horses had lacked the mental stimulus, and even I felt rather exhausted.

On the bridge I stopped, threw the blankets over the horses, and fed. Somehow this seemed to be the best place to do it. There was no snow to speak of and I did not know yet what might follow. The horses were drooping, and I gave them an additional ten minutes' rest. Then I slowly made ready. I did not really expect any serious trouble.

We turned at a walk, and the chasm of the bush road opened up. Instantly I pulled the horses in. What I saw, baffled me for a moment so completely that I just sat there and gasped. There was no road. The trees to both sides were not so overly high, but the snow had piled in level with their tops; the drift looked like a gigantic barricade. It was that fleeting sight of the telephone posts over again, though on a slightly smaller scale; but this time it was in front. Slowly I started to whistle and then looked around. I remembered now. There was a newly cut-out road running north past the school which lay embedded in the bush. It had offered a lane to the wind; and the wind, going there, in cramped space, at a doubly furious stride, had picked up and carried along all the loose snow from the grassy glades in its path. The road ended abruptly just north of the drift, where the east-west grade sprang up. When the wind had reached this end of the lane, where the bush ran at right angles to its direction, it had found itself in something like a blind alley, and, sweeping upward, to clear the obstacle, it had dropped every bit of its load into the shelter of the brush, gradually, in the course of three long days, building up a ridge that buried underbrush and trees. I might have known it, of course. I knew enough about snow; all the conditions for an exceptionally large drift were provided for here. But it had not occurred to me, especially after I had found the northern fringe of the marsh so well sheltered. Here I felt for a moment as if all the snow of the universe had piled in. As I said, I was so completely baffled that I could have turned the horses then and there.

But after a minute or two my eyes began to cast about. I turned to the south, right into the dense underbrush and towards the creek which here swept south in a long, flat curve. Peter was always intolerant of anything that moved underfoot. He started to bolt when the dry and hard-frozen stems snapped and broke with reports resembling pistol shots. But since Dan kept quiet, I held Peter well in hand. I went along the drift for maybe three to four hundred yards, reconnoitering. Then the trees began to stand too dense for me to proceed without endangering my cutter. Just beyond I saw the big trough of the creek bed, and though I could not make out how conditions were at its bottom, the drift continued on its southern bank, and in any case it was impossible to cross the hollow. So I turned; I had made up my mind to try the drift.

About a hundred and fifty yards from the point where I had turned off the road there was something like a fold in the flank of the drift. At its foot I stopped. For a moment I tried to explain that fold to myself. This is what I arrived at. North of the drift, just about where the new cut-out joined the east-west grade, there was a small clearing caused by a bush fire which a few years ago had penetrated thus far into this otherwise virgin corner of the forest. Unfortunately it stood so full of charred stumps that it was impossible to get through there. But the main currents of the wind would have free play in this opening, and I knew that, when the blizzard began, it had been blowing from a more northerly quarter than later on, when it veered to the northwest. And though the snow came careering along the lane of the cut-out, that is, from due north, its "throw" and therefore, the direction of the drift would be determined by the direction of the wind that took charge of it on this clearing. Probably, then, a first, provisional drift whose long axis lay nearly in a north-south line, had been piled up by the first, northerly gale. Later a second, larger drift had been superimposed upon it at an angle, with its main axis running from the northwest to the southeast. The fold marked the point where the first, smaller drift still emerged from the second larger one. This reasoning was confirmed by a study of the clearing itself which I came to make two or three weeks after.

Before I called on the horses to give me their very last ounce of strength, I got out of my cutter once more and made sure that my lines were still sound. I trusted my ability to guide the horses even in this crucial test, but I dreaded nothing so much as that the lines might break; and I wanted to guard against any accident. I should mention that, of course, the top of my cutter was down, that the traces of the harness were new, and that the cutter itself during its previous trials had shown an exceptional stability. Once more I thus rested my horses for five minutes, and they seemed to realize what was coming. Their heads were up, their ears were cocked. When I got back into my cutter, I carefully brushed the snow from moccasins and trousers, laid the robe around my feet, adjusted my knees against the dashboard, and tied two big loops into the lines to hold them by.

Then I clicked my tongue. The horses bounded upward in unison. For a moment it looked as if they intended to work through, instead of over, the drift. A wild shower of angular snow-slabs swept in upon me. The cutter reared up and plunged and reared again—and then the view cleared. The snow proved harder than I had anticipated—which bespoke the fury of the blow that had piled it. It did not carry the horses, but neither—once we had reached a height of five or six feet—did they sink beyond their bellies and out of sight. I had no eye for anything except them. What lay to right or left, seemed not to concern me. I watched them work. They went in bounds, working beautifully together. Rhythmically they reared, and rhythmically they plunged. I had dropped back to the seat, holding them with a firm hand, feet braced against the dashboard; and whenever they got ready to rear, I called to them in a low and quiet voice, "Peter—Dan—now!" And their muscles played with the effort of desperation. It probably did not take more than five minutes, maybe considerably less, before we had reached the top, but to me it seemed like hours of nearly fruitless endeavour. I did not realize at first that we were high. I shall never forget the weird kind of astonishment when the fact came home to me that what snapped and crackled in the snow under the horses' hoofs, were the tops of trees. Nor shall the feeling of estrangement, as it were—as if I were not myself, but looking on from the outside at the adventure of somebody who yet was I—the feeling of other-worldliness, if you will pardon the word, ever fade from my memory—a feeling of having been carried beyond my depth where I could not swim—which came over me when with two quick glances to right and left I took in the fact that there were no longer any trees to either side, that I was above that forest world which had so often engulfed me.

Then I drew my lines in. The horses fought against it, did not want to stand. But I had to find my way, and while they were going, I could not take my eyes from them. It took a supreme effort on my part to make them obey. At last they stood, but I had to hold them with all my strength, and with not a second's respite. Now that I was on top of the drift, the problem of how to get down loomed larger than that of getting up had seemed before. I knew I did not have half a minute in which to decide upon my course; for it became increasingly difficult to hold the horses back, and they were fast sinking away.

During this short breathing spell I took in the situation. We had come up in a northeast direction, slanting along the slope. Once on top, I had instinctively turned to the north. Here the drift was about twenty feet wide, perfectly level and with an exfoliated surface layer. To the east the drift fell steeply, with a clean, smooth cliff-line marking off the beginning of the descent; this line seemed particularly disconcerting, for it betrayed the concave curvature of the down-sweep. A few yards to the north I saw below, at the foot of the cliff, the old logging-trail, and I noticed that the snow on it lay as it had fallen, smooth and sheer, without a ripple of a drift. It looked like mockery. And yet that was where I had to get down.

The next few minutes are rather a maze in my memory. But two pictures were photographed with great distinctness. The one is of the moment when we went over the edge. For a second Peter reared up, pawing the air with his forefeet; Dan tried to back away from the empty fall. I had at this excruciating point no purchase whatever on the lines. Then apparently Peter sat or fell down, I do not know which, on his haunches and began to slide. The cutter lurched to the left as if it were going to spill all it held. Dan was knocked off his hind feet by the drawbar and we plunged. . . . We came to with a terrific jolt that sent me in a heap against the dashboard. One jump, and I stood on the ground. The cutter—and this is the second picture which is etched clearly on the plate of my memory—stood on its pole, leaning at an angle of forty-five degrees against the drift. The horses were as if stunned. "Dan, Peter!" I shouted, and they struggled to their feet. They were badly winded, but otherwise everything seemed all right. I looked wistfully back and up at the gully which we had torn into the flank of the drift.

I should gladly have breathed the horses again, but they were hot, the air was at zero or colder, the rays of the sun had begun to slant. I walked for a while alongside the team. They were drooping sadly. Then I got in again, driving them slowly till we came to the crossing of the ditch. I had no eye for the grade ahead. On the bush road the going was good—now and then a small drift, but nothing alarming anywhere. The anti-climax had set in. Again the speckled trunks of the balm poplars struck my eye, now interspersed with the scarlet stems of the red osier dogwood. But they failed to cheer me—they were mere facts, unable to stir moods. . . .

I began to think. A few weeks ago I had met that American settler with the French sounding name who lived alongside the angling dam further north. We had talked snow, and he had said, "Oh, up here it never is bad except along this grade,"—we were stopping on the last east-west grade, the one I was coming to—"there you cannot get through. You'd kill your horses. Level with the tree-tops." Well, I had had just that a little while ago—I could not afford any more of it. So I made up my mind to try a new trail, across a section which was fenced. It meant getting out of my robes twice more, to open the gates, but I preferred that to another tree-high drift. To spare my horses was now my only consideration. I should not have liked to take the new trail by night, for fear of missing the gates; but that objection did not hold just now. Horses and I were pretty well spent. So, instead of forking off the main trail to the north we went straight ahead.

In due time I came to the bridge which I had to cross in order to get up on the dam. Here I saw—in an absentminded, half unconscious, and uninterested way—one more structure built by architect wind. The deep master ditch from the north emptied here, to the left of the bridge, into the grade ditch which ran east and west. And at the corner the snow had very nearly bridged it—so nearly that you could easily have stepped across the remaining gap. But below it was hollow—nothing supported the bridge—it was a mere arch, with a vault underneath that looked temptingly sheltered and cosy to wearied eyes.

The dam was bare, and I had to pull off to the east, on to the swampy plain. I gave my horses the lines, and slowly, slowly they took me home! Even had I not always lost interest here, to-day I should have leaned back and rested. Although the horses had done all the actual work, the strain of it had been largely on me. It was the after-effect that set in now.

I thought of my wife, and of how she would have felt had she been able to follow the scenes in some magical mirror through every single vicissitude of my drive. And once more I saw with the eye of recent memory the horses in that long, endless plunge through the corner of the marsh. Once more I felt my muscles a-quiver with the strain of that last wild struggle over that last, inhuman drift. And slowly I made up my mind that the next time, the very next day, on my return trip, I was going to add another eleven miles to my already long drive and to take a different road. I knew the trail over which I had been coming so far was closed for the rest of the winter—there was no traffic there—no trail would be kept open. That other road of which I was thinking and which lay further west was the main cordwood trail to the towns in the south. It was out of my way, to be sure, but I felt convinced that I could spare my horses and even save time by making the detour.

Being on the east side of the dam, I could not see school or cottage till I turned up on the correction line. But when at last I saw it, I felt somewhat as I had felt coming home from my first big trip overseas. It seemed a lifetime since I had started out. I seemed to be a different man.

Here, in the timber land, the snow had not drifted to any extent. There were signs of the gale, but its record was written in fallen tree trunks, broken branches, a litter of twigs—not in drifts of snow. My wife would not surmise what I had gone through.

She came out with a smile on her face when I pulled in on the yard. It was characteristic of her that she did not ask why I came so late; she accepted the fact as something for which there were no doubt compelling reasons. "I was giving our girl a bath," she said; "she cannot come." And then she looked wistfully at my face and at the horses. Silently I slipped the harness off their backs. I used to let them have their freedom for a while on reaching home. And never yet but Peter at least had had a kick and a caper and a roll before they sought their mangers. To-day they stood for a moment knock-kneed, without moving, then shook themselves in a weak, half-hearted way and went with drooping heads and weary limbs straight to the stable.

"You had a hard trip?" asked my wife; and I replied with as much cheer as I could muster, "I have seen sights to-day that I did not expect to see before my dying day." And taking her arm, I looked at the westering sun and turned towards the house.

Frederick Philip Grove won the Governor General's Award for his autobiography, In Search of Myself *(1946). He is best known for his novels—especially* Settlers of the Marsh, Fruits of the Earth *and* A Search for America*—though many believe his best writing is to be found in* Over Prairie Trails, *from which "Snow" is taken.*

MELVIN ARBUCKLE'S FIRST COURSE IN SHOCK THERAPY

W. O. MITCHELL

LAST YEAR, LIKE THOUSANDS OF OTHER FORMER KHARTOUMIANS, I returned to Khartoum, Saskatchewan, to help her celebrate her Diamond Jubilee year. In the Elks' Bar, on the actual anniversary date, September 26, the Chamber of Commerce held a birthday get-together, and it was here that Roddy Montgomery, Khartoum's mayor, introduced me to a man whose face had elusive familiarity.

"One of Khartoum's most famous native sons," Roddy said with an anticipatory smile. "Psychiatrist on the West Coast. Portland."

I shook hands; I knew that I should remember him from the litmus years of my prairie childhood. As soon as he spoke I remembered: Miss Coldtart first, then *Pippa Passes*—then Melvin Arbuckle.

I was tolled back forty years: Melvin Arbuckle, only son of Khartoum's electrician, the boy who had successfully frustrated Miss Coldtart through all our Grade Four reading classes. Then, and today it seemed, he was unable to say a declarative sentence; he couldn't manage an exclamatory or imperative one either. A gentle-spoken and utterly stubborn woman with cream skin and dyed hair, Miss Coldtart called upon Melvin to read aloud every day of that school year, hoping against hope that one of his sentences would not turn up at the end like the sandal toes of an *Arabian Nights* sultan. The very last day of Grade Four she had him read *Pippa Passes* line for line after her. He did—interrogatively down to the last "God's in His Heaven?—All's right with the world?"

And forty years later it seemed quite fitting to me that Melvin was a psychiatrist, especially when I recalled Melvin's grandfather who lived with the Arbuckles, a long ropey octogenarian with buttermilk eyes and the sad and equine face of William S. Hart. I liked Melvin's grandfather. He claimed that he had been imprisoned by Louis Riel in Fort Garry when the Red River Rebellion started, that he was a close friend of Scott whom Riel executed in 1870. He said that he was the first man to enter Batoche after it fell, that he'd sat on the jury that condemned Riel to hang in '85. By arithmetic he could have been and done these things, but Melvin said his grandfather was an historical liar.

Melvin's grandfather had another distinction: saliva trouble. He would gather it, shake it back and forth from cheek to cheek, the way you might rattle dice in your hand before making a pass—then spit. He did this every twenty seconds. Also he wandered a great deal, wearing a pyramid-peaked hat of RCMP or boy scout issue, the thongs hanging down either cheek, a lumpy knapsack high between his shoulder-blades, a peeled and varnished willow-root cane in his hand. Since the Arbuckles' house stood an eighth of a mile apart from the eastern edge of Khartoum, it was remarkable that the old man never got lost on the empty prairie flung round three sides. Years of wilderness travel must have drawn him naturally towards habitation: Melvin's after-fours were ruined with the mortification of having to knock on front doors in our end of town, asking people if they'd seen anything of his lost grandfather. All his Saturdays were unforgivably spoiled too, for on these days Melvin's mother went down to the store to help his father, and Melvin had to stay home to see that his grandfather didn't get lost.

No one was ever able to get behind Melvin's grandfather; he sat always in a corner with two walls at his back; this was so in the house or in the Soo Beer Parlour. Melvin's mother had to cut her father's hair, for he refused to sit in Leon's barber chair out in the unprotected centre of the shop. If he met someone on the street and stopped to talk, he would circle uneasily until he had a building wall or a hedge or a fence at his back; sometimes he would have to settle for a tree. He had a very sensible reason for this: they were coming to get him one day, he said. It was never quite clear who was coming to get him one day, but I suspected revengeful friends of the man he called the half-breed renegade, Dumont. He may have been an historical liar, as Melvin said, but there was no doubting that he was afraid—afraid for his life.

I sincerely believed that someone was after him: nobody could have spent as much time as he did in the Arbuckle privy if somebody weren't after him. From mid-April, when the sun had got high and strong, to harvest he spent more time out there with four walls closing safe around him than he did in the house. I can hardly recall a visit to Melvin's place that there wasn't blue smoke threading from the diamond cutout in the backhouse door. Melvin's grandfather smoked natural-leaf Quebec tobacco that scratched with the pepper bitterness of burning willow root. He had the wildest smell of any man I had ever known, compounded of wine and iron tonic, beer, natural leaf, wood smoke, buckskin and horses. I didn't mind it at all.

He was a braggarty sort of old man, his words hurrying out after each other as though he were afraid that if he stopped he wouldn't be permitted to start up again—and also as though he knew that no one was paying attention to what he was saying anyway, so that he might just as well settle for getting it *said* as quickly as possible. Even Miss Coldtart would have found many of his expressions colourful: "she couldn't cook guts for a bear"; "spinnin' in the wind like the button on a backhouse door"; "so stubborn she was to drown'd you'd find her body upstream"; "when he was borned they set him on the porch to see if he barked or cried." Even though you felt he was about to embarrass you by spitting or lying, I found Melvin's grandfather interesting.

Yet I was glad that he was Melvin's grandfather and not mine. Even though he kept dragging his grandfather into conversation, Melvin was ashamed of him. He was always reminding us of his grandfather, not because he wanted to talk about him but just as though he were tossing the old man at our feet for a dare. I can't remember any of us taking him up on it. Perhaps now that he is a psychiatrist out on the West Coast, he has decided what compelled him to remind us continually of the grandfather he was ashamed of.

The summer that I have in mind was the year that Peanuts moved to Khartoum from Estevan, where his father was an engineer for a coal strip-mining company. Some sort of cousin of the Sweeneys, Peanuts had immigrated to Canada from England just the year before. He'd only had three months in Khartoum to pick up the nickname, Peanuts. He was not a peanuts sort of boy, quite blocky, very full red cheeks, hemp fair hair and wax blue eyes. At ten years of age, I suppose John Bull must have looked a great deal like Peanuts. His given name was actually Geoffrey.

He was quite practical, and could give all kinds of sensible reasons why a project could not work; this unwillingness to suspend disbelief tore illusion and spoiled pretend games. He had no sense of humour at all, for he seldom laughed at anything Fat said; English into the bargain, he should have been the most unpopular boy in Khartoum. However, he had piano-wire nerves which made up for his shortcomings. When we held our circus that July, he slipped snake after snake down the throat of his blouse, squirmed them past his belt and extricated them one by one from the legs of his stovepipe British woollen pants. They were only garter snakes, but a week later to settle a horticultural argument in Ashford's Grove, he ate a toadstool raw. Just because he didn't die was not proof that he was right and that we were wrong, for immediately after he pulled up and ate two bouquets of wild horseradish, with instantaneous emetic effect.

Now that I think back to a late August day that year, I can see that Peanuts has to share with Melvin's grandfather the credit or the responsibility for Melvin's being today a leading West Coast psychiatrist. It was a day that promised no excitement. The Khartoum Fair was past; Johnny J. Jones's circus had come and gone a month before, its posters already nostalgic and wind-tattered on shed and fence and barn walls. We couldn't duck or bottom it in the little Souris River, for it was filled with rusty bloodsuckers and violet-coloured algae that caused prairie itch. The bounty was off gopher tails for the rest of the year so there was no point in hunting them.

There was simply nothing to do but sprawl in the adequate shade of McGoogan's hedge, eating clover heads and caragana flowers. With bored languor we looked out over Sixth Street lifting and drifting in the shimmering heat. Without interest we saw the town wagon roll by, darkening the talcum-fine dust with spray; moments later the street was thirsty again, smoking under the desultory August wind.

Fin pulled out the thick glass from a flashlight, focused it to a glowing bead on his pant leg. A thin streamer of smoke was born and we idly watched a fusing spark eat through the cloth until its ant sting bit Fin's knee. He put the glass back into his pocket and said, "Let's go down to the new creamery and chew tar." Someone said, "Let's go look for beer bottles and lead instead"; someone else said, "How about fooling around in the loft of Fat's uncle's livery stable"; someone else said, "The hell with it."

About that time we all got to our feet, for an ice dray came down the street, piled high with frozen geometry. When the leather-chapped driver had chipped and hoisted a cake of ice over his shoulder and left for delivery, we went to the back of the dray. We knew we were welcome to the chips on the floor, and as we always did we popped into our mouths chunks too big for them. The trick was to suck in warm air around the ice until you could stand it no longer, then lower your head, eject and catch.

Someone said, "Let's go over and see Melvin stuck with his grandfather." Inhibited by ice and the cool drool of it, no one agreed or disagreed. We wandered up Sixth Street, past the McKinnon girls and Noreen Robins darting in and out of a skipping rope, chanting: "Charlie Chaplin—went to—France—teach the—ladies—how to dance . . ." At the corner of Bison and Sixth we turned east and in two blocks reached the prairie. I think it was the tar-papered and deserted shack between the town's edge and the Arbuckles' house that gave us the idea of building a hut. By the time we had reached Melvin's, we had decided it might be more fun to dig a cave, which would be lovely and cool.

Melvin was quite agreeable to our building the cave in his backyard; there were plenty of boards for covering it over; if we all pitched in and started right away, we might even have it finished before his grandfather had wakened from his nap. Shovel and spade and fork plunged easily through the eighteen inches of topsoil; but the clay subsoil in this dry year was heart—and back—breaking. Rock-hard, it loosened under pick and bar in reluctant sugar lumps. Stinging with sweat, our shoulder sockets aching, we rested often, reclining at the lip of our shallow excavation. We idly wished: "If a fellow only had a fresno and team, he could really scoop her out . . ."

"If a fellow could soak her good . . . run her full of water—soften her up. Easy digging then."

"If a fellow could only blow her out . . ."

"How?"

"Search me."

"Stumping powder—dynamite . . ."

"Oh," Peanuts said, "yes—dynamite."

"Whumph and she'd blow our cave for us," Fin said.

"She sure would," Fat said.

Melvin said, "Only place I know where they got dynamite—CPR sheds."

"I have dynamite," Peanuts said. "I can get dynamite."

We looked at each other; we looked at Peanuts. Knowing Peanuts, I felt a little sick; Fat and Fin and Melvin didn't look so happy either. We had never even seen a stick of dynamite; it simply did not belong in our world. It had been quite *imaginary* dynamite that we had been tossing about in conversation.

Fat said, "We can't go swiping dynamite."

Fin said, "We don't know a thing about handling dynamite."

"I do," Peanuts said.

"Isn't our yard," Fat said. "We can't set off dynamite in Mel's yard." Peanuts got up purposefully. "Can we, Mel?"

"The cave's a hundred yards from the house," Peanuts said. "Nothing dangerously near it at all." He turned to Melvin. "Are you frightened?"

"Well—no," Melvin said.

"My father has a whole case of 60 per cent," Peanuts said. "From the mine. While I get it you have them do the hole."

"What hole?" Melvin said.

"For the dynamite—with the bar—straight down about four feet, I should say."

"The whole goddam case!" Fin said.

"Dead centre, the hole," Peanuts said and started for his house.

"He bringing back the whole case?" Fin said.

Fat got up. "I guess I better be getting on my way . . ." His voice fainted as he looked down at us and we looked up at him. "I guess I better—we better—start punching—down that hole," he finished up. "Like Peanuts said." It was not what Fat had started out to say at all.

Peanuts brought back only three sticks of dynamite, and until his return the hole went down rather slowly. He tossed the sticks on the ground by the woodpile and took over authority. He did twice his share of digging the dynamite hole; from time to time he estimated how much further we had to go down. When it seemed to suit him he dropped two of the sticks down the hole, one on top of the other. There was no tenderness in the way he handled that dynamite, inserted the fuse end into the copper tube detonator, crimped it with his teeth, and used a spike to work a hole into the third stick to receive the cap and fuse. He certainly knew how to handle dynamite. We watched him shove loose clay soil in around the sticks, tamp it firm with the bar. With his jackknife he split the free end of the fuse protruding from the ground. He took a match from his pocket.

"Hold on a minute," Melvin said. "Where do we—what do we—how long do we . . ."

"Once it's going there'll be three minutes," Peanuts said. "Plenty of time to take cover."

"What cover?" Fat said.

"Round the corner of the house," Peanuts said. "You may go there now if you wish. I'll come when the fuse is started. They're hard to start—it will take several matches."

We stayed. The fuse took life at the third match. Fat and Fin and Melvin and I ran the hundred yards to the house. We looked around the corner to Peanuts coming towards us. He did it by strolling. I had begun to count to myself so that I could have a rough notion of when the fuse was near the end of its three minutes. I had reached fifty-nine when I heard the Arbuckle screen door slap the stillness.

Fin said, "Judas Priest!"

Melvin said, "He's headed for the backhouse!"

Fat said, "He's got his knapsack and his hat and his cane on—maybe he's just going out to get lost."

Melvin started round the corner of the house but Fin grabbed him. "Let him keep goin', Mel! Let him keep goin' so's he'll get in the clear!"

"I'll get him," Peanuts said.

"He's my grandfather!" Melvin said.

Fin said, "There ain't even a minute left!" I had no way of telling, for I'd stopped counting.

The site of our proposed cave and, therefore, of the dynamite with its burning fuse, was halfway between the back of the Arbuckle house and the privy. Melvin's grandfather stopped by the woodpile. He shook his head and he spat. Peanuts launched himself around the corner of the house, belly to the ground towards the old man. Melvin's grandfather must have thought the running footsteps behind him were those of either Louis Riel or Gabriel Dumont, for without looking back he covered the open ground to the privy in ten seconds, jumped inside and slammed the door. Right in stride, Peanuts pounded past and out to the prairie beyond. There he was still running with his head back, chin out, arms pumping, knees high, when the dynamite let go.

The very first effect was not of sound at all. Initially the Arbuckle yard was taken by one giant and subterranean hiccup. An earth fountain spouted; four cords of wood took flight; the privy leaped straight up almost six feet; two clothesline posts javelined into the air, their wires still stretched between them in an incredible aerial cat's cradle. Not until then did the lambasting explosion seem to come. For several elastic seconds all the airborne things hung indecisively between the thrust of dynamite and the pull of gravity. Gravity won.

The privy was the first thing to return to earth, and when it fell its descent obeyed Newton's Law of Falling Backhouses, which says: "A falling privy shall always come to rest upon the door side." The corollary: "A loved one trapped within cannot be taken out on the vertical, only through the hole and upon the horizontal."

At the back of the house we looked at each other wildly; we swallowed to unbung our ears, heard the Japanese chiming of glass shards dropping from Arbuckle windows, the thud of wood chunks returning to earth. I saw Melvin lick with the tip of his tongue at twin blood yarns coming down from his nostrils. No one said anything; we simply moved as a confused body in the direction of the privy. We skirted the great shallow saucer the dynamite had blown, and I remember thinking they would never fill it in: the dirt was gone forever. At the very centre it was perhaps ten feet deep; it would have taken all the lumber from a grain elevator to roof it over for a cave.

"Grampa—Grampa—" Melvin was calling—"Please, Grampa. Please, Grampa."

"We'll have to tip it up," Fin said, "so's we can open the door."

"You're not supposed to move injured people," Fat said.

Melvin squatted down beside the fallen privy and put his face to the hole. His frightened voice sounded cistern-hollow. "Grampa!" Then he really yelled as the tip of the varnished willow cane caught him across the bridge of the nose. He straightened up and he said, "He's still alive. Give me a hand."

It took all of us to upright the privy and Melvin's grandfather. He swung at us with his cane a couple of times when we opened the door, then he let us help him to the house and into his own room off the kitchen. Seated there on a Winnipeg couch, he stared straight ahead of himself as Melvin removed the boy scout hat, slipped off the packsack. With an arm around the old man's shoulders, Melvin eased him down on the pillow, then motioned us out of the room. Before we got to the door the old man spoke.

"Melvin."

"Yes, Grampa?"

"Sure they're all cleared out now?"

"Yes, Grampa."

He released a long sigh. "Get word to General Middleton."

"For help, Grampa?"

"Not help." The old man shook his head. "Sharply engaged enemy. Routed the bastards!"

We were all whipped that evening, and the balance of our merciful catharsis was earned over a month's quarantine, each in his own yard. When his month's isolation was up, Melvin gained a freedom he'd never known before; he didn't have to knock on another door, for his grandfather never wandered again. He sat at the Arbuckle living-room window for the next three years, then died.

One of Khartoum's most famous native sons, Roddy Montgomery had called him at the Chamber of Commerce birthday party in the Elks' Bar: Dr. Melvin Arbuckle, Portland psychiatrist and mental health trail-blazer—in shock therapy, of course.

W.O. Mitchell's classic novel Who Has Seen the Wind *has sold over half a million copies in Canada alone. His two short story collections* Jake and the Kid *and* According to Jake and the Kid *won the Stephen Leacock Award for Humour. He also wrote other novels and plays, and was a renowned performance artist and teacher of writing.*

ONE'S A HEIFER

Sinclair Ross

My uncle was laid up that winter with sciatica, so when the blizzard stopped and still two of the yearlings hadn't come home with the other cattle, Aunt Ellen said I'd better saddle Tim and start out looking for them.

"Then maybe I'll not be back tonight," I told her firmly. "Likely they've drifted as far as the sandhills. There's no use coming home without them."

I was thirteen, and had never been away like that all night before, but, busy with the breakfast, Aunt Ellen said yes, that sounded sensible enough, and while I ate, hunted up a dollar in silver for my meals.

"Most people wouldn't take it from a lad, but they're strangers up towards the hills. Bring it out independent-like, but don't insist too much. They're more likely to grudge you a feed of oats for Tim."

After breakfast I had to undress again, and put on two suits of underwear and two pairs of thick, home-knitted stockings. It was a clear, bitter morning. After the storm the drifts lay clean and unbroken to the horizon. Distant farm-buildings stood out distinct against the prairie as if the thin sharp atmosphere were a magnifying glass. As I started off Aunt Ellen peered cautiously out of the door a moment through a cloud of steam, and waved a red and white checkered dish-towel. I didn't wave back, but conscious of her uneasiness rode erect, as jaunty as the sheepskin and two suits of underwear would permit.

We took the road straight south about three miles. The calves, I reasoned, would have by this time found their way home if the blizzard hadn't carried them at least that far. Then we started catercornering across fields, riding over to straw-stacks where we could see cattle sheltering, calling at farmhouses to ask had they seen any strays. "Yearlings," I said each time politely. "Red with white spots and faces. The same almost except that one's a heifer and the other isn't."

Nobody had seen them. There was a crust on the snow not quite hard enough to carry Tim, and despite the cold his flanks and shoulders soon were steaming. He walked with his head down, and sometimes, taking my sympathy for granted, drew up a minute for breath.

My spirits, too, began to flag. The deadly cold and the flat white silent miles of prairie asserted themselves like a disapproving presence. The cattle round the straw-stacks stared when we rode up as if we were intruders. The fields stared, and the sky stared. People shivered in their doorways, and said they'd seen no strays.

At about one o'clock we stopped at a farmhouse for dinner. It was a single oat sheaf half thistles for Tim, and fried eggs and bread and tea for me. Crops had been poor that year, they apologized, and though they shook their heads when I brought out my money I saw the woman's eyes light greedily a second, as if her instincts of hospitality were struggling hard against some urgent need. We too, I said, had had poor crops lately. That was why it was so important that I find the calves.

We rested an hour, then went on again. "Yearlings," I kept on describing them. "Red with white spots and faces. The same except that one's a heifer and the other isn't."

Still no one had seen them, still it was cold, still Tim protested what a fool I was.

The country began to roll a little. A few miles ahead I could see the first low line of sandhills. "They'll be there for sure," I said aloud, more to encourage myself than Tim. "Keeping straight to the road it won't take a quarter as long to get home again."

But home now seemed a long way off. A thin white sheet of cloud spread across the sky, and though there had been no warmth in the sun the fields looked colder and bleaker without the glitter on the snow. Straw-stacks were fewer here, as if the land were poor, and every house we stopped at seemed more dilapidated than the one before.

A nagging wind rose as the afternoon wore on. Dogs yelped and bayed at us, and sometimes from the hills, like the signal of our approach, there was a thin, wavering howl of a coyote. I began to dread the miles home again almost as much as those still ahead. There were so many cattle straggling across the fields, so many yearlings just like ours. I saw them for sure a dozen times, and as often choked my disappointment down and clicked Tim on again.

AND THEN AT LAST I REALLY SAW THEM. It was nearly dusk, and along with fifteen or twenty other cattle they were making their way towards some buildings that lay huddled at the foot of the sandhills. They passed in single file less than fifty yards away, but when I pricked Tim forward to turn them back he floundered in a snowed-in water-cut. By the time we were out they were a little distance ahead, and on account of the drifts it was impossible to put on a spurt of speed and pass them. All we could do was take our place at the end of the file, and proceed at their pace towards the buildings.

It was about half a mile. As we drew near I debated with Tim whether we should ask to spend the night or start off right away for home. We were hungry and tired, but it was a poor, shiftless-looking place. The yard was littered with old wagons and machinery; the house was scarcely distinguishable from the stables. Darkness was beginning to close in, but there was no light in the windows.

Then as we crossed the yard we heard a shout, "Stay where you are," and a man came running towards us from the stable. He was tall and ungainly, and, instead of the short sheepskin that most farmers wear, had on a long black overcoat nearly to his feet. He seized Tim's bridle when he reached us, and glared for a minute as if he were going to pull me out of the saddle. "I told you to stay out," he said in a harsh, excited voice. "You heard me, didn't you? What do you want coming round here anyway?"

I steeled myself and said, "Our two calves."

The muscles of his face were drawn together threateningly, but close to him like this and looking straight into his eyes I felt that for all their fierce look there was something about them wavering and uneasy. "The two red ones with the white faces," I continued. "They've just gone into the shed over there with yours. If you'll give me a hand getting them out again I'll start for home now right away."

He peered at me a minute, let go the bridle, then clutched it again. "They're all mine," he countered. "I was over by the gate. I watched them coming in."

His voice was harsh and thick. The strange wavering look in his eyes steadied itself for a minute to a dare. I forced myself to meet it and insisted, "I saw them back a piece in the field. They're ours all right. Let me go over a minute and I'll show you."

With a crafty tilt of his head he leered, "You didn't see any calves. And now, if you know what's good for you, you'll be on your way."

"You're trying to steal them," I flared rashly. "I'll go home and get my uncle and the police after you—then you'll see whether they're our calves or not."

My threat seemed to impress him a little. With a shifty glance in the direction of the stable he said, "All right, come along and look them over. Then maybe you'll be satisfied." But all the way across the yard he kept his hand on Tim's bridle, and at the shed made me wait a few minutes while he went inside.

The cattle shed was a lean to on the horse stable. It was plain enough: he was hiding the calves before letting me inside to look around. While waiting for him, however, I had time to reflect that he was a lot bigger and stronger than I was, and that it might be prudent just to keep my eyes open, and not give him too much insolence.

He reappeared carrying a smoky lantern. "All right," he said pleasantly enough, "come in and look around. Will your horse stand, or do you want to tie him?"

We put Tim in an empty stall in the horse stable, then went through a narrow doorway with a bar across it to the cattle shed. Just as I expected, our calves weren't there. There were two red ones with white markings that he tried to make me believe were the ones I had seen, but, positive I hadn't been mistaken, I shook my head and glanced at the doorway we had just come through. It was narrow, but not too narrow. He read my expression and said, "You think they're in there. Come on, then, and look around."

The horse stable consisted of two rows of open stalls with a passage down the centre like an aisle. At the far end were two box-stalls, one with a sick colt in it, the other closed. They were both boarded up to the ceiling, so that you could see inside them only through the doors. Again he read my expression, and with a nod towards the closed one said, "It's just a kind of harness room now. Up till a year ago I kept a stallion."

But he spoke furtively, and seemed anxious to get me away from that end of the stable. His smoky lantern threw great swaying shadows over us; and the deep clefts and triangles of shadow on his face sent a little chill through me, and made me think what a dark and evil face it was.

I was afraid, but not too afraid. "If it's just a harness room," I said recklessly, "why not let me see inside? Then I'll be satisfied and believe you."

He wheeled at my question, and sidled over swiftly to the stall. He stood in front of the door, crouched down a little, the lantern in front of him like a shield. There was a sudden stillness through the stable as we faced each other. Behind the light from his lantern the darkness hovered vast and sinister. It seemed to hold its breath, to watch and listen. I felt a clutch of fear now at my throat, but I didn't move. My eyes were fixed on him so intently that he seemed to lose substance, to loom up close a moment, then recede. At last he disappeared completely, and there was only the lantern like a hard hypnotic eye.

It held me. It held me rooted, against my will. I wanted to run from the stable, but I wanted even more to see inside the stall. Wanting to see and yet afraid of seeing. So afraid that it was a relief when at last he gave a shamefaced laugh and said, "There's a hole in the floor—that's why I keep the door closed. If you didn't know, you might step into it—twist your foot. That's what happened to one of my horses a while ago."

I nodded as if I believed him, and went back tractably to Tim. But regaining control of myself as I tried the saddle girths, beginning to feel that my fear had been unwarranted, I looked up and said, "It's ten miles home, and we've been riding hard all day. If we could stay a while—have something to eat, and then get started—"

The wavering light came into his eyes again. He held the lantern up to see me better, such a long, intent scrutiny that it seemed he must discover my designs. But he gave a nod finally, as if reassured, brought oats and hay for Tim, and suggested, companionably, "After supper we can have a game of checkers."

Then, as if I were a grown-up, he put out his hand and said, "My name is Arthur Vickers."

INSIDE THE HOUSE, rid of his hat and coat, he looked less forbidding. He had a white nervous face, thin lips, a large straight nose, and deep uneasy eyes. When the lamp was lit I fancied I could still see the wavering expression in them, and decided it was what you called a guilty look.

"You won't think much of it," he said apologetically, following my glance around the room. "I ought to be getting things cleaned up again. Come over to the stove. Supper won't take long."

It was a large, low-ceilinged room that for the first moment or two struck me more like a shed or granary than a house. The table in the centre was littered with tools and harness. On a rusty cook-stove were two big steaming pots of bran. Next to the stove stood a grindstone, then a white iron bed covered with coats and horse blankets. At the end opposite the bed, weasel and coyote skins were drying. There were guns and traps on the wall, a horse collar, a pair of rubber boots. The floor was bare and grimy. Ashes were littered around the stove. In a corner squatted a live owl with a broken wing.

He walked back and forth a few times looking helplessly at the disorder, then cleared off the table and lifted the pots of bran to the back of the stove. "I've been mending harness," he explained. "You get careless, living alone like this. It takes a woman anyway."

My presence, apparently, was making him take stock of the room. He picked up a broom and swept for a minute, made an ineffective attempt to straighten the blankets on the bed, brought another lamp out of a cupboard and lit it. There was an ungainly haste to all his movements. He started unbuckling my sheepskin for me, then turned away suddenly to take off his own coat. "Now we'll have supper," he said with an effort at self-possession. "Coffee and beans is all I can give you—maybe a little molasses."

I replied diplomatically that that sounded pretty good. It didn't seem right, accepting hospitality this way from a man trying to steal your calves, but theft, I reflected, surely justified deceit. I held my hands out to the warmth and asked if I could help.

There was a kettle of plain navy beans already cooked. He dipped out enough for our supper into a frying pan, and on top laid rashers of fat salt pork. While I watched that they didn't burn he rinsed off a few dishes. Then he set out sugar and canned milk, butter, molasses, and dark heavy biscuits that he had baked himself the day before. He kept glancing at me so apologetically all the while that I leaned over and sniffed the beans, and said at home I ate a lot of them.

"It takes a woman," he repeated as we sat down to the table. "I don't often have anyone here to eat with me. If I'd known, I'd have cleaned things up a little."

I was too intent on my plateful of beans to answer. All through the meal he sat watching me, but made no further attempts at conversation. Hungry as I was, I noticed that the wavering, uneasy look was still in his eyes. A guilty look, I told myself again, and wondered what I was going to do to get the calves away. I finished my coffee and he continued:

"It's worse even than this in the summer. No time for meals—and the heat and flies. Last summer I had a girl cooking for a few weeks, but it didn't last. Just a cow she was—just a big stupid cow—and she wanted to stay on. There's a family of them back in the hills. I had to send her home."

I wondered should I suggest starting now, or ask to spend the night. Maybe when he's asleep, I thought, I can slip out of the house and get away with the calves. He went on, "You don't know how bad it is sometimes.

Weeks on end and no one to talk to. You're not yourself—you're not sure what you're going to say or do."

I remembered hearing my uncle talk about a man who had gone crazy living alone. And this fellow Vickers had queer eyes all right. And there was the live owl over in the corner, and the grindstone standing right beside the bed. "Maybe I'd better go now," I decided aloud. "Tim'll be rested, and it's ten miles home."

But he said no, it was colder now, with the wind getting stronger, and seemed so kindly and concerned that I half forgot my fears. "Likely he's just starting to go crazy," I told myself, "and it's only by staying that I'll have a chance to get the calves away."

When the table was cleared and the dishes washed he said he would go out and bed down the stable for the night. I picked up my sheepskin to go with him, but he told me sharply to stay inside. Just for a minute he looked crafty and forbidding as when I first rode up on Tim, and to allay his suspicions I nodded compliantly and put my sheepskin down again. It was better like that anyway, I decided. In a few minutes I could follow him, and perhaps, taking advantage of the shadows and his smoky lantern, make my way to the box-stall unobserved.

But when I reached the stable he had closed the door after him and hooked it from the inside. I walked round a while, tried to slip in by way of the cattle shed, and then had to go back to the house. I went with a vague feeling of relief again. There was still time, I told myself, and it would be safer anyway when he was sleeping.

So that it would be easier to keep from falling asleep myself I planned to suggest coffee again just before we went to bed. I knew that the guest didn't ordinarily suggest such things, but it was no time to remember manners when there was someone trying to steal your calves.

WHEN HE CAME IN FROM THE STABLE WE PLAYED CHECKERS. I was no match for him, but to encourage me he repeatedly let me win. "It's a long time now since I've had a chance to play," he kept on saying, trying to convince me that his short-sighted moves weren't intentional. "Sometimes I used to ask her to play, but I had to tell her every move to make. If she didn't win she'd upset the board and go off and sulk."

"My aunt is a little like that too," I said. "She cheats sometimes when we're playing cribbage—and, when I catch her, says her eyes aren't good."

"Women talk too much ever to make good checker players. It takes concentration. This one, though, couldn't even talk like anybody else."

After my long day in the cold I was starting to yawn already. He noticed it, and spoke in a rapid, earnest voice, as if afraid I might lose interest soon and want to go to bed. It was important for me too to stay awake, so I crowned a king and said, "Why don't you get someone, then, to stay with you?"

"Too many of them want to do that." His face darkened a little, almost as if warning me. "Too many of the kind you'll never get rid of again. She did, last summer when she was here. I had to put her out."

There was silence for a minute, his eyes flashing, and wanting to placate him I suggested, "She liked you, maybe."

He laughed a moment, harshly. "She liked me all right. Just two weeks ago she came back—walked over with an old suitcase and said she was going to stay. It was cold at home, and she had to work too hard, and she didn't mind even if I couldn't pay her wages."

I was getting sleepier. To keep awake I sat on the edge of the chair where it was uncomfortable and said, "Hadn't you asked her to come?"

His eyes narrowed. "I'd had trouble enough getting rid of her the first time. There were six of them at home, and she said her father thought it time that someone married her."

"Then she must be a funny one," I said. "Everybody knows that the man's supposed to ask the girl."

My remark seemed to please him. "I told you didn't I?" he said, straightening a little, jumping two of my men. "She was so stupid that at checkers she'd forget whether she was black or red."

We stopped playing now. I glanced at the owl in the corner and the ashes littered on the floor, and thought that keeping her would maybe have been a good idea after all. He read it in my face and said, "I used to think that too sometimes. I used to look at her and think nobody knew now anyway and that she'd maybe do. You need a woman on a farm all right. And night after night she'd be sitting there where you are—right there where you are, looking at me, not even trying to play—"

The fire was low, and we could hear the wind. "But then I'd go up in the hills, away from her for a while, and start thinking back the way things used to be, and it wasn't right even for the sake of your meals ready and your house kept clean. When she came back I tried to tell her that, but all the family are the same, and I realized it wasn't any use. There's nothing you can do when you're up against that sort of thing. The mother talks just like a child of ten. When she sees you coming she runs and hides. There are six of them, and it's come out in every one."

It was getting cold, but I couldn't bring myself to go over to the stove. There was the same stillness now as when he was standing at the box-stall door. And I felt the same illogical fear, the same powerlessness to move. It was the way his voice had sunk, the glassy, cold look in his eyes. The rest of his face disappeared; all I could see were his eyes. And they filled me with a vague and overpowering dread. My own voice a whisper, I asked, "And when you wouldn't marry her—what happened then?"

He remained motionless a moment, as if answering silently; then with an unexpected laugh like a breaking dish said, "Why, nothing happened. I just told her she couldn't stay. I went to town for a few days—and when I came back she was gone."

"Has she been back to bother you since?" I asked.

He made a little silo of checkers. "No—she took her suitcase with her."

To remind him that the fire was going down I went over to the stove and stood warming myself. He raked the coals with the lifter and put in poplar, two split pieces for a base and a thick round log on top. I yawned again. He said maybe I'd like to go to bed now, and I shivered and asked him could I have a drink of coffee first. While it boiled he stood stirring the two big pots of bran. The trouble with coffee, I realized, was that it would keep him from getting sleepy too.

I undressed finally and got into bed, but he blew out only one of the lamps, and sat on playing checkers with himself. I dozed a while, then sat up with a start, afraid it was morning already and that I'd lost my chance to get the calves away. He came over and looked at me a minute, then gently pushed my shoulders back on the pillow. "Why don't you come to bed too?" I asked, and he said, "Later I will—I don't feel sleepy yet."

It was like that all night. I kept dozing on and off, wakening in a fright each time to find him still there sitting at his checker board. He would raise his head sharply when I stirred, then tiptoe over to the bed and stand close to me listening till satisfied again I was asleep. The owl kept wakening too. It was down in the corner still where the lamplight scarcely reached, and I could see its eyes go on and off like yellow bulbs. The wind whistled drearily around the house. The blankets smelled like an old granary. He suspected what I was planning to do, evidently, and was staying awake to make sure I didn't get outside.

Each time I dozed I dreamed I was on Tim again. The calves were in sight, but far ahead of us, and with the drifts so deep we couldn't overtake them. Then instead of Tim it was the grindstone I was straddling, and that was the reason, not the drifts, that we weren't making better progress.

I wondered what would happen to the calves if I didn't get away with them. My uncle had sciatica, and it would be at least a day before I could be home and back again with some of the neighbours. By then Vickers might have butchered the calves, or driven them up to a hiding place in the hills where we'd never find them. There was the possibility, too, that Aunt Ellen and the neighbours wouldn't believe me. I dozed and woke—dozed and woke—always he was sitting at the checker board. I could hear the dry tinny ticking of an alarm clock, but from where I was lying couldn't see it. He seemed to be listening to it too. The wind would sometimes creak the house, and then he would give a start and sit rigid a moment with his eyes fixed on the window. It was always the window, as if there was nothing he was afraid of that could reach him by the door.

Most of the time he played checkers with himself, moving his lips, muttering words I couldn't hear, but once I woke to find him staring fixedly across the table as if he had a partner sitting there. His hands were clenched in front of him, there was a sharp, metallic glitter in his eyes. I lay transfixed, unbreathing. His eyes as I watched seemed to dilate, to brighten, to harden like a bird's. For a long time he sat contracted, motionless, as if gathering himself to strike, then furtively he slid his hand an inch or two along the table towards some checkers that were piled beside the board. It was as if he were reaching for a weapon, as if his invisible partner were an enemy. He clutched the checkers, slipped slowly from his chair and straightened. His movements were sure, stealthy, silent like a cat's. His face had taken on a desperate, contorted look. As he raised his hand the tension was unbearable.

It was a long time—a long time watching him the way you watch a finger tightening slowly in the trigger of a gun—and then suddenly wrenching himself to action he hurled the checkers with such vicious fury that they struck the wall and clattered back across the room.

And everything was quiet again. I started a little, mumbled to myself as if half-awakened, lay quite still. But he seemed to have forgotten me, and after standing limp and dazed a minute got down on his knees and started looking for the checkers. When he had them all, he put more wood in the stove, then returned quietly to the table and sat down. We were alone again; everything was exactly as before. I relaxed gradually, telling myself that he'd just been seeing things.

The next time I woke he was sitting with his head sunk forward on the table. It looked as if he had fallen asleep at last, and huddling alert among the bed-clothes I decided to watch a minute to make sure, then dress and try to slip out to the stable.

While I watched, I planned exactly every movement I was going to make. Rehearsing it in my mind as carefully as if I were actually doing it, I climbed out of bed, put on my clothes, tiptoed stealthily to the door and slipped outside. By this time, though, I was getting drowsy, and relaxing among the blankets I decided that for safety's sake I should rehearse it still again. I rehearsed it four times altogether, and the fourth time dreamed that I hurried on successfully to the stable.

I fumbled with the door a while, then went inside and felt my way through the darkness to the box-stall. There was a bright light suddenly and the owl was sitting over the door with his yellow eyes like a pair of lanterns. The calves, he told me, were in the other stall with the sick colt. I looked and they were there all right, but Tim came up and said it might be better not to start for home till morning. He reminded me that I hadn't paid for his feed or my own supper yet, and that if I slipped off this way it would mean that I was stealing, too. I agreed, realizing now that it wasn't the calves I was looking for after all, and that I still had to see inside the stall that was guarded by the owl. "Wait here," Tim said, "I'll tell you if he flies away," and without further questioning I lay down in the straw and went to sleep again. . . . When I woke coffee and beans were on the stove already, and though the lamp was still lit I could tell by the window that it was nearly morning.

We were silent during breakfast. Two or three times I caught him watching me, and it seemed his eyes were shiftier than before. After his sleepless night he looked tired and haggard. He left the table while I was still eating and fed raw rabbit to the owl, then came back and drank another cup of coffee. He had been friendly and communicative the night before, but now, just as when he first came running out of the stable in his long black coat, his expression was sullen and resentful. I began to feel that he was in a hurry to be rid of me.

I took my time, however, racking my brains to outwit him still and get the calves away. It looked pretty hopeless now, his eyes on me so suspiciously, my imagination at low ebb. Even if I did get inside the box-stall to see the calves—was he going to stand back then and let me start off home with them? Might it not more likely frighten him, make him do something desperate, so that I couldn't reach my uncle or the police? There was the owl over in the corner, the grindstone by the bed. And with such a queer fellow you could never tell. You could never tell, and you had to think about your own skin too. So I said politely, "Thank you, Mr. Vickers, for letting me stay all night," and remembering what Tim had told me took out my dollar's worth of silver.

He gave a short dry laugh and wouldn't take it. "Maybe you'll come back," he said, "and next time stay longer. We'll go shooting up in the hills if you like—and I'll make a trip to town for things so that we can have better meals. You need company sometimes for a change. There's been no one here now quite a while."

His face softened again as he spoke. There was an expression in his eyes as if he wished that I could stay on now. It puzzled me. I wanted to be indignant, and it was impossible. He held my sheepskin for me while I put it on, and tied the scarf around the collar with a solicitude and determination equal to Aunt Ellen's. And then he gave his short dry laugh again, and hoped I'd find my calves all right.

He had been out to the stable before I was awake, and Tim was ready for me, fed and saddled. But I delayed a few minutes, pretending to be interested in his horses and the sick colt. It would be worth something after all, I realized, to get just a glimpse of the calves. Aunt Ellen was going to be sceptical enough of my story as it was. It could only confirm her doubts to hear me say I hadn't seen the calves in the box-stall, and was just pretty sure that they were there.

So I went from stall to stall, stroking the horses and making comparisons with the ones we had at home. The door, I noticed, he had left wide open, ready for me to lead out Tim. He was walking up and down the aisle, telling me which horses were quiet, which to be careful of. I came to a nervous chestnut mare, and realized she was my only chance.

She crushed her hips against the side of the stall as I slipped up to her manger, almost pinning me, then gave her head a toss and pulled back hard on the halter shank. The shank, I noticed, was tied with an easy slip-knot that the right twist and a sharp tug would undo in half a second. And the door was wide open, ready for me to lead out Tim—and standing as she was with her body across the stall diagonally, I was for the moment screened from sight.

It happened quickly. There wasn't time to think of consequences. I just pulled the knot, in the same instant struck the mare across the nose. With a snort she threw herself backwards, almost trampling Vickers, then flung up her head to keep from tripping on the shank and plunged outside.

It worked as I hoped it would. "Quick," Vickers yelled to me, "the gate's open—try and head her off"—but instead I just waited till he himself was gone, then leaped to the box-stall.

The door was fastened with two tight-fitting slide-bolts, one so high that I could scarcely reach it standing on my toes. It wouldn't yield. There was a piece of broken whiffle-tree beside the other box-stall door. I snatched it up and started hammering on the pin. Still it wouldn't yield. The head of the pin was small and round, and the whiffle-tree kept glancing off. I was too terrified to pause a moment and take careful aim.

Terrified of the stall though, not of Vickers. Terrified of the stall, yet compelled by a frantic need to get inside. For the moment I had forgotten Vickers, forgotten even the danger of his catching me. I worked blindly, helplessly, as if I were confined and smothering. For a moment I yielded to panic, dropped the piece of whiffle-tree and started kicking at the door. Then, collected again, I forced back the lower bolt, and picking up the whiffle-tree tried to pry the door out a little at the bottom. But I had wasted too much time. Just as I dropped to my knees to peer through the opening Vickers seized me. I struggled to my feet and fought a moment, but it was such a hard, strangling clutch at my throat that I let myself go limp and blind. In desperation then I kicked him, and with a blow like a reflex he sent me staggering to the floor.

But it wasn't the blow that frightened me. It was the fierce, wild light in his eyes.

Stunned as I was, I looked up and saw him watching me, and, sick with terror, made a bolt for Tim. I untied him with hands that moved incredibly, galvanized for escape. I knew now for sure that Vickers was crazy. He followed me outside, and, just as I mounted, seized Tim again by the bridle. For a second or two it made me crazy too. Gathering up the free ends of the rein I lashed him hard across the face. He let go of the bridle, and, frightened and excited too now, Tim made a dash across the yard and out of the gate. Deep as the snow was, I kept him galloping for half a mile, pommelling him with my fists, kicking my heels against his sides. Then of his own accord he drew up short for breath, and I looked around to see whether Vickers was following. He wasn't—there was only snow and the hills, his buildings a lonely little smudge against the whiteness—and the relief was like a stick pulled out that's been holding up tomato vines or peas. I slumped across the saddle weakly, and till Tim started on again lay there whimpering like a baby.

We were home by noon. We didn't have to cross fields or stop at houses now, and there had been teams on the road packing down the snow so that Tim could trot part of the way and even canter. I put him in the stable without taking time to tie or unbridle him, and ran to the house to tell Aunt Ellen. But I was still frightened, cold and a little hysterical, and it was a while before she could understand how everything had happened. She was silent a minute, indulgent, then helping me off with my sheepskin said kindly, "You'd better forget about it now, and come over and get warm. The calves came home themselves yesterday. Just about an hour after you set out."

I looked up at her. "But the stall, then—just because I wanted to look inside he knocked me down—and if it wasn't the calves in there—"

She didn't answer. She was busy building up the fire and looking at the stew.

Sinclair Ross won acclaim for his works of prairie realism many years after his now classic novel, As for Me and My House, *first appeared in 1941. His collection of stories* The Lamp at Noon and Other Stories *was published in 1968.*

HORSES OF THE NIGHT

Margaret Laurence

I NEVER KNEW I HAD DISTANT COUSINS WHO LIVED UP NORTH, until Chris came down to Manawaka to go to high school. My mother said he belonged to a large family, relatives of ours, who lived at Shallow Creek, up north. I was six, and Shallow Creek seemed immeasurably far, part of a legendary winter country where no leaves grow and where the breath of seals and polar bears snuffled out steamily and turned to ice.

"Could plain people live there?" I asked my mother, meaning people who were not Eskimos. "Could there be a farm?"

"How do you mean?" she said, puzzled. "I told you. That's where they live. On the farm. Uncle Wilf—that was Chris's father, who died a few years back—he got the place as a homestead, donkey's years ago."

"But how could they grow anything? I thought you said it was up north."

"Mercy," my mother said, laughing, "it's not *that* far north, Vanessa. It's about a hundred miles beyond Galloping Mountain. You be nice to Chris, now, won't you? And don't go asking him a whole lot of questions the minute he steps inside the door."

How little my mother knew of me, I thought. Chris had been fifteen.

He could be expected to feel only scorn towards me. I detested the fact that I was so young. I did not think I would be able to say anything at all to him.

"What if I don't like him?"

"What if you don't?" my mother responded sharply. "You're to watch your manners, and no acting up, understand? It's going to be quite difficult enough without that."

"Why does he have to come here, anyway?" I demanded crossly. "Why can't he go to school where he lives?"

"Because there isn't any high school up there," my mother said. "I hope he gets on well here, and isn't too homesick. Three years is a long time. It's very good of your grandfather to let him stay at the Brick House."

She said this last accusingly, as though she suspected I might be thinking differently. But I had not thought of it one way or another. We were all having dinner at the Brick House because of Chris's arrival. It was the end of August, and sweltering. My grandfather's house looked huge and cool from the outside, the high low-sweeping spruce trees shutting out the sun with their dusky out-fanned branches. But inside it wasn't cool at all. The woodstove in the kitchen was going full blast, and the whole place smelled of roasting meat.

Grandmother Connor was wearing a large mauve apron. I thought it was a nicer colour than the dark bottle-green of her dress, but she believed in wearing sombre shades lest the spirit give way to vanity, which in her case was certainly not much of a risk. The apron came up over her shapeless bosom and obscured part of her cameo brooch, the only jewellery she ever wore, with its portrait of a fiercely bearded man whom I imagined to be either Moses or God.

"Isn't it nearly time for them to be getting here, Beth?" Grandmother Connor asked.

"Train's not due until six," my mother said. "It's barely five-thirty now. Has Father gone to the station already?"

"He went an hour ago," my grandmother said.

"He would," my mother commented.

"Now, now, Beth," my grandmother cautioned and soothed.

At last the front screen door was hurled open and Grandfather Connor strode into the house, followed by a tall lanky boy. Chris was wearing a white shirt, a tie, grey trousers. I thought, unwillingly, that he looked handsome. His face was angular, the bones showing through the brown skin. His grey eyes were slightly slanted, and his hair was the colour of couchgrass at the end of summer when it has been bleached to a light yellow by the sun. I had not planned to like him, not even a little, but somehow I wanted to defend him when I heard what my mother whispered to my grandmother before they went into the front hall.

"Heavens, look at the shirt and trousers—must've been his father's, the poor kid."

I shot out into the hall ahead of my mother, and then stopped and stood there.

"Hi, Vanessa," Chris said.

"How come you knew who I was?" I asked.

"Well, I knew your mother and dad only had one of a family, so I figured you must be her," he replied, grinning.

The way he spoke did not make me feel I had blundered. My mother greeted him warmly but shyly. Not knowing if she were expected to kiss him or to shake hands, she finally did neither. Grandmother Connor, however, had no doubts. She kissed him on both cheeks and then held him at arm's length to have a proper look at him.

"Bless the child," she said.

Coming from anyone else, this remark would have sounded ridiculous, especially as Chris was at least a head taller. My grandmother was the only person I have ever known who could say such things without appearing false.

"I'll show you your room, Chris," my mother offered.

Grandfather Connor, who had been standing in the living room doorway in absolute silence, looking as granite as a statue in the cemetery, now followed Grandmother out to the kitchen.

"Train was forty minutes late," he said weightily.

"What a shame," my grandmother said. "But I thought it wasn't due until six, Timothy."

"Six!" my grandfather cried. "That's the mainline train. The local's due at five-twenty."

This was not correct, as both my grandmother and I knew. But neither of us contradicted him.

"What on earth are you cooking a roast for, on a night like this?" my grandfather went on. "A person could fry an egg on the sidewalk, it's that hot. Potato salad would've gone down well."

Privately I agreed with this opinion, but I could never permit myself to acknowledge agreement with him on anything. I automatically and emotionally sided with Grandmother in all issues, not because she was inevitably right but because I loved her.

"It's not a roast," my grandmother said mildly. "It's mock-duck. The stove's only been going for an hour. I thought the boy would be hungry after the trip."

My mother and Chris had come downstairs and were now in the living room. I could hear them there, talking awkwardly, with pauses.

"Potato salad," my grandfather declaimed, "would've been plenty good enough. He'd have been lucky to get it, if you ask me anything. Wilf's family hasn't got two cents to rub together. It's me that's paying for the boy's keep."

The thought of Chris in the living room, and my mother unable to explain, was too much for me. I sidled over to the kitchen door, intending to close it. But my grandmother stopped me.

"No," she said, with unexpected firmness. "Leave it open, Vanessa."

I could hardly believe it. Surely she couldn't want Chris to hear? She herself was always able to move with equanimity through a hurricane because she believed that a mighty fortress was her God. But the rest of us were not like that, and usually she did her best to protect us. At the time I felt only bewilderment. I think now that she must have realised Chris would have to learn the Brick House sooner or later, and he might as well start right away.

I had to go into the living room. I had to know how Chris would take my grandfather. Would he, as I hoped, be angry and perhaps even speak out? Or would he, meekly, only be embarrassed?

"Wilf wasn't much good, even as a young man," Grandfather Connor was trumpeting. "Nobody but a simpleton would've taken up a homestead in a place like that. Anybody could've told him that land's no use for a thing except hay."

Was he going to remind us again how well he had done in the hardware business? Nobody had ever given him a hand, he used to tell me. I am sure he believed that this was true. Perhaps it even was true.

"If the boy takes after his father, it's a poor lookout for him," my grandfather continued.

I felt the old rage of helplessness. But as for Chris—he gave no sign of feeling anything. He was sitting on the big wing-backed sofa that curled into the bay window like a black and giant seashell. He began to talk to me, quite easily, just as though he had not heard a word my grandfather was saying.

This method proved to be the one Chris always used in any dealings with my grandfather. When the bludgeoning words came, which was often, Chris never seemed, like myself, to be holding back with a terrible strained force for fear of letting go and speaking out and having the known world unimaginably fall to pieces. He would not argue or defend himself, but he did not apologise, either. He simply appeared to be absent, elsewhere. Fortunately there was very little need for response, for when Grandfather Connor pointed out your shortcomings, you were not expected to reply.

But this aspect of Chris was one which I noticed only vaguely at the time. What won me was that he would talk to me and wisecrack as though I were his same age. He was—although I didn't know the phrase then—a respecter of persons.

On the rare evenings when my parents went out, Chris would come over to mind me. These were the best times, for often when he was supposed to be doing his homework, he would make fantastic objects for my amusement, or his own—pipecleaners twisted into the shape of wildly prancing midget men, or an old set of Christmas-tree lights fixed onto a puppet theatre with a red velvet curtain that really pulled. He had skill in making miniature things of all kinds. Once for my birthday he gave me a leather saddle no bigger than a matchbox, which he had sewn himself, complete in every detail, stirrups and horn, with the criss-cross lines that were the brand name of his ranch, he said, explaining it was a reference to his own name.

"Can I go to Shallow Creek sometime?" I asked one evening.

"Sure. Some summer holidays, maybe. I've got a sister about your age. The others are all grown up."

I did not want to hear. His sisters—for Chris was the only boy—did not exist for me, not even as photographs, because I did not want them to exist. I wanted him to belong only here. Shallow Creek existed, though, no longer filled with ice mountains in my mind but as some beckoning country beyond all ordinary considerations.

"Tell me what it's like there, Chris."

"My gosh, Vanessa, I've told you before, about a thousand times."

"You never told me what your house is like."

"Didn't I? Oh well—it's made out of trees grown right there beside the lake."

"Made out of trees? Gee. Really?"

I could see it. The trees were still growing, and the leaves were firmly and greenly on them. The branches had been coaxed into formations of towers and high-up nests where you could look out and see for a hundred miles or more.

"That lake, you know," Chris said. "It's more like an inland sea. It goes on for ever and ever amen, that's how it looks. And you know what? Millions of years ago, before there were any human beings at all, that lake was full of water monsters. All different kinds of dinosaurs. Then they all died off. Nobody knows for sure why. Imagine them—all those huge creatures, with necks like snakes, and some of them had hackles on their heads, like a rooster's comb only very tough, like hard leather. Some guys from Winnipeg came up a few years back, there, and dug up dinosaur bones, and they found footprints in the rocks."

"Footprints in the *rocks*?"

"The rocks were mud, see, when the dinosaurs went trampling through, but after trillions of years the mud turned into stone and there were these mighty footprints with the claws still showing. Amazing, eh?"

I could only nod, fascinated and horrified. Imagine going swimming in those waters. What if one of the creatures had lived on?

"Tell me about the horses," I said.

"Oh, them. Well, we've got these two riding horses. Duchess and Firefly. I raised them, and you should see them. Really sleek, know what I mean? I bet I could make racers out of them."

He missed the horses, I thought with selfish satisfaction, more than he missed his family. I could visualise the pair, one sorrel and one black, swifting through all the meadows of summer.

"When can I go, Chris?"

"Well, we'll have to see. After I get through high school, I won't be at Shallow Creek much."

"Why not?"

"Because," Chris said, "what I am going to be is an engineer, civil engineer. You ever seen a really big bridge, Vanessa? Well, I haven't either, but I've seen pictures. You take the Golden Gate Bridge in San Francisco now. Terrifically high—all those thin ribs of steel, joined together to go across this very wide stretch of water. It doesn't seem possible, but it's there. That's what engineers do. Imagine doing something like that, eh?"

I could not imagine it. It was beyond me.

"Where will you go?" I asked. I did not want to think of his going anywhere.

"Winnipeg, to college," he said with assurance.

The Depression did not get better, as everyone had been saying it would. It got worse, and so did the drought. That part of the prairies where we lived was never dustbowl country. The farms around Manawaka never had a total crop failure, and afterwards, when the drought was over, people used to remark on this fact proudly, as though it had been due to some virtue or special status, like the Children of Israel being afflicted by Jehovah but never in real danger of annihilation. But although Manawaka never knew the worst, what it knew was bad enough. Or so I learned later. At the time I saw none of it. For me, the Depression and drought were external and abstract, malevolent gods whose names I secretly learned although they were concealed from me, and whose evil I sensed only superstitiously, knowing they threatened us but not how or why. What I really saw was only what went on in our family.

"He's done quite well all through, despite everything," my mother said. She sighed, and I knew she was talking about Chris.

"I know," my father said. "We've been over all this before, Beth. But quite good just isn't good enough. Even supposing he managed to get a scholarship, which isn't likely, it's only tuition and books. What about room and board? Who's going to pay for that? Your father?"

"I see I shouldn't have brought up the subject at all," my mother said in an aloof voice.

"I'm sorry," my father said impatiently. "But you know, yourself, he's the only one who might possibly—"

"I can't bring myself to ask Father about it, Ewen. I simply cannot do it."

"There wouldn't be much point in asking," my father said, "when the answer is a foregone conclusion. He feels he's done his share, and actually, you know, Beth, he has, too. Three years, after all. He may not have done it gracefully, but he's done it."

We were sitting in the living room, and it was evening. My father was slouched in the grey armchair that was always his. My mother was slenderly straight-backed in the blue chair in which nobody else ever sat. I was sitting on the footstool, beige needlepoint with mathematical roses, to which I had staked own claim. This seating arrangement was obscurely satisfactory to me, perhaps because predictable, like the three bears. I was pretending to be colouring into a scribbler on my knee, and from time to time my lethargic purple crayon added a feather to an outlandish swan. To speak would be to invite dismissal. But their words forced questions in my head.

"Chris isn't going away, is he?"

My mother swooped, shocked at her own neglect.

"My heavens—are you still up, Vanessa? What am I thinking of?"

"Where is Chris going?"

"We're not sure yet," my mother evaded, chivvying me up the stairs. "We'll see."

He would not go, I thought. Something would happen, miraculously, to prevent him. He would remain, with his long loping walk and his half-slanted grey eyes and his talk that never excluded me. He would stay right here. And soon, because I desperately wanted to, and because every day mercifully made me older, quite soon I would be able to reply with such a lightning burst of knowingness that it would astound him, when he spoke of the space or was it some black sky that never ended anywhere beyond this earth. Then I would not be innerly belittled for being unable to figure out what he would best like to hear. At that good and imagined time, I would not any longer be limited. I would not any longer be young.

I was nine when Chris left Manawaka. The day before he was due to go, I knocked on the door of his room in the Brick House.

"Come in," Chris said. "I'm packing. Do you know how to fold socks, Vanessa?"

"Sure. Of course."

"Well, get folding on that bunch there, then."

I had come to say goodbye, but I did not want to say it yet. I got to work on the socks. I did not intend to speak about the matter of college, but the knowledge that I must not speak about it made me uneasy. I was afraid I would blurt out a reference to it in my anxiety not to. My mother had said, "He's taken it amazingly well—he doesn't even mention it, so we mustn't either."

"Tomorrow night you'll be in Shallow Creek," I ventured.

"Yeh." He did not look up. He went on stuffing clothes and books into his suitcase.

"I'll bet you'll be glad to see the horses, eh?" I wanted him to say he didn't care about the horses any more and that he would rather stay here.

"It'll be good to see them again," Chris said. "Mind handing over those socks now, Vanessa? I think I can just squash them in at the side here. Thanks. Hey, look at that, will you? Everything's in. Am I an expert packer or am I an expert packer?"

I sat on his suitcase for him so it would close, and then he tied a piece of rope around it because the lock wouldn't lock.

"Ever thought what it would be like to be a traveller, Vanessa?" he asked.

I thought of Richard Halliburton, taking an elephant over the Alps and swimming illicitly in the Taj Mahal lily pool by moonlight.

"It would be keen," I said, because this was the word Chris used to describe the best possible. "That's what I'm going to do someday."

He did not say, as for a moment I feared he might, that girls could not be travellers.

"Why not?" he said. "Sure you will, if you really want to. I got this theory, see, that anybody can do anything at all, anything, if they really set their minds to it. But you have to have this total concentration. You have to focus on it with your whole mental powers, and not let it slip away by forgetting to hold it in your mind. If you hold it in your mind, like, then it's real, see? You take most people, now. They can't concentrate worth a darn."

"Do you think I can?" I enquired eagerly, believing that this was what he was talking about.

"What?" he said. "Oh—sure. Sure I think you can. Naturally."

Chris did not write after he left Manawaka. About a month later we had a letter from his mother. He was not at Shallow Creek. He had not gone back. He had got off the northbound train at the first stop after Manawaka, cashed in his ticket, and thumbed a lift with a truck to Winnipeg. He had written to his mother from there, but had given no address. She had not heard from him since. My mother read Aunt Tess's letter aloud to my father. She was too upset to care whether I was listening or not.

"I can't think what possessed him, Ewen. He never seemed irresponsible. What if something should happen to him? What if he's broke? What do you think we should do?"

"What can we do? He's nearly eighteen. What he does is his business. Simmer down, Beth, and let's decide what we're going to tell your father."

"Oh Lord," my mother said. "There's that to consider, of course."

I went out without either of them noticing. I walked to the hill at the edge of the town, and down into the valley where the scrub oak and poplar grew almost to the banks of the Wachakwa River. I found the oak where we had gone last autumn, in a gang, to smoke cigarettes made of dried leaves and pieces of newspaper. I climbed to the lowest branch and stayed there for a while.

I was not consciously thinking about Chris. I was not thinking of anything. But when at last I cried, I felt relieved afterwards and could go home again.

Chris departed from my mind, after that, with a quickness that was due to the other things that happened. My Aunt Edna, who was a secretary in Winnipeg, returned to Manawaka to live because the insurance company cut down on staff and she could not find another job. I was intensely excited and jubilant about her return, and could not see why my mother seemed the opposite, even though she was as fond of Aunt Edna as I was. Then my brother Roderick was born, and that same year Grandmother Connor died. The strangeness, the unbelievability, of both these events took up all of me.

When I was eleven, almost two years after Chris had left, he came back without warning. I came home from school and found him sitting in our living room. I could not accept that I had nearly forgotten him until this instant. Now that he was present, and real again, I felt I had betrayed him by not thinking of him more.

He was wearing a navy-blue serge suit. I was old enough now to notice that it was a cheap one and had been worn a considerable time. Otherwise, he looked the same, the same smile, the same knife-boned face with no flesh to speak of, the same unresting eyes.

"How come you're here?" I cried. "Where have you been, Chris?"

"I'm a traveller," he said. "Remember?"

He was a traveller all right. One meaning of the word *traveller* in our part of the world, was a travelling salesman. Chris was selling vacuum cleaners. That evening he brought out his line and showed us. He went through his spiel for our benefit, so we could hear how it sounded.

"Now look, Beth," he said, turning the appliance on and speaking loudly above its moaning roar, "see how it brightens up this old rug of yours? Keen, eh?"

"Wonderful," my mother laughed. "Only we can't afford one."

"Oh well—" Chris said quickly, "I'm not trying to sell one to you. I'm only showing you. Listen, I've only been in this job a month, but I figure this is really a going thing. I mean, it's obvious, isn't it? You take all those old wire carpet-beaters of yours, Beth. You could kill yourself over them and your carpet isn't going to look one-tenth as good as it does with this."

"Look, I don't want to seem—" my father put in, "but, hell, they're not exactly a new invention, and we're not the only ones who can't afford—"

"This is a pretty big outfit, you know?" Chris insisted. "Listen, I don't plan to stay, Ewen. But a guy could work at it for a year or so, and save—right? Lots of guys work their way through university like that."

I needed to say something really penetrating, something that would show him I knew the passionate truth of his conviction.

"I bet—" I said, "I bet you'll sell a thousand, Chris."

Two years ago, this statement would have seemed self-evident, unquestionable. Yet now, when I had spoken, I knew that I did not believe it.

The next time Chris visited Manawaka, he was selling magazines. He had the statistics worked out. If every sixth person in town would get a subscription to *Country Guide*, he could make a hundred dollars in a month. We didn't learn how he got on. He didn't stay in Manawaka a full month. When he turned up again, it was winter. Aunt Edna phoned.

"Nessa? Listen, kiddo, tell your mother she's to come down if it's humanly possible. Chris is here, and Father's having fits."

So in five minutes we were scurrying through the snow, my mother and I, with our overshoes not even properly done up and our feet getting wet. We need not have worried. By the time we reached the Brick House, Grandfather Connor had retired to the basement, where he sat in the rocking chair beside the furnace, making occasional black pronouncements like a subterranean oracle. These loud utterances made my mother and aunt wince, but Chris didn't seem to notice any more than he ever had. He was engrossed in telling us about the mechanism he was holding. It had a cranker handle like an old-fashioned sewing machine.

"You attach the ball of wool here, see? Then you set this little switch here, and adjust this lever, and you're away to the races. Neat, eh?"

It was a knitting machine. Chris showed us the finished products. The men's socks he had made were coarse wool, one pair in grey heather and another in maroon. I was impressed.

"Gee—can I do it, Chris?"

"Sure. Look, you just grab hold of the handle right here."

"Where did you get it?" my mother asked.

"I've rented it. The way I figure it, Beth, I can sell these things at about half the price you'd pay in a store, and they're better quality."

"Who are you going to sell them to?" Aunt Edna enquired.

"You take all these guys who do outside work—they need heavy socks all year round, not just in winter. I think this thing could be quite a gold mine."

"Before I forget," my mother said, "how's your mother and the family keeping?"

"They're okay," Chris said in a restrained voice. "They're not short of hands, if that's what you mean, Beth. My sisters have their husbands there."

Then he grinned, casting away the previous moment, and dug into his suitcase.

"Hey, I haven't shown you—these are for you, Vanessa, and this pair is for Roddie."

My socks were cherry-coloured. The very small ones for my brother were turquoise.

Chris only stayed until after dinner, and then he went away again.

AFTER MY FATHER DIED, the whole order of life was torn. Nothing was known or predictable any longer. For months I lived almost entirely within myself, so when my mother told me one day that Chris couldn't find any work at all because there were no jobs and so he had gone back to Shallow Creek to stay, it made scarcely any impression on me. But that summer, my mother decided I ought to go away for a holiday. She hoped it might take my mind off my father's death. What, if anything, was going to take her mind off his death, she did not say.

"Would you like to go to Shallow Creek for a week or so?" she asked me. "I could write to Chris's mother."

Then I remembered, all in a torrent, the way I had imagined it once, when he used to tell me about it—the house fashioned of living trees, the lake like a sea where monsters had dwelt, the grass that shone like green wavering light while the horses flew in the splendour of their pride.

"Yes," I said. "Write to her."

The railway did not go through Shallow Creek, but Chris met me at Challoner's Crossing. He looked different, not only thinner, but—what was it? Then I saw that it was the fact that his face and neck were tanned red-brown, and he was wearing denims, farm pants, and a blue plaid shirt open at the neck. I liked him like this. Perhaps the change was not so much in him as in myself, now that I was thirteen. He looked masculine in a way I had not been aware of, before.

"C'mon, kid," he said. "The limousine's over here."

It was a wagon and two horses, which was what I had expected, but the nature of each was not what I had expected. The wagon was a long and clumsy one, made of heavy planking, and the horses were both plough horses, thick in the legs, and badly matched as a team. The mare was short and stout, matronly. The gelding was very tall and gaunt, and he limped.

"Allow me to introduce you," Chris said. "Floss—Trooper—this is Vanessa."

He did not mention the other horses, Duchess and Firefly, and neither did I, not all the fortnight I was there. I guess I had known for some years now, without realising it, that the pair had only ever existed in some other dimension.

Shallow Creek wasn't a town. It was merely a name on a map. There was a grade school a few miles away, but that was all. They had to go to Challoner's Crossing for their groceries. We reached the farm, and Chris steered me through the crowd of aimless cows and wolfish dogs in the yard, while I flinched with panic.

It was perfectly true that the house was made out of trees. It was a fair-sized but elderly shack, made out of poplar poles and chinked with mud. There was an upstairs, which was not so usual around here, with three bedrooms, one of which I was to share with Chris's sister, Jeannie, who was slightly younger than I, a pallid-eyed girl who was either too shy to talk or who had nothing to say. I never discovered which, because I was so reticent with her myself, wanting to push her away, not to recognise her, and at the same time experiencing a shocked remorse at my own unacceptable feelings.

Aunt Tess, Chris's mother, was severe in manner and yet wanting to be kind, worrying over it, making tentative overtures which were either ignored or repelled by her older daughters and their monosyllabic husbands. Youngsters swam in and out of the house like shoals of nameless fishes. I could not see how so many people could live here, under the one roof, but then I learned they didn't. The married daughters had their own dwelling places, nearby, but some kind of communal life was maintained. They wrangled endlessly but they never left one another alone, not even for a day.

Chris took no part at all, none. When he spoke, it was usually to the children, and they would often follow him around the yard or to the barn, not pestering but just trailing along in clusters of three or four. He never told them to go away. I liked him for this, but it bothered me, too. I wished he would return his sisters' bickering for once, or tell them to clear out, or even yell at one of the kids. But he never did. He closed himself off from squabbling voices just as he used to do with Grandfather Connor's spearing words.

The house had no screens on the doors or windows, and at meal times the flies were so numerous you could hardly see the food for the iridescent-winged blue-black bodies squirming all over it. Nobody noticed my squeamishness except Chris, and he was the only one from whom I really wanted to conceal it.

"Fan with your hand," he murmured.

"It's okay," I said quickly.

For the first time in all the years we had known each other, we could not look the other in the eye. Around the table, the children stabbed and snivelled, until Chris's oldest sister, driven frantic, shrieked, *Shut up shut up shut up*. Chris began asking me about Manawaka then, as though nothing were going on around him.

They were due to begin haying, and Chris announced that he was going to camp out in the bluff near the hayfields. To save himself the long drive in the wagon each morning, he explained, but I felt this wasn't the real reason.

"Can I go, too?" I begged. I could not bear the thought of living in the house with all the others who were not known to me, and Chris not here.

"Well, I don't know—"

"Please. Please, Chris. I won't be any trouble. I promise."

Finally he agreed. We drove out in the big hayrack, its slatted sides rattling, its old wheels jolting metallically. The road was narrow and dirt, and around it the low bushes grew, wild rose and blueberry and wolf willow with silver leaves. Sometimes we would come to a bluff of pale-leaved poplar trees, and once a red-winged blackbird flew up out of the branches and into the hot dusty blue of the sky.

Then we were there. The hayfields lay beside the lake. It was my first view of the water which had spawned saurian giants so long ago. Chris drove the hayrack through the fields of high coarse grass and on down almost to the lake's edge, where there was no shore but only the green rushes like floating meadows in which the water birds nested. Beyond the undulating reeds the open lake stretched, deep, green-gray, out and out, beyond sight.

No human word could be applied. The lake was not lonely or untamed. These words relate to people, and there was nothing of people here. There was no feeling about the place. It existed in some world in which man was not yet born. I looked at the grey reaches of it and felt threatened. It was like the view of God which I had held since my father's death. Distant, indestructible, totally indifferent.

Chris had jumped down off the hayrack.

"We're not going to camp *here*, are we?" I asked and pleaded.

"No. I just want to let the horses drink. We'll camp up there in the bluff." I looked. "It's still pretty close to the lake, isn't it?"

"Don't worry," Chris said, laughing. "You won't get your feet wet."

"I didn't mean that."

Chris looked at me.

"I know you didn't," he said. "But let's learn to be a little tougher, and not let on, eh? It's necessary."

Chris worked through the hours of sun, while I lay on the half-formed stack of hay and looked up at the sky. The blue air trembled and spun with the heat haze, and the hay on which I was lying held the scents of grass and dust and wild mint.

In the evening, Chris took the horses to the lake again, and then he drove the hayrack to the edge of the bluff and we spread out our blankets underneath it. He made a fire and we had coffee and a tin of stew, and then we went to bed. We did not wash, and we slept in our clothes. It was only when I was curled up uncomfortably with the itching blanket around me that I felt a sense of unfamiliarity at being here, with Chris only three feet away, a self-consciousness I would not have felt even the year before. I do not think he felt this sexual strangeness. If he wanted me not to be a child—and he did—it was not with the wish that I would be a woman. It was something else.

"Are you asleep, Vanessa?" he asked.

"No. I think I'm lying on a tree root."

"Well, shift yourself, then," he said. "Listen, kid, I never said anything before, because I didn't really know what to say, but—you know how I felt about your dad dying, and that, don't you?"

"Yes," I said chokingly. "It's okay. I know."

"I used to talk with Ewen sometimes. He didn't see what I was driving at, mostly, but he'd always listen, you know? You don't find many guys like that."

We were both silent for a while.

"Look," Chris said finally. "Ever noticed how much brighter the stars are when you're completely away from any houses? Even the lamps up at the farm, there, make enough of a glow to keep you from seeing properly like you can out here. What do they make you think about, Vanessa?"

"Well—"

"I guess most people don't give them much thought at all, except maybe to say—*very pretty*—or like that. But the point is, they aren't like that. The stars and planets, in themselves, are just not like that, not *pretty*, for heaven's sake. They're gigantic—some of them burning—imagine those worlds tearing through space and made of pure fire. Or the ones that are absolutely dead—just rock or ice and no warmth in them. There must be some, though, that have living creatures. You wonder what *they* could look like, and what they feel. We won't ever get to know. But somebody will know, some day. I really believe that. Do you ever think about this kind of thing at all?"

He was twenty-one. The distance between us was still too great. For years I had wanted to be older so I might talk with him, but now I felt unready.

"Sometimes," I said, hesitantly, making it sound like *Never*.

"People usually say there must be a God," Chris went on, "because otherwise how did the universe get here? But that's ridiculous. If the stars and planets go on to infinity, they could have existed forever, for no reason at all. Maybe they weren't ever created. Look—what's the alternative? To believe in a God who is brutal. What else could He be? You've only got to look anywhere around you. It would be an insult to Him to believe in a God like that. Most people don't like talking about this kind of thing—it embarrasses them, you know? Or else they're not interested. I don't mind. I can always think about things myself. You don't actually need anyone to talk to. But about God, though—if there's a war, like it looks there will be, would people claim that was planned? What kind of a God would pull a trick like that? And yet, you know, plenty of guys would think it was a godsend, and who's to say they're wrong? It would be a job, and you'd get around and see places."

He paused, as though waiting for me to say something. When I did not, he resumed.

"Ewen told me about the last war, once. He hardly ever talked about it, but this once he told me about seeing the horses into the mud, actually going under, you know? And the way their eyes looked when they realised they weren't going to get out. Ever seen horses' eyes when they're afraid, I mean really berserk with fear, like in a bush-fire? Ewen said a guy tended to concentrate on the horses because he didn't dare think what was happening to the men. Including himself. Do you ever listen to the news at all, Vanessa?"

"I—"

I could only feel how foolish I must sound, still unable to reply as I would have wanted, comprehendingly. I felt I had failed myself utterly. I could not speak even the things I knew. As for the other things, the things I did not know, I resented Chris's facing me with them. I took refuge in pretending to be asleep, and after a while Chris stopped talking.

Chris left Shallow Creek some months after the war began, and joined the Army. After his basic training he was sent to England. We did not hear from him until about a year later, when a letter arrived for me.

"Vanessa—what's wrong?" my mother asked.

"Nothing."

"Don't fib," she said firmly. "What did Chris say in his letter, honey?"

"Oh—not much."

She gave me a curious look and then she went away. She would never have demanded to see the letter. I did not show it to her and she did not ask about it again.

Six months later my mother heard from Aunt Tess. Chris had been sent home from England and discharged from the Army because of a mental breakdown. He was now in the provincial mental hospital and they did not know how long he would have to remain there. He had been violent, before, but now he was not violent. He was, the doctors had told his mother, passive.

Violent. I could not associate the word with Chris, who had been so much the reverse. I could not bear to consider what anguish must have catapulted him into that even greater anguish. But the way he was now seemed almost worse. How might he be? Sitting quite still, wearing the hospital's grey dressing-gown, the animation gone from his face?

My mother cared about him a great deal, but her immediate thought was not for him.

"When I think of you, going up to Shallow Creek that time," she said, "and going out camping with him, and what might have happened—"

I, also, was thinking of what might have happened. But we were not thinking of the same thing. For the first time I recognised, at least a little, the dimensions of his need to talk that night. He must have understood perfectly well how impossible it would be, with a thirteen-year-old. But there was no one else. All his life's choices had grown narrower and narrower. He had been forced to return to the alien lake of home, and when finally he saw a means of getting away, it could only be into a turmoil which appalled him and which he dreaded even more than he knew. I had listened to his words, but I had not really heard them, not until now. It would not have made much difference to what happened, but I wished it were not too late to let him know.

Once when I was on holiday from college, my mother got me to help her clean out the attic. We sifted through boxes full of junk, old clothes, schoolbooks, bric-a-brac that once had been treasures. In one of the boxes I found the miniature saddle that Chris had made for me a long time ago.

"Have you heard anything recently?" I asked, ashamed that I had not asked sooner.

She glanced up at me. "Just the same. It's always the same. They don't think there will be much improvement."

Then she turned away.

"He always used to seem so—hopeful. Even when there was really nothing to be hopeful about. That's what I find so strange. He *seemed* hopeful, didn't you think?"

"Maybe it wasn't hope," I said.

"How do you mean?"

I wasn't certain myself. I was thinking of all the schemes he'd had, the ones that couldn't possibly have worked, the unreal solutions to which he'd clung because there were no others, the brave and useless strokes of fantasy against a depression that was both the world's and his own.

"I don't know," I said. "I just think things were always more difficult for him than he let on, that's all. Remember that letter?"

"Yes."

"Well—what it said was that they could force his body to march and even to kill, but what they didn't know was that he'd fooled them. He didn't live inside it any more."

"Oh Vanessa—" my mother said. "You must have suspected right then."

"Yes, but—"

I could not go on, could not say that the letter seemed only the final heartbreaking extension of that way he'd always had of distancing himself from the absolute unbearability of battle.

I picked up the tiny saddle and turned it over in my hand.

"Look. His brand, the name of his ranch. The Criss-Cross."

"What ranch?" my mother said, bewildered.

"The one where he kept his racing horses. Duchess and Firefly."

Some words came into my head, a single line from a poem I had once heard. I knew it referred to a lover who did not want the morning to come, but to me it had another meaning, a different relevance.

Slowly, slowly, horses of the night—

The night must move like this for him, slowly, all through the days and nights. I could not know whether the land he journeyed through was inhabited by terrors, the old monster-kings of the lake, or whether he had discovered at last a way for himself to make the necessary dream perpetual.

I put the saddle away once more, gently and ruthlessly, back into the cardboard box.

Margaret Laurence was born in Neepawa, Manitoba, and studied in Winnipeg. She is widely celebrated for her African novels and especially for her Manawaka novels: The Stone Angel, A Jest of God, The Fire-Dwellers, A Bird in the House *and* The Diviners.

THE GREAT ELECTRICAL REVOLUTION

K EN M ITCHELL

I was only a little guy in 1937 but I can still remember Grandad being out of work. Nobody had any money to pay him and, as he said, there wasn't much future in bricklaying as a charity. So mostly he just sat around in his suite above the hardware store and listened to the radio. We all listened to it when there was nothing else to do, which was most of the time, unless you happened to be going to school like me. Grandad stuck right there through it all, soap operas, weather reports and quiz shows. Unless he came across a bit of cash somewhere, and then he and Uncle Fred would go down to the beer parlour at the King William Hotel.

Grandad and Grandma came out from the Old Country long before I was born. When they arrived in Moose Jaw all they had was three children—Uncle Fred, Aunt Thecla and my dad—a trunk full of working clothes and a twenty-six pound post maul for putting up fences to keep "rogues" off Grandad's land. Rogues meant Orangemen, cattle rustlers, and capitalists. All the way on the train out from Montreal, he glared out the Pullman window at the endless flat, saying to his family, "I came out here for land, b'Christ, and none of them's going to sly it on me!" He had sworn to carve a mighty estate from the raw Saskatchewan prairie, though he had never handled so much as a garden hoe in his life before leaving Dublin.

When he stepped off the train at the CPR station in Moose Jaw, it looked like he was thinking of tearing it down and seeding the site to oats. It was two o'clock in the morning, but he kept striding up and down the lobby of the station, his chest puffed out like a bantam rooster in a chicken run. My dad and Uncle Fred and Aunt Thecla sat on the trunk while Grandma pleaded with him to go out and find them a place to stay. It was only later they realized he was afraid to step outside the station. But he finally quit strutting long enough to find a porter to carry their trunk to a hotel across the street.

The next day they went to the government land office to secure their homestead. Then Grandad and his two sons rented a democrat buggy and set out to inspect the land they'd sailed halfway round the world to claim. Grandma and Aunt Thecla were told to stay in the hotel room and thank the Blessed Virgin for deliverance. They were still offering their prayers some four hours later when Grandad burst into the room, his eyes wild and his face trembling. "Sweet Jesus Christ," he shouted. "There's too much of it! There's just too damned much of it out there." He staggered around the room in circles, knocking against the walls and moaning, "Miles and miles of nothing but miles and miles." He collapsed onto one of the beds and lay staring at the ceiling. "It'd drive us all witless in a week."

The two boys came in and told the story of their expedition to the countryside. Grandad had started out fine, perhaps just a bit nervous. But the further they went from town the more agitated and distraught he became. Soon he quit urging the horse along and let it drift to a stop. They were barely five miles from Moose Jaw when they turned around and came back with Uncle Fred driving. Grandad could only crouch on the floor of the democrat, trying to hide from the enormous sky and whispering at Fred to go faster. Grandad had come five thousand miles to the wide open spaces—only to discover he suffered from agoraphobia.

That was his last excursion onto the open prairie, though he did make one special trip to the town of Bulkhead in 1928 to fix Aunt Thecla's chimney. But that was a family favour and even then Uncle Fred had to drive him in an enclosed Ford sedan in the middle of the night, with newspapers taped to the windows so he couldn't see out. So Grandad abandoned the dream of a country manor. He took up his old trade of bricklaying in the town of Moose Jaw, where there were trees and tall buildings to protect him from the vastness. Maybe it was a fortunate turn of fate. Certainly he prospered until the Depression hit, about the time I was born.

Yet Grandad always felt somehow guilty about not settling on the land. Perhaps it was his faith in the rural life that prompted him to send my dad out to work at a cattle ranch in the hills the day after he turned sixteen. He married Aunt Thecla off to a Norwegian wheat farmer at Bulkhead. Uncle Fred was the eldest and an apprentice bricklayer so he stayed in town and lived with Grandad and Grandma in the suite above the hardware store.

I don't remember much about the ranch my father eventually took over, except whirls of dust and skinny animals dragging themselves from one side of the range to the other. Finally there were no more cattle and nothing to feed them if we did have them except wild foxtail and Russian thistle. So we moved into Moose Jaw with Grandad and Grandma and went on relief. It was better than the cattle ranch where there was nothing to do but watch tumbleweeds roll through the yard. We would've had to travel into town to collect our salted fish and government pork anyway. Grandad was happy to have us, because when my Dad went down to the rail sheds to collect our rations, he got Grandad's food as well. My Dad never complained about waiting in line for the handout, but Grandad would've starved to death first.

"Damned government drives us all to the edge. Then they expect us to queue up for the damn swill they're poisoning us with."

That was when we spent so much time listening to Grandad's radio, a great slab of black walnut he had practically stolen—or so he claimed—from a second-hand dealer on River Street. A green incandescent bulb glowed in the center of it to show when the tubes were warming up. There was a row of knobs with elaborate initials and a dial with cities like Tokyo, Madrid and Chicago. Try as we might on long winter evenings to tune the needle in and hear a show in Russian or Japanese, all we ever got was CHMJ Moose Jaw, the Buckle of the Wheat Belt.

Even so, I spent many hours on the floor in front of the cloth-covered speakers, lost to another world of mystery and imagination. When the time came that Grandad could find no more bricks to lay, he set a kitchen chair in front of the radio and sat there, not moving except to go to the King William Hotel with Uncle Fred. My Dad managed to get relief work with the city, gravelling streets for fifty cents a day.

But things grew worse. One night in the fall of 1937, the Moose Jaw Electric Light and Power Company came around and cut off our electricity for non-payment. It was hard on Grandad not to have his radio. Not only did he have nothing to do, but he had to spend all day thinking about it. So he stared out the parlour window at the back alley behind our building, and at the loading dock of the Rainbow Laundry.

That's what he was doing the day of his discovery, about the time of the Feast of the Immaculate Conception. My Dad and Uncle Fred were arguing over who had caused the Depression—R.B. Bennett or the CPR. Suddenly Grandad turned from the window with a strange look on his face. "Where does that wire go?"

"What wire?" my dad said.

"This wire, running right past the window."

He pointed to a double strand of power line that run from the pole in the back alley to the side of our building. It was a lead-in for the hardware store below.

"Holy Moses Cousin Harry," Grandad said, grinning crazily. "Isn't that a sight now?"

"You're nuts," Uncle Fred told him. "You'll never get a tap off that line there. And if you did, they'd find you out in nothing flat."

"Now father," Grandma called from the kitchen. "Don't you go and do some foolishness will get us all electrinated."

"By Jaysus." He rarely paid attention to her advice. "Cut off my power, will they?"

That night when I went to bed, I listened to him and Uncle Fred banging and scraping as they bored a hole through the parlour wall. My dad wouldn't have anything to do with it, and took my mother out to a free movie at the Co-op. He said Grandad was descending to the level of the Moose Jaw Light and Power Company.

Actually, Grandad had some experience as an electrician. He had known for a long time how to run a wire from one side of the meter around to the other, to cheat the power company. I had often watched him under the meter, teetering on the rungs of our broken stepladder, yelling at Grandma to lift the damned holy candle higher, so he could see what the hell he was doing.

The next day Grandad and Uncle Fred were like a couple of children, snorting and giggling and jabbing each other in the ribs. They were waiting for the King William beer parlour to open so they could go down and tell their friends about Grandad's revenge on the power company. There they spent the afternoon like heroes, telling over and over how Grandad had spied the lead-in and how they'd bored the hole through the wall, and how justice had finally crushed the capitalist leeches. They came home for supper, but headed back immediately to the King William, where everybody was treating them to free beer.

Grandma didn't think much of their efforts, though she admitted to enjoying the music on the radio. The line came through the hole in our wall and snaked across the living room floor to the kitchen. Other cords were attached which led to the two bedrooms. Grandma muttered angrily when she had to sweep around the black tangle of wires and sockets. Never one for labour-saving gadgets, she had that quaint old country belief that electricity leaked from all the connections and swirled about the floor like demons and banshees. And with six of us living in the tiny suite, somebody was always tripping on the cords and knocking things over. But we lived with all that, because Grandad was happy again. And we might all have lived happily ever after, if Grandad and Uncle Fred could have kept their mouths shut about their revenge on the power company.

One night about a week later, we were listening to Fibber McGee and Molly, when there was a knock at the door. It was Mrs. Pizak, who lived in a tiny room down the hallway.

"Goot even," she said. "I see your power has turnt beck on."

"Ha!" Grandad barked. "We turned it on *for* 'em. Damned rogues."

"Come in and listen to the show with us," Grandma said.

Mrs. Pizak kept looking at the wires running back and forth across the parlour, and at Grandad's radio.

"Dey shut off my power too. Now I can't hear de church music."

"The dirty brigands. They'd steal pennies from the eyes of the dead!"

"So you vill turn my power beck on?"

"Hmm!" Grandad said, trying to hear Fibber and the Old-Timer. Mrs. Pizak wasn't listening to the show. Grandma and my dad watched him, not listening either. Finally he couldn't stand it. "All right, Fred. Go and fetch the brace and bit."

They bored a hole through a bedroom wall into Mrs. Pizak's cubicle and then she was on Grandad's power grid too. In fact it didn't take long before all the neighbours in the block discovered the free electricity. They all wanted to hook up. There were two whole floors of apartments above the hardware store, and soon the walls and ceilings of Grandad's suite were as full of holes as a colander, with wires running in all directions like black spaghetti. For the cost of a bottle of whiskey, people could run their lights twenty-four hours a day if they wanted. By Christmas Day, even those neighbours who paid their bills had given notice to the power company. So we enjoyed a tolerable Christmas at the end of a bad year, and Grandad and Uncle Fred got credit for it. There was a lot of celebration up and down the halls, where they were feasted as honoured guests and heroes. A euphoric feeling ran through our block, like being in a state of siege or revolution, led by my Grandad.

ONE LATE AFTERNOON just after New Year's I was lying on the parlour floor, reading a second-hand *Book of Knowledge* Aunt Thecla had sent for Christmas. Grandma and my mother were knitting socks, and all three of us were listening to Major Bowes' Amateur Hour. Out of the corner of my eye, I thought I saw the radio move. I blinked and stared at it, but the big console just sat there talking about Geritol. I turned a page. Again it seemed to move with a jerk.

"Grandma, the radio moved!"

She looked up from her knitting, not believing a word I might have to say. I gave up and glared at the stupid machine. As I watched, it slid at least six inches across the parlour floor.

"Grandma, it is moving! All by itself!"

She stood up and looked at the radio, the tangle of wires across the floor, and out the parlour window.

"Larry-boy. You'd better run down the hall and fetch your grandfather. He's at the McBrides'. Number eight!"

I sprinted down the hall and pounded at the door, which someone within opened the width of a crack. "Is my Grandad in there?"

He stepped out with a glass of whiskey in his hand. "What is it, Larry?"

"Grandma says for you to come right now. There's something funny with the radio."

"My radio!" He began walking down the hall, broke into a trot then a steady gallop, holding the glass of whiskey out front so it wouldn't spill. He burst into the apartment and skidded to a halt in front of the radio, which sat in its traditional majesty, but maybe a foot to the left of his chair.

"By the Holy Toenails of Moses. What is it, woman?"

Grandma jerked her chin ominously toward the window.

Her quiet firmness usually calmed him but now in two fantastic bounds, Grandad stood glaring out the window. He turned to me with a pale face. "Larry, run and fetch your Uncle Fred."

I ran down the hallway again to number eight and fetched Uncle Fred. When we got back, Grandad was pacing in a fury, and my mother's knitting needles clattered like telegraph keys. "Have a gawk at this, Fred."

Uncle Fred and I crowded past him to see out the window. There on a pole only twenty feet from our parlour window, practically facing us eye-to-eye, was a lineman from the power company. He was replacing glass insulators along the line. God knows why he was doing it in the dead of winter, but he obviously hadn't noticed our homemade lead-in, or he would have already been pounding at our door. We could only pray he wouldn't look at the line too closely.

Once, he lifted his eyes to our window, where we stood gaping at him in the growing darkness. He raised his hand in a salute. He thought we were admiring his work!

"Wave back!" Grandad ordered and the three of us waved frantically at the lineman to make him think we appreciated his efforts, though Grandad was muttering some very ugly things about the man's ancestry.

"Look at him—as dumb as two sticks. He has to be an Orangeman. May the High King of Glory give him the mange!"

Finally, to our relief, the lineman got ready to descend the pole. He reached out his hand for support, and my heart stopped beating as his weight hung on the contraband line. Behind me, I could hear the radio slide another foot across the parlour floor. The lineman stared at the wire in his hand. He tugged experimentally, his eyes following it up to the hole through our wall. He looked at Uncle Fred and Grandad and me, standing there at the lit-up window, with our horror-struck grins and our arms frozen above our heads in grotesque waves. Understanding spread slowly across his face.

He scrambled around to the opposite side of the pole and braced himself to give a mighty pull on our line. Simultaneously Grandad leaped into action, grabbing the wire on our side of the wall. He wrapped it round his hands and braced his feet against the baseboard. "He'll never take it from us!" The lineman gave his first vicious yank and it almost jerked Grandad smack against the wall. I remember thinking what a powerful man he must be to do that to my Grandad!

"Fred, you feather-brained idiot! Get over here and *haul* before the black-hearted son of a bitch pulls me through the wall."

Uncle Fred ran to the wire just in time, as the man on the pole gave another, mightier heave. I could see him stiffen with rage. The slender wire sawed through the hole in the wall for at least ten minutes, first one side, then the other, getting advantage. The curses on our side got very loud and bitter. I couldn't hear the lineman, but I could see him, with his mouth twisted in an awful snarl, throwing terrible looks at me and heaving on the line. He was not praying to St. Jude.

Grandad's cursing would subside periodically when Grandma warned:

"Now now, Father, not in front of the boy." Then she would go back to her knitting and pretend the whole affair wasn't happening and Grandad's blasphemies would soar to monumental heights. The lineman must have been in excellent condition because our side began to play out. Grandad yelled at Grandma and my mother, even at me, to throw ourselves on the line and help. But the women refused to leave their knitting and would not allow me to be corrupted.

Grandad and Uncle Fred kept losing ground until the huge radio had slid all the way across the room and stood at their backs, hampering their exertions. "Larry. Is he weakenin' any?" He wanted desperately for me to say yes, but it was useless. "It doesn't look like it." Grandad burst out in a froth of curses I'd never heard before. A fresh attack on the line pulled his knuckles to the wall, and scraped them badly. He looked tired and beaten. All the slack in the line was taken up. He was against the wall, his head twisted, looking at me. A light flared in his eyes.

"All right, Fred. If he wants the damned thing so bad—let him have it!" They both jumped back—and nothing happened.

I could see the lineman, completely unaware of his impending disaster, literally winding himself up for an all-out assault on our wire. I wanted, out of human kindness, to shout a warning at him. But it was too late. With an incredible backward lunge, he disappeared from sight behind the power pole.

A shattering explosion of noise blasted around us, like a bomb had fallen in Grandad's suite. Every electric appliance and light they owned flew into the parlour, ricocheting off the walls, and smashing against each other. A table lamp from the bedroom careened off Uncle Fred's knee. The radio collided against the wall and was ripped off its wire. Sparking and flashing, all of Grandma's things hurled themselves against the parlour wall, popping like a string of firecrackers as the cords went zipping through the hole.

A silence fell, like a breath of air to a drowning man. The late afternoon darkness settled through the room. "Sweet Jesus," Grandad said. Then came a second uproar, a bloodcurdling series of roars and shouts as all our neighbours recovered from seeing their lamps, radios, irons, and toasters leap from their tables and collect in ruined piles of junk around the "free power" holes in their walls. Uncle Fred turned white as a sheet.

I looked out the window. The lineman sat at the foot of his pole, dazed. He looked up at me with one more hateful glare, then snipped our wire with a pair of cutters, taped the end, and marched away into the night.

Grandad stood in the darkened ruins, trying to examine his beloved radio for damage. Grandma sat in her rocking chair, knitting socks and refusing to acknowledge the disaster. It was Grandad who finally broke the silence.

"Well, they're lucky," he said. "It's just damned lucky for them they didn't scratch my radio!"

Ken Mitchell is the author of over twenty novels, collections of short fiction, screenplays, dramas and works of poetry. He is a professor of English at the University of Regina. In 1999 he was awarded the Order of Canada for his work teaching Canadian literature in Canada and abroad. Ken Mitchell's books include Wandering Rafferty, The Meadowlark Connection *and* Everybody Gets Something Here.

REQUIEM FOR BIBUL

JACK LUDWIG

Once upon a time—if we counted time not by calendars but by assimilated history and scientific change I'd be tempted to say four or five thousand years ago: before total war and all-out war, before death camps, Nagasaki, before fusion and fission, jets, moon shots, aeronauts, Luniks in orbit, before antibiotics, polio vaccine, open-heart surgery, before TV, carburetors and other wonders of automation, before dead-faced hoods on motorcycles, dead-faced beatniks on maldecycles—once upon *that* kind of time lived a boy and his horse.

The year was 1939. This is no pastoral tale. The boy and the horse are both dead.

Twenty years late, counting time by the calendar, I write you of this boy Bibul and his horse Malkeh, of Bibul's ambition and his sad sad end. In time-sorrowed perspective I record for you the imprint Bibul left on my mind and feeling—his tic-like blink, his coal-black hair in bangs over his forehead, his emerycloth shaver's shadow, his ink-stained mouth, his immutable clothes that wouldn't conform to style or the seasons: always black denim Relief-style pants whitened by wear and washing, always a brown pebbled cardigan coiled at the wrists and elbows with unravelled wool, always a leather cap with bent visor, split seams, matching the colour and texture of Bibul's hair. An old ruined Malkeh, scorned before lamented, making her daily round under Bibul's urging, dragging his creak of a fruit-peddler's wagon through Winnipeg's 'island' slum north of the Canadian Pacific Railway Yards.

Bibul peddled while my time burned: in 1939 all of us high-school boys owlish with sixteen- and seventeen-year-old speculation, almost missed seeing this Bibul foxy with world-weary finagling. We were out to save the world, Bibul a buck. Hip-deep in reality, trying to beat tricky suppliers, weasely competitors, haggling customers, Bibul couldn't believe in us vaguesters. Peddling had forced him to see, hear, and judge everything. By his practical measure we were simply unreal. We'd speculate: Bibul would respond with *yeh-yeh*—the Yiddish double affirmative that makes a negative. He didn't have to say a word, or raise sceptical eyebrow, or even frown with that tic. His smell alone argued a reality out of reach of our politely neutral Lux, Lifebuoy, Vitalis middle-class sweetness: 'effluvium Bibul' we called that mixture of squashed berries, bad turnips, dank pineapple crates, straw, chickens, sad old horsey Malkeh. Bibul had a grand gesture to sweep away our irrelevance, a sudden movement of the hand like a farmwife's throwing feed to chickens, his nose sniffing disgust, his sour mouth giving out a squelching sound, 'aaaa.' Sometimes he sounded like a goat, other times a baby lamb—just 'aaaa,' but enough to murder our pushy pretensions.

We were a roomful of competitive sharks—math sharks, physics sharks, English, Latin, history sharks, secretly, often openly, sure we surpassed our teachers in brain and knowhow. Joyfully arrogant we shook off the restricting label high-school student, considering ourselves pros—mathematicians, scientists, writers, artists. In our own minds we had already graduated from the University, had passed through Toronto or Oxford, were entangled in public controversies with great names in our respective fields, ending right but humble, modestly triumphant. But where was Bibul in this league? As loud as we pros hollered Bibul heard nothing. He only yawned, slouched, even snoozed, gave out with that killing *yeh-yeh*, poked his greyish nose into his peddler's notebook red with reality's ooze of tomato.

'Bibul,' we'd say in the break between classes, 'do semantics mean nothing to your knucklehead? An intellectual revolution's coming. You've got to stand up and be counted. What'll it be? Are you *for* Count Korzybski or against him?'

'Aaaa,' aaed Bibul, and his chicken-feeding motion sent us back to ivory towers.

'You' nuddin' bud gids,' he'd say haughtily whenever we disturbed his audit of fruit-and-vegetable reality, 'a 'ell of a lod you guys know aboud live.'

Though we jeered and mocked, treated him like a clown, he was one of us, so how could we disown him? Kings of St. John's High, lording it from our third-floor eminence over the giants and dwarfs living the underground life in the school's basement ascreech with whirling lathes and milling machines, or those second-floor, salt-of-the-earth commercial students dedicated to bookkeeping, typing, the sensible life, we of course wanted to pass our nobility on to Bibul. We ran the yearbook and could have established him there—but on the 'island' English ran a poor second to Ukrainian, Polish, German, or in his case, Hebrew. We could have made him captain of the debating team, but peddling wrecked that: wrought up he stammered, angry he slobbered, no way to win arguments. Being a businessman, like his breed he had no time for politics; being tone-deaf he was a flop at glee-club try-outs. At sports he was dreadful. He couldn't swim a stroke, or skate, was flubbyknuckled at baseball, slashing pigeon-toed at soccer, truly kamikaze going over a hurdle. And women? He had no time for them in his practical life: his old mare Malkeh and the ladies who haggled with him were the only females Bibul knew.

In recognition of his memo-book involvement we made Bibul our room treasurer.

After classes we theoreticians sprawled on the school green and took pleasure from long-limbed, heavy-thighed, large-breasted girls thwarting an educator's pious wish that the serge tunic neutralize the female form. Bibul was never with us. At the closing bell he'd run off to his horse and wagon, set to run the gauntlet of his customers (*shnorrers,* pigs he called them); and early on a morning, when we theoreticians-turned-lover, weary after a long night of girl-gaming, sat in Street Railways waiting houses knocking ourselves out over noisy reading of Panurge's adventure with the Lady of Paris, Bibul, up and dressed since 4:00 A.M., struggled at the Fruit Row for bruised fruit and battered vegetables in competition with wizened peddlers and their muscular sons. At nine, bleary-eyed all, theoretician and practical man rose to greet the morn with a mournful *O Canada*.

Lost in abstraction, and me, I thought little of Bibul in those days. He was a clown. A mark. A butt. The peddling was part of the sad desperate struggle for money every family in the depression knew. Bibul was the eldest of four children, his widowed ma supporting them on what she could make out of a tiny grocery store, doing the best she could, the dear lady, known throughout the 'island' as 'The Golden Thumb' and the 'Adder,' the latter reference ambiguous, meaning either snakes or computation, Bibul's ma being famous for a mathematical theorem that said $5 + 6 = 12$ or 13, whichever was higher.

Not till the year of our graduation did I discover why Bibul peddled with such dedication, why he rode out like a teen-age Don Quixote to do battle with those abusive, haggling, thieving *shnorrers*.

And what a riding-out that was! His paintless wagon listed like a sinking ship, sounded like resinless fiddles in the hands of apes, each wheel a circle successfully squared. Bibul sat on a tatter of leatherette bulging at the ends like a horsehair creampuff; over his wilted greens and culled fruit Bibul's faultless-in-his-favour scales made judgement, this battered tin scoop more dented than a tin B-B target. And what was more fitting than a nag like Malkeh to drag that crumbling wagon on its progress?

As grim as Don Quixote's Rosinante would look next to elegant Pegasus, that's how Malkeh would have looked next to Rosinante: she was U-shaped in side view, as if permanently crippled by the world's fattest knight lugging the world's heaviest armour. She sagged like a collapsed sofa with stuffing hanging low. She was bare as buffed mohair, her shoulders tanned from the rub of reins, her colour an unbelievable combination of rust, maroon, purple, bronze, found elsewhere only in ancient sun-drenched velvets. Her tail was a Gibson Girl's worn discarded feather boa, its fly-discouraging movements ritualistic, perfunctory, more to let flies know that Malkeh wasn't dead than that she was alive. Her legs, like a badly carpentered table, were of assorted lengths, which made Malkeh move by shuffling off like a pair of aged soft-shoe dancers in final farewell. Her hooves were fringed with fuzzy hairs like a frayed fiddle-bow abandoned to rain and sun, her horseshoes dime-thin, rusty as the metal hinges on her wagon's tail-gate. To encourage Malkeh to see Bibul covered her almost-blind eyes with a pair of snappy black racing-horse blinkers trimmed with shiny silver rivets, a touch to her décor like a monocle in the eye of a Bowery bum.

Out of compassion, out of loyalty to this wreck of a horse, Bibul let his wagon go to ruin: wood could be camouflaged with paint or varnish but where was covering to hide or revive said old mortal Malkeh?

One day I came to school early, and saw her.

She was the horse version of 'The Dying Gaul.' On Bibul's 'island' Malkeh suffered no invidious comparisons, but on a main thoroughfare like St. John's High's Salter Street Malkeh was exposed to the cruelty of horse hierarchy, and her submarginal subproletariat hide was bared. High-stepping, glossy-flanked, curried and combed T. Eaton Company horses, middle-class cousins of aristocratic thoroughbreds seen only on race tracks, veered their rumps sharply as they passed, hooves steelringing, traces white as snow. Their tails were prinked out with red ribbon, their wagons chariots sparkling in red, white, gold against blue-blackness that could mean only good taste. These bourgeois horses had the true bourgeois comforts—warm blankets, stables with hay wall-to-wall, feedbags that offered privacy and nourishment. Their drivers looked like sea-captains, neat contrast to a slop like Bibul. And their commercial feed was gastronomical compared with the bad lettuce, wilted carrot tops, shrivelled beets Bibul shoved at Malkeh in a ripped old postman's pouch.

Malkeh took their snubs without flinching. It was part of the class struggle. What hurt was the heavy powerful working-class Percherons and their stinking garbage scows, when *they* avoided kinship with Malkeh, acting like a guest at a high-toned party ignoring a waiter who's a close relative.

Pity old Malkeh's vengeful heart: the only pleasure she got from her enforced station on Salter Street came from knowing flies used her as an aerodrome from which to launch vicious attacks on the elegant department-store horses passing.

I saw her. The Principal too saw her, slouched with resignation, a 'Don't' in an SPCA exhibit, her right foreleg flatteringly fettered by a cracked curling stone to give Malkeh the impression she had the vim and youth to turn runaway horse. Malkeh died a long time ago, but years before she did the Principal had her one visit gnomically memorialized and graven in metal: early next morning, where Malkeh had stood, this marker went up: 'No Parking At Any Time.'

Bibul never again brought her to school.

Which is not to say that life on the 'island' was without its grim side: what accounted for an almost-blind horse wearing blinkers? *Shnorrers!* Those women with bare feet stuck hurriedly into their husbands' outsize felt slippers, their hair uncombed, faces unmade, women in nightgowns at four on a sunshiny afternoon, hands clenching pennies and silver Bibul had to charm away from them with hard-sell and soft-soap. Singly they waited, in concert plotted, en masse moved in on him. Their purpose was simple—*get much, pay little.* To the victor went Bibul's spoiled spoils.

'Giddy ahb, Malgeh,' Bibul would holler from his high seat on the wagon, and his cry sounded to a *schnorrer's* ears like a warring clarion.

Into the lists Malkeh dragged the keening wagon, onto the 'island' in ruins like a mediaeval town (Canadian history is short but our buildings add spice by getting older faster). Foundationless hovels kids might have built out of assorted-sized decks of cards sagged, leaned at crazy-house angles to astound Pisa. Gates tipsy as Malkeh's wagon swung on one hinge from a last lost post; dry, cracking wood fences leaned in surrender towards the ground, begging like old men in sight of a grave to be allowed to fall the rest of the way; windows were tarpaper-patched, like pirates' eyes, ominous as the blackness left in the streets by uninsured fires.

Behind every window or screen opaque with dust, behind every door splintered from kids' kicking waited the *shnorrers,* trying to make Bibul anxious, make him sweat a little, a cinch for persistent hagglers.

'Ebbles, ebbles, den boundz f'a quadder,' Bibul shouted.

Crafty with stealth the *shnorrers* didn't bite.

Unflustered, unfooled, Bibul took advantage of the phony war, biting off the only three unspotted cherries in his entire stock while Malkeh dragged the exposed tin rims of the wagonwheels into the frost heaves and back-lane crevices. That cramped stinking back lane was mutually agreeable as a Compleat Battlefield—for Bibul because the solid pall of chicken droppings and horse dung was fine camouflage for the imperfections Time and Decay wrought his produce, for the *shnorrers* because the narrow quarters made tampering with the scale easier, detection harder, filching a hot possibility.

'Whoa beg, whoa der Malgeh,' Bibul ordered, oblivious of the spying women.

There, among rusted bedsprings hung up like huge harps, torn mattresses resembling giant wads of steel wool, in a boneyard of Model T's, Malkeh and the wagon rested. Dogs scooted in darts of nervous yapping, cats hissed down from rust-streaked corrugated rooftops, pigeons wheeled high above Bibul's untroubled head, resuming to perch on overhanging eaves like fans anxious to get close to a scene of scuffle.

The *shnorrers* tried to read Bibul's face: the text was that Sphinx-like tic of a blink. Stalling he made entries into that memo-book, peeled an orange, scratched himself with casual but maddening thoroughness.

The *shnorrers'* united front crumbled. A foot slipped out from behind a door. Then a head.

'Wha' you gonna cheat me on t'day, Bibul?' rasped out of an impatient throat.

The war was on! Horseflies, the depression having made pickings so sparse they dropped their high standards and declared Malkeh a host, left the depressing fare of uncovered garbage cans (each lid long ago commandeered to be target in the minor-league jousts of the *shnorrers'* unknightly kids), and, hiding behind the *shnorrers* sneaking up to do Bibul battle, launched assault on old Malkeh's flat weak flanks.

The siege began, swiftly, deftly: a red-haired old woman flipped two-cent oranges into the one-cent bins, her other hand pointed up at the sky to make Bibul raise his eyes and predict weather.

Her accomplice brought Bibul back to reality, picking the bargains up before they'd even stopped rolling.

'Boyaboy Bibul, you god good tings in y' usually stinkin' stock, look here, Mrs. Gilfix, at such oranges.'

Bibul's tic-like blink snapped like a camera shutter on their mischief.

'Give over here dem oniges,' he reproved them, *'yoisher,* show a liddle resdraind,' and the sad old innocents watched the two-cent numbers fall back into the two-cent bins.

On the other side of the wagon a pair of raspberry hands crushed away at lettuce greens.

'How much off f'damaged goods?' the criminal hollered, wiping lettuce juice off on her gaping nightgown.

But the red-haired old woman hadn't given up on oranges.

'Black head means black heart, robber,' she cried out, 'Perls d'fruit man who has a white head and eight kids and supports two unmarried sisters in Russia, from *him* I get fresher cheaper by two coppers—ha come, ha? Ha come?'

'My oniges are Sundgizd, Blue Gooze,' Bibul, a sucker for brand names, came back huffily, 'Berls' oniges grow on ebble drees.'

One man's quarrel is another woman's smoke screen. The *shnorrers* moved in, squeezing the fruit, poking, tapping, complaining with shrieks and curses that sent the pigeon-hearted pigeons high off their perches. Like a bucket brigade the ladies passed fruit up and down the length of the wagon, each nose an inspector, those with teeth taking their duties more seriously, tasters whose opinions Bibul could live without.

'*Schnorrers* dad youz are,' he hollered, holding up a nipped apple, a chewed-up orange, 'you god no gare vor my broyids?'

'Look how he's independent,' mocked the red-haired one, lunging fruitless after a fistful of cherries, 'look how he holds hisself big! His fadder's a doctor, maybe? Or the mayor?'

Bibul was a lone guard defending his fortress from desperate pillagers; ubiquitous as Churchill, many-handed as Shiva, he had to be compassionate as Schweitzer. Though I didn't know what Bibul's dedication to peddling was all about, the *schnorrers* did: Bibul was saving up to become a Rabbi. Bibul immersed himself in the practical, pedestrian, material life because of a Great

Cause—the Yeshiva in New York, eventual immersion in a spiritual life dedicated to comfort suffering mankind.

How the *shnorrers* used that Great Cause in their war with Bibul! It was all double: in sincerity they poured out their hearts to him—an educated boy, soon to be a Rabbi, maybe he'd understand *their* side—the husband who had taken off and never come back, the bad-hearted rich relatives, the ungrateful kids, the treacherous friends, root, trunk, branch of a Jewish Seven Deadly Sins. They dizzied him with complicated stories, unsettled his strong stomach with demonstrations of human frailty—missing teeth, crossed eyes, wens, tumours, needed operations.

As a bonus to sincerity they hoped the tales would divert Bibul long enough for their aprons to fill with filched fruit.

Crying real tears Bibul would free an apricot from a fist already stained with cherry.

'A religious you call yourself?' the caught thief howled. 'God should strike me dead if I stole ever in my life one thing!'

Glancing up at the sky she moved closer to the other ladies: who knew what kind of pull with God a boy-studying-to-be-a-Rabbi had?

'Bibul, sveethard,' cooed one Mrs Itzcher, blemished but bleached, 'give off ten cents a dozen by oranges and Tillie'll show plenty appreciation.'

Bibul used his chickenfeed gesture to ward off temptation.

The *shnorrers* prayed God to give Bibul good enough ears to hear their laments but to compensate with a little dimming of the eyes so he wouldn't catch them stealing. When they lost they cursed in tones loud enough to be heard above the world's fishwifery in action.

No wonder Bibul considered us sharks irrelevant. After those *shnorrers* poured it on what was left to be said?

'My brudder's second wibe's kid wid da hump in back, Rabbi Bibul, has already her third miscarriage.'

In the midst of haggle they rained down proofs of suffering and absurdity—banged heads, cut knees, singed eyelashes, hands caught in wringers, slippery floors, broken steps, toppling ladders. The compensation they asked was meagre. Pity, a buy on a busted watermelon.

When we sharks, hot for culture, cool for Schoenberg, long on judgements, short on facts, turned our abstract expressions Bibul's way how else could he respond but with that 'aaaa'? What did our books and ideas have to compete with a *schnorrer's* lament? Now when I think of that 'aaaa' I translate it 'When I was a child I spake as a child . . .' (may Bibul forgive me for quoting Saint Paul); 'aaaa' said 'vanity of vanities; all is vanity'; in explanation of the term for Mammon so that the rest would be with Abraham, Isaac, and Jacob; 'aaaa' said 'To everything there is a season, and a time to every purpose under the heaven.'

On St. John's High School's Graduation Day Bibul was already at least half a Rabbi. The cardigan was gone, so too the denims and the black leather cap. He wore a fancy blue serge suit so new it still smelled of smoke. His sideburns were growing religiously into side curls, his emerycloth shadow was now a beardlike reality. But it was Bibul's eyes I remember, excited, gay, snapping under that tic. He looked incredibly happy.

'Bibul,' I said seriously, 'you look beautiful in that suit!'

'Damorra, Joe,' he said low and secretive, 'damorra I go d'Noo Yorick an' d'Yeshiva.'

I talked to him without clowning. He told me what he wanted, explained the peddling.

'Bibul,' I said as we were walking out to our waiting parents, 'doesn't the idea of a city the size of New York scare you? You'll be strange. Winnipeg's a village—'

'Wadz t'be asgared?' Bibul said with that wave of his hand. 'Beoble iz beoble. I zeen all ginds aready.'

He told me he'd sold Malkeh to Perls the peddler. His mother walked proudly towards Bibul as we reached the street.

'Bibul,' I shouted as parents came between us, 'you'll be a terrific Rabbi! Good luck!'

He gave that chickenfeed flourish, but with new style, and with modesty.

'Aaaa,' I heard above the shouting congratulations of parents, the last time I heard or saw Bibul.

That fall we sharks entered the University, and Canada the war.

Winnipeg was transformed, full of aircrew trainees from places I knew about before only through postage stamps, men with yellow skins, red, brown, black, Maori tribesmen from New Zealand, bushmen from Australia, strange-sounding South Africans, carved-faced Indians thronging the streets and beer parlours. But far off in New York, Bibul, who had known war with the *shnorrers,* paid little attention to this latest struggle. He studied Torah and Talmud. He made his spending money selling fruit to Lower East Side *shnorrers* at the Essex Street Market.

Bibul's old Winnipeg customers haggled half-heartedly with old man Perls and old horse Malkeh, the one mercifully deaf, the other nearly blind. The depression seemed over: money came easier.

Once in a long while I checked in at Bibul's mother's store and, gleaning news of Bibul, let her weigh me up a light pound of corned beef. She wore her hair Buster Brown, carried a huge buxom body on little feet in gray-white tennis shoes.

She shoved a letter at me.

'Look how a educated boy writes?' she said, pugnaciously proud. 'Who but a Rabbi could understand such words?'

She pulled it back before I could answer.

'See him only, just look,' she pushed a picture at my eyes.

Bibul huddled against a bare Williamsburg wall grinning the same grin as the three other Bibuls in the picture, all of them bearded and wild as Russians, in black beaver hats bought with money they had earned tutoring the Americanized grandchildren of rich Chassidim.

'Some boy, my Bibul,' his mother called to me as I was leaving.

Winter passed and the war grew grimmer. Spring was beautiful, the war more dreadful. Summer was hot, particularly in New York where Bibul divided his time between the Yeshiva and Essex Street's *shnorrers.* For days the temperature was in the high nineties. Bibul had never known such heat. He couldn't study, sleep, sell. In desperation he took himself one evening to the 'Y,' forgetting in the heat that he'd never learned to swim.

An attendant, going off duty, warned Bibul away, told him not to enter the pool. Who can be blind to Bibul's response?

'Aaaa,' and that gesture.

He drowned.

His *shnorrers* on the 'island,' being told, wept and lamented. We sharks, even in the midst of war's casualties, were moved and stricken. Bibul was the first of us to die.

I cannot find Bibul's like in Winnipeg today.

Somebody waved a T-square wand over the old 'island,' bringing it the ninety-degree angle unknown in Bibul's far-off day. Progress pretends Bibul's 'island' never really existed: the lanes are paved, the rot-wood of wall and fence has been sloshed over with paint. A few sneaky signs of the old world are around: a clothesline pole, exhausted from long years of soggy fleece-lined underwear to support, seems ready to give up the ghost; an outside staircase, impermanent as a hangman's scaffold, mocks the fire commission that asked for greater safety and got greater danger.

Malkeh is dead. The wagon is all bits and crumble.

Motorized peddlers in trucks like Brink's Cars zoom through the reformed 'island' late at night with the remnants of produce picked over by ringed and braceleted hands on the day route—River Heights, Silver Heights, Garden City, places of Togetherness, Betterness, Spotlessness, the polite answers Comfort has given to the sad old questions of Civilization.

'Apples, apples, two pounds for a quarter,' the peddlers call, but not too loudly, and the women once poor enough to be *shnorrers* (few are still alive), the women who have replaced the departed *shnorrers* in remodelled rebuilt houses, look over the fruit and vegetables (ironically like Bibul's old rejects and reduced-to-clears because of prior though elegant pawing), buy a little, haggle not at all, or withdraw with a snub at peddling, a bow in favour of the superior refrigeration of supermarkets.

Through the streets old Malkeh drew that creaking wagon urged on by leather-capped Bibul, chrome-trimmed cars speed in unending gaggle, their sport-capped, stylishly-hatted drivers in control of power the equivalent of four hundred un-Malkeh horses. The Mayor tells Winnipeggers to 'Think Big,' bid for the Pan-American Games, hang out more flags and buntings.

Slums like Bibul's 'island' and the City Hall are fortunately doomed: Winnipeg is obviously a better place to live in.

Who doesn't welcome prosperity?

But the fact remains: I cannot find Bibul's like in Winnipeg today.

And that is why here and now, in this, his and my city, I write you this requiem for Bibul, for his face, for his Great Cause, his tic, his wave, his 'aaaa.' In love and the joy of remembering I sing you this Bibul and all that's past and passing but not to come.

When the City Hall is torn down they will build Winnipeg a new one; but where, O where shall we find more Bibuls?

Jack Ludwig has authored three novels—Confusions, Above Ground *and* A Woman of Her Age—*and five works of nonfiction, including* Five Ring Circus. *His story "Requiem for Bibul" received an* Atlantic Monthly *award, and he has twice won O. Henry Prize awards. He was a co-founder and editor of* The Noble Savage.

THE SKATING PARTY

MERNA SUMMERS

Our house looked down on the lake. From the east windows you could see it: a long sickle of blue, its banks hung with willow. Beyond was a wooded ridge, which, like all such ridges in our part of the country, ran from northeast to southwest.

In another part of the world, both lake and ridge would have had names. Here, only people had names. I was Maida; my father was Will, my mother was Winnie. Take us all together and we were the Singletons. The Will Singletons, that is, as opposed to the Dan Singletons, who were my grandparents and dead, or Nathan Singleton, who was my uncle and lived in the city.

We were north of the Battle and south of the Saskatchewan and the Vermilion River flowed nearby, but that was about it for named parts of the landscape. In the books I read, lakes and hills had names, and so did ponds and houses. Their names made them more real to me, of greater importance, than the hills and lakes and sloughs that I saw every day. I was eleven years old before I learned that the hill on which our house was built had once had a name. It was called Stone Man Hill. My parents had never thought to tell me that.

It was my uncle, Nathan Singleton, who told me. Uncle Nathan was a bachelor. He had been a teacher before he came to Willow Bunch, but he had wanted to be a farmer. He had farmed for a few years when he was a young man, on a quarter that was now part of our farm. His quarter was just south of what had been my grandfather's home place, and was now ours. But then he had moved to the city and become a teacher again.

In some ways it seemed as if he had never really left Willow Bunch. He spent all his holidays at our place, taking walks with me, talking to my mother, helping my father with such chores as he hadn't lost the knack of performing. Our home was his home. I found it hard to imagine him as I knew he must be in his classroom: wearing a suit, chalk dust on his sleeve, putting seat work on the blackboard. He didn't even talk like a teacher.

Uncle Nathan was older than my father, quite a lot older, but he didn't seem so to me. In some ways he seemed younger, for he told me things and my father did not. Not that my father was either silent or unloving. He talked as much as anybody, and he was fond of some people—me included—and showed it. What he did not give away was information.

Some children are sensitive: an eye and an ear and a taking-in of subtleties. I wasn't like that. I wanted to be told. I wanted to know how things really were and how people really acted. Sometimes it seemed to me that collecting the facts was uphill work. I persisted because it was important for me to have them. I wanted to know who to praise and who to blame. Until I was in my mid-teens, that didn't seem to me to be too much to ask.

Perhaps my father had a reluctance to look at things too closely himself. He wanted to like people, and he may have found it easier to do if he kept them a little out of focus. Besides that, he believed that life was something that children should be protected from knowing about for as long as possible.

I got most of my information from my mother. She believed that knowledge *was* protection: that children had a right to know and parents had an obligation to teach. She didn't know all there was to know, but what she did know she intended to pass on to me.

I knew this because I heard her say so one night after I had gone to bed. Uncle Nathan, who was at the farm for the weekend, saw things my mother's way. "What you don't know *can* hurt you," he said. "Especially what you don't know about yourself."

So my mother and my uncle talked to me, both as a sort of innoculation against life and because, I now believe, both of them liked to talk anyway. I was always willing to listen. My father listened too. He might feel that my mother told me too much, but his conviction wasn't strong enough to stop her.

It was Uncle Nathan, talking for pleasure, not policy, who gave me the pleasure of knowing that I lived in a place with a name. Stone Man Hill was so named, he said, because long ago there had existed on the slopes below our house the shape of a man, outlined in fieldstones.

"He was big," Uncle Nathan said. "Maybe fifteen yards, head to foot."

It was a summer afternoon. I was eleven. My father, in from the fields for coffee, was sitting at the kitchen table. His eyelashes were sooty with field dust. My mother was perched on a kitchen stool by the cupboard, picking over berries.

"He must have been quite a sight," my father said.

I walked to the east window of the kitchen and looked out, trying to imagine our hillside field of brome as unbroken prairie sod, trying to picture what a stone man would look like stretched out among the buffalo beans and gopher holes, his face to the sky.

"You get me a writing pad and I'll show you what he looked like," Uncle Nathan said.

I got the pad and Uncle Nathan sat down at the table opposite my father. I sat beside him, watching as he began to trace a series of dots. His hand worked quickly, as if the dots were already visible, but only to his eyes. The outline of a man took shape.

"Who made the stone man?" I asked.

"Indians," Uncle Nathan said. He held the picture up, as if considering additions. "But I don't know when and I don't know why."

"He could have been there a hundred years," my father said. "Maybe more. There was no way of telling."

"I used to wonder why the Indians chose this hill," Uncle Nathan said. "I still do."

He got up and walked to the window, looking out at the hill and the lake and the ridge. "It may be that it was some sort of holy place to them," he said.

My mother left the cupboard and came across to the table. She picked up Uncle Nathan's drawing. Looking at it, the corners of her mouth twitched upwards.

"You're sure you haven't forgotten anything?" she asked. "Your mother used to say that the stone man was *very* complete."

Uncle Nathan returned her smile. "The pencil's right here, Winnie," he said. "You're welcome to it."

My father spoke quickly. "It was too bad the folks didn't have a camera," he said. "It would have been nice to have a picture of the stone man."

My mother went back to her berries.

"I've always been sorry I was too young to remember him," my father said. "Before he turned into a rock pile, that is."

I hadn't yet got around to wondering about the stone man's disappearance. Now I did. He should still have been on his hillside for me to look at. My father had been a baby when his people came to Willow Bunch, and he couldn't remember the stone man. My uncle had been a young man and could. But the difference in their ages and experience hadn't kept them from sharing a feeling of excitement at the thought of a stone man on our hillside. Why had my grandfather been insensible to this appeal? Hadn't he liked the stone man?

"Liking wouldn't enter into it," my father said. "Your grandfather had a family to feed. He knew where his duty lay."

"There was thirty acres broke when Pa bought this place," Uncle Nathan said. "He thought he needed more. And this hill was the only land he could break without brushing it first."

Somebody else had owned our place before my grandfather, hadn't they? I asked. He hadn't turned the stone man into a rock pile.

"He was a bachelor," my father said.

"The way your grandfather saw it," Uncle Nathan said, "it was a case of wheat or stones. And he chose wheat."

"Which would you have chosen?" I asked Uncle Nathan. "Which did you want?"

"I wanted both," Uncle Nathan said.

"The choice wasn't yours to make." My mother spoke as if she were defending him.

"That's what I thought then," Uncle Nathan said.

"I thought when Pa told me to get those rocks picked, that that was what I had to do. I think now I should have spoken up. I know for years I felt guilty whenever I remembered that I had done just what was expected of me."

He looked up, a half-smile on his face. "I know it sounds crazy," he said, "but I felt as if the stone man had more claim on me than my own father did."

"We all of us think some crazy things sometimes," my father said.

FROM MY POINT OF VIEW, Uncle Nathan had only one peculiarity. He had never married. And though I sometimes asked him why, I never found any satisfaction in his answers.

"Maybe it wasn't every girl who took my eye," he told me once. "I'd pity the girl who had to count on me to take care of her," he said another time.

Then my mother told me about the skating party. It had been a dark night in November, and my mother, five years old, had come to our lake with her parents, and spent the night pushing a kitchen chair in front of her across the ice, trying to learn to skate. The party was being held in honour of Uncle Nathan and a girl called Eunice Lathem. They were to be married soon, and their friends planned, after the skating, to go up to the house and present a gift to them. The gift and the fact that the party was in her honour were to be a surprise to Eunice. Nathan, for some reason, had been told about it.

There had been cold that year but no snow, so you could skate all over the lake. My mother remembered them skimming by, the golden lads and girls who made up the world when she was small, and Nathan and Eunice the most romantic of all. Nathan was handsome and Eunice was beautiful and they were very much in love, she said.

She remembered the skaters by moonlight, slim black shapes mysterious against the silver fields. There were a lot of clouds in the sky that night and when the moon went behind one of them, friends, neighbours and parents' friends became alike: all equally unknown, unidentifiable.

My grandfather and Uncle Nathan had built a big wood fire at the near end of the lake. My mother said that it was a grand experience to skate off into the darkness and the perils and dangers of the night, and then turn and come back toward the light, following the fire's reflection on the ice.

Late on, when some people were already making their way up the hill to the house, Eunice Lathem went skating off into the darkness with her sister. They didn't skate up the middle of the lake as most of the skaters had been doing. Instead they went off toward the east bank. There is a place there where a spring rises and the water is deep, but they didn't know that. The ice was thinner there. They broke through.

Near the fire, people heard their cries for help. A group of the men skated out to rescue them. When the men got close to the place where the girls were in the water, the ice began to crack under their feet.

All the men lay down then and formed a chain, each holding the ankles of the man in front of him. Uncle Nathan was at the front. He inched forward, feeling the ice tremble beneath his body, until he came to the point where he could reach either of two pairs of hands clinging to the fractured edge.

It was dark. He couldn't see the girls' faces. All he could do was grasp the nearest pair of wrists and pull. The men behind him pulled on his feet. Together they dragged one girl back to safety. But as they were doing it, the ice broke away beneath them and the second girl went under. The moon came out and they saw it was Eunice Lathem's sister they had saved. They went back to the hole, but Eunice had vanished. There wasn't any way they could even get her body.

"It was an awful thing to have happen on our place," my father said.

"Your Uncle Nathan risked his life," my mother said. Her voice was earnest, for she too believed in identifying heroes and villains.

"There was no way on earth he could save both girls," she said. "The ice was already breaking, and the extra weight of the first one was bound to be too much for it."

Why hadn't he saved Eunice first?

"I told you," my mother said. "He couldn't see their faces."

It troubled me that he hadn't had some way of knowing. I would have expected love to be able to call out to love. If it couldn't do that, what was it good for? And why had the moon been behind a cloud anyway?

"Your grandmother used to say that the Lord moves in a mysterious way," my father said.

"What does that mean?" I asked.

"It means that nobody knows," my mother said.

I'd seen Eunice Lathem's name on a grave in the yard of St. Chad's, where we attended services every second Sunday. If I'd thought of her at all, it was as a person who had always been dead. Now she seemed real to me, almost like a relative. She was a girl who had loved and been loved. I began to make up stories about her. But I no longer skated on the lake alone.

Eunice Lathem's sister, whose name was Delia Sykes, moved away from Willow Bunch right after the accident. She didn't wait until her husband sold out; she went straight to Edmonton and waited for him there. Even when they buried Eunice in the spring, she didn't come back.

Years later, someone from Willow Bunch had seen her in Edmonton. She didn't mention Eunice or the accident or even Willow Bunch.

"It must have been a short conversation," my mother said practically.

Is it surprising that I continued to wonder why Uncle Nathan didn't marry? Some people remember their childhoods as a time when they thought of anybody over the age of twenty-five as being so decrepit as to be beyond all thought of romance or adventure. I remember feeling that way about *women,* but I never thought of men that way, whatever their ages. It seemed to me that Uncle Nathan could still pick out a girl and marry her if he set his mind to it.

"No," he said when I asked him. "Not 'still' and not 'pick out a girl.' A person doesn't have that much say in the matter. You can't love where you choose."

And then, making a joke of it, "See that you remember that when your time comes," he said.

ONE DAY MY MOTHER SHOWED ME a picture of Eunice Lathem and her sister. Two girls and a pony stood looking at the camera. Both girls were pretty. The one who wasn't Eunice was laughing; she looked like a girl who loved to laugh. Eunice was pretty too but there was a stillness about her, almost a sternness. If she hadn't been Eunice Lathem, I would have said she was sulking.

I felt cheated. Was the laughing one also prettier?

"She may have been," my mother said. "I remember Eunice Lathem as being beautiful. But since Delia Sykes was married, I don't suppose I gave her looks a thought one way or the other."

AS I GREW OLDER I spent less time wondering about the girl who'd been Eunice Lathem. I'd never wondered about her sister, and perhaps never would have if I hadn't happened to be with Uncle Nathan the day he heard that Delia Sykes had died.

It was the spring I was fifteen. My parents were away for the weekend, attending a silver wedding in Rochfort Bridge. Uncle Nathan and I were alone on the farm and so, if he wanted to talk about Delia Sykes, he hadn't much choice about who to talk to.

It was a morning for bad news. The frost was coming out of the ground, setting the very ditches and wheel ruts to weeping. Out in the barn, a ewe was mourning her lost lamb. We had put her in a pen by herself and we were saving the dead lamb, so we could use its skin to dress another lamb in case one of the ewes died in lambing or had no milk.

Uncle Nathan and I left the barn and walked out to the road to pick up the mail. The news of Delia's death was in the local paper. "Old-timers will be saddened to learn of the death in Duncan, B.C. of Mrs. Delia Sykes, a former resident of this district," the paper said.

Uncle Nathan shook his head slowly, as if he found the news hard to believe. "So Delia's gone," he said. "She was a grand girl, Delia Sykes. No matter what anybody said, she was a grand girl."

There was a picture of Mrs. Sykes with the death notice. I saw a middle-aged woman who had gone from the hairdresser's to the photographer's. Her cheeks were as firm and round as two peach halves, and she had snappy eyes. She was wearing a white dress. She looked as if she might have belonged to the Eastern Star or the Rebekahs.

Uncle Nathan looked at the picture too. "Delia always was a beauty," he said.

He sat in silence for a while, and then, bit by bit, he began to tell me the story of how he had met Delia Sykes and before her, her husband.

"Only I didn't realize that he was her husband," Uncle Nathan said. "I thought when I met her that she was single; that was the joke of it."

It was late July and late afternoon. Uncle Nathan was teaching school, to make enough money to live on until his farm got going. But he was hoping to get out of it.

"The land was new then and we thought there was no limit to how rich we were all going to be some day. Besides that," he added, "what I wanted to do was farm. School-teaching seemed to me to be no proper job for a man."

There were two things Uncle Nathan wanted. One was to stop teaching. The other was to find a wife.

There were more men than girls around then, he told me, so the man who wanted a good selection had to be prepared to cover a lot of territory.

"Harold Knight and I took in dances and ball games as far away as Hasty Hills," he said.

They'd already seen a fair sampling, but there were still girls they hadn't seen.

"I had a pretty fair idea of what I was looking for," Uncle Nathan said. "I imagine it was the same sort of thing every young fellow thinks he's looking for, but I thought I had standards. I wasn't willing to settle for just anyone."

IT WAS WITH THE IDEA of looking over another couple of girls that he went to see Harold Knight that late July afternoon. A family with two daughters was rumoured to have moved in somewhere near Morningside School. He'd come to suggest to Harold that they take in the church service at the school the next Sunday.

The Knights, Uncle Nathan said, had hay and seed wheat to sell to people with the money to buy it. When Uncle Nathan walked into their yard that day, he saw that Mr. Knight was talking to a buyer. It was a man he'd never seen before, but he guessed by the cut of the man's rig that he must be well fixed.

"Nathan," Mr. Knight said, "meet Dobson Sykes."

Mr. Sykes was a straight-standing man with greying hair. He put out his hand and Uncle Nathan shook it.

"His driving horses," Uncle Nathan said, "were as showy a team as I'd ever seen—big bays with coats the colour of red willow."

"You'd go a long way before you'd find a better-matched team than that," Mr. Knight said.

"Oh, they match well enough." Dobson Sykes spoke as if that was a matter of little importance to him, as if no effort was made in the acquiring of such a team. "I'd trade them in a minute if something better came along," he said carelessly. "I have a job to keep Spark, here, up to his collar."

"I had a fair amount of respect then for men who'd done well in life," Uncle Nathan told me. "This man was about my father's age, old enough to have made it on his own. When a man like that came my way, I studied him. I thought if I was going to be a farmer instead of a teacher, I'd have to start figuring out how people went about getting things in life.

"I wasn't really surprised when Mr. Knight said that Sykes had a crew of men—men he was paying—putting up a set of buildings for him on a place he'd bought near Bannock Hill. He looked like a man with that kind of money."

"We're not building anything fancy," Dobson Sykes said. "If I'd wanted to stay farming on a big scale, I wouldn't have moved from Manitoba."

After a while Uncle Nathan left the two older men talking and walked out toward the meadow, where Harold was fetching a load of hay for Mr. Sykes.

It was on the trail between buildings and meadow that he met Delia Sykes.

He didn't see her at first because she wasn't sitting up front with Harold.

She must have been lying back in the hay, Uncle Nathan said, just watching the clouds drift by overhead. She sat up.

Uncle Nathan saw at once that she was not very old; he had girls almost as old as she was in his classroom. But there was nothing of the schoolgirl about Delia. She was young but womanly. Everything about her curved, from the line of her cheek to the way she carried her arms.

Uncle Nathan saw all this in the instant that she appeared looking down over the edge of the load. He saw too that she had a kind of class he'd never seen around Willow Bunch. She looked like a girl perfectly suited to riding around the country behind a team of perfectly matched bays.

She reached behind her into the hay and came up with a crown of French-braided dandelions. She set it on top of her hair and smiled.

He knew right then, Uncle Nathan said, that his voice wouldn't be among those swelling the hymns at Morningside School next Sunday. And he felt as if he understood for the first time how men must feel when they are called to the ministry. Choosing and decision and standards have nothing to do with it. You're called or you're not called, and when you're called you know it.

The girl smiled and opened her arms as if to take in the clouds in the sky and the bees buzzing in the air and the red-topped grasses stirring in the wind. Then she spoke.

"You've got no worries on a load of hay," she said.

Those were the first words Uncle Nathan heard Delia Sykes say. "You've got no worries on a load of hay."

There was a patch of milkweed blooming near the path where Uncle Nathan was standing. In late July, small pink blossoms appear and the milk, rich and white, is ready to run as soon as you break the stalk. Uncle Nathan picked a branch, climbed the load of hay, and presented it to the girl.

"It's not roses," he said, "but the sap is supposed to cure warts."

She laughed. "My name is Delia Sykes," she said.

"I THOUGHT SHE WAS DOBSON'S DAUGHTER," Uncle Nathan said, "and it crossed my mind to wonder if he'd have traded her off if she hadn't moved along smart in her harness.

"There didn't seem to be much fear of that. You could see right away she had spirit. If she had too much, it was nothing that marriage to a good man wouldn't cure, I thought."

Uncle Nathan gave a rueful smile. "Of course when we got back to the yard I found out that she wasn't Dobson's daughter but his wife. Later I wondered why she hadn't introduced herself as *Mrs.* Sykes. And she'd called me *Nathan* too, and girls didn't do that then.

"The truth is," Uncle Nathan said, "I had kind of fallen for her."

Did she feel the same way about him?

If she did, Uncle Nathan wasn't willing to say so. "Delia was only nineteen," he said. "I don't think she knew what she wanted."

He was silent for a while. Then he went on with his story. "Once I knew she was married," he said, "I knew right away what I had to do. I remember I gave myself a good talking to. I said, 'If you can fall in love in twenty minutes, you can fall out of love just as fast.'"

"And could you?"

"Some people could, I guess," Uncle Nathan said. "It seemed to take me a bit longer than that."

The story stopped then because we had to go out to the barn to check the sheep. While we'd been in the house, another ewe had dropped her lamb. We heard it bleat as we came in the barn, and the ewe whose lamb had died heard it too. It was at the far end of the barn, out of sight, but at the sound of it, milk began to run from her udder. She couldn't help herself.

We checked the rest of the sheep, and then we went back into the house. I made us a pot of tea.

"I was afraid to go to see Dobson and Delia after they got moved in," Uncle Nathan said. "I think I was afraid somebody would read my mind."

He went, he said, because Delia soon made her house a gathering place for all the young people of the district, and he didn't see how he could be the only one to stay away. Delia didn't make things any easier for him.

"She used to keep saying she'd only been married three months . . . as if that made it any less final. And when she spoke of anything they had—whether it was a buggy or a kitchen safe or the pet dog—she would say 'my buggy' or 'my kitchen safe' or 'my dog.' 'We' and 'us' were words she didn't use at all."

I poured our tea then, trying to imagine the house that Delia Sykes had lived in.

"It was something of a showplace for its time," Uncle Nathan told me. Everything in it was the best of its kind, he said, from the Home Comfort stove in the kitchen to the pump organ in the parlour. What puzzled Uncle Nathan was Delia's attitude to her things. She'd picked them out herself in Winnipeg and ordered them sent, but when they got here, she seemed to feel they weren't important.

"The more things you've got, the more things you've got to take care of," she said. She didn't even unpack most of her trunks.

Dobson was worried. He thought that moving away from her family had unsettled her. "Delia wasn't like this in Manitoba," he said.

"I kept wondering," Uncle Nathan said, "where we would go from here. It never occurred to me that there could be another girl for me. And then Eunice came along."

It was on an October afternoon, Uncle Nathan said, that he met Eunice Lathem.

The sun was low in the southwest when he drove into the Sykes yard, and Dobson, as usual, was out around the buildings showing the younger men his grinding mill, his blacksmith shop, his threshing machine.

Uncle Nathan remembered that the trees were leafless except for the plumes of new growth at the top. He tied up his horse and, as he headed for the house, saw that the afternoon sun was turning the west-facing walls all gold and blue. It looked like a day for endings, not beginnings. But he went into the house, and there stood Eunice Lathem.

Eunice was a year or two older than Delia but she looked just like her. Uncle Nathan noticed that she was quieter.

Supper was already on the table when Uncle Nathan got there. The news of Eunice's arrival had attracted such a company of bachelors that there weren't enough plates or chairs for everybody to eat at once.

"I don't know about anybody else, but I'm starving," Delia announced, taking her place at the head of the table. Eunice, though she was the guest of honour, insisted on waiting until the second sitting.

As the first eaters prepared to deal with their pie, Eunice began to ladle water out of a stonewear crock into a dishpan. Uncle Nathan went to help her. He said something funny and she laughed.

Delia's voice startled them both. "I invited Eunice out here to find a husband," she said with a high-pitched laugh. "I said to myself, 'With all the bachelors we've got around, if she can't find a husband here, there's no hope for her.'"

Delia spoke as if she were making a joke, and there was a nervous round of laughter. Blood rose in Eunice's face.

"If I'd known that was why you were asking me," Eunice said, "I would never have come."

And indeed, Uncle Nathan said, Eunice wasn't the sort of girl to need anyone's help in finding a husband. She was, if anything, prettier than Delia. Not as showy, perhaps, perhaps not as rounded. But if you went over them point by point comparing noses, chins, teeth and all the rest of it, Eunice might well have come out on top.

Later, when the others had gone, Delia apologized. "I shouldn't have said that," she said. "It sounded awful." She didn't even claim to have been making a joke.

"I want you two to be friends," she said.

In the weeks that followed, Uncle Nathan saw that Delia was pushing her sister his way. He didn't know why, but he didn't find the idea unpleasant.

"I suppose I liked Eunice at first because she looked so much like Delia," he said, "but as I got to know her better it seemed to me that she might be easier to get along with in the long run. I wouldn't be the first man to marry the sister of the girl who first took his fancy, nor the last one either.

"It seemed to me that a man could love one girl as easily as another if he put his mind to it. I reasoned it out. How much did the person matter anyway? That was what I asked myself. It seemed to me that when all was said and done, it would be the life that two people made together that would count, not who the people were.

"I remember thinking that getting married would be like learning to dance. Some people are born knowing how; they have a natural beat. Other people have to make an effort to learn. But all of them, finally, are moving along to the music one way or the other.

"Anyway," Uncle Nathan said, "I spoke to Eunice, and she agreed, and we decided to be married at Christmas.

"It was September, I think, when we got engaged," Uncle Nathan said. "I remember thinking about telling Dobson and Delia. I could imagine the four of us—Dobson and Delia, Eunice and me—living side by side, spending our Sundays together, raising children who would be cousins and might even look like each other.

"I came over early on the Sunday and we told them. Delia didn't have very much to say then. But in the afternoon when quite a crowd had gathered and Eunice and I were waiting for the rest of them to get there before we made our announcement, a strange thing happened.

"The day before, Dobson had brought home a new saddle pony and Delia had wanted to ride it. Dobson didn't know how well broke it was, or if it could be trusted, and he refused. I guess that refusal rankled. Delia didn't like to be told she couldn't do a thing or have a thing she had set her heart on.

"Anyway, on Sunday afternoon Eunice was sitting at the pump organ playing for us, and she looked beautiful. We were all sitting around looking at her.

"And then somebody happened to glance out of the window," Uncle Nathan said. "And there was Delia on the pony, and the pair of them putting on a regular rodeo.

"She didn't break her neck, which was a wonder. By the time she finally got off the pony, we were all out in the yard, and somebody had the idea of taking a picture of Delia and Eunice and the pony."

After that, Uncle Nathan said, Delia seemed to want to get the wedding over with as soon as possible. She hemmed sheets and ordered linen and initialed pillowcases. When November finally came and the neighbours decided on a skating party for Eunice and Uncle Nathan, it was Delia who sewed white rabbit fur around the sleeves and bottom of Eunice's coat, so that it would look like a skating dress.

The night of the party was dark. There was a moon, but the sky was cloudy. They walked down the hill together, all those young people, laughing and talking.

"One minute you could see their faces and the next they would all disappear," Uncle Nathan said. "I touched a match to a bonfire we had laid in the afternoon, and we all sat down to screw on our skates.

"I skated first with Eunice. She wanted to stay near the fire so we could see where we were going. I skated with several other girls, putting off, for some reason, the time when I would skate with Delia. But then she came gliding up to me and held out her hands, and I took them and we headed out together into the darkness.

"As soon as we turned our backs on the fire it was as if something came over us. We wanted to skate out farther and farther. It seemed to me that we could keep on like this all our lives, just skating outward farther and farther, and the lake would keep getting longer and longer so that we would never come to the end of it."

Uncle Nathan sighed. "I didn't know then that in three days Delia would have left Willow Bunch for good, and in six months I would have followed her," he said.

Why had he given up farming?

"Farming's no life for a man alone," he said. "And I couldn't imagine ever wanting to marry again."

He resumed his story. "Once the moon came out and I could see Delia's face, determined in the moonlight.

"'Do you want to turn back?' I asked her.

"'I'm game as long as you are,' she said.

"Another time, 'I don't ever want to turn back,' she said.

"I gave in before Delia did," Uncle Nathan said.

"'If we don't turn around pretty soon,' I told her, 'we're going to be skating straight up Pa's stubble fields.'

"We turned around then, and there was the light from the fire and our feet already set on its path. And I found I wanted to be back there with all the people around me. Eunice deserved better, and I knew it."

As they came toward the fire, Eunice skated out to meet them. "I might as well have been someplace else for all the attention she paid me," Uncle Nathan said. Her words were all for Delia.

"If this is what you got me out here for," Eunice said, "you can just forget about it. I'm not going to be your window blind."

"I don't know what you're talking about," Delia said.

She looked unhappy. "She knew as well as I did," Uncle Nathan said, "that whatever we were doing out there, it was more than just skating."

"We were only skating," Delia said. And then her temper rose. "You always were jealous of me," she said.

"Who would you say was jealous now?" Eunice asked.

"We were far enough away from the fire for the girls not to be heard," Uncle Nathan said. "At least I hoped we were.

"What was worrying me was the thought of Eunice having to meet all the people up at the house, and finding out she was the guest of honour, and having to try to rise to the occasion.

"That was why I suggested that the two of them go for a skate. I thought it would give them a chance to cool down. Besides," he added, "I couldn't think of anything else to do."

The girls let themselves be persuaded. They skated off together and Uncle Nathan watched them go. First he could see their two silhouettes, slim and graceful against the silver lake. Then all he could see was the white fur on Eunice's coat. And then they were swallowed up by the darkness.

"It was several minutes before we heard them calling for help," Uncle Nathan said.

Uncle Nathan and I sat silent for some time then: he remembering, I pondering. "If only you could have seen how beautiful she was," he said at last, and I didn't know whether it was Eunice he was speaking of, or Delia.

"I wonder if I would have felt any better about it if I'd got Eunice instead of Delia," he said. I realized that he'd been trying to make the judgment for thirty years.

"You didn't have any choice," I reminded him. "It was dark. You couldn't see their faces."

"No," Uncle Nathan said. "I couldn't see their faces." The sound of old winters was in his voice, a sound of infinite sadness.

"But I could see their hands on the edge of the ice," he said. "The one pair of arms had white fur around them.

"And I reached for the other pair."

Merna Summers is the author of three collections of short stories, The Skating Party, Calling Home, *and* North of the Battle. *Her writing has won numerous literary prizes, including the Marian Engel Award, the Katherine Anne Porter Prize for Short Fiction, an Ohio State Award and two Writers Guild of Alberta awards for the year's best collection of short stories.*

THE FLOOD

Sandra Birdsell

Maurice Lafreniere stood on the fire escape on the south side of the hotel and looked with awe at the litter-strewn lake which spread out where the town had been only two weeks ago.

"My God," he said, because he needed to hear the sound of his own voice. He felt abandoned, as though he were the only remaining human on earth.

Across the street, a chunk of dirt-riddled ice battered against the Bank of Montreal. The wind had swept the ice into town during the night. He'd lain shivering in bed, listening to that ice crashing like a battering ram against everything that was his. And his thoughts had run together, had overflowed: his submerged business, the barber chairs bolted to the floor, one hundred years old, at least. Brought up from St. Paul on a steamboat, bequeathed to him by Henry Roy who had been like a father to him and who had also taught him his barbering trade. Mika, in Choritza, awaiting the birth of their sixth child. His other five children, cut off, wood chips floating about until the flood would subside. And his mother. When exhaustion had overcome the noise of the ice, he'd dreamed of his mother who was not dead, but alive in his dream, standing beside the river. She was gathering willow branches for her baskets. She'd looked up suddenly and she was not as he'd remembered, defeated and broken, eyes turned **inward**. Her broad face was strong and serious, her black eyes demanding his attention. If you have a large family, she said, you will need a bigger boat.

He thought of his boat moored below and smiled. They didn't come any smaller than his rowboat. He pulled his tweed cap tighter on his head and made his way carefully down the ice-coated fire escape. One slip and he'd be gone. Two minutes was all a person could hope for in the icy water even if he could get the hipwaders off. And then the little woman would be a widow, his children fatherless. The town would rush in for a woman like Mika. The town thought Mika had taken him in hand and with her clean habits and Mennonite ways had made him what he was today.

His boat rose and fell with the waves, its wood squeaking and protesting against the piece of wooden sidewalk he'd lashed to the bottom of the fire escape to serve as a dock. Water, as far as the eye could see. Who would have thought that their tired, narrow river could have come to this? He told himself that he was anxious to see how the men at the courthouse had endured the ice. Damned fools, he called them, for letting a few rats in the hotel frighten them from sleeping safely as he did. But he knew his real anxiety. It had surfaced during the night and he needed to reassure himself that this flood had happened gradually, others knew about it too. It was not something that had happened overnight to him alone. He was not the only human being left in the world.

He crouched, moved low in the boat and seated himself in the center of it. No one accused him of being a careless person anymore. He still took chances, certainly, but not until he was sure everything was shipshape first. He untied the knot which moored his boat to the fire escape. He pushed off from the sidewalk with the oar and sliced deeply through the ice slush floating on the surface as he headed out toward the center of Main Street. He wondered what condition the courthouse basement would be in. It was not what you'd call shipshape. No matter what Bill Livingston said, he would try and persuade the others to move into the hotel before it was too late.

Up and down the wide street, there wasn't another boat to be seen, no human sounds, just the wind and water rushing against the buildings. He stopped rowing, let the oars sink deep into the water and stared for a moment at the bottom of the boat where his boots had crushed through the film of muddy ice. He felt the oar scrape against one of the drowned vehicles that had been parked on Main Street and he shuddered. It was like disturbing the dead, bumping into submerged things. He began rowing against the current which swept down from the mouth of the Agassiz River, across the cemetery and into town. The bottom of the hotel sign bobbed the water. The sign had been sheared off by the ice during the night, one of the sounds that had kept him awake. He'd been kept awake all spring by the sounds of the ice cracking and groaning like a woman about to give birth. What are you up to? he'd asked the river. Gather up your skirts, it's time, he said, fancying the sound of his thoughts, the idea that the river was a pregnant woman. But its deep complaining rumble made him uneasy. Then, when the weather turned on them, becoming bitterly cold with freezing rain and snowstorms, he sent his children away and only he and Mika remained. They'd been prepared. The flood hadn't taken him by surprise. The last of the townspeople had been evacuated only three days ago, taken like cattle in boats with the few things they had time to pack and loaded onto railcars at the CN line. Evacuees, flood victims, the *Winnipeg Free Press* called them.

Agassiz evacuation climaxes grim saga, the headline read. The saga of the rivers. The Agassiz and the Red meeting headlong in the north end of town, each carrying full loads into the late-melting tributaries. The pincer-like movement caused the waters near the mouth of the Agassiz to back up in twenty-four hours and run across Main Street at Agassiz Bridge. The saga of the government engineer's stupidity: "We expect nothing this year to approach the '48 flood."

"Expect?" Maurice had said and smacked the report in the newspaper with the back of his hand. "How can anyone expect things from the river? You listen and watch and you can feel what's going to happen. You don't go by charts and expect. It's unpredictable."

The barbershop had become the meeting place for the daily discussions about the possibilities of the river's flooding. Maurice, standing at the barber chair cutting hair, had remained silent until now. He was surprised by his outburst, to find himself throwing aside the need to be agreeable and to keep the peace with all around him at any cost. But if he knew anything well, it was the river. The knowledge was hidden inside him and flowed out naturally when he put his mind to it. The conversation which had centered around Bill Livingston, Agassiz's mayor, trailed away. The men stared at Maurice.

He was standing on an edge. His word on the line. "I'm telling you. If you know what's good for you, then get ready for a doozer of a flood."

In the same tone of voice Bill Livingston had used thirty odd years ago when he'd pulled the blanket up over Maurice's mother's face and said to those present, "Now that's drunk. Dead drunk. But what can you expect?" he got up from the bench, walked over to the barber chair and stuck his red face into Maurice's. "Horse shit," he said. "You'll have everyone running for the hills."

Maurice caught sight of his own reflection in the mirror above the bench where the men had gathered. He moved around the chair gracefully, he was light on his feet. He wore his thick black hair swept back, it made him look taller. He saw the slender back of himself, the blue birthmark on his neck, while in the plate glass mirror above his marble sinks, he could see the front of himself. Mika fed him well. He had the beginning of a double chin and a slight paunch. He saw himself begin to gesture expansively, his hand extended, palm up in a sweeping motion. Look here, he was going to say to Livingston, I'm an agreeable man. He dropped his arm quickly.

"Use your head. Forget what they're saying in Winnipeg. Those dumbbells can't forecast a flood until they're up to their asses in water. I predict that it'll be the worst flood ever."

Maurice's breath came faster now as he rowed against a small side current where the water swept between two buildings. He'd said it. His word had stood and one by one the men had begun to trust his knowledge and come to him for advice. He passed by the barbershop. He passed by the movie theater. The sign on the marquee, THE LADY TAKES A SAILOR, used to make him laugh, but because of the ferocity of the flood, now seemed to him to have been a portent filled with meaning.

Freed of the metal graveyard of drowned vehicles that had been parked down Main Street, Maurice stopped rowing. He started up the small outboard motor that Flood Control had issued him. Engine straining, he moved out faster into the current, the bow whacking against the choppy water. And he saw the lights of the courthouse beaming out at him from the tall narrow windows. So, the basement, she'd held. The courthouse had been built up on its foundation. It was entrenched behind sandbags, but water lapped inches from the top of the dike. He heard the sound of another motor and tension fled from his muscles. He wasn't alone. A boat moved out from behind the courthouse, its hull cutting a deep V down into the water. It veered suddenly in his direction. He shut down his motor and waited. There were three men in the boat, two of them farmers from the area, and Woods, a young RCMP officer whose cap appeared to be held in place by his ears.

"What's up?" Maurice asked.

Stevens, the younger one of the farmers, motioned wearily to the west. All three men looked alike, unshaven, complexions gray from too much coffee and too little sleep. Maurice saw the rifles on the floor of their boat.

"He's got fifty head of Herefords," Woods said. His voice to an excited screech. "They're stranded. Haven't been able to get feed into them. Not sure they'll even be there, not after this ice."

"That was some night," Maurice said. "Have you checked the basement?"

"It's tighter than a drum," Woods said, echoing a Livingston pronouncement.

That was the whole damned trouble. It was too tight. There was too much pressure on the walls. They should flood the basement or the whole thing would pop inward. Damned farmers. The closest they'd been to water before the flood was the dugouts they'd led their cows down to and Woods was still wet behind his big flapping ears.

"What's the situation with the livestock?" he asked.

Stevens lifted one of the rifles and laid it across his knees.

"Plain damned shame. Something should be done," Maurice said. He'd told Stevens, ship 'em out. If you don't, may as well shoot them now. "We're all in the same condition," he said. "My shop, your cattle. We'll have to start over, that's all." He was surprised by his own sudden optimism. It was what

Henry Roy would have said. He'd dispensed good will like pills when the going got tough.

"Sure we will," the farmer said. "With what? The money I'll get from this year's crop?"

Maurice said, "Wait and see, the government will come through in the end."

The farmer spat. "Laurent doesn't even know where Agassiz is," he said. "And all they care about on Broadway is making sure the houses on Wellington Crescent don't get wet."

"Watch, watch," Maurice called out suddenly as a sharp piece of ice swept close to their boats. He angled his craft away into the waves. The ice slid inches from the hull of the other boat and then was gone. The three men watched it pass by. Maurice could tell they were unaware of the danger. It was a wonder there hadn't been a serious accident, what with the mayor heading up the flood control committee. He had a bulldozer for a brain. Ran over people who didn't agree with him. Sent people running off half-cocked to do what they damned well should have done a month ago.

"If that one had hit, you'd have been able to drive a grain truck through the hole," Maurice said. He felt strong, in control. "Keep your eyes open out there. An aluminum boat is no damned good in this stuff." Old Man River. That was the name they'd given to him since his prediction of the flood had come true. Maurice Lafreniere reads the river like it was a newspaper. When the going gets tough, the tough get going, he told himself. And he'd proven himself. Why do you have stay, now of all times, Mika had asked. And he couldn't explain to her that for once he didn't want to be on the outside, left out, but dead center. Because Mika didn't know otherwise. He was the one who went out each morning to check the waters' rising, measured on a pole at Agassiz Bridge, and took the reading to the courthouse where the police radioed it into Winnipeg.

"Why don't you come with us?" Woods asked.

Hold your hand, you mean. "I'm going to take the reading and then cruise around a bit, see what damage I can do. Was there any breakfast? Could eat a horse."

"We'll bring you one," Stevens said.

Maurice chuckled at the bad joke. His spirits rose. He watched the three men head out across the open field. It was just a case of numbers to Ottawa: 28:1. If they could get the real story. Drop Laurent down in the middle of this hell, get his feet wet and he wouldn't say, "No aid for the flood victims."

He tied the boat to the railing on the bridge. He didn't dare venture into the river channel, it was choked with debris. He took the binoculars from beneath the seat and lifted them. The water rose and fell at the level of 29:3 on the pole. He predicted that the crest was days away. Three more feet of water and even the tops of the trees, the only remaining indication of where the river's bank used to be, would be under. They were like scrawny black fingers now, pointing out the sweep and curve of the shoreline where he'd spent that terrible summer hiding from the priest who would take him to be with his brothers in the convent in the city. The memory caught at him suddenly like a camouflaged barb hooking an unsuspecting fish.

He turned the glasses toward the cemetery. His hands shook with the cold. All the grave stones had vanished, had been tumbled by the waves or cut down by the ice and scattered like broken teeth at the bottom of the lake. He lowered the glasses. His eyes stung. His mother and father were there. They were side by side, locked into their early middle years behind the frozen ground. First his father; a railroad accident. And there had been no town clamoring to rescue that widow. She'd been ignored. Left alone to feed three kids with the money she made sewing and from her baskets. And a month later, they buried her. Dead drunk. Lying on her back in the center of the bed, her head in a pool of gray vomit. Perspiration ran down between his shoulder blades.

Hey, boy, do you want to keep these? Livingston had asked, holding up his mother's beaded moccasins. He'd come with a number of other men, now forgotten, to help carry her away and to poke around through the remains of his family. The wind rose and the icy blast of it seemed to bore straight through his skull. He wished suddenly that he'd been able to find one place for his children instead of shipping them off, piece by piece, to live out the flood among strangers. The ice slush was like crushed glass as it slid swiftly beneath and around his boat. He rowed steadily. His arms began to ache. The sound of a shrill whistle jarred him. He turned quickly and saw the huge white hull of a fishing vessel bearing down on him. It was the *Apex,* bringing supplies to Agassiz.

They plucked Maurice from his rowboat and towed his boat back to town. They took him back to the courthouse, unloaded the supplies, had something to eat, and then Maurice, by virtue of his title, Old Man River, was invited to come along on a cruise about the town to show a newspaper reporter who had come to see for himself what damage had been done.

"This is incredible," the man said. His name was Charles Medlake. The tall thin man spoke to them as though they hadn't already known that the flood was incredible, devastating, all the fancy words he used to describe what had happened to their town. "I've never seen anything like this," he kept saying.

He thinks he pays us a compliment, Maurice thought. Being ten feet under is a great accomplishment. He stood at the railing on the stern of the *Apex* with Bill Livingston and the reporter, listening to their conversation with growing impatience.

"I bloody well hope that we never do again, either," said Bill Livingston, but there was a strange tone of pride in his booming voice. "But according to an Indian legend, this happens every hundred years."

Medlake's hands shook as he cupped them and lit another cigarette. He drew deeply on it and expelled shreds of blue smoke which were snatched by the wind. "Have many people left the area for good?" he asked.

"Hell no. We're tough chickens."

Maurice shifted from one foot to another as the reporter asked the mayor many questions. According to an Indian legend? That was the first he'd heard of it. What Indian? Outwardly, he appeared solid and calm. His parka was unzipped, revealing his green curling sweater with the white rearing bucks on it. Mika's mother had knit it for him. He chewed thoughtfully on a toothpick, moving it from one side of his mouth to the other.

"This isn't the worst of it," the mayor said. "We haven't been east of town yet. The ice took out three or four houses."

"I've seen enough for now," the man said. He flicked his half-smoked cigarette over the stern. "Listen, the luckiest house in Agassiz is the worst hit in Winnipeg. I never saw anything this bad in the city."

"Really?" the mayor said.

It was what Maurice had suspected. Once they'd figured it out, that the same river that was flooding Agassiz would eventually flood Winnipeg, they screamed bloody murder. Squeaky wheel gets the grease.

"I'd like to get back to the courthouse and call the paper to send out a photographer. This should be recorded."

Livingston called out directions to the pilot. The fishing boat began a slow wide turn.

"The feds have got to open their eyes to this," Livingston said. "Pictures would help. We estimate that property damage alone will be close to five million dollars. Then there's the months of lost revenue to consider." He turned suddenly to Maurice. "How long has it been since you've earned a cent, Maurie?"

"Eh?" He was jolted loose from his tumbling thoughts.

"I said, how are you going to manage to feed the kiddies when they get home? Let alone afford the lumber to rebuild the house and buy new furniture?"

"Well, I . . . ," Maurice began and stopped. I was prepared. My furniture is high and dry. We took what was left of the preserves to Mika's sister's place. But there was something in Livingston's tone of voice that kept him quiet. He sensed that there was more here than an innocent question.

Livingston didn't wait for his reply. "We must be compensated. We're going to need money and lots of it. Interest-free money for the business community to replace their inventory. I've lost my entire stock of hardware. The farmers, their seed and fertilizer. And people like Maurie, here, they'll need money to feed and clothe the family. He's got six kids."

"Five," Maurice said. "I've got five." He was stung. Money for people like Maurie, here. How are you going to feed your family? A straightforward question. But it rankled. It was intended to remind him that at one time he'd swept their floors, carried out their shit pails and shoveled clean the barns. He'd fallen down drunk in the street. He'd been looked upon with pity or scorn. And that he had risen only so far in twenty years that his main concern would be how to feed six mouths, nothing more. He sees me as being another flood victim, same as all the others. Maurice freed his hands from his parka pockets and cut the air in front of the two men in an impatient motion.

"Compensation, to be sure," he said.

"What was that?" Charles Medlake spoke directly to him for the first time.

"Compensation, to be sure. By all means." His was the quiet reasonable voice of Henry Roy, his mentor. He hoped it was the voice of someone who would listen for so long to the clamor of others and then, with a few chosen words, bring clarity to their ramblings so as to make them look ridiculous. "But look here, compensation and interest-free loans are only a small part of the whole picture," he continued.

The newsman moved in closer. He began to make notes on a tablet. "Just what do you think should be done?"

"Many things. Certainly, I could use a hand just as everyone else in this town could use a hand. I'm a businessman too. I've lost more than furniture." He avoided Livingston's eyes. "But I personally wouldn't care if I didn't get a penny from the government if we could take steps to make certain that this here flood will never happen again."

Livingston laughed outright and turned away.

"But how is that possible?" Medlake asked.

Maurice was unsettled by the laughter. He shoved his hands back into his pockets. They were heading back toward the courthouse. They had circled the town and approached the stone building from behind, moving slowly down Elm Avenue. The trees were bare, bark black with orange rusty-looking growths in the crooks of limbs. A chair was caught in the lower branches of one tree. Maurice cleared his throat to speak. Build a sewage treatment plant so we no longer shit and piss on the river. We didn't have floods like this one until we got the running water. My God, the river, she doesn't pretend to be beautiful, but some honor is due, eh? Lure the goldeye and pickerel back with clean water. Forget the Indian legend that says we have no say in the matter. We should remember the river. She gave this region its life. But he knew they saw the river with different eyes. To them it was heavy, sluggish and ugly, a breeding ground for mosquitoes and eels.

"It's impossible to prevent flooding," Livingston said. He took Medlake by the elbow and attempted to steer him away by pointing out some particular damage.

"Wait, let him finish," Medlake said.

"We need to look to the future," Maurice said.

"How?"

"With all our minds, we should be able to come up with something instead of just saying it happens every hundred years. We should think about building a permanent dike around the town, for instance, or dig drainage ditches in the country to let the spring run-off enter into the Red further downstream."

"Winnipeg would never go for that," Livingston interrupted. "Because it would mean more water for them."

He speaks as though he has just bit into a lemon, Maurice thought.

"There must be a way around it," Medlake said.

The boat nudged slowly into the courthouse yard toward a large oak tree in the center of it. The pilot cut the engine and Maurice was jolted forward as the craft met bark with a hollow thud. The *Apex* whistled its arrival. Dark shapes appeared at the window and then the back door swung open. Woods and Stevens stepped out on the stairs. They climbed into Maurice's rowboat and began rowing toward them. Woods cupped his hands to his mouth. "Survivors," he shouted. "We found two women and a child stranded on the roof of a granary."

"Listen," Medlake said to Maurice. "I'd like to talk to you later on. What you say makes good sense."

Maurice felt the careful attentive posture of Livingston's large body. "Suits me," he said, trying to sound casual.

"Where can I find you?"

"If I'm not here—"

"He's over at the hotel," the mayor finished. "Maurie here doesn't like our company. He's always been what you might call a lone wolf."

Maurice's face grew warm. "Shoot, it's not that," he said. He felt as though his mouth was full of marbles. He juggled words in his mind. "It's not that. It's the basement. She's going to cave in."

"What?" Medlake asked. "And you're taking me in there?"

"He doesn't know what he's talking about," Livingston said. "The walls are two feet thick. This place is built like a brick shithouse."

The rowboat came alongside and they got into it. Maurice sat between the two men, slouched down into his parka, his fists curled tightly inside his pockets. Blow, goddammit, he urged as they approached the courthouse. Now. He imagined walls crumbling.

They removed their hipwaders in the basement. Maurice sat on the cot in the jail cell and leaned against the rough Tyndalstone wall and closed his eyes.

"Well, Maurie," Livingston said and laughed. "Drainage ditches, eh? It looks as though the wrong one ran for mayor."

Maurice didn't answer. He could see his parents' fresh graves, a mixture of yellow clay and topsoil. This room carried the memory. The priest had found him beside the river, trying to build a raft so that he could float downstream to his mother's people. And had agreed, Maurice could stay. He didn't have to join his brothers in the convent in the city. He'd sat in this very cell, tracing the outlines of strange creatures locked in the stone without knowing what they were while the men of the town decided his fate. Send for his mother's people, the priest advised. And so he waited it out in this room for a full week. They didn't want me? he asked. Henry Roy winked. You wouldn't have wanted them, he said. I never sent the message. And he took Maurice in and gave him work in the hotel. It would have turned out well if it hadn't been that it took too long for a town to forget a person who would die suffocating on their own vomit. Dead drunk.

"Come on, Old Man River," Livingston said and clapped him on the shoulder. "Let's go on up and meet those survivors."

Maurice followed him into the main hall. Two women and the child huddled beneath blankets within the circle of men. The men parted to let Maurice and Livingston through. The women and child were of mixed blood, Maurice realized instantly. Mongrels. The women had identical expressions, wide smiles, like fools, displaying their rotting teeth. Don't let anyone tell you different, Henry Roy had said, mongrels don't make better dogs. But the child studied Maurice with the same serious black eyes as his mother had in his dream last night. If you're going to have a large family, she said, you will need a bigger boat. These people didn't even have a boat. Not even a small one. The men seemed to be waiting for him to do something.

"Do you speak French?" Maurice asked the women.

They laughed and covered the gaping holes in their teeth with hands that looked to be tinged by wood smoke.

Maurice felt the floor move.

"No, no, not French," Livingston said. "You never know. You could be related. Say something to them in Indian."

"In a pig's ass," Maurice said, his anger breaking loose in upraised fists. The floor tilted. And then there was a sound, like thunder, beneath them. Relief flooded every part of his body and his knees suddenly felt weak. He felt like laughing hysterically.

Stevens ran into the room. "Clear out," he yelled. "The basement just went."

The reporter scrambled for his parka. Maurice led the women and child to the back door. They were calm. They pulled their blankets about themselves and walked slowly, as though they were accustomed to calamities. Bill Livingston ran to the tables, gathered papers to his chest, set them back down again. Maurice heard the roar of the water filling the basement, flooding the little room. He lifted the child quickly and handed her to Stevens. When she saw the boat, she clung to Maurice's sweater and began to cry. He peeled her loose and handed her down. I was right, he told himself. Once again, I was right. He felt like laughing and he felt like crying. Thank God, the *Apex* was big enough, it would hold them all. It would carry the whole damned works of them to the hills.

Sandra Birdsell's books include the short story collections Night Travellers *and* Ladies of the House *and the novels* The Chrome Suite *and* The Missing Child. The Two-Headed Calf *appeared in 1998. She has won the Gerald Lampert Award and has been nominated for the Governor General's Award.*

DIAMOND GRILL

Fred Wah
From *Diamond Grill*

IN THE DIAMOND, AT THE END OF A long green vinyl aisle between booths of chrome, Naugahyde, and Formica, are two large swinging wooden doors, each with a round hatch of face-sized window. Those kitchen doors can be kicked with such a slap they're heard all the way up to the soda fountain. On the other side of the doors, hardly audible to the customers, echoes a jargon of curses, jokes, and cryptic orders. Stack a hots! Half a dozen fry! Hot beef san! Fingers and tongues all over the place jibe and swear You mucka high!—Thloong you! And outside, running through and around the town, the creeks flow down to the lake with, maybe, a spring thaw. And the prairie sun over the mountains to the east, over my family's shoulders. The journal journey tilts tight-fisted through the gutter of the book, avoiding a place to start—or end. Maps don't have beginnings, just edges. Some frayed and hazy margin of possibility, absence, gap. Shouts in the kitchen. Fish an! Side a fries! Over easy! On brown! I pick up an order and turn, back through the doors, whap! My foot registers more than its own imprint, starts to read the stain of memory.

Thus: a kind of heterocellular recovery reverberates through the busy body, from the foot against that kitchen door on up the leg into the torso and hands, eyes thinking straight ahead, looking through doors and languages, skin recalling its own reconnaissance, cooked into the steamy food, replayed in the folds of elsewhere, always far away, tunneling through the centre of the earth, mouth saying can't forget, mouth saying what I want to know can feed me, what I don't can bleed me.

Mixed Grill is an entrée
    at the Diamond

and, as in most Chinese-Canadian restaurants in western Canada, is your typical improvised imitation of Empire cuisine. No kippers or kidney for the Chinese cafe cooks, though. They know the authentic mixed grill alright. It is part of their colonial cook's training, learning to serve the superior race in Hong Kong and Victoria properly, mostly as chefs in private elite clubs and homes. But, as the original lamb chop, split lamb kidney, and pork sausage edges its way onto every small town cafe menu, its ruddy countenance has mutated into something quick and dirty, not grilled at all, but fried.

Shu composes his mixed grill on top of the stove. He throws on a veal chop, a rib-eye, a couple of pork sausages, bacon, and maybe a little piece of liver or a few breaded sweetbreads if he has those left over from the special. While the meat's sizzling he adds a handful of sliced mushrooms and a few slices of tomato to sauté alongside. He shovels it all, including the browned grease, onto the large oblong platters used only for this dish and steak dinners, wraps the bacon around the sausages, nudges on a scoop of mashed potatoes, a ladle of mixed steamed (actually canned and boiled) vegetables, a stick of celery, and sometimes a couple of flowered radishes. As he lifts the finished dish onto the pickup counter he wraps the corner of his apron around his thumb and wipes the edge of the platter clean, pushes a button that rings a small chime out front, and shouts loudly into the din of the kitchen, whether there's anyone there or not, *mixee grill!*

THE MUFFLED SCRAPING OF
THE SNOW PLOW DOWN

on Baker Street is what he hears first. Then Coreen's deep breathing. Warmth. Shut off the alarm, quick, before she wakes up. Four forty-five, still dark, the house chilled. Dream-knot to Asia, dark and umbilical, early morning on the Pearl Delta, light the grass fire under the rice, ginger taste, garlic residue dampened. Here, on the other side of the world (through that tunnel all the way to China), in long-johns and slippers, quietly to the basement to stoke the furnace with a couple shovelfuls of coal and then wash up. Shave. He talks silently to himself (in English?) as he moves through the routine in near darkness: Who gave me this Old Spice last Christmas? One of the girls at work? Think I'll wear that rayon shirt today. Where's that pack of Players? My pen in the shirt pocket. Light brown gabardines. Start the day with less than a buck's worth of change in the right pocket. Clean hanky in the back pocket. The heavy Health Spot shoes the kids shined last night, by the kitchen door. Overcoat. Overshoes. Out the door into the morning that is still night.

Haven't plowed Victoria Street yet. Not too bad, but it's still snowing. The curling broom out of the trunk. Brush the snow off hood and windows. So quiet, he almost hates to start the Pontiac. Purr. Brr! First tracks on the street this morning, so clean. Lightly, lightly—don't lock the brakes down the hill. Good (still talking to himself), Baker Street's done. Guess I'll park out front until they get the alley plowed. Boy, the town's so quiet now. And the lights. Won't get home for a nap this afternoon. Weekend before Christmas'll be too busy for that.

The buzz of his busy day has, as every other day, kicked in through a muffled dialogue of place, person, and memory translated over an intersection of anxiety, anger, and wonder at the possibility of a still new world. At least another New Year.

As he unlocks the swinging front doors of the Diamond Grill he can see the light in the kitchen at the back of the cafe and he says to himself (in Chinese?), good, Shu's already at work.

Yet languageless. Mouth always a gauze, words locked

behind tongue, stopped in and out, what's she saying, what's she want, why's she mad, this woman-silence stuck, struck, stopped—there and back, English and Chinese churning ocean, her languages caught in that loving angry rip tide of children and coercive tradition and authority. Yet.

Grampa Wah's marriage to Florence Trimble is a surprise to most of the other Chinamen in the cafes around southern Saskatchewan, but not to his wife back in China. Kwan Chungkeong comes to Canada in 1892, returns to his small village in Hoiping County in 1900, and stays just long enough to marry a girl from his village and father two daughters and a son. When he returns to Canada in 1904 he has to leave his family behind because the head tax has, in his absence, been raised to five hundred dollars (two years' Canadian wages). He realizes he'll never be able to get his family over here so, against the grain for Chinamen, he marries a white woman (Scots-Irish from Trafalgar, Ontario), the cashier in his cafe. They have three boys and four girls and he never goes back to China again.

I don't know how Grampa Wah talks her into it (maybe he doesn't) but somehow Florence lets two of her children be sent off to China as recompense in some patriarchal deal her husband has with his Chinese wife. He rationalizes to her the Confucian idea that a tree may grow as tall as it likes but its leaves will always return to the ground. Harumph, she thinks, but to no avail.

Fred and his older sister Ethel are suddenly one day in July 1916 taken to the train station in Swift Current, their train and boat tickets and identities pinned to their coats in an envelope. My grandfather had intended to send number one son but when departure day arrives Uncle Buster goes into hiding. Grampa grabs the next male in line, four-year-old Fred, and, because he is so young, nine-year-old Ethel as well, to look after him. He has the word of the conductor that the children will be delivered safely to the boat in Vancouver and from there the connections all the way to Canton have been arranged. Fred, Kwan Foo-lee, and Ethel, Kwan An-wa, spend the next eighteen years, before returning to Canada, being raised by their Chinese step-mother alongside two half-sisters and a half-brother.

Yet, in the face of this patrimonial horse-trading it is the women who turn it around for my father and Aunty Ethel. Back in Canada my grandmother, a deeply religious lady, applies years of Salvation Army morality to her heathen husband to bring her children home. But he is a gambler and, despite his wife's sadness and Christian outrage, he keeps gambling away the money that she scrapes aside for the kids' return passage.

Meanwhile, the remittance money being sent from Canada to the Chinese wife starts to dwindle when the depression hits. She feels the pinch of supporting these two half-ghosts and, besides, she reasons with my grandfather, young Foo-lee is getting dangerously attracted to the opium crowd. As a small landholder she sells some land to help buy his way back to Canada.

Aunty Ethel's situation is different. She is forced to wait while, back in Canada, Fred convinces his father to arrange a marriage for her with a Chinaman in Moose Jaw. She doesn't get back to Canada until a year later, 1935.

Yet the oceans of women migrant-tongued words in a double-bind of bossy love and wary double-talk forced to ride the waves of rebellion and obedience through a silence that shutters numb the traffic between eye and mouth and slaps across the face of family, yet these women forced to spit, out of bound-up feet and torsoed hips made-up yarns and foreign scripts unlucky colours zippered lips—yet, to spit, when possible, in the face of the father the son the holy ticket safety-pinned to his lapel—the pileup of twisted curtains intimate ink pious pages partial pronouns translated letters shore-to-shore Pacific jetsam pretending love forgotten history braided gender half-breed loneliness naive voices degraded miscourse racist myths talking gods fact and fiction remembered faces different brothers sisters misery tucked margins whisper zero crisscross noisy mothers absent fathers high muckamuck husbands competing wives bilingual I's their unheard sighs, their yet still-floating lives.

DIRTY HEATHENS, GRANNY ERICKSON
    THINKS OF THE CHINESE,

the whole bunch of them, in their filthy cafes downtown. Just because that boy dresses up and has a little money, she throws herself at him. She and those other girls, they're always horsing around, looking for fun, running off to Gull Lake for a basketball game, a bunch of little liars, messing around in those cars, I know, not getting home until late at night, all fun and no work. I know what they're doing, they can't fool me, oof dah, that Coreen, she'll ruin herself, you wait and see, she'll be back here for help soon enough. Well she can look out for herself, she's not going to get any more of my money, she can just take her medicine, now that she's living with that Chinaman, nobody'll speak to her, the little hussy.

Chinese sausage? When I'm in
          Chinatown I see

it hanging in the butcher windows in bunches, candled together with twine. My mouth waters at the sight of the dried sausages marbled with fat. I still call Chinese sausage foong cheng, that's what my Granny Wah called it. And granny cooked foong cheng nearly all the time, a real delicacy. We'd have family meals in her and Grampa's little house and there was usually a large group of people at the table, uncles and aunts and cousins. I'd watch her at the stove when she opened up the rice pot, peek at the glistening steamed sausages so red and juicy on top of the white rice. She cooked one foong cheng for each person. Everybody got served one sausage on top of their rice, and so did I, but I always had one underneath too. Granny put an extra one under my rice for me. Special.

To top it off, his birth
          certificate has

been destroyed in the Medicine Hat city hall fire so his parents can't prove he's Canadian. Half Chinese, speaking only Chinese and no English, arriving on a boat from Hong Kong during the paranoia of the Chinese

Immigration (Exclusion) Act, my father and therefore his father can't be trusted. He's jailed in the immigration cells in Victoria, B.C., on Juan de Fuca Strait for three months while his parents try to convince immigration officials to let their son back in. They finally find some papers—his baptism records or the 1912 census—so he makes it through. His mother has her son back, his father winks, smiles, and thinks of those Confucian leaves that can be blown great distances in a strong wind.

Fred Wah is a Governor General's Award recipient for poetry and winner of the Howard O'Hagan Award for Diamond Grill. *His most recent book is* Faking It: Poetics and Hybridity, Critical Writing, 1984–1999. *Fred Wah teaches creative writing at the University of Calgary.*

EDEN

Sharon Butala

ELINOR LIFTED HER SHOULDERS as high as they would go and then forced them down, trying to ease the cramp in her neck. In the distance ahead a line of blue cliffs wavered and danced, sometimes stretching high, sometimes flattening to a thin blue line. It's a mirage, she thought, pleased with herself for recognizing it, yet aware that if this could appear to be what it was not, so could other things. She seemed to be travelling across a high plateau cut by valleys on three sides. She could picture the land dropping off from the edge ahead of her, the bleached prairie grass giving way to stony brown clay slopes that fell sharply downward, then curving out to olive-coloured thorny bushes and to clumps of featherlike, dusty sage, and finally, to an imaginary narrow brown river with gnarled trees, perhaps a kind of olive, like those she had seen in Spain, growing up from its banks.

She blinked rapidly several times, then rubbed her eyes with the back of her hand. She had been driving for over four hours through an almost empty countryside, was no longer sure she had a destination. She glanced into the rearview mirror hoping for the satisfaction of seeing the road, arrowstraight and thin, dwindling behind her, proof that she was making progress across the vast landscape, but saw instead only a long, billowing cloud of yellow-brown dust hanging in the air long after she had passed.

Ahead of her, on her left, were the promised red wagonwheels fastened upright on either side of a narrow side road. Her stomach tightened and sweat broke out on her temples. She stepped on the brake too hard; the ballooning dust caught up with her. She gripped the steering wheel fiercely as she turned it, and bumped for a short distance down a dirt road flanked on each side by old, dying cottonwoods, till a farmyard came into sight between the trees.

She had expected more than this: a small, frame house, the bottom half painted bright blue, the top half white, a gravel patch for parking by the back door, a vegetable garden beside the house, some round, silvery-coloured grain bins, a few small red wooden buildings, and all this framed by a neat double row of poplars.

As soon as she pulled up on the gravel the screen door opened and a stout woman wearing a print housedress, her grey hair pulled back in a bun, rushed out and started down the porch stairs, letting the door bang shut behind her. It opened once again and a short, heavy-set man walked slowly out, his hands shoved into the pockets of his striped overalls.

Elinor's hands had begun to tremble. The pain in her neck shot upward through the back of her head; even her jaws ached. She set her sunglasses carefully on the dash, opened the car door and immediately a blanket of heat rushed at her, enveloping her. Inside the car with the air conditioning on, she hadn't realized how intensely hot it was. She arranged her numb face into what she hoped was a smile, and put her hand out to Mrs. Hackett who thumped down the last step, her bosom giving one final, leaden heave.

"Goodness!" she said, before Elinor could speak, "you must be tired. Harold, come and get her suitcases. Watch that step, it's a little higher than the others. All the way from Toronto in one day. We keep meaning to get it fixed, but there's always so many things that need doing. I'd have known you anywhere you look so much like your mother." She propelled a startled Elinor up the stairs and into the kitchen. "Supper's on, I'll just show you your . . ." Elinor caught a confused glimpse of a white cloth on a table set with blue plates and cups, red enamelled pots on the stove, clouds of steam rising from them, plaster ducks flying heavenward across the kitchen wall, a bouquet of artificial pink roses sitting on a crocheted doily on a hall table, before Mrs. Hackett, still talking, had shown her her room and then left her at the bathroom door. ". . . used to be Judy's room. I'd have given you Billy's, but . . ." Mr. Hackett, who had thumped along behind them, set her suitcases down and went back down the hall without speaking. "Now, there's the bathroom. When you're ready . . ." Mrs. Hackett turned, still talking, and followed him to the kitchen. Elinor could hear her voice rising and falling, punctuated by the clink and rattle of pots and dishes.

She shut the bathroom door and locked it. Sweat was trickling between her shoulder blades. Her slacks were sticking to her thighs. Homesickness for her own small, quiet apartment, the door shut and locked behind her, swept over her. And was followed instantly by her father's low moaning, his emaciated yellow face, by the look in his deep-sunk, dark eyes that seemed to see right through her. Quickly, fumbling, she put the plug in the sink and turned both taps on full, the water splashing up onto her slacks and blouse. She washed her face and hands, emptied the sink, and rinsed it. Patting herself dry with the towel, her face buried in its soft, sweet-smelling folds, she tried breathing deeply, exhaling slowly, the way the therapist had told her.

Mrs. Hackett was draining vegetables in the sink.

"Did you have a good trip?" she asked. "What time did you have to get up this morning? Early, I'll wager. Are you far from the airport? It's such a long drive from Regina. I don't know how you did it all alone like that, of course, you young people . . ." She set a steaming bowl of carrots and one of green beans on the table and sat down herself. "When your mother was your age she was the prettiest thing. A little more meat on her bones than you." She paused to pour gravy on her potatoes, her lips pursed, her glasses slipping down her nose. "Then she went off to Normal School and the next thing we heard she was marrying this engineer." She offered Elinor the platter of meat. "He took a long time dying," she said. Elinor froze, her hand on the platter. "When your mother phoned and asked if you could come for a visit, you could have knocked me over with a feather, I was that surprised." Mrs. Hackett sighed. "It's hard on everybody," she said. "Those long cancer deaths. Stomach, wasn't it? I hated to ask Amy."

Elinor nodded. The heavy, rich smell of roast beef permeated the air. Mr. Hackett cut and chewed methodically, his eyes on his food.

"All those trips to the hospital. Waiting. Watching a loved one suffer. What a blessing your mother had you with her. I can imagine you were a comfort to her in her time of sorrow."

"I . . . I was . . . working most of the time," Elinor said. I couldn't bear to see him, I invented excuses to stay away. Aloud, she went on, "Mother is so strong. She never seemed to . . . it never seemed to be too much for her."

"Librarian, your mother said. You'll have to see our library. I don't use it myself but Judy and Billy used to when they were in school. I'll show it to you." Mr. Hackett was buttering a slice of bread on the palm of his hand. He didn't appear to be listening. Mrs. Hackett rattled on. "I remember when Harold's sister died. Cancer. With her husband gone and no children, I spent all my waking hours at the hospital for the last month. Especially the last week. Didn't know anybody. Couldn't talk. But she held onto my hand, just gripped it, like that, wouldn't let go. I had to pry it loose when I left at night." She shook her head. "Poor thing. I know what you've been through. They need you when they're dying. You don't know what they're thinking or even if they know who you are, but they seem to need you."

Elinor began to cry.

"Excuse me," she said, her hand over her face, and hurried to the bathroom where she shut the door, then leaned against it, her hand still over her eyes. She tried again to breathe slowly and deeply. After a moment of this she stopped crying, although her hands still trembled. When she went back to her place at the table Mrs. Hackett said, leaning toward her, "You'll get used to it, dear. Crying doesn't hurt a bit." She handed the potatoes to Mr. Hackett. "The living have to go on."

MORNING. The light through the eastern windows flooded the bedroom. The sheets crackled when she turned. The white spread, the smooth beige carpet, Judith's picture on the polished dresser, all gleamed in the clear morning light. Elinor sat up, frightened for a moment. Outside her window birds were chirping noisily. Then she remembered where she was and in the morning brightness, with the birds chirruping gaily, felt a twinge of hope.

After breakfast she went for a walk. Mr. Hackett, lowering his newspaper, his face expressionless, had said, "Better go now. Soon be hot as hades out there. Hot as hades all day, cold as sin at night." Then he'd lifted his paper in front of his face again.

She pushed open the screen door and stepped outside, pausing on the porch, her hands on the railing, feeling the morning sun on her arms. She lifted her face and closed her eyes, and was surprised to find herself smiling. The air smelled faintly spicy, a scent she didn't recognize. She wandered down the steps and across the yard toward the grain bins and the barn.

She wove in and out of the huge round steel bins, touching their dusty, corrugated surfaces with her hands. Already they were beginning to be warmed by the sun. Behind them, the prairie, sculptured into long brown furrows as far as she could see, rose to the sky. What a strange, spare countryside, she thought.

She walked on past the open barn door, a musky, pungent odour from its dark interior cutting the lighter morning air around her, and found a path leading along the edge of the poplars that bordered the yard. She followed it, strolling slowly, trying not to get dust on her sandals and thinking about Mr. Hackett whose gruffness intimidated her and whose appearance did nothing to reassure her. There was something lying on the path up ahead.

A rat. A dead rat. It lay on the path at her feet, its long tail curling in a hieroglyph in the dirt, its pointed snout tilted upward. She screamed, a short, choked-off shriek. The rodent's flesh was ripped apart, its bloody guts spilled in the dirt. The other picture leaped in front of her, she couldn't stop it: the bloody cavern that had been her father's stomach, her father's detached, darkened eyes watching her as she stood frozen, staring, as though she were not his daughter, but some stranger. Till the nurse, lifting one reddened, gloved hand from his belly, jerked the curtain shut.

She clutched her abdomen, bent, and vomited in the dirt. Suddenly a warm, heavy arm circled her shoulders.

"Now, now," Mrs. Hackett said. "Goodness, throwing up the little you did eat! No wonder you're so thin. Now you come right into the house and let me clean you up. That's only a rat. The dogs must have killed it in the night. That's what we keep them for. Thought we were rid of them, but every once in a while you see signs. Harold'll have to put out some more poison." Elinor, trying not to cry, let herself be led back to the house where Mrs. Hackett sponged her face and tried to clean the front of her blouse.

"I imagine a person can live forever in the city and not see a thing die," she said, wringing out the washcloth and scrubbing again at the stains while Elinor stood obediently, like a small child. "Concrete all over everything. Little squares of grass the size of a postage stamp. The smell so bad even the birds got more sense than to stay around." She scrubbed and scolded. "I suppose you've just never seen anything dead before."

In her room, the acrid taste of vomit still burning the back of her throat, she put on a clean blouse, fumbling with the buttons. How kind Mrs. Hackett is, she thought humbly. How . . . decent. She imagined herself day after day, holding her mother's hand at her father's bedside, talking with quiet authority with the nurses and the doctor, sending her mother away from the hospital for a meal and a rest. Like Mrs. Hackett would have done. She stared at her reflection in the mirror, at her smooth, unlined pale skin, at her wide, light eyes, her fine, childish blonde hair, and was overcome by despair at her own weakness, at her cowardice.

ELINOR AND MRS. HACKETT were bumping over a roughly plowed field in an old red and white truck. Mrs. Hackett drove with white-knuckled intensity, forward and squinting out the windshield, her jaw set. She applied the brake and the gas with indiscriminate force so that they were either flying over the summerfallow, bouncing clear of their seats, or else they were crashing to a stop, Elinor managing to keep from shattering her head against the windshield only by hanging onto the dash. She almost laughed when she noticed it was the first time Mrs. Hackett had stopped talking since she'd arrived.

They reached the far side of the summerfallow and drove onto a smooth strip of prairie. They were going slowly now, winding through the Hacketts' small herd of cows.

"Herefords," Mrs. Hackett threw at Elinor out of the corner of her mouth, not turning her head. The cows stood motionless, watching the truck approach. At the last second, switching their tails, mooing in an annoyed tone, they lumbered reluctantly out of the way. Calves watched their progress, then suddenly spun and galloped off a few feet and came to a dead stop on their tiny hooves, to gaze up at the truck, their tails erect, their small white faces gleaming like daisies in the short yellow grass.

They climbed a low hill and she could see Mr. Hackett below them driving a machine with a long wheel in front of it like the paddlewheel of a steamboat. The hayfield formed an island of green in the tawny landscape. Behind him, a narrow brown river, its banks thick with tall grasses and weeds, wound haphazardly around the field. A few stunted willows stood in clumps here and there along its banks.

Mrs. Hackett stopped the truck on the crest of the hill and Elinor climbed out. The sun blazed above them: cast its glittering bronze net to hold the summer prairie captive. Far beyond them, through the undulating heat waves, she could see the elevators of a distant town and beyond that, those same blue cliffs shimmering in the distant sky above the shelf of land.

When Mr. Hackett noticed them, he lifted the wheel from the hay and stopped the machine. Elinor started down the slope toward the swather while Mr. Hackett leaned on the steering wheel and gazed off into the distance. Mrs. Hackett had said, although Elinor doubted that it was true, that Mr. Hackett wanted her to ride around on the swather with him. Elinor had said quickly, "Why how nice. I'd love to," wanting to make up for the way she had acted over the rat. Now she jumped across two rows of cut hay and climbed up on the idling machine.

"Hang on," Mr. Hackett said, and put the swather into gear. It started with a jerk. He lowered the wheel; it started turning with a high whine and the hay began to fall. Conversation was impossible for the engine's noise, and the motor threw off so much heat Elinor wondered how Mr. Hackett could stand it all day. Over their heads a tattered sun umbrella, the red faded to pink, fluttered its frayed edges to give their only protection against the sun.

The wheel turned, a heavy, sweet aroma rose from the clover and alfalfa, and behind them, in their wake, a thick, neat row of cut hay emerged from beneath the machine. She watched, fascinated. She perched against the railing, hanging on with both hands. The light breeze lifted her short blonde hair under the straw hat Mrs. Hackett had lent her. Now and then birds flew up from the field and insects skittered across the top of the tall grass, lighting on the blue and yellow flowers. The earth is a humming factory, she thought; insects, plants, animals, thriving and reproducing in the steady rays of the sun.

Suddenly a partridge threw itself upward into the sky from under the paddlewheel. It had only one leg. A trail of silver beads marked its path against the blue. Suddenly the other leg dropped from the bird into the hay. It beat its wings frantically trying to rise and then plummeted downward, disappearing in the thick tangle of grasses. Mr. Hackett stopped the swather so quickly that Elinor lurched forward and almost fell off.

"I'll kill it," he said, as he clambered past her. He waded into the hip-deep hay, parting it with his hands, searching this way and that. Elinor stood rigid, one hand on the swather railing, the other flat on her chest. They had cut off the bird's legs.

She climbed down, her hands trembling and sweating on the hot metal railing, her heart thudding in her ears, wanting only to get away. The hay reached to her waist and seemed to cling to her, holding her back. The sweet, cloying smell of clover rose around her and nausea started in her stomach, rose to her throat. The scent mingled with, was indistinguishable from, the odour in her father's bedroom just before her mother had finally given in and sent him to the hospital to die.

She plowed through the hay like a swimmer, retching and coughing, trying to get away from the sickening smell. When she reached the edge of the field, she looked back and saw Mr. Hackett, a dark, solid figure, standing in hay up to his hips, his arms making a wringing motion.

She began to run. Running was easy on the prairie, and she ran as fast as she could, she ran like the wind. Her hat blew off and billowed out like a parachute behind her. She ran, gasping for air; she ran till her lungs burned. When she couldn't run anymore, she stumbled to a walk and then sat down on the grass. Away from the smell of the clover, her nausea gradually passed.

The sun beat down on her. Sweat stained her blouse under the arms, down her backbone. Her yellow slacks were smudged, grass-stained, and dusty. Looking down at her ruined clothes she found herself wondering why she insisted on wearing expensive, thin cotton slacks and sandals to ride on the swather, to go walking across the prairie, to sit on the dry, prickly yellow grass. Even her feet and hands were dirtier than she could ever remember them having been. It seemed to her odd, eccentric, that she should be so clean, a way that she had never before thought of herself as being. She sat for a long time in the dusty grass looking at the dirt on the palms of her thin white hands.

ELINOR AND THE HACKETTS were driving back from the neighbours where they had gone for supper.

"What a beautiful night," she said. "You never see the stars in the city."

"You don't!" Mrs. Hackett said. "Imagine that! Not seeing the stars!" The most casual remark Elinor made about city life always struck the Hacketts as amazing. "They have no conception," Elinor wrote to her mother, "of what life is like for most people. It is beyond them to imagine that anyone would ever deliberately choose to live in the city. They feel sorry for anybody who has to live in the city. They think city-dwellers are people who were driven out of the Garden of Eden."

They drove into the yard, parked, and Mr. and Mrs. Hackett went into the house. Elinor stopped on the back porch for one last look at the stars. The farm buildings stood outlined knife-sharp against the luminous night sky. She began to pick out the stars, at first the few bright ones, then clusters of smaller ones, then the Milky Way galaxy. As she watched, faint pinpoints of light began to emerge where at first she had seen only the resonant blue-black of space. The longer she looked, the more stars appeared. The universe goes on forever, she thought, tonight in India, in Africa, in all those poor countries in South America, people are dying. They are dying by the thousands on the streets of villages and cities, in the fields, on the mountainsides, and no one even knows their names. No one will mourn them.

The night air was cool, goose-bumps were prickling her bare arms, and she shivered and hurried inside.

"Would you like to spend the day in town with us?" Mrs. Hackett asked her. Over the hiss of bacon Elinor could hear the birds chattering to one another.

"It's so lovely out here, I hate to leave," she said. Mrs. Hackett bustled to the table with the coffee pot.

"We'll be gone all day," she said. "You won't mind staying by yourself?" She looked carefully at Elinor over her glasses.

"Not at all," Elinor said, smiling. Out here she never felt alone as she did in the city. No, she wouldn't mind being alone.

Later, after they had gone, she went out for a walk. She set off in the direction of the river, strolling, looking off in the distance at the elevators ten miles away and at the panorama of yellow, black, and green rectangles spread out before her, stopping now and then to examine a diminutive plant growing in the short dusty grass. Beauty on the prairie, she saw, was in either brilliant, gargantuan sweeps of land and sky, or in microscopic detail of tiny flowering plants that sprang up with each sparse rain, and then disappeared again when the dryness and heat returned.

She was approaching the Hacketts' cows. They lay motionless in the noon heat, their calves curled up beside them. Mr. Hackett, in his longest speech, had said that they were more afraid of her than she was of them, and that as long as she didn't get between one of them and its calf, she had nothing to be afraid of. It seemed that on a day as perfect as this, there could be no fear in the world.

At the edge of the field she got down on her knees and crawled under the barbed wire fence, the peppery scent of sage catching her and then drifting away as she rose. She stood, carelessly slapping at her knees to brush off the dust, and tried to decide which way to go. A light breeze lifted her hair, cooling her neck. A few horned larks rose from a nearby coulee and fluttered away. The familiar path lay to her left. She had taken it before, once to pick saskatoons by the river with Mrs. Hackett, and once by herself. She decided to find a way down to the water by angling to her right where she knew the river curved out of sight down below her, and where she hadn't been before.

The land was rougher here, more hilly, and clumps of wild rose bushes, wild gooseberries, and chokecherries grew in the hollows. She climbed a rise and started down the other side when she saw a cow lying on its side on the far slope of the hollow. Elinor looked around for its calf. She didn't see one anywhere. She started down the slope, keeping her eye on the cow which lifted its head and mooed, but didn't get up. Usually the cows heaved themselves to their feet and ran whenever anybody came near them. Perhaps it was caught in something, barbed wire, maybe. It was thrusting with its head now, as though it were trying to rock to its feet. It gave a prolonged but feeble moo, then dropped its head. Something was definitely wrong. Elinor walked closer to it, her curiosity overcoming her timidity.

When the cow saw her coming near, she lifted her head again and made a violent effort to get up. This time she managed to get her front legs to a kneeling position while she thrust upward with her back legs. After a long, shuddering moment she wavered, then toppled over on her side.

Elinor circled her cautiously. Every rib showed; there was a deep hollow in front of her hip bone; her nose was blackened and peeling as though she had been burned somehow. Big flakes of skin hung off her blackened udders and most of the white hair had fallen out from her chest, face, and belly and there were patches of blisters where the white hair had been. Even Elinor could see that the cow was sick, possibly dying.

She was overcome by the desire to stroke the cow, to murmur to her soothingly, and to give her comfort, but every time she took a step closer, the cow struggled pathetically to rise, then fell heavily back. Elinor found herself whispering, "Oh, no," each time she fell, and once she put out her hand as if to stop the fall.

Elinor squatted down on her haunches, certain now that the cow was dying. Her eyes were sinking deeper into her head, her long tongue lolled out, her ribs heaved with her efforts to breathe. She no longer seemed aware of Elinor's presence.

The mid-day had grown very quiet. The breeze had died. The birds were silent, no insect hummed. The only sound was the air whistling in and out of the cow's lungs.

Elinor moved a little closer and squatted down again. Now she was inside the radiant circle of heat from the cow's body. The cow lifted her head and looked at Elinor. Elinor stared back, unable to move her eyes away. The cow lay her head down, her legs thrashed out once, she coughed, choked, and died. Blood seeped from her nose and then stopped. Her eyes, fastened on Elinor, retreated, and the stare went glassy and blank.

For a long time Elinor didn't move. The carcass lay in front of her, hollow, and growing rigid. After a while a fly settled on one eye. Then Elinor stood up, paused, and walked on down to the river.

Pushing aside the tangled weeds and grasses, she sat on a rock at the edge of the stream. It was so hot that trickles of sweat ran down her neck from her hair and she felt dizzy from the heat. The dry scent of weeds and grasses rose around her. She began to take off her clothes, first her blouse and shoes, then her slacks, her bra, her panties. When she was naked she stepped carefully into the water and waded out till it came to the middle of her thighs. Standing still, she thought she could hear the sun as the water, the plants, birds and insects quivered to its song.

She waded further out into the water till it lapped softly around her waist, rocking her. The river bottom was soft. It had a delicate, silky feel under her feet. A water bird rose from its hiding place among the weeds on the bank and flapped noisily away. She watched its awkward flight.

She crouched till the water reached her chin. It flowed around her, cooling her, lifting her. She stretched out, letting her legs float upward, spreading her arms. The accusal in her father's eyes as they met hers, and yet did not seem to see her. Perhaps it was only the recognition of death, she thought.

She turned over, swam a few strokes, then floated on her back again for a while. Then she climbed out of the water. When the sun had dried her, she dressed.

She followed the stream till she came to the path she had taken on her other trips to the river and started up the slope. Behind her, a shining perch broke the surface of the water and dived, spreading silver rings toward each bank. She paused to watch a herd of antelope, pale brown and white, skim across a distant hillside. On the other side of the hills, near the body of the cow, a thin grey coyote trotted, its long tail brushing the dust, its nose to the ground.

Sharon Butala was born in Nipawin, Saskatchewan, and has lived for the last twenty-five years on a ranch near Eastend, Saskatchewan. She is the author of six novels, two short story collections and three works of nonfiction, the latest of which is Wild Stone Heart: An Apprentice in the Fields. *She has been the recipient of the Marian Engel Award for Women Writers.*

WHERE IS THE VOICE COMING FROM?

RUDY WIEBE

THE PROBLEM IS TO MAKE THE STORY.

One difficulty of this making may have been excellently stated by Teilhard de Chardin: "We are continually inclined to isolate ourselves from the things and events which surround us . . . as though we were spectators, not elements, in what goes on." Arnold Toynbee does venture, "For all that we know, Reality is the undifferentiated unity of the mystical experience," but that need not here be considered. This story ended long ago; it is one of finite acts, of orders, or elemental feelings and reactions, of obvious legal restriction and requirements.

Presumably all the parts of the story are themselves available. A difficulty is that they are, as always, available only in bits and pieces. Though the acts themselves seem quite clear, some written reports of the acts contradict each other. As if these acts were, at one time, too well known; as if the original nodule of each particular fact had from somewhere received non-factual accretions; or even more, as if, since the basic facts were so clear, perhaps there were a larger number of facts than any one reporter, or several, or even any reporter had ever attempted to record. About facts that are simply told by this mouth to that ear, of course, even less can be expected.

An affair seventy-five years old should acquire some of the shiny transparency of an old man's skin. It should.

Sometimes it would seem that it would be enough—perhaps more than enough—to hear the names only. The grandfather One Arrow; the mother Spotted Calf; the father Sounding Sky; the wife (wives rather, but only one of them seems to have a name, though their fathers are Napaise, Kapahoo, Old Dust, The Rump)—the one wife named, of all things, Pale Face; the cousin Going-Up-To-Sky; the brother-in-law (again, of all things) Dublin. The names of the police sound very much alike; they all begin with Constable or Corporal or Sergeant, but here and there an Inspector, then a Superintendent and eventually all the resonance of an Assistant Commissioner echoes down. More. Herself: Victoria, by the Grace of God, etc., etc., QUEEN, defender of the Faith, etc., etc.; and witness "Our Right Trusty and Right Well-beloved Cousin and Councillor the Right Honourable Sir John Campbell Hamilton-Gordon, Earl of Aberdeen; Viscount Formartine, Baron Haddo, Methlic, Tarves and Kellie in the Peerage of Scotland; Viscount Gordon of Aberdeen, County of Aberdeen in the Peerage of the United Kingdom; Baronet of Nova Scotia, Knight Grand Cross of Our Most Distinguished Order of Saint Michael and Saint George, etc., Governor General of Canada." And of course himself: in the award proclamation named "Jean-Baptiste" but otherwise known only as Almighty Voice.

But hearing cannot be enough; not even hearing all the thunder of A Proclamation: "Now Hear Ye that a reward of FIVE HUNDRED DOLLARS will be paid to any person or persons who will give such information as will lead . . . (etc., etc.) this Twentieth day of April, in the year of Our Lord one thousand eight hundred and ninety-six, and the Fifty-ninth year of Our Reign . . ." etc. and etc.

Such hearing cannot be enough. The first item to be seen is the piece of white bone. It is almost triangular, slightly convex—concave actually as it is positioned at this moment with its corners slightly raised—graduating from perhaps a strong eighth to a weak quarter of an inch in thickness, its scattered pore structure varying between larger and smaller on its polished, certainly shiny surface. Precision is difficult since the glass showcase is at least thirteen inches deep and therefore an eye cannot be brought as close as the minute inspection of such a small, though certainly quite adequate, sample of skull would normally require. Also, because of the position it cannot be determined whether the several hairs, well over a foot long, are still in some manner attached to it or not.

The seven-pounder cannon can be seen standing almost shyly between the showcase and the interior wall. Officially it is known as a gun, not a cannon, and clearly its bore is not large enough to admit a large man's fist. Even if it can be believed that this gun was used in the 1885 Rebellion and that on the evening of Saturday, May 29, 1897 (while the nine-pounder, now unidentified, was in the process of arriving with the police on the special train from Regina), seven shells (all that were available in Prince Albert at that time) from it were sent shrieking into the poplar bluffs as night fell, clearly such shelling could not and would not disembowel the whole earth. Its carriage is now nicely lacquered, the perhaps oak spokes of its petite wheels (little higher than a knee) have been recently scraped, puttied and varnished; the brilliant burnish of its brass breeching testifies with what meticulous care charmen and women have used nationally advertised cleaners and restorers.

Though it can also be seen, even a careless glance reveals that the same concern has not been expended on the one (of two) .44 calibre 1866 model Winchesters apparently found at the last in the pit with Almighty Voice. It is also preserved in a glass case; the number 1536735 is still, though barely, distinguishable on the brass cartridge section just below the brass saddle ring. However, perhaps because the case was imperfectly sealed at one time (though sealed enough not to warrant disturbance now), or because of simple neglect, the rifle is obviously spotted here and there with blotches of rust and the brass itself reveals discolorations almost like mildew. The rifle bore, the three long strands of hair themselves, actually bristle with clots of dust. It may be that this museum cannot afford to be as concerned as the other; conversely, the disfiguration may be something inherent in the items themselves.

The small building which was the police guardroom at Duck Lake,

Saskatchewan Territory, in 1895 may also be seen. It had subsequently been moved from its original place and used to house small animals, chickens perhaps, or pigs—such as a woman might be expected to have under her responsibility. It is, of course, now perfectly empty, and clean so that the public may enter with no more discomfort than a bend under the doorway and a heavy encounter with disinfectant. The door-jamb has obviously been replaced; the bar network at one window is, however, said to be original; smooth still, very smooth. The logs inside have been smeared again and again with whitewash, perhaps paint, to an insistent point of identity-defying characterlessness. Within the small rectangular box of these logs not a sound can be heard from the streets of the, probably dead, town.

Hey Injun you'll get hung for stealing that steer
Hey Injun for killing that government cow you'll
get three weeks on the woodpile
Hey Injun

The place named Kinistino seems to have disappeared from the map but the Minnechinass Hills have not. Whether they have ever been on a map is doubtful but they will, of course, not disappear from the landscape as long as the grass grows and the rivers run. Contrary to general report and belief, the Canadian prairies are rarely, if ever, flat and the Minnechinass (spelled five different ways and translated sometimes as "The Outside Hill," sometimes as "Beautiful Bare Hills") are dissimilar from any other of the numberless hills that everywhere block out the prairie horizon. They are bare; poplars lie tattered along their tops, almost black against the straw-pale grass and sharp green against the grey soil of the ploughing laid in half-mile rectangular blocks upon their western slopes. Poles holding various wires stick out of the fields, back down the bend of the valley; what was once a farmhouse is weathering into the cultivated earth. The poplar bluff where Almighty Voice made his stand has, of course, disappeared.

The policemen he shot and killed (not the ones he wounded, of course) are easily located. Six miles east, thirty-nine miles north in Prince Albert, the

English cemetery. Sergeant Colin Campbell Colebrook, North West Mounted Police Registration Number 605, lies presumably under a gravestone there. His name is seventeenth in a very long "list of non-commissioned officers and men who have died in the service since the inception of the force." The date is October 29, 1895, and the cause of death is anonymous: "Shot by escaping Indian prisoner near Prince Albert." At the foot of this grave are two others: Constable John R. Kerr, No. 3040, and Corporal C.H.S. Hockin, No. 3106. Their cause of death on May 28, 1897, is even more anonymous, but the place is relatively precise: "Shot by Indians at Min-etchinass Hills, Prince Albert District."

The gravestone, if he has one, of the fourth man Almighty Voice killed is more difficult to locate. Mr. Ernest Grundy, postmaster at Duck Lake in 1897, apparently shut his window the afternoon of Friday, May 28, armed himself, rode east twenty miles, participated in the second charge into the bluff at about 6:30 P.M., and on the third sweep of that charge was shot dead at the edge of the pit. It would seem that he thereby contributed substantially not only to the Indians' bullet supply, but his clothing warmed them as well.

The burial place of Dublin and Going-Up-To-Sky is unknown, as is the grave of Almighty Voice. It is said that a Métis named Henry Smith lifted the latter's body from the pit in the bluff and gave it to Spotted Calf. The place of burial is not, of course, of ultimate significance. A gravestone is always less evidence than a triangular piece of skull, provided it is large enough.

Whatever further evidence there is to be gathered may rest on pictures. There are, presumably, almost numberless pictures of the policemen in the case, but the only one with direct bearing is one of Sergeant Colebrook who apparently insisted on advancing to complete an arrest after being warned three times that if he took another step he would be shot. The picture must have been taken before he joined the force; it reveals him a large-eared young man, hair brush-cut and ascot tie, his eyelids slightly drooping, almost hooded under thick brows. Unfortunately a picture of Constable R. C. Dickson, into whose charge Almighty Voice was apparently committed in that guardroom and who after Colebrook's death was convicted of negligence, sentenced to two months hard labour and discharged, does not seem to be available.

There are no pictures to be found of either Dublin (killed early by rifle fire) or Going-Up-To-Sky (killed in the pit), the two teen-age boys who gave their ultimate fealty to Almighty Voice. There is, however, one said to be of Almighty Voice, Junior. He may have been born to Pale Face during the year, two hundred and twenty-one days that his father was a fugitive. In the picture he is kneeling before what could be a tent, he wears striped denim overalls and displays twin babies whose sex cannot be determined from the double-laced dark bonnets they wear. In the supposed picture of Spotted Calf and Sounding Sky, Sounding Sky stands slightly before his wife; he wears a white shirt and a striped blanket folded over his left shoulder in such a manner that the arm in which he cradles a long rifle cannot be seen. His head is thrown back; the rim of his hat appears as a black half-moon above eyes that are pressed shut as if in profound concentration; above a mouth clenched thin in a downward curve. Spotted Calf wears a long dress, a sweater which could also be a man's dress coat, and a large fringed and embroidered shawl which would appear distinctly Doukhobor in origin if the scroll patterns on it were more irregular. Her head is small and turned slightly towards her husband so as to reveal her right ear. There is what can only be called a quizzical expression on her crumpled face; it may be she does not understand what is happening and that she would have asked a question, perhaps of her husband, perhaps of the photographers, perhaps even of anyone, anywhere in the world if such questioning were possible for a Cree woman.

There is one final picture. That is one of Almighty Voice himself. At least it is purported to be of Almighty Voice himself. In the Royal Canadian Mounted Police Museum on the Barracks Grounds just off Dewdney Avenue in Regina, Saskatchewan, it lies in the same showcase, as a matter of fact immediately beside that triangular piece of skull. Both are unequivocally labelled, and it must be assumed that a police force with a world-wide reputation would not label *such* evidence incorrectly. But here emerges an ultimate problem in making the story.

There are two official descriptions of Almighty Voice. The first reads:

"Height about five feet, ten inches, slight build, rather good looking, a sharp hooked nose with a remarkably flat point. Has a bullet scar on the left side of his face about 1 ½ inches long running from near corner of mouth towards ear. The scar cannot be noticed when his face is painted but otherwise is plain. Skin fair for an Indian." The second description is on the Award Proclamation: "About twenty-two years old, five feet, ten inches in height, weight about eleven stone, slightly erect, neat small feet and hands; complexion inclined to be fair, wavey dark hair to shoulders, large dark eyes, broad forehead, sharp features and parrot nose with flat tip, scar on left cheek running from mouth towards ear, feminine appearance."

So run the descriptions that were, presumably, to identify a well-known fugitive in so precise a manner that an informant could collect five hundred dollars—a considerable sum when a police constable earned between one and two dollars a day. The nexus of the problems appears when these supposed official descriptions are compared to the supposed official picture. The man in the picture is standing on a small rug. The fingers of his left hand touch a curved Victorian settee, behind him a photographer's backdrop of scrolled patterns merges to vaguely paradisiacal trees and perhaps a sky. The moccasins he wears make it impossible to deduce whether his feet are "neat small." He may be five feet, ten inches tall, may weigh eleven stone, he certainly is "rather good looking" and, though it is a frontal view, it may be that the point of his long and flaring nose could be "remarkably flat." The photograph is slightly over-illuminated and so the unpainted complexion could be "inclined to be fair"; however, nothing can be seen of a scar, the hair is not wavy and shoulder-length but hangs almost to the waist in two thick straight braids worked through with beads, fur, ribbons and cords. The right hand that holds the corner of the blanket-like coat in position is large and, even in the high illumination, heavily veined. The neck is concealed under coiled beads and the forehead seems more low than "broad."

Perhaps, somehow, these picture details could be reconciled with the official description if the face as a whole were not so devastating.

On a cloth-backed sheet two feet by two and one-half feet in size, under the Great Seal of the Lion and the Unicorn, dignified by the names of the

Deputy of the Minister of Justice, the Secretary of State, the Queen herself and all the heaped detail of her "Right Trusty and Right Well-beloved Cousin," this description concludes: "feminine appearance." But the picture: any face of history, any believed face that the world acknowledges as *man*— Socrates, Jesus, Attila, Genghis Khan, Mahatma Gandhi, Joseph Stalin—no believed face is more *man* than this face. The mouth, the nose, the clenched brows, the eyes—the eyes are large, yes, and dark, but even in this watered-down reproduction of unending reproductions of that original, a steady look into those eyes cannot be endured. It is a face like an axe.

IT IS NOW EVIDENT that the de Chardin statement quoted at the beginning has relevance only as it proves itself inadequate to explain what has happened. At the same time, the inadequacy of Aristotle's much more famous statement becomes evident: "The true difference *between the historian and the poet* is that one relates what *has* happened, the other what *may* happen." These statements cannot explain the storymaker's activity since, despite the most rigid application of impersonal investigation, the elements of the story have now run me aground. If ever I could, I can no longer pretend to objective, omnipotent disinterestedness. I am no longer *spectator* of what *has* happened or what *may* happen: I am become *element* in what is happening at this very moment.

For it is, of course, I myself who cannot endure the shadows on that paper which are those eyes. It is I who stand beside this broken veranda post where two corner shingles have been torn away, where barbed wire tangles the dead weeds on the edge of this field. The bluff that sheltered Almighty Voice and his two friends has not disappeared from the slope of the Minnechinass, no more than the sound of Constable Dickson's voice in that guardhouse is silent. The sound of his speaking is there even if it has never been recorded in an official report:

hey injun you'll get
hung
for stealing that steer

hey injun for killing that government
cow you'll get three
weeks on the woodpile hey injun

The unknown contradictory words about an unprovable act that move a boy to defiance, an implacable Cree warrior long after the three-hundred-and-fifty-year war is ended, a war already lost the day the Cree watch Cartier hoist his guns ashore at Hochelaga and they begin the long retreat west; these words of incomprehension, of threatened incomprehensible law are there to be heard just as the unmoving tableau of the three-day siege is there to be seen on the slopes of the Minnechinass. Sounding Sky is somewhere not there, under arrest, but Spotted Calf stands on a shoulder of the Hills a little to the left, her arms upraised to the setting sun. Her mouth is open. A horse rears, riderless, above the scrub willow at the edge of the bluff, smoke puffs, screams tangle in rifle barrage, there are wounds, somewhere. The bluff is so green this spring, it will not burn and the ragged line of seven police and two civilians is staggering through, faces twisted in rage, terror, and rifles sputter. Nothing moves. There is no sound of frogs in the night; twenty-seven policemen and five civilians stand in cordon at thirty-yard intervals and a body also lies in the shelter of a gully. Only a voice rises from the bluff:

We have fought well
You have died like braves
I have worked hard and am hungry
Give me food

but nothing moves. The bluff lies, a bright green island on the grassy slope surrounded by men hunched forward rigid over their long rifles, men clumped out of rifle-range, thirty-five men dressed as for fall hunting on a sharp spring day, a small gun positioned on a ridge above. A crow is falling out of the sky into the bluff, its feathers sprayed as by an explosion. The first gun and the second gun are in position, the beginning and end of the bristling surround of thirty-five Prince Albert Volunteers, thirteen civilians and fifty-six policemen in position relative to the bluff and relative to the unnumbered whites astride their horses, standing up in their carts, staring and pointing across the valley, in position relative to the bluff and the unnumbered Cree squatting silent along the higher ridges of the Hills, motionless mounds, faceless against the Sunday morning sunlight edging between and over them down along the tree tips, down into the shadows of the bluff. Nothing moves. Beside the second gun the red-coated officer has flung a handful of grass into the motionless air, almost to the rim of the red sun.

And there is a voice. It is an incredible voice that rises from among the young poplars ripped of their spring bark, from among the dead somewhere lying there, out of the arm-deep pit shorter than a man; a voice rises over the exploding smoke and thunder of guns that reel back in their positions, worked over, serviced by the grimed motionless men in bright coats and glinting buttons, a voice so high and clear, so unbelievably high and strong in its unending wordless cry.

THE VOICE OF "GITCHIE-MANITOU WAYO"—interpreted as "voice of the Great Spirit"—that is, The Almighty Voice. His death chant no less incredible in its beauty than in its incomprehensible happiness.

I say "wordless cry" because that is the way it sounds to me. I could be more accurate if I had a reliable interpreter who would make a reliable interpretation. For I do not, of course, understand the Cree myself.

Rudy Wiebe won the Governor General's Award for his novels The Temptations of Big Bear *and* A Discovery of Strangers. River of Stone: Fictions and Memories *is his most recent collection of short fiction and essays.*

IN THE SIXTIES

Greg Hollingshead

Four rooms, off-white and stipple, empty of furniture except a waterbed, a vanity, a scarred round table with a lamp. Two or three straight-backed chairs. Everything else was boxes of books and scattered items of Zochie's clothing, medicine, make-up, notes. The topic of furniture had never come up. When Nelson moved in he gave her a framed A.Y. Jackson print for the bedroom. She smashed it during their big first fight, after which she filled the wall it had hung on with anti-Nelson lipstick graffiti.

"Zochie, it's me! Don't you remember? I live here too!"

"I am sorry. I was sleeping."

Zochie unchained the door and kissed him. Sleep and smoke, old heat. Nelson hugged her, or tried to.

"Be careful of my cigarette!" she cried, brushing away ashes.

"Sorry. Can I open the drapes?"

"Drapes? It is Americans who say drapes."

"It is also Canadians who say drapes." He threw them open.

"Ooh, it's so bright," she said, searching for the hole.

"I'm sorry."

"I don't care about my clothes. You don't like this anyway. You haven't said one word about it. Don't you think it's nice?"

It was a tiger-skin print dressing gown, in silk.

"Sure. "

"Screw you. Who cares. What I wear means nothing to me."

"You're beautiful anyway."

Zochie lit a cigarette, exhaled. "I know I'm beautiful," she said. "But I'm fucked up."

Nelson opened the balcony door. She had spent another day in bed. "That's right," he said. "You're more than a pretty face, you're insane."

"I was napping." The ashtray by the waterbed bloomed with crushed cigarettes, orange peels were scattered around the sheets and floor, and a cord ran from the wall outlet to under the pillow. "That is not my problem. Won't you like some coffee?"

"No thanks." In the fridge he found margarine, an egg, cream cheese yellow along the edges, a bit of Gruyère, a withered eggplant, a saucer of crystalized anchovies. The egg he stirred with dry buckwheat in a hot skillet. When the grains were separate he poured in boiling water. The water went crazy on contact with the skillet. As the hissing and spitting died to boiling and the steam cloud started to move down the wall, he heard the vibrator from the bedroom. He clamped the lid on the skillet.

Zochie was propped against two pillows, one hand and the head of the machine between her legs. Nelson sat at her vanity and watched her face. She opened her eyes and smiled.

Nelson placed his ankle on his knee.

Zochie was moving her hips in a slow circle. She closed her eyes.

Nelson went to check the kasha. He stood on the balcony and looked down on rush-hour life. Moving right along. He wished every tree he saw could be in leaf. He wished he was under them, in green sunlight, green shadow. No, higher than the tip of the highest. Breathing sky. Breathing stars. The vibrator clicked off. Five more minutes for the kasha. He was hunting for butter when Zochie appeared at the kitchen door smoking a cigarette.

"I am so sexy because I am nervous about my examinations." She took a long drag. "Nelson, I am going to fail."

"That's my department."

"I am going to fail. It's not my intelligence, it's my English. You know how badly I write it, how slowly. I should have studied mathematics purely. I am going to fail. I will have to sleep with my professor. I will kill myself first. When will you fuck me? It doesn't matter. I am sore from the machine. I have used up orgasms for three days."

Zochie stood smoking and looking out over the city while Nelson ate.

"Have some kasha," he said.

NELSON SLIPPED THE KEY into the lobby door of the apartment building then walked back across the driveway to the oval of lawn in front, took off his shoes and socks, and dragged his feet through the dew, hands in his pockets, wanting Zochie to be home. He stretched out on the grass, dew soaking through his shirt.

"NELSON! What are you doing here? Nelson!" Zochie was kneeling to feel the grass. "It is too wet. You are drunk!"

He got up shivering. "Did you screw him?"

She was opening the door to the building with the key he had left in the lock. Swaying slightly. "Who?"

"Your professor."

"No. How could I go through with it. He is like potatoes."

"Did he try?"

"Yes. I was very nice to him. He thinks he will. That should be enough. He is so boring."

"Where'd you go?"

She shrugged. "The waiters sing there. His French is very bad."

They were riding the elevator.

"My French is bad too."

"Yes. But you are not like potatoes."

Nelson was shivering.

"You will have a cold sleeping on the grass."

While Zochie showered, Nelson stood in the darkened living room watching the lights of the city.

"Good night, Zochie!" he called when she went into the bedroom.

"Come in and kiss me goodnight."

He kissed her.

"Nelson, why don't you love me? Why do you despise me? I would like once to know."

Nelson looked at his watch. "Super says no fights after eleven."

Later he went out for a walk. When he got back, Zochie was gone. So was her toothbrush.

TOWARDS NOON THE NEXT DAY he collapsed on his way to shower. Nausea, mottled face in the mirror. Back to bed where he was when Zochie did not come home that night. Next morning he sat by the glass doors to the balcony in pale spring sunlight looking down on the street, eating toast and drinking tea.

And then he must have slept again. Zochie was in the bedroom, undressing to shower. "Hello my love. Did you have a nice time without me?"

"I caught flu."

"Oh, I'm sorry. Don't give it to me."

She disappeared into the bathroom. Emerging to dry herself, she said, "I am sorry you have caught flu."

Next morning he was standing on the balcony in his dressing gown when Zochie called goodbye. Goodbye. The sun was warm. He dressed and sat in it, spent most of the week like that, or in bed, while his body fought the sickness. Weeping as he watched the sun unfold delicate leaves the colour of lime Freshie, the rush hour traffic stall and honk down below, Zochie come in, shower, drink coffee, go out again.

WHEN NELSON RECOVERED he bought chickpeas, tahini, pita, a lemon. Four months after moving in he had found a blender under the sink, behind the garbage bucket. "Of course it works," Zochie had said. "I never use it because it makes too much noise. Cooking bores me."

"What are you doing?" she asked now.

"Making humous. Any paprika? It doesn't matter. How's the work?"

"Oh," lighting a cigarette, standing on one bare foot. "It's all right. I will pass."

"Perfect."

"No, not perfect. A miserable high second."

Nelson turned on the blender to cream the chickpeas, added more tahini. Zochie left and returned with a drink. Nelson was bent over watching creamed chickpea crawl towards the blades.

"What are you drinking?" he asked when he turned off the machine.

"Dubonnet. And I think I will have more."

"Go easy on me, Zochie, or I'll go out. Hey, there's lemon. There's ice." He made her a proper drink.

She picked the lemon slice off the rim and threw it into the sink. "Bourgeois shit."

When the humous was ready Nelson sprinkled cayenne on it to resemble paprika and carried it and a plate of hot pita into the living room. Zochie was hipshot at the window with an empty glass in her hand.

A knock at the door. With the plate on his knees, Nelson looked to Zochie, but she was on her way to the bedroom.

It was a woman named Dagmar. Nelson had met her at a party. She was standing in the hall radiating light in a six-inch aura. Nelson stepped back and she entered, removing gloves, shawls, wraps, scarves, embroidery-heavy Tibetan vest, motorcycle helmet. She passed the whole pile to Nelson.

"Watch my earrings," she said. "They're in the helmet."

Entering the living room, she said, "Oh. Are you just moving in?"

"Not really." As he passed down the hall to hang Dagmar's stuff in a closet, Zochie kicked shut the bedroom door.

"Is there someone else here?" Dagmar called from the living room.

"Yes."

"Oh. I thought you said you lived alone."

"I didn't think I said that."

Sound of breaking glass from the bedroom.

Zochie was half-dressed, holding a high heel. She had just smashed the mirror over her vanity. Her face was scarcely visible for cigarette smoke. Nelson moved warily, closing the door behind him. "What's the matter?"

"You were talking about me."

"Do you want her to leave?"

"No. I want to meet her. Why is she here?"

"To score. Please don't break anything else."

"No, my love."

"Zochie, she's absurd."

"Tell *her* this."

Nelson went back to the kitchen.

"What was it?" Dagmar called from the balcony.

"That was Zochie. She broke a mirror."

"On purpose?"

"She'll be out in a minute. Have some humous."

"Do you have anything to drink?"

"Water?"

"City water?" Dagmar asked, her eyes following Zochie from the bedroom to the kitchen where a cupboard door opened. Zochie was pouring herself a drink.

"I think maybe there's some Dubonnet here," Nelson called to Dagmar. "Would you like some of that?"

"Dubonnet?" Dagmar asked.

Zochie appeared from the kitchen. "Dubonnet," she said, hand on her hip, raising her glass.

Nelson introduced them.

Zochie was wearing cream-coloured leather pants, a black silk top, high-heeled cork sandals.

The women smiled at each other.

"Could I try some?" Dagmar said.

"Of course," Zochie replied.

When Nelson placed the drink in her hand Dagmar smelled it. "It's alcoholic," she said.

Zochie looked at Nelson.

"Why, yes," he said. "I suppose Dubonnet is."

"I couldn't," Dagmar said, handing it back. "I can't meditate when I do, and I'm no good for anything when I don't meditate."

Zochie choked on her cigarette.

DAGMAR SCORED A HALF OUNCE of Nepalese and had to rush away. At the door she turned, helmet in hand, and invited them both to dinner on Sunday. Nelson wrote down the address while Zochie stood deep in the room smoking. When the door closed Zochie went to the kitchen for a Dubonnet. A knock on the door. Dagmar was back for her earrings. She found them in her helmet and left again. Zochie sat at the table with her drink and a cigarette.

"That was Dagmar," Nelson said.

"Will you fuck her?"

"Only if you're there."

"I will not be."

"I'd rather you were. She makes me nervous."

"No. I have an exam on Monday. You go. I will stay here."

After a shower Nelson squeezed two oranges, added a little water and Vitamin C crystals, and sat with a glass of the results beside Zochie who moved only to light another cigarette.

"Nicotine kills vitamins," Nelson said at last, softly.

"Fuck off."

"I won't sleep with Dagmar. I prefer you."

"It is a choice? Do I prevent you?"

"No."

"So do it."

Zochie finished her drink on the way to the kitchen. She returned with a half inch of red wine, had emptied the Dubonnet. "You have no love for me," Zochie said.

"Christ."

"Nelson, it is *true!*"

"Then I should leave."

"*No!*"

"Zochie, they make flips this way."

"I am not a flip!" Zochie cried.

"I didn't say you were a flip."

"You said that you will be a flip if you stay here." She began to sob.

Nelson moved around the table, caught some wine in the face. *"Don't touch me!"* She ran to the bedroom and slammed the door. A few seconds later glass cracked. Nelson went to the balcony, to see a bullet-sized hole in the bedroom window. Her high heel again. Was she smashing her way out? He knocked on the door. The waterbed sloshed.

He returned to the living room and sat looking up at the stars. He got his winter coat from the closet and put it on over his pajamas and dressing gown and found a pair of stinking work socks in the clothes basket in the kitchen. Don't ask him why the kitchen. He put a pair of galoshes on over them and carried a chair onto the balcony where he sat in the spring night and watched for falling stars. An hour later he undressed in the hallway and crept into the bedroom. He undressed her—kissing her breasts—and climbed in beside her. The bed went heaving. She was snoring. He turned her onto her side and lay on his back, feeling the heat radiate from her back and legs down his side. He shut his eyes. Zochie was a soft bathtub, the engine of a melting car, a warm river. She moved. The raft rocked gently.

DINNER FOLLOWED BY A VERY STRANGE, almost furtive hour on the floor and in bed with Dagmar, who declined an orgasm because her current lover was psychically attuned to her body, and Nelson was letting himself into the apartment building at midnight. He would shower. Zochie would be studying, have the door on the latch. She did. He knocked. She took a long time to come to the door and a long time to unfasten the latch. Avoiding his eyes, she returned to a fan of books and papers on the floor under a circle of light cast by the lamp, which sat on the very edge of the scarred round table.

"Hello," he said and noticed an empty mickey of gin on the table. "How's the work?"

"Could you pass me my cigarettes. Thanks. It is all right. I don't care about it. I have decided to go home. I hate this city."

Immediately the fear went thrilling up and down the backs of Nelson's legs. Three slow beats of his heart and it was into his throat. He swallowed. "Maybe you'll feel different after your exams."

"No." She exhaled. "I am going home."

"I don't want you to."

"No. You never loved me."

Her eyes were averted. Nelson went into the bedroom and closed the door. Methodically he undressed and got into bed. He lay on his stomach with the pillow over his head and cried. Got up, washed his face, and climbed back into bed. Lay on his back thinking how scared he was, until she crept in beside him, found his mouth with hers, all smoke and gin, and slipped him inside.

"Oh love," he said. "Oh love oh love oh love."

When his body was quiet she kissed his cheek. She went for a cigarette and smoked it lying with her back to him. When she finished the cigarette, she put the ashtray on the floor and turned towards him. He fell asleep, holding her in his arms, with the smell of her hair.

When he woke up the room was dark and Zochie was not there. He found her in the living room, leaned against the scarred little table, just outside the circle of light from the lamp. She was sitting on one foot, with the tiger-skin gown loose around her shoulders, her head bowed as if she were studying the hand that lay palm upwards in her lap.

"Zochie, what are you doing? Come to bed."

Her head swung up and she looked at him as if trying to remember who he was. Suddenly she laughed. The arm that was not in her lap lay heavy on the table. She tried to swing it clear of the lamp to salute him with her glass, but she clipped the lampshade and the lamp teetered. The circle of light shifted and the shadows went swaying. "What am I doing?" she said. "What is Zochie doing? She is asking herself why her love does not love her. Why this boy who is too simple to be bad treats her like a whore."

"Oh shit, Zochie, please! Come to bed. You're drunk."

"Yes, I am drunk."

"Will you come to bed?"

She laughed. "Didn't you know, my love? Whores never sleep at night."

Nelson returned to bed thinking how theatrical she was, how difficult; thinking what a relief to be free from that inexorable mind. But he could not stop being afraid. Suddenly he gave a start and was wide awake—like Zochie herself often, or like a child—with a night terror, but there was nothing, no vision, only the continuing darkness and the crack of light under the door. And then there was something there, something small and potent, blossoming.

He found her in the living room curled in the circle of light with her knees up and her arms against her breasts. At first he thought the darkness by her head was a shadow cast by the lamp, but it was not. She was cuddled into what might have been a pool of blood if her notes and dressing gown had not been under to soak it up. He held the lamp to her face. He rummaged through the kitchen drawer for clean dish towels. He wrapped her wrists. He found an empty bottle of barbituates but could not tell how many she had taken. He phoned a cab—an ambulance would have meant it was too serious—and was still fussing with dressing her when the buzzer sounded.

In the cab she came to consciousness begging him please not to blame her, not to be mad, to forgive her, not to let them take her to the hospital. He told her they were going to the hospital because she had swallowed pills.

"Not too many. Only to forget. Don't be angry. Please forgive me. I love you so much."

Nelson shut his eyes.

An orderly was sitting in a wheelchair just inside the Emergency doors. He got up and beckoned Zochie into the seat as if she had come in for a haircut. The smell of hospital was suffocating. For Nelson it was frightening and reassuring but reassuring in a way that was also frightening. The orderly wheeled Zochie down a broad corridor. A nurse appeared from a doorway, glanced at Zochie, and said something to the orderly. Nelson started towards her but was called back by another nurse, who asked for Zochie's date of birth, name, address, what she had swallowed, how much approximately, and how long she had been drinking. The other nurse reached for the information sheet. Nelson was told to sit down.

He crossed and uncrossed his legs in a moulded plastic chair across from a very pale old man asleep in his coat with his hat on his lap. He shuffled magazines on an arborite table without thinking. He got up to walk around, afraid the reception nurse would order him back to his seat. The sounds that he, and he alone, it seemed, was hearing from down the corridor were Zochie's gagging, wailed objections to having her stomach pumped. A nurse was shouting at her. The gagging, objections, and reprimands went on for a long time. Periodically the nurse gave an instruction to someone else. Twenty minutes after all noise had suddenly ended, the orderly returned with the wheelchair and told Nelson he would find her through the third door on the left.

Zochie was at the near end of an apparently uninhabited, shadowy room filled with beds half obscured by white curtains. She was strapped onto a high narrow bed with wheels. The clothes he had dressed her in were jumbled underneath in a metal lattice like a shopping basket. She was wearing a hospital nightgown in two shades of faded blue check, tied at the back. A white sheet, drawn under her arms, was spattered with vomit. Her wrists had been bandaged.

"Come to see me tomorrow," she said. She was very pale, her eyes hardly open at all.

"Sure."

"I'm sorry."

"It's OK."

"Don't despise me."

"I don't despise you."

"I am ashamed."

"It doesn't matter."

"They will try to commit me."

"No they won't."

"They will deport me."

"No."

"Come to see me tomorrow."

Back at Zochie's, Nelson scrubbed the kitchen sink and filled it with cold water to soak her tiger-skin dressing gown. He wiped blood off her notes in the bathroom sink and spread them flat on newspaper in the living room. He opened the curtains and got into bed as the sun paused on the horizon a moment to perfect itself before lifting off.

Greg Hollingshead has published three collections of stories—Famous Players, White Buick, *and* The Roaring Girl, *which won the 1995 Governor General's Award for Fiction. His novel* The Healer *won the Rogers Fiction Prize and was shortlisted for the Giller Prize. He teaches creative writing at the University of Alberta and is the director of writing programs at the Banff Centre for the Arts.*

HEAD

Edna Alford

Coming home I discovered there was no home left nor would there ever be again. Spruce and poplar and scrub were all in place along the way exactly as I had left them but my head was not where I had left it. I left it on a rock in the sun at the corner of the home quarter, the part not yet broke although I see there's been some breaking done on the next quarter to it. I left it on the big rock because I had never in all the years of my growing up seen the snow cover that rock. I don't know why. Maybe it had something to do with the wind.

At first I thought I might nestle it between some of the smaller rocks in the stone pile but then I remembered the snow even though it was very hot that day I left the head out in the field. And the head could smell the buffalo beans and the mustard and the stubby growth of wolf willow barely poking up out of the tall slough grass.

I wouldn't be so upset if I had thought about it before, about the chance the head might not be there when I got back. But I always kind of banked on its being there all that time looking out over the fields toward the sky, clear and cold most of the time. The clarity is what I mostly thought about. That there still was a place somewhere in the world where I could see things clear and from a long way off, like stars, I guess, or trees along the coulee hill, things like that and maybe more.

For it always seemed to me that if you could see one kind of thing clear and from far off—real things, natural things, trees and stars and such—then you could probably see the other kinds of things too, things you couldn't touch, ideas and feelings and who knows what, clear and from a long way off. I thought about that for years after I left the prairie, right up to now in fact. And I wasn't the only one who had that notion. Most of us did.

I met a fellow once in a Vancouver bar and he was reading a paper and he read me a story about city dwellers, how after a long time living in the city, they lose what they call their long-distance vision. These experts had figured it out. It's apparently because city people don't have to look so far, because they've always got something in the way of their looking, like brick buildings or glass skyscrapers or things like that. They get used to looking close; some of them, it seemed to me when I was there, got so bad they pretty well looked at their shoes most of the time or maybe it was the cracks in the sidewalk they were looking at and some of them in fact didn't seem to be looking out at anything at all. They seemed to be looking at themselves, as if their eyes had kind of revolved inside their heads and faced the wrong way altogether—toward their own insides—which is about as far away from long-distance vision as a person can get.

I was pretty smug in those days, knowing all the time I had my head back there on the bald-headed prairie—looking out at the sky and the fields any time I felt like it. Never anything to get in its way, maybe a storm some days, snow or rain or something, but always afterward the sun came back and all the clear clear sky lit up fine and green or even better, white and clean and fiercely clear. And all the time in the city when I'd see folks on their way to work looking at the grey pavement or the cracks in the concrete sidewalks or the buildings made of marble or cement like headstones, or maybe even at windows that gave them back a likeness of themselves, flat, without flesh, and sometimes wavy like the mermaids in the sea might look to a drowning man, I'd think to myself: *Now if only you could see the world the way I see it.*

I even told the guy in the bar in Vancouver about it. About the prairie and the way a man could see better there than anywhere and he laughed and picked up his glass and made a toast to the province of Saskatchewan and then he laughed again and emptied his glass, said the whole coast was nothing but a haven for prairie dogs like me and he said if things were so much better back there, how come the coast's full of all you stubble-jumpers. Half the province of British Columbia is from the province of Saskatchewan. Which is why he was toasting it in the first place he says. And he says he doesn't mind having to look at the buildings or the roads, which he hears still aren't so hot back there, much less cedars and mountains and such—anything, he says, has got to beat nothing six different ways. And he says he's from around Swift Current himself and why don't I tell him another one.

I never gave a second thought to him or what he said till now. When the mill shut down this fall, I finally come back to the prairie, to see the folks mostly. Then too, I guess I had it in the back of my mind I'd take a drive out to the home place and poke around some. And also I guess I had it in my mind to just take a quick check on the head while I was out there.

Which was how I come to see they'd burned the home place down and planted rape. And when I come to the stone pile down by the slough, I see the birds have picked my whole head clean as a whistle, like one of those buffalo skulls you see in the museums. And in the holes that used to be the eyes, I see somebody took a couple of little stones from the pile and stuck them in. They'd hung a pair of spectacles with wire frames on it. Only there was no glass in them, no glass at all. Nothing a fellow could see through even if he did have eyes.

Edna Alford is the author of two short fiction collections, A Sleep Full of Dreams *and* The Garden of Eloise Loon. *She has received the Gerald Lampert Award and the Marian Engel Award. A former editor of* Dandelion *and* Grain, *Edna Alford serves as associate director for writing programs at the Banff Centre for the Arts.*

KOLLA, TICKS

Kristjana Gunnars

JULY TWENTY ONE.

The ticks must be gone now. In the Wasagaming Museum they say the active time for ticks is between the middle of June and the middle of July. They had a bloated one in a plastic box. It was bigger than a lima bean. They said it came from a dog and was finished sucking up the lymph and blood. It must be the stupidest insect. It's got no head at all, just a large bloated torso. The disgusting thing about ticks it that they're parasites. Some insects spin webs or dig burrows or build honeycombs. But this one can't do anything except latch onto an animal and suck the life out of it.

June seventeen must be just the time for ticks. We never think of that. We always have to celebrate June seventeenth in the country by Pense. There have to be open fires in the dusk and races in burlap sacks in the afternoon and walks down a country road. It's dusty and crickets croak in the tall grass by the wayside. Far away a tractor pokes into a field in a dust cloud. Behind you someone laughs loudly. A joke about Gudbrandur Erlendsson whose cow sank into a quagmire in eighteen eighty. The air is dry. Straws crack, blackbirds fidget. Grasshoppers pounce across the road. For once the huldupeople are visible. People you've heard about and never seen. That day you see them. Next day they're gone. It's like that every year. They say things don't last in Canada. They're wrong.

Stories get told on June seventeen. Stories that never made it into English or into print. I know why. It's the odd people they show. You think your great grandparents must have been superstitious. I guess they were. That Johannes Bjarnason from Stykkisholmur, say. He stayed with Jonas Schaldemoes in a cabin by Lake Winnipegosis in nineteen sixteen. I heard that story five weeks ago in Pense when we got together for our yearly fest. They say Canada's too new for folktales and legends. That only natives have real legends here. They're wrong.

I'm sitting on the bank of the Lake Waskesiu panhandle in north Saskatchewan, here alone. I brought no provisions except for a tent and sleeping bag. There are patches of wild strawberry just below my tent site and saskatoons closer to the lake. My plan was to pick those and fish for the rest of my needs. I've got a licence and it's a good fishing lake. I just haven't made the gear yet. I've picked the branches and root fibres, but it's all still raw in the camp. This morning I put a sheet of birch bark into the lake to soften it up. I'm going to make a spoon and a bowl with it when it's smooth enough. I'm back to feel it, but it's not ready. I planned this trip a month ago. Now that I'm here I'm angry. Maybe I didn't sleep well enough. It was the first night. You have to expect to be nervous on the first night, but it's made me bad. I feel bad.

Maybe it's the ugly ticks. You come up here to think about beauty. To hear warblers in the morning and wind in the birch leaves overhead. But then you end up thinking about mites and ticks with lymph-sucking pipes that cut open your skin and dig inside. There they hang, getting big on your own blood. You don't think of purple hyssops or scarlet shootingstars or swallows swooping by. You think of white or yellow or brown ticks that don't have any shape or colour or character. It's mean. The whole thing is mean. Those pests don't have a right to lay eight thousand eggs all over the grass with nothing to do but climb onto a straw and wait for you to walk by.

Maybe you get that way when you're by yourself and everything is raw. That Johannes Bjarnason up in Lake Winnipegosis was like that. He got strange. Maybe it's in the family. He's supposed to be related on my mother's side. He stayed in this cabin with Schaldemoes' family, a wife and daughter, on a promontory into the lake. He was new in Manitoba, fresh from Iceland. The idea was that he'd help Jonas put the nets into the lake in the fall and gather firewood for winter. They were going to fish the nets out when the lake froze over. To do that, they hacked out bald spots in the ice and threaded a string underneath. Later they pulled the nets out of the holes, took the fish out, and put them back in. They had almost seventy nets and they lifted twenty of them every day.

If my folks knew about this they'd have a search party out for me. Maybe they've got one out anyway. It's a big argument with them, that I don't know enough to do something like this. It's dangerous for a girl who's only seventeen. But what about the first pioneers? What did they know about fishing in prairie lakes or camping in poplar stands? There isn't anything remotely like this in Iceland. You've got to be brave about life. You can't test yourself unless you step outside. It's true, I don't know what I'm doing, but I'll learn. I figure I'll be able to catch northern pike or yellow perch here. Pike are supposed to get so big that one catch might do me for a couple of days. They come where the water is shallow in the morning. You can probably just pick them up from the water-weeds. Otherwise you can put a worm on your hook and use a button for a lure. A shiny one, anyway. And perch are supposed to be around all the time. You can catch it from the banks, especially at noon or in the evening. It shouldn't be hard.

This Johannes, my great-uncle. In November the Schaldemoes family went to Winnipegosis town and he stayed in the cabin alone while they were gone. It was on Hunter's Island, twenty miles away and three miles from the nearest neighbour. Jonas Schaldemoes kept asking him if he felt all right about being alone, and told him not to work after dark and to stay overnight in the neighbour's cabin instead of sleeping alone. Friday morning the family left and Johannes went to work on the lake. It was slow work, lifting nets alone, but he didn't want to quit until he'd done enough to call it a day's work. So he didn't get back to the cabin till after dark. He was uncomfortable when he got there, but the discomfort vanished as soon as he started preparing supper for himself. He made the lunch-pack for the following day and went to sleep.

Next morning he went to work early and stayed on the lake till it was dark again. The hoarfrost was thick in the air and there was a dark heavy fog when he got back. He tried to open the door to the cabin, but it was as if someone pushed it against him from inside. He tried to get in twice, but both times the door slammed shut in his face. He thought about following Jonas' advice and going to the neighbour's cabin, but then he decided that would be cowardly. He'd slept all right in this one the night before. So he collected his energy, opened the door and walked in. As soon as he'd lit the lamp, he stood for a while and looked around. It occurred to him that he wasn't alone in the cabin. He couldn't see anybody else, but he felt sure he wasn't alone.

They say a tick goes through three stages. It's as if it's got three lives and in each one it has to latch onto an animal and gorge itself with blood. First it's the larva, then it's the nymph, then it's the adult. Each time it's bigger and takes more blood than before, and in the end it's so big that the shield on the outside of the body just about cracks. That's when it drops to the grass again. Then it's had enough. The lousy parasite. It isn't enough to have thousands of eggs from each one, but every one of those eggs gets you three times before it's dead. They're all over. There's no such thing as being alone in the wilds, is there? There's lots of company.

Johannes pulled himself out of his cowardice and started preparing supper. Stewing catfish, maybe. He knew he wouldn't get any sleep so he sat down to write a letter home. He didn't finish the letter till after midnight, but by that time he felt calm and tired. So he went to bed. There was a window over his bed and the stove stood on the other side of the room, a few feet away. He turned his face to the wall and lay still for a while. Then he looked over his shoulder onto the floor. There stood a man, halfway between the bed and the stove. Half a man, because the top half was missing. The legs, feet, and hips were there, but the rest was gone. He sat up in bed and stared at the apparition, but then it vanished.

You'd think he was getting bush fever already on his second night. Maybe it doesn't take longer than that. The trick is to stay organized and keep your mind on something specific. Like the birch bark. Even if a tree is dead, you can use the bark. The bark stays alive in a way. You just have to soak it in water and it'll work. Anything can be made with it: cups and bowls and plates. Pots too, with the dark side out so it won't catch fire. I'm going to fold this piece up into a rectangle and glue the ends up with sap. Then I'll roll up a small wad for a spoon and slide it into the slit of a twig. I'll tie it with roots. It's easy.

That man. He should have thought of something else when he lay down again after the figure was gone. Keeping your mind on something like that makes it come again. Sure enough, a little later he saw the same half-man on the floor. When he stood up, the vision was gone. He lay down for the third time, and soon he saw it again. Three times it came to him during the night. After that he couldn't stay in bed. He got up and paced the floor for the rest of the night. By six in the morning he was so tired that he lay down. Just as he was about to fall asleep, he heard a man call just outside his window: "Ho, ho, ho." He thought it was Hjalmar, Jonas' cousin from the next cabin. Hjalmar used to visit on Sunday mornings. But then he realized it was too early for a visitor. Johannes went outside and walked around the cabin, but he couldn't see anyone. The strange voice had sounded most like an Indian's call.

By noon the family was back home at the cabin. They asked Johannes how he'd been and he said nothing about what he'd seen. Some days later, when they were at work on the lake, Jonas asked again if he hadn't seen anything while they were gone. Then Johannes told him everything. After all, they said he'd been strange when they got back. Jonas got more thoughtful after hearing the story of the split man in the cabin. Then he told his guest what it was he'd seen.

That's the way ticks are. You don't see them on the grass. You walk into them and they jump on you. You don't see them until they're burrowing into your skin and you have to get them out. The only way to do it is to stick a burning twig at the insect. That'll make it curl up and drop off. If you force it out or pull it, the mouthparts stay in your skin. But the whole thing doesn't sound as dangerous as they make it out to be. A few bloodsuckers can't do anything when they're that small. I guess they can give you diseases or sores or ulcers. That's what happens to cows and sheep. In the Rockies, the chipmunks and rabbits have spotted fever from ticks. People can get that too. But it sounds worse than it is. Just put some oil on the pest and it'll let go.

That birch bark still isn't ready. I didn't realize there were so many layers to a piece of bark when I cut it off the tree. Where do you stop with all those layers? They keep going. You don't know where the bark ends and the meat of the trunk begins. Maybe I didn't peel off enough layers. You peel one sheet, then another, some darker, some lighter. They alternate, but they always come back. Maybe I took too many and that's why it's so stiff. Maybe it's never ready.

Like that Indian on Lake Winnipegosis. He may never stop calling. Jonas said that a few years earlier, an Indian had been working on the lake during the winter. He moved fish bundles across the lake on a sled pulled by two horses. It was early in the winter and the ice was rotten. He disappeared on that trip and people said he'd fallen through. But no one knew what really happened. Next spring, when the ice loosened up, a man's corpse washed up just below Jonas' cabin. They decided it must have been the Indian who had vanished, but they couldn't be sure. The body wasn't recognizable any more. It was cut in half. All they found was the bottom half.

You'd think it was the top half calling for the bottom half. Looking for itself forever. But what harm can half a ghost do anybody? Without a head, without arms, it has to be harmless. But there's no real body there. Even if it were a real ghost, it'd be easy to shrug off. Just light a fire in the hearth and you won't see it any more. But what if it keeps coming back? Every spring it's there and you have to listen to the calls and the knocks clattering on your floor. By winter it's under the ice again. It only comes around when somebody's alone in a cabin and it wants to talk.

Maybe I've got my information wrong. Maybe you don't soak the bark in water at all. I guess I'll try a young tree next time, one with soft moist bark you can just rip off. Maybe I'm too mad to do anything right. It's only the second day. I'll come around. I didn't sleep after all. This sort of thing takes time. You have to move one step at a time. First you set up a tent, then you make a fire. Then you make the implements, one at a time. Soon you'll have them all. Bowls and spoons and plates and knives'll be dangling on the branches all around your tent. Like the sheep ticks. You don't see them, don't hear them, hardly feel them. But suddenly they're there. Right on you. They say in Europe the cows can have so many ticks hanging on them that they clatter and rattle when they walk. What a load. Think of having to take them off, one at a time. Burning them off with brands.

It's mean. The whole thing is mean. Like the name they gave me. Kolla. That's short for Kolbrun. I got it because I'm darker than the rest of them, as if I were the black sheep or something. Maybe they got the idea I'd be moody already when they had me in the crib. Kolbrun. That means brown as coal. Coal. That's a burnt forest, isn't it? It's mean.

Waskesiu, Wasagaming, Regina, 1978-79

Kristjana Gunnars is the author of six books of poetry, two collections of short stories and four books of cross-genre fiction and nonfiction. As well, she has translated two books and edited a collection of essays on Margaret Laurence and diasporic fiction. Gunnars' book of poems Exiles Among You *won the Stephan G. Stephansson Alberta Book of the Year Award. Her novel* The Prowler *won the McNally Robinson–Manitoba Book of the Year Award and her nonfiction work* Zero Hour *was nominated for the Governor General's Award and the Wilfred Eggleston Award for Nonfiction.* The Rose Garden: Reading Marcel Proust *won the George Bugnet Award for Fiction. Her short fiction and essays have appeared widely in anthologies and in Spanish, Chinese, Icelandic and Danish translation. She teaches creative writing at the University of Alberta.*

GOD IS NOT A FISH INSPECTOR

W.D. Valgardson

Although Emma made no noise as she descended, Fusi Bergman knew his daughter was watching him from the bottom of the stairs.

"God will punish you," she promised in a low, intense voice.

"Render unto Caesar what is Caesar's," he snapped. "God's not a fish inspector. He doesn't work for the government."

By the light of the front ring of the kitchen stove, he had been drinking a cup of coffee mixed half and half with whisky. Now, he shifted in his captain's chair so as to partly face the stairs. Though he was unable to make out more than the white blur of Emma's nightgown, after living with her for 48 years he knew exactly how she would look if he turned on the light.

She was tall and big boned with the square, pugnacious face of a bulldog. Every inch of her head would be crammed with metal curlers and her angular body hidden by a plain white cotton shift that hung from her broad shoulders like a tent. Whenever she was angry with him, she always stood rigid and white lipped, her hands clenched at her sides.

"You prevaricate," she warned. "You will not be able to prevaricate at the gates of Heaven."

He drained his cup, sighed, and pulled on his jacket. As he opened the door, Fusi said, "He made fish to catch. There is no place in the Bible where it says you can't catch fish when you are three score and ten."

"You'll be the ruin of us," she hissed as he closed the door on her.

She was aggressive and overbearing, but he knew her too well to be impressed. Behind her forcefulness, there was always that trace of self-pity nurtured in plain women who go unmarried until they think they have been passed by. Even if they eventually found a husband, the self-pity returned to change their determination into a whine. Still, he was glad to have the door between them.

This morning, as every morning, he had wakened at three. Years before, he had trained himself to get up at that time and now, in spite of his age, he never woke more than five minutes after the hour. He was proud of his early rising for he felt it showed he was not, like many of his contemporaries, relentlessly sliding into the endless blur of senility. Each morning, because he had become reconciled to the idea of dying, he felt, on the instant of his awakening, a spontaneous sense of amazement at being alive. The thought never lasted longer than the brief time between sleep and consciousness, but the good feeling lingered throughout the day.

When Fusi stepped outside, the air was cold and damp. The moon that hung low in the west was pale and fragile and very small. 50 feet from the house, the breakwater that ran along the rear of his property loomed like the purple spine of some great beast guarding the land from a lake which seemed, in the darkness, to go on forever.

Holding his breath to still the noise of his own breathing, Fusi listened for a cough or the scuff of gravel that would mean someone was close by, watching and waiting, but the only sound was the muted rubbing of his skiff against the piling to which it was moored. Half a mile away where the land was lower, rows of gas boats roped five abreast lined the docks. The short, stubby boats with their high cabins, the grey surface of the docks and the dark water were all tinged purple from the mercury lamps. At the harbour mouth, high on a thin spire, a red light burned like a distant star.

Behind him, he heard the door open and, for a moment, he was afraid Emma might begin to shout, or worse still, turn on the back-door light and alert his enemies, but she did neither. Above all things, Emma was afraid of scandal, and would do anything to avoid causing an unsavoury rumour to be attached to her own or her husband's name.

Her husband, John Smith, was as bland and inconsequential as his name. Moon faced with wide blue eyes and a small mouth above which sat a carefully trimmed moustache, he was a head shorter than Emma and a good 50 pounds lighter. Six years before, he had been transferred to the Eddyville branch of the Bank of Montreal. His transfer from Calgary to a small town in Manitoba was the bank's way of letting him know that there would be no more promotions. He would stay in Eddyville until he retired.

A year after he arrived, Emma had married him and instead of her moving out, he had moved in. For the last two years, under Emma's prodding, John had been taking a correspondence course in theology so that when he no longer worked at the bank he could be a full-time preacher.

On the evenings when he wasn't balancing the bank's books, he laboured over the multiple-choice questions in the Famous Preacher's course that he received each month from the One True and Only Word of God Church in Mobile, Alabama. Because of a freak in the atmosphere one night while she had been fiddling with the radio, Emma had heard a gospel hour advertising the course and, although neither she nor John had ever been south of Minneapolis and had never heard of the One True and Only Word of God Church before, she took it as a sign and immediately enrolled her husband in it. It cost $500.

John's notes urged him not to wait to answer His Call but to begin ministering to the needy at once for the Judgment Day was always imminent. In anticipation of the end of the world and his need for a congregation once he retired, he and Emma had become zealous missionaries, cramming their Volkswagen with a movie projector, a record-player, films, trays of slides, religious records for every occasion, posters and pamphlets, all bought or rented from the One True and Only Word of God Church. Since the townspeople were obstinately Lutheran, and since John did not want to give offence to any of his bank's customers, he and Emma hunted converts along the grey dirt roads that led past tumble-down farmhouses, the inhabitants of which were never likely to enter a bank.

Fusi did not turn to face his daughter but hurried away because he knew he had no more than an hour and a half until dawn. His legs were fine as he crossed the yard, but by the time he had mounted the steps that led over the breakwater, then climbed down fifteen feet to the shore, his left knee had begun to throb.

Holding his leg rigid to ease the pain, he waded out, loosened the ropes and heaved himself away from the shore. As soon as the boat was in deep water, he took his seat, and set both oars in the oar-locks he had carefully muffled with strips from an old shirt.

For a moment, he rested his hands on his knees, the oars rising like too-small wings from a cumbersome body, then he straightened his arms, dipped the oars cleanly into the water and in one smooth motion pulled his hands toward his chest. The first few strokes were even and graceful but then as a speck of pain like a grain of sand formed in his shoulder, the sweep of his left oar became shorter than his right. Each time he leaned against the oars, the pain grew until it was, in his mind, a bent shingle-nail twisted and turned in his shoulder socket.

With the exertion, a ball of gas formed in his stomach, making him uncomfortable. As quickly as a balloon being blown up, it expanded until his lungs and heart were cramped and he couldn't draw in a full breath. Although the air over the lake was cool, sweat ran from his hairline.

At his two-hundredth stroke, he shipped his left oar and pulled a coil of rope with a large hook from under the seat. After checking to see that it was securely tied through the gunwale, he dropped the rope overboard and once more began to row. Normally, he would have had a buoy made from a slender tamarack pole, a block of wood and some lead weights to mark his net, but he no longer had a fishing licence so his net had to be sunk below the surface where it could not be seen by the fish inspectors.

Five more strokes of the oars and the rope went taut. He lifted both oars into the skiff, then, standing in the bow, began to pull. The boat responded sluggishly but gradually it turned and the cork line that lay hidden under two feet of water broke the surface. He grasped the net, freed the hook and began to collect the mesh until the lead line appeared. For once he had been lucky and the hook had caught the net close to one end so there was no need to backtrack.

Hand over hand he pulled, being careful not to let the corks and leads bang against the bow, for on the open water sound carried clearly for miles. In the first two fathoms there was a freshly caught pickerel. As he pulled it toward him, it beat the water with its tail, making light, slapping sounds. His fingers were cramped, but Fusi managed to catch the fish around its soft middle and, with his other hand, work the mesh free of the gills.

It was then that the pain in his knee forced him to sit. Working from the seat was awkward and cost him precious time, but he had no choice, for the pain had begun to inch up the bone toward his crotch.

He wiped his forehead with his hand and cursed his infirmity. When he was twenty, he had thought nothing of rowing five miles from shore to lift five and six gangs of nets and then, nearly knee deep in fish, row home again. Now, he reflected bitterly, a quarter of a mile and one net were nearly beyond him. Externally, he had changed very little over the years. He was still tall and thin, his arms and legs corded with muscle. His belly was hard. His long face, with its pointed jaw, showed his age the most. That and his hands. His face was lined until it seemed there was nowhere the skin was smooth. His hands were scarred and heavily veined. His hair was grey but it was still thick.

While others were amazed at his condition, he was afraid of the changes that had taken place inside him. It was this invisible deterioration that was gradually shrinking the limits of his endurance.

Even in the darkness, he could see the distant steeple of the Lutheran church and the square bulk of the old folk's home that was directly across from his house. Emma, he thought grimly, would not be satisfied until he was safely trapped in one or carried out of the other.

He hated the old folk's home. He hated the three stories of pale yellow brick with their small, close-set windows. He hated the concrete porch with its five round pillars and the large white buckets of red geraniums. When he saw the men poking at the flowers like a bunch of old women, he pulled his blinds.

The local people who worked in the home were good to the inmates, tenants they called them, but there was no way a man could be a man in there. No whisky. Going to bed at ten. Getting up at eight. Bells for breakfast, coffee and dinner. Bells for everything. He was surprised that they didn't have bells for going to the toilet. Someone watching over you every minute of every day. It was as if, having earned the right to be an adult, you had suddenly, in some inexplicable way, lost it again.

The porch was the worst part of the building. Long and narrow and lined with yellow and red rocking-chairs, it sat ten feet above the ground and the steps were so steep that even those who could get around all right were afraid to try them. Fusi had lived across from the old folk's home for 40 years and he had seen old people, all interchangeable as time erased their identities, shuffling and bickering their way to their deaths. Now, most of those who came out to sleep in the sun and to watch the world with glittering, jealous eyes, were people he had known.

He would have none of it. He was not afraid of dying, but he was determined that it would be in his own home. His licence had been taken from him because of his age, but he did not stop. One net was not thirty, but it was one, and a quarter-mile from shore was not five miles, but it was a quarter-mile.

He didn't shuffle and he didn't have to be fed or have a rubber diaper pinned around him each day. If anything, he had become more cunning for, time and again, the inspectors had come and destroyed the illegal nets of other fishermen, even catching and sending them to court to be fined, but they hadn't caught him for four years. Every day of the fishing season, he pitted his wits against theirs and won. At times, they had come close, but their searches had never turned up anything and, once, to his delight, when he was on the verge of being found with freshly caught fish on him, he hid them under a hole in the breakwater and then sat on the edge of the boat, talked about old times, and shared the inspectors' coffee. The memory still brought back a feeling of pleasure and excitement.

As his mind strayed over past events, he drew the boat along the net in fits and starts for his shoulder would not take the strain of steady pulling.

Another good-sized fish hung limp as he pulled it to him, but then as he slipped the mesh from its head, it gave a violent shake and flew from his hands. Too stiff and slow to lunge for it, he could do nothing but watch the white flash of its belly before it struck the water and disappeared.

He paused to knead the backs of his hands, then began again. Before he was finished, his breath roared in his ears like the lake in a storm, but there were four more pickerel. With a sigh that was nearly a cry of pain, he let the net drop. Immediately, pulled down by the heavy, rusted anchors at each end, it disappeared. People were like that, he thought. One moment they were here, then they were gone and it was as if they had never been.

Behind the town, the horizon was a pale, hard grey. The silhouette of rooftops and trees might have been cut from a child's purple construction paper.

The urgent need to reach the shore before the sky became any lighter drove Fusi, for he knew that if the inspectors saw him on the water they would catch him as easily as a child. They would take his fish and net, which he did not really mind, for there were more fish in the lake and more nets in his shed, but he couldn't afford to lose his boat. His savings were not enough to buy another.

He put out the oars, only to be unable to close the fingers of his left hand. When he tried to bend his fingers around the handle, his whole arm began to tremble. Unable to do anything else, he leaned forward and pressing his fingers flat to the seat, he began to relentlessly knead them. Alternately, he prayed and cursed, trying with words to delay the sun.

"A few minutes," he whispered through clenched teeth. "Just a few minutes more." But even as he watched, the horizon turned red, then yellow and a sliver of the sun's rim rose above the houses.

Unable to wait any longer, he grabbed his left hand in his right and forced his fingers around the oar, then braced himself and began to row. Instead of cutting the water cleanly, the left oar skimmed over the surface, twisting the handle in his grip. He tried again, not letting either oar go deep. The skiff moved sluggishly ahead.

Once again, the balloon in his chest swelled and threatened to gag him, making his gorge rise, but he did not dare stop. Again and again, the left oar skipped across the surface so that the bow swung back and forth like a wounded and dying animal trying to shake away its pain. Behind him, the orange sun inched above the sharp angles of the roofs.

When the bow slid across the sand, he dropped the oars, letting them trail in the water. He grasped the gunwale, but as he climbed out, his left leg collapsed and he slid to his knees. Cold water filled his boots and soaked the legs of his trousers. Resting his head against the boat, he breathed noisily through his mouth. He remained there until gradually his breathing eased and the pain in his chest closed like a night flower touched by daylight. When he could stand, he tied the boat to one of the black pilings that was left from a breakwater that had long since been smashed and carried away.

As he collected his catch, he noticed the green fisheries department truck on the dock. He had been right. They were there. Crouching behind his boat, he waited to see if anyone was watching him. It seemed like a miracle that they had not already seen him, but he knew that they had not for if they had, their launch would have raced out of the harbour and swept down upon him.

Bending close to the sand, he limped into the deep shadow at the foot of the breakwater. They might, he knew, be waiting for him at the top of the ladder, but if they were, there was nothing he could do about it. He climbed the ladder and, hearing and seeing nothing, he rested near the top so that when he climbed into sight, he wouldn't need to sit down.

No-one was in the yard. The block was empty. With a sigh of relief, he crossed to the small shed where he kept his equipment and hefted the fish onto the shelf that was nailed to one wall. He filleted his catch with care, leaving none of the translucent flesh on the back-bone or skin. Then, because they were pickerel, he scooped out the cheeks, which he set aside with the roe for his breakfast.

As he carried the offal across the backyard in a bucket, the line of gulls that gathered every morning on the breakwater broke into flight and began to circle overhead. Swinging back the bucket, he flung the guts and heads and skin into the air and the gulls darted down to snatch the red entrails and iridescent heads. In a thrumming of white and grey wings, those who hadn't caught anything descended to the sand to fight for what remained.

Relieved at being rid of the evidence of his fishing—if anyone asked where he got the fillets he would say he had bought them and the other fishermen would lie for him—Fusi squatted and wiped his hands clean on the wet grass.

There was no sign of movement in the house. The blinds were still drawn and the high, narrow house with its steep roof and faded red-brick siding looked deserted. The yard was flat and bare except for the dead trunk of an elm, which was stripped bare of its bark and wind polished to the colour of bone.

He returned to the shed and wrapped the fillets in a sheet of brown waxed paper, then put the roe and the cheeks into the bucket. Neither Emma nor John were up when he came in and washed the bucket and his food, but as he started cooking, Emma appeared in a quilted housecoat covered with large, purple tulips. Her head was a tangle of metal.

"Are you satisfied?" she asked, her voice trembling. "I've had no sleep since you left."

Without turning from the stove, he said, "Leave. Nobody's making you stay."

Indignantly, she answered, "And who would look after you?"

He grimaced and turned over the roe so they would be golden brown on all sides. For two weeks around Christmas he had been sick with the flu and she never let him forget it.

"Honour thy father and mother that thy days may be long upon this earth."

He snorted out loud. What she really wanted to be sure of was that she got the house.

"You don't have to be like this," she said, starting to talk to him as if he was a child. "I only want you to stop because I care about you. All those people who live across the street, they don't. . . ."

"I'm not one of them," he barked.

"You're 70 years old. . . ."

"And I still fish," he replied angrily, cutting her off. "And I still row a boat and lift my nets. That's more than your husband can do and he's just 50." He jerked his breakfast off the stove. Because he knew it would annoy her, he began to eat out of the pan.

"I'm 70," he continued between bites, "and I beat the entire fisheries department. They catch men half my age, but they haven't caught me. Not for four years. And I fish right under their noses." He laughed with glee and laced his coffee with a finger of whisky.

Emma, her lips clamped shut and her hands clenched in fury, marched back up the stairs. In half an hour both she and John came down for their breakfast. Under Emma's glare, John cleared his throat and said, "Emma, that is we, think—" He stopped and fiddled with the knot of his tie. He always wore light grey ties and a light grey suit. "If you don't quit breaking the law, something will have to be done." He stopped and looked beseechingly at his wife, but she narrowed her eyes until little folds of flesh formed beneath them. "Perhaps something like putting you in custody so you'll be saved from yourself."

Fusi was so shocked that for once he could think of nothing to say. Encouraged by his silence, John said, "It will be for your own good."

Before either of them realized what he was up to, Fusi leaned sideways and emptied his cup into his son-in-law's lap.

The coffee was hot. John flung himself backward with a screech, but the back legs of his chair caught on a crack in the linoleum and he tipped over with a crash. In the confusion Fusi stalked upstairs.

In a moment he flung an armload of clothes down. When his daughter rushed to the bottom of the stairs, Fusi flung another armload of clothes at her.

"This is my house," he bellowed. "You're not running it yet."

Emma began grabbing clothes and laying them flat so they wouldn't wrinkle. John, both hands clenched between his legs, hobbled over to stare.

Fusi descended the stairs and they parted to let him by. At the counter, he picked up the package of fish and turning toward them, said, "I want you out of here when I get back or I'll go out on the lake and get caught and tell everyone that you put me up to it."

His fury was so great that once he was outside he had to lean against the house while a spasm of trembling swept over him. When he was composed, he rounded the corner. At one side of the old folk's home there was an enclosed fire escape that curled to the ground like a piece of intestine. He headed for the kitchen door under it.

Fusi had kept on his rubber boots, dark slacks and red turtle-neck sweater, and because he knew that behind the curtains, eyes were watching his every move, he tried to hide the stiffness in his left leg.

Although it was early, Rosie Melysyn was already at work. She always came first, never missing a day. She was a large, good natured widow with grey hair.

"How are you today, Mr. Bergman?" she asked.

"Fine," he replied. "I'm feeling great." He held out the brown paper package. "I thought some of the old people might like some fish." Although he had brought fish for the last four years, he always said the same thing.

Rosie dusted off her hands, took the package and placed it on the counter.

"I'll see someone gets it," she assured him. "Help yourself to some coffee."

As he took the pot from the stove, she asked, "No trouble with the inspectors?"

He always waited for her to ask that. He grinned delightedly, the pain of the morning already becoming a memory. "No trouble. They'll never catch me. I'm up too early. I saw them hanging about, but it didn't do them any good."

"Jimmy Henderson died last night," Rosie offered.

"Jimmy Henderson," Fusi repeated. They had been friends, but he felt no particular sense of loss. Jimmy had been in the home for three years. "I'm not surprised. He wasn't more than 68 but he had given up. You give up, you're going to die. You believe in yourself and you can keep right on going."

Rosie started mixing oatmeal and water.

"You know," he said to her broad back, "I was with Jimmy the first time he got paid. He cut four cords of wood for 60¢ and spent it all on hootch. He kept running up and down the street and flapping his arms, trying to fly.

When he passed out, we hid him in the hayloft of the stable so his old man couldn't find him."

Rosie tried to imagine Jimmy Henderson attempting to fly and failed. To her, he was a bent man with a sad face who had to use a walker to get to the dining-room. What she remembered about him best was coming on him unexpectedly and finding him silently crying. He had not seen her and she had quietly backed away.

Fusi was lingering because after he left, there was a long day ahead of him. He would have the house to himself and after checking the vacated room to see that nothing of his had been taken, he would tie his boat properly, sleep for three hours, then eat lunch. In the afternoon he would make a trip to the docks to see what the inspectors were up to and collect information about their movements.

The back door opened with a swish and he felt a cool draft. Both he and Rosie turned to look. He was shocked to see that instead of it being one of the kitchen help, it was Emma. She shut the door and glanced at them both, then at the package of fish.

"What do you want?" he demanded.

"I called the inspectors," she replied, "to tell them you're not responsible for yourself. I told them about the net."

He gave a start, but then was relieved when he remembered they had to actually catch him fishing before they could take the skiff. "So what?" he asked, confident once more.

Quietly, she replied, "You don't have to worry about being caught. They've known about your fishing all along."

Suddenly frightened by her calm certainty, his voice rose as he said, "That's not true."

"They don't care," she repeated. "Inspector McKenzie was the name of the one I talked to. He said you couldn't do any harm with one net. They've been watching you every morning just in case you should get into trouble and need help."

Emma stood there, not moving, her head tipped back, her eyes benevolent.

He turned to Rosie. "She's lying, isn't she? That's not true. They wouldn't do that?"

"Of course, she's lying," Rosie assured him.

He would have rushed outside but Emma was standing in his way. Since he could not get past her, he fled through the swinging doors that led to the dining-room.

As the doors shut, Rosie turned on Emma and said, "You shouldn't have done that." She picked up the package of fish with its carefully folded wrapping. In the artificial light, the package glowed like a piece of amber. She held it cupped in the hollows of her hands. "You had no right."

Emma seemed to grow larger and her eyes shone.

"The Lord's work be done," she said, her right hand partly raised as if she were preparing to give a benediction.

W.D. Valgardson is the author of thirteen books. In the last six years he has published five books for children including Garbage Creek *and* The Divorced Kids Club. *His most recent book is a young adult novel. He is currently chair of the writing department at the University of Victoria.*

MAN DESCENDING

GUY VANDERHAEGHE

IT IS SIX-THIRTY; my wife returns home from work. I am shaving when I hear her key scratching at the lock. I keep the door of our apartment locked at all times. The building has been burgled twice since we moved in and I don't like surprises. My caution annoys my wife; she sees it as proof of a reluctance to approach life with the open-armed camaraderie she expected in a spouse. I can tell that this bit of faithlessness on my part has made her unhappy. Her heels click down our uncarpeted hallway with a lively resonance. So I lock the door of the bathroom to forestall her.

I do this because the state of the bathroom (and my state) will only make her unhappier. I note that my dead cigarette butt has left a liverish stain of nicotine on the edge of the sink and that it has deposited droppings of ash in the basin. The glass of Scotch standing on the toilet tank is not empty. I have been oiling myself all afternoon in expectation of the New Year's party that I would rather not attend. Since Scotch is regarded as a fine social lubricant, I have attempted, to the best of my ability, to get lubricated. Somehow I feel it hasn't worked.

My wife is rattling the door now. "Ed, are you in there?"

"None other," I reply, furiously slicing great swaths in the lather on my cheeks.

"Goddamn it, Ed," Victoria says angrily. "I asked you. I asked you *please* to be done in there before I get home. I have to get ready for the party. I told Helen we'd be there by eight."

"I didn't realize it was so late," I explain lamely. I can imagine the stance she has assumed on the other side of the door. My wife is a social worker and has to deal with people like me every day. Irresponsible people. By now she has crossed her arms across her breasts and inclined her head with its shining helmet of dark hair ever so slightly to one side. Her mouth has puckered like a drawstring purse, and she has planted her legs defiantly and solidly apart, signifying that she will not be moved.

"Ed, how long are you going to be in there?"

I know that tone of voice. Words can never mask its meaning. It is always interrogative, and it always implies that my grievous faults of character could be remedied. *So why don't I make the effort?*

"Five minutes," I call cheerfully.

Victoria goes away. Her heels are brisk on the hardwood.

My thoughts turn to the party and then naturally to civil servants, since almost all of Victoria's friends are people with whom she works. Civil servants inevitably lead me to think of mandarins, and then Asiatics in general. I settle on Mongols and begin to carefully carve the lather off my face, intent on leaving myself with a shaving-cream Fu Manchu. I do quite a handsome job. I slit my eyes.

"Mirror, mirror on the wall," I whisper. "Who's the fiercest of them all?"

From the back of my throat I produce a sepulchral tone of reply. "You Genghis Ed, Terror of the World! You who raise cenotaphs of skulls! You who banquet off the backs of your enemies!" I imagine myself sweeping out of Central Asia on a shaggy pony, hard-bitten from years in the saddle, turning almond eyes to fabulous cities that lie pliant under my pitiless gaze.

Victoria is back at the bathroom door. "Ed!"

"Yes, dear?" I answer meekly.

"Ed, explain something to me," she demands.

"Anything, lollipop," I reply. This assures her that I have been alerted to danger. It is now a fair fight and she does not have to labour under the feeling that she has sprung upon her quarry from ambush.

"Don't get sarcastic. It's not called for."

I drain my glass of Scotch, rinse it under the tap, and stick a toothbrush in it, rendering it innocuous. The butt is flicked into the toilet, and the nicotine stain scrubbed out with my thumb. "I apologize," I say, hunting madly in the medicine cabinet for mouthwash to disguise my alcoholic breath.

"Ed, you have nothing to do all day. Absolutely nothing. Why couldn't you be done in there before I got home?"

I rinse my mouth. Then I spot my full, white Fu Manchu and begin scraping. "Well, dear, it's like this," I say. "You know how I sweat. And I do get nervous about these little affairs. So I cut the time a little fine. I admit that. But one doesn't want to appear at these affairs too damp. I like to think that my deodorant's power is peaking at my entrance. I'm sure you see—"

"Shut up and get out of there," Victoria says tiredly.

A last cursory inspection of the bathroom and I spring open the door and present my wife with my best I'm-a-harmless-idiot-don't-hit-me smile. Since I've been unemployed I practise my smiles in the mirror whenever time hangs heavy on my hands. I have one for every occasion. This particular one is a faithful reproduction, Art imitating Life. The other day, while out taking a walk, I saw a large black Labrador taking a crap on somebody's doorstep. We established instant rapport. He grinned hugely at me while his body trembled with exertion. His smile was a perfect blend of physical relief, mischievousness, and apology for his indiscretion. A perfectly suitable smile for my present situation.

"Squeaky, pretty-pink clean," I announce to my wife.

"Being married to an adolescent is a bore," Victoria says, pushing past me into the bathroom. "Make me a drink. I need it."

I hurry to comply and return in time to see my wife lowering her delightful bottom into a tub of scalding hot, soapy water and ascending wreaths of steam. She lies back and her breasts flatten; she toys with the tap with delicate ivory toes.

"Christ," she murmurs, stunned by the heat.

I sit down on the toilet seat and fondle my drink, rotating the transparent cylinder and its amber contents in my hand. Then I abruptly hand Victoria her glass and as an opening gambit ask, "How's Howard?"

My wife does not flinch, but only sighs luxuriantly, steeping herself in the rich heat. I interpret this as hardness of heart. I read in her face the lineaments of a practised and practising adulteress. For some time now I've suspected that Howard, a grave and unctuously dignified psychologist who works for the provincial Department of Social Services, is her lover. My wife has taken to working late and several times when I have phoned her office, disguising my voice and playing the irate beneficiary of the government's largesse, Howard has answered. When we meet socially, Howard treats me with the barely concealed contempt that is due an unsuspecting cuckold.

"Howard? Oh, he's fine." Victoria answers blandly, sipping at her drink. Her body seems to elongate under the water, and for a moment I feel justified in describing her as statuesque.

"I like Howard," I say. "We should have him over for dinner some evening."

My wife laughs. "Howard doesn't like you," she says.

"Oh?" I feign surprise. "Why?"

"You know why. Because you're always pestering him to diagnose you. He's not stupid, you know. He knows you're laughing up your sleeve at him. You're transparent, Ed. When you don't like someone you belittle their work. I've seen you do it a thousand times."

"I refuse," I say, "to respond to innuendo."

This conversation troubles my wife. She begins to splash around in the tub. She cannot go too far in her defence of Howard.

"He's not a bad sort," she says. "A little stuffy, I grant you, but sometimes stuffiness is preferable to complete irresponsibility. You, on the other hand, seem to have the greatest contempt for anyone whose behaviour even remotely approaches sanity."

I know my wife is now angling the conversation toward the question of employment. There are two avenues open for examination. She may concentrate on the past, studded as it is with a series of unmitigated disasters, or on the future. On the whole I feel the past is safer ground, at least from my point of view. She knows that I lied about why I was fired from my last job, and six months later still hasn't got the truth out of me.

Actually, I was shown the door because of "habitual uncooperativeness". I was employed in an adult extension program. For the life of me I couldn't master the terminology, and this created a rather unfavourable impression. All that talk about "terminal learners", "life skills", etc., completely unnerved me. Whenever I was sure I understood what a word meant, someone decided it had become charged with nasty connotations and invented a new "value-free term". The place was a goddamn madhouse and I acted accordingly.

I have to admit, though, that there was one thing I liked about the job. That was answering the phone whenever the office was deserted, which it frequently was since everyone was always running out into the community "identifying needs". I greeted every caller with a breezy "College of Knowledge. Mr. Know-It-All here!" Rather juvenile, I admit, but very satisfying. And I was rather sorry I got the boot before I got to meet a real, live, flesh-and-blood terminal learner. Evidently there were thousands of them out in the community and they were a bad thing. At one meeting in which we were trying to decide what should be done about them, I suggested, using a bit of Pentagon jargon I had picked up on the late-night news, that if we ever laid hands on any of them or their ilk, we should have them "terminated with extreme prejudice".

"By the way," my wife asks nonchalantly, "were you out looking today?"

"Harry Wells called," I lie. "He thinks he might have something for me in a couple of months."

My wife stirs uneasily in the tub and creates little swells that radiate from her body like a disquieting aura.

"That's funny," she says tartly. "I called Harry today about finding work for you. He didn't foresee anything in the future."

"He must have meant the immediate future."

"He didn't mention talking to you."

"That's funny."

Victoria suddenly stands up. Venus rising from the bath. Captive water sluices between her breasts, slides down her thighs.

"Damn it, Ed! When are you going to begin to tell the truth? I'm sick of all this." She fumbles blindly for a towel as her eyes pin me. "Just remember," she adds, "behave yourself tonight. Lay off my friends."

I am rendered speechless by her fiery beauty, by this many-times-thwarted love that twists and turns in search of a worthy object. Meekly, I promise.

I DRIVE TO THE PARTY, my headlights rending the veil of thickly falling, shimmering snow. The city crews have not yet removed the Christmas decorations; strings of lights garland the street lamps, and rosy Santa Clauses salute with good cheer our wintry silence. My wife's stubborn profile makes her disappointment in me palpable. She does not understand that I am a man descending. I can't blame her because it took me years to realize that fact myself.

Revelation comes in so many guises. A couple of years ago I was paging through one of those gossipy newspapers that fill the news racks at supermarkets. They are designed to shock and titillate, but occasionally they run a factual space-filler. One of these was certainly designed to assure mothers that precocious children were no blessing, and since most women are the mothers of very ordinary children, it was a bit of comfort among gloomy predictions about San Francisco toppling into the sea or Martians making off with tots from parked baby carriages.

It seems that in eighteenth-century Germany there was an infant prodigy. At nine months he was constructing intelligible sentences; at a year and a half he was reading the Bible; at three he was teaching himself Greek and Latin. At four he was dead, likely crushed to death by expectations that he was destined to bear headier and more manifold fruits in the future.

This little news item terrified me. I admit it. It was not because this child's brief passage was in any way extraordinary. On the contrary, it was because it followed such a familiar pattern, a pattern I hadn't until then realized existed. Well, that's not entirely true. I had sensed the pattern, I knew it was there, but I hadn't really *felt* it.

His life, like every other life, could be graphed: an ascent that rises to a peak, pauses at a particular node, and then descends. Only the gradient changes in any particular case; this child's was steeper than most, his descent swifter. We all ripen. We are all bound by the same ineluctable law, the same mathematical certainty.

I was twenty-five then; I could put this out of my mind. I am thirty now, still young I admit, but I sense my feet are on the down slope. I know now that I have begun the inevitable descent, the leisurely glissade which will finally topple me at the bottom of my own graph. A man descending is propelled by inertia; the only initiative left him is whether or not he decides to enjoy the passing scene.

Now, my wife is a hopeful woman. She looks forward to the future, but the same impulse that makes me lock our apartment door keeps me in fear of it. So we proceed in tandem, her shoulders tugging expectantly forward, my heels digging in, resisting. Victoria thinks I have ability; she expects me, like some arid desert plant that shows no promise, to suddenly blossom before her wondering eyes. She believes I can choose to be what she expects. I am intent only on maintaining my balance.

Helen and Everett's house is a blaze of light, their windows sturdy squares of brightness. I park the car. My wife evidently decides we shall make our entry as a couple, atoms resolutely linked. She takes my arm. Our host and hostess greet us at the door. Helen and Victoria kiss, and Everett, who distrusts me, clasps my hand manfully and forgivingly, in a holiday mood. We are led into the living-room. I'm surprised that it is already full. There are people everywhere, sitting and drinking, even a few reclining on the carpet. I know almost no one. The unfamiliar faces swim unsteadily for a moment, and I begin to realize that I am quite drunk. Most of the people are young, and, like my wife, public servants.

I spot Howard in a corner, propped against the wall. He sports a thick, rich beard. Physically he is totally unlike me, tall and thin. For this reason I cannot imagine Victoria in his arms. My powers of invention are stretched to the breaking-point by the attempt to believe that she might be unfaithful to my body type. I think of myself as bearish and cuddly. Sex with Howard, I surmise, would be athletic and vigorous.

Someone, I don't know who, proffers a glass and I take it. This is a mistake. It is Everett's party punch, a hot cider pungent with cloves. However, I dutifully drink it. Victoria leaves my side and I am free to hunt for some more acceptable libation. I find a bottle of Scotch in the kitchen and pour myself a stiff shot, which I sample. Appreciating its honest taste (it is obviously liquor; I hate intoxicants that disguise their purpose with palatability), I carry it back to the living-room.

A very pretty, matronly young woman sidles up to me. She is one of those kind people who move through parties like wraiths, intent on making late arrivals comfortable. We talk desultorily about the party, agreeing it is wonderful and expressing admiration for our host and hostess. The young woman, who is called Ann, admits to being a lawyer. I admit to being a naval architect. She asks me what I am doing on the prairies if I am a naval architect. This is a difficult question. I know nothing about naval architects and cannot even guess what they might be doing on the prairies.

"Perspectives," I say darkly.

She looks at me curiously and then dips away, heading for an errant husband. Several minutes later I am sure they are talking about me, so I duck back to the kitchen and pour myself another Scotch.

Helen finds me in her kitchen. She is hunting for olives.

"Ed," she asks, "have you seen a jar of olives?" She shows me how big with her hands. Someone has turned on the stereo and I sense a slight vibration in the floor, which means people are dancing in the living-room.

"No," I reply. "I can't see anything. I'm loaded," I confess.

Helen looks at me doubtfully. Helen and Everett don't really approve of drinking—that's why they discourage consumption by serving hot cider at parties. She smiles weakly and gives up olives in favour of employment. "How's the job search?" she asks politely while she rummages in the fridge.

"Nothing yet."

"Everett and I have our ears cocked," she says. "If we hear of anything you'll be the first to know." Then she hurries out of the kitchen carrying a jar of gherkins.

"Hey, you silly bitch," I yell, "those aren't olives, those are gherkins!"

I wander unsteadily back to the living-room. Someone has put a waltz on the stereo and my wife and Howard are revolving slowly and serenely in the limited available space. I notice that he has insinuated his leg between my wife's thighs. I take a good belt and appraise them. They make a handsome couple. I salute them with my glass but they do not see, and so my world-weary and cavalier gesture is lost on them.

A man and a woman at my left shoulder are talking about Chile and Chilean refugees. It seems that she is in charge of some and is having problems with them. They're divided by old political enmities; they won't learn English; one of them insists on driving without a valid operator's licence. Their voices, earnest and shrill, blend and separate, separate and blend. I watch my wife, skilfully led, glide and turn, turn and glide. Howard's face floats above her head, an impassive mask of content.

The wall clock above the sofa tells me it is only ten o'clock. One year is separated from the next by two hours. However, they pass quickly because I have the great good fortune to get involved in a political argument. I know nothing about politics, but then neither do any of the people I am arguing with. I've always found that a really lively argument depends on the ignorance of the combatants. The more ignorant the disputants, the more heated the debate. This one warms nicely. In no time several people have denounced me as a neo-fascist. Their lack of objectivity pleases me no end. I stand beaming and swaying on my feet. Occasionally I retreat to the kitchen to fill my glass and they follow, hurling statistics and analogies at my back.

It is only at twelve o'clock that I realize the extent of the animosity I have created by this performance. One woman genuinely hates me. She refuses a friendly New Year's buss. I plead that politics should not stand in the way of fraternity.

"You must have learned all this stupid, egotistical individualism from Ayn Rand," she blurts out.

"Who?"

"The writer. Ayn Rand."

"I thought you were referring to the corporation," I say.

She calls me an ass-hole and marches away. Even in my drunken stupor I perceive that her unfriendly judgement is shared by all people within hearing distance. I find myself talking loudly and violently, attempting to justify myself. Helen is wending her way across the living-room toward me. She takes me by the elbow.

"Ed," she says, "you look a little the worse for wear. I have some coffee in the kitchen."

Obediently I allow myself to be led away. Helen pours me a cup of coffee and sits me down in the breakfast nook. I am genuinely contrite and embarrassed.

"Look, Helen," I say, "I apologize. I had too much to drink. I'd better go. Will you tell Victoria I'm ready to leave?"

"Victoria went out to get some ice," she says uneasily.

"How the hell can she get ice? She doesn't drive."

"She went with Howard."

"Oh . . . okay. I'll wait."

Helen leaves me alone to ponder my sins. But I don't dwell on my sins; I dwell on Victoria's and Howard's. I feel my head, searching for the nascent bumps of cuckoldry. It is an unpleasant joke. Finally I get up, fortify myself with another drink, find my coat and boots, and go outside to wait for the young lovers. Snow is still falling in an unsettling blur. The New Year greets us with a storm.

I do not have long to wait. A car creeps cautiously up the street, its headlights gleaming. It stops at the far curb. I hear car doors slamming and then laughter. Howard and Victoria run lightly across the road. He seems to be chasing her, at least that is the impression I receive from her high-pitched squeals of delight. They start up the walk before they notice me. I stand, or imagine I stand, perfectly immobile and menacing.

"Hi, Howie," I say. "How's tricks?"

"Ed," Howard says, pausing. He sends me a curt nod.

"We went for ice," Victoria explains. She holds up the bag for proof.

"Is that right, Howie?" I ask, turning my attention to the home-breaker. I am uncertain whether I am creating this scene merely to discomfort Howard, whom I don't like, or because I am jealous. Perhaps a bit of both.

"The name is Howard, Ed."

"The name is Edward, Howard."

Howard coughs and shuffles his feet. He is smiling faintly. "Well, Ed," he says, "what's the problem?"

"The problem, Howie, is my wife. The problem is cuckoldry. Likewise the incredible amount of hostility I feel toward you this minute. Now, you're the psychologist, Howie, what's the answer to my hostility?"

Howard shrugs. The smile which appears frozen on his face is wrenched askew with anger.

"No answer? Well, here's my prescription. I'm sure I'd feel much better if I bopped your beanie, Bozo," I say. Then I begin to do something very stupid. In this kind of weather I'm taking off my coat.

"Stop this," Victoria says. "Ed, stop it right now!"

Under this threat of violence Howard puffs himself up. He seems to expand in the night; he becomes protective and paternal. Even his voice deepens; it plumbs the lower registers. "I'll take care of this, Victoria," he says gruffly.

"Quit acting like children," she storms. "Stop it!"

Poor Victoria. Two wilful men, rutting stags in the stilly night.

Somehow my right arm seems to have got tangled in my coat sleeve. Since I'm drunk, my attempt to extricate myself occupies all my attention. Suddenly the left side of my face goes numb and I find myself flat on my back. Howie towers over me.

"You son of a bitch," I mumble, *"that* is not cricket." I try to kick him in the family jewels from where I lie. I am unsuccessful.

Howard is suddenly the perfect gentleman. He graciously allows me to get to my feet. Then he ungraciously knocks me down again. This time the force of his blow spins me around and I make a one-point landing on my nose. Howie is proving more than I bargained for. At this point I find myself wishing I had a pipe wrench in my pocket.

"Had enough?" Howie asks. The rooster crowing on the dunghill.

I hear Victoria. "Of course he's had enough. What's the matter with you? He's drunk. Do you want to kill him?"

"The thought had entered my mind."

"Just you let me get my arm loose, you son of a bitch," I say. "We'll see who kills who." I *have* had enough, but of course I can't admit it.

"Be my guest."

Somehow I tear off my coat. Howard is standing waiting, bouncing up on his toes, weaving his head. I feel slightly dizzy trying to focus on his frenetic motion. "Come on," Howard urges me. "Come on."

I lower my head and charge at his midriff. A punch on the back of the neck pops my tongue out of my mouth like a released spring. I pitch head first into the snow. A knee digs into my back, pinning me, and punches begin to rain down on the back of my head. The best I can hope for in a moment of lucidity is that Howard will break a hand on my skull.

My wife saves me. I hear her screaming and, resourceful girl that she is, she hauls Howie off my back by the hair. He curses her; she shouts; they argue. I lie on the snow and pant.

I hear the front door open, and I see my host silhouetted in the doorframe.

"Jesus Christ," Everett yells, "what's going on out here?"

I roll on my back in time to see Howard beating a retreat to his car. My tigress has put him on the run. He is definitely piqued. The car roars into life and swerves into the street. I get to my feet and yell insults at his tail-lights.

"Victoria, is that you?" Everett asks uncertainly.

She sobs a yes.

"Come on in. You're upset."

She shakes her head no.

"Do you want to talk to Helen?"

"No."

Everett goes back into the house nonplussed. It strikes me what a remarkable couple we are.

"Thank you," I say, trying to shake the snow off my sweater. "In five years of marriage you've never done anything nicer. I appreciate it."

"Shut up."

"Have you seen my coat?" I begin to stumble around searching for my traitorous garment.

"Here." She helps me into it. I check my pockets. "I suspect I've lost the car keys," I say.

"I'm not surprised." Victoria has calmed down and is drying her eyes on her coat sleeves. "A good thing too, you're too drunk to drive. We'll walk to Albert Street. They run buses late on New Year's Eve for drunks like you."

I fall into step with her. I'm shivering with cold but I know better than to complain. I light a cigarette and wince when the smoke sears a cut on the inside of my mouth. I gingerly test a loosened tooth with my tongue.

"You were very brave," I say. I am so touched by her act of loyalty I take her hand. She does not refuse it.

"It doesn't mean anything."

"It seems to me you made some kind of decision back there."

"A perfect stranger might have done the same."

I allow that this is true.

"I don't regret anything," Victoria says. "I don't regret what happened between Howard and me; I don't regret helping you."

"Tibetan women often have two husbands," I say.

"What is that supposed to mean?" she asks, stopping under a streetlight.

"I won't interfere any more."

"I don't think you understand," she says, resuming walking. We enter a deserted street, silent and white. No cars have passed here in hours, the snow is untracked.

"It's New Year's Eve," I say hopefully, "a night for resolutions."

"You can't change, Ed." Her loss of faith in me shocks me.

I recover my balance. "I could," I maintain. "I feel ready now. I think I've learned something. Honestly."

"Ed," she says, shaking her head.

"I resolve," I say solemnly, "to find a job."

"Ed, no."

"I resolve to tell the truth."

Victoria actually reaches up and attempts to stifle my words with her mittened hands. I struggle. I realize that, unaccountably, I am crying. "I resolve to treat you differently," I manage to say. But as I say it, I know that I am not capable of any of this. I am a man descending and I should not make promises that I cannot keep, not to her—of all people.

"Ed," she says firmly, "I think that's enough. There's no point any more."

She is right. We walk on silently. Injuries so old could likely not be healed. Not by me. The snow seems to fall faster and faster.

Guy Vanderhaeghe won the Governor's General Award for his first collection of stories, Man Descending. *His novel* The Englishman's Boy *won the Governor General's Award and was shortlisted for the Giller Prize.*

WAITING FOR THE RODEO

Aritha van Herk

WARNING: DO NOT COME TO CALGARY. THERE IS NO CRIME, NO MONEY, NO DISEASE. THE CITY HAS BECOME COMPLETELY CONVENTIONAL AND SHOULD BE AVOIDED. BY ORDER OF CALGARY CITY COUNCIL. SIGNED, MAYOR RALPH KLEIN.

TIP DID NOT CONSCIOUSLY DECIDE to ignore the posters, the newspaper ads, the radio and television bulletins. She was going to Calgary and she went, without much consideration of the consequences. That was the way she travelled; when the moment came, she followed it. If she had been one to listen to horror stories, she would never have gone anywhere. Every city had its drawbacks, its white-gloved commissionaires and fungus epidemics, its travelling magic shows. Audiences watched magicians like hawks; if they could detect a trick, the magician's apprentice was allowed to saw the magician in half, a ritual accompanied by goatish shouts and bellows. Too, Tip had once contracted a bad case of the staggers in Regina and had only been able to pull herself out of it by flying to Amsterdam and walking the cobblestones for a week. That had given her a bad scare and she never wanted to see Saskatchewan again. But it didn't stop her following her life's lust—to live in every Canadian city substantially enough to flaunt its markings in public. Everyone else wore their armbands and tattoos with a tribal loyalty; they only travelled when they were looking for trouble or because there was a rash of work.

For the last five years Calgary had been swollen with outsider markings, so much so that it would have been hard to find a native, but now, Tip knew from the television, the streets were empty and the wind howled down the glass coulees without ruffling much more than cement dust. Everyone had played Monopoly, tossing their dice on the sidewalks in front of the buildings they were gambling for. But the game had tired and the players packed up their Chance and Opportunity Knocks cards and went west, leaving behind the hopscotch outline of their chalked dice squares.

Tip always ran with the climate; when a city boasted a high suicide, divorce, and amputation rate, she was one of the first to move there, knowing that it would be a hot spot, a pride place to live. But now the deterring ads yearned her toward Calgary. She had never stopped there, only passed through on the TransCanada. And her life was getting predictable; it might be more fun to play in an unfashionable city. Most of all, she wanted to evade plot.

Tip owned a rusty U-haul for her moves. She never actually unpacked it, just pulled it up on the sidewalk in front of her crash. She had shoved all the stuff to the back and lived in it a few times when she hit a city with a housing shortage. It held the masked and intermittent objects that she had collected, had narrowed her eyes and imagined a future use for. She towed it behind her Ford.

Tip arrived in Calgary two weeks before Rodeo. As an economic joust, she decided to turn her pennies in. She went to the bank and asked for penny rolls. The teller brought her a dozen.

"Oh, that won't be enough."

"How meny dew yew wand?"

"A hundred." Each roll held fifty pennies.

The teller squinted. "A hunderd?"

"Yes. I've been saving them." For four years, she might have added, chunking them into her ten piggy banks, clinking them into empty mayonnaise jars. Now they waited, fat and heavy, to be emptied; for the plugs, the slots, the lids to release their copperbrown stream. Tip anticipated the ritual, shaking each container onto a heap on the floor, kneeling to count by fistfuls, rolling them into the brown cylinders. It was an afternoon's occupation and by the end of it her hands would be greenish, she would roll the last fifty and fold the ends down with satisfaction. She saved it up for herself the same way she saved the pennies, caching them in her piggy banks once a week or when she sorted her purse. She was never one who said to the cashier, "Oh, I have two pennies." She took them home for deposit in her own poor box, surreptitious pleasure in their accumulation.

She waited for a rainy afternoon, then bundled in an old woolen sweater with frayed wrists, she began to heap the pennies, tipping them into a noisy pile on the floor. She stood to cascade the piggybanks empty, rattle them from a satisfying height. Then, on her knees, she began to count and roll. Occasionally, she would stop to add the accumulating cylinders—fourteen, thirty-seven, fifty-five, sixty (she stopped for a cup of tea and streaked black across her face), ninety-two, and finally one hundred. There was still a small heap left and she separated it into piles. Eighteen, she would have to get more rolls. One hundred and eighteen rolls, fifty-nine dollars. She rocked back on her heels and stroked the neat cylinders with her palm. She would turn them in, all that extra weight shed, and use the paper bills to entertain a day. She divided the pennies between three plastic grocery bags and scrubbed her face and hands, feeling that she had completed her move, that she was settled.

The bags were so heavy she had trouble lugging them into the bank and she set them down on the teller's counter with a terrific clunk. The teller scowled. "Yew cand hand doze in all ad onze."

"Why not?"

"We don wand dem. Dere's doo many."

"What am I supposed to do, drag them off and bring them back two at a time?"

The teller shrugged.

"You're a bank, you're supposed to take them." Tip began hauling rolls out of the bags, slamming them down on the teller's desk pad. "Twofoursix eighttentwelvefourteensixteeneighteentwenty—"

"Hew many are there?"

"Hundred and eighteen—twentytwotwentyfourtwentysixtwentyeight-thirty—"

"All ride. Slew down." She counted, then re-counted them and put them back into the grocery bags before hauling them one at a time into the vault, wincing. When she returned to her computer stool she looked at Tip as if she were part of a hold-up. "Yeh?"

"You haven't given me the money. Fifty-nine dollars."

"Oh yeh." She opened her drawer and reluctantly extracted four tens, two fives and nine ones, crumpled and well-circulated. Several of the ones were criss-crossed with scotchtape.

"Don't you have any new money?"

"Newp."

Tip folded the bills once and tucked them into her hip pocket. She felt light as the dust that the wind was blowing across the parking lot in front of her feet.

To compound her re-location, she hung all her clothes up in her new mirrored closet and began to sort them, moving the hangers in a complicated chess of different seasons and occupations. Play clothes, work clothes, dress-up clothes, costume clothes, evening clothes, sexy clothes, maneuver clothes, impractical clothes, wornout but loved clothes. Then she re-sorted them according to their function. Pants, jeans, skirts, dresses, suits, blouses, ties, scarves, belts, sweaters, t-shirts, underwear. And then, began to tear them from their hangers, hold each considered item up for her critical eye; keep it or pitch it? It was hard for Tip to get rid of clothes—they had a past, they lacked the safe anonymity of pennies. Sorting clothes was unsettling; once the pile of hangers lay flung beside the pile of clothes to be discarded, she had doubts. Would she never wear that purple velvet again? Were those silk slacks really splitting at the seam, couldn't they be mended? The pile lay on the floor while she speculated, sometimes returning an item to a hanger and place in the closet, sometimes flinging even more onto the pile. Until she was utterly sick of the process, swept the bundle up in her arms and carried it down to the car wanting to be done with it once and for all. But then had to scan the yellow pages searching for where to abandon it: Goodwill, the Salvation Army? And thinking of that, had to consider consignment shops. Would someone else actually pay for her old clothes? She reviewed her discards again. She could take them to an amateur theatre; they must need costumes. The clothes wrinkled in the back window of the car while Tip tried to make up her mind. Finally, she stuffed them into the nearest clothing box in the nearest shopping center, not caring how wrinkled or stained they would get or who would parade them on the streets. And driving away, she saw in her rearview mirror the leg of a pair of red pants executing a limp kick out of the box's chute door.

She had worn those pants when she was the magician's apprentice, when she stood behind him on the stage after he had seduced the audience by conjuring rabbits and scarves and flights of paper birds, after he sawed her in half. He had insisted that she wear red pants, that she wear red pants with a black scarf, that she conceal within her pant legs the accoutrements of his trade. They were filled with pockets, huge expanding pockets, and driving away, Tip was worried that someone would try the pants on and discover themselves the magician's apprentice without any real wish to follow that profession, without agreement or their own volition. But she had to get them out of her life, until she discarded them she would always be reminded of her role as his sidekick, the cantor to his liturgical exercises. The job had paid well, but night after night she grew increasingly tense as time for the concluding act drew near. His finale was to place her in a kind of pine coffin and saw the box in half, all very realistically, the saw rasping at the wood, the crumbs of sawdust flying so that the audience, certain of the act's authenticity, thrilled to be watching the terrible demise of what they took to be an endless stream of magician's girls (all tarts who had no life beyond magic), watching for a trickle of blood to appear on the floor under the coffin (which was always balanced each end on a straight-backed chair); they held their breath as the magician finished his laborious work, would knock the two halves of the coffin apart and wave his hand, whereupon Tip was supposed to spring up, the two halves of enclosing wood falling away from her red pants, her sexy bosom. The truth was that the coffins (a new one delivered by the local coffin-maker every day) were slightly larger than they appeared, so that she could tuck up her legs and curl herself into a ball in one half of the coffin; but every night she watched and listened to the progress of the saw so close to her ear, her unseeing eye, that the job began to wear on her. One night, unforgivably, right before the magician's finale, she stole the gate receipts and ran away, changing her name, her hair colour, her way of dressing so that he could not trace her. She even gained weight and consciously altered her walk. Magician's apprentices are not allowed to quit their jobs. They know too much. If he found her she was in trouble. And now he had. So the red flag of her discarded apprentice pants signalled both relief and worry. If he happened to see them walking down the street on a body's legs, he would know she lived here in Calgary now; on the other hand, they cast a sinister light on the rest of her closet and she was glad to abandon them to thrift shops and second-hand dealers. She wanted no reminders of her failed vocation.

Next, she had to learn money machine etiquette. When she first came to Calgary, she barged up without waiting her turn, looked over people's shoulders and was surprised when they turned and snarled at her. The rules were unbendable. You came up while someone was using the machine. You stood exactly three feet behind them, directly behind them so that they could use their back as a shield, and if they glanced over their shoulder at you, you looked away into the distance. You were no machine thief, you had no intention of watching them punch in their number and then bashing them on the head in order to steal their card and commit computer crime, emptying their programmed and helpless accounts of their programmed limit.

While break-in artists left polite lists of what they had taken (for insurance purposes) and homeowners left a chicken in the fridge for hungry break-in artists, the elaborate ritual of money machines was played out 1900 times an hour all over Calgary, customers brandishing their punch-in cards, their key numbers cleverly memorized (one street in from the back door, the fourteen stations of the cross, subtract the last digit of my birthdate from the first), all following the indelible etiquette of the money machines, protocol as rigid and unyielding as the plastic and metal consoles it was performed for, an elaborate punctilio. Tip tried to ignore rules but the behavior proved infectious and she averted her eyes with as much disdainful courtesy as everyone else. "Who, me? I'm not trying to see your number. I'm just waiting my turn." Nobody knew where the money came from although everyone used the money machines and everyone had a different limit, seemed to have a different monetary designation. Trading numbers and cards had become a gambling racket—you threw yours in the pile to see if you could come off with a higher limit. Even better, the money that the machines doled out was always crisp and new, a pleasure to riffle between the fingers. Money machines were illegal down across the line.

Still, Tip needed a job. The most prevalent occupation in Calgary was that of doorman. Most places had at least one doorman; high class places two or three, a head doorman, an under-doorman, who stood a few steps in front of the head doorman, and a street doorman, who stood at sidewalk level. They were all dressed in top hats and tails, with gold-headed canes across the arms of the head doormen and whistles around the necks of the street doormen. The whistles were to summon rickshaws. The doormen, whose primary employment was staying on their feet, were always yawning, huge molar-displaying yawns that would crack a normal person's jaw, but the doormen were used to it. The problem was that the yawns were contagious, and if you passed a doorman you were sure to catch yourself in the middle of a yawn half a block farther. It got so that people would avert their faces when they passed, all the doormen saw were the backs of heads and determinedly walking bodies. Of course, when you came out of a cave at eleven o'clock at night, pitch black and raining hailstones, there were no doormen around, they were all in the back gambling or trying on each other's uniforms. The biggest union issues were changes of colour and cut for the tailcoats.

The big event came. Rodeo, when the city went naked, resulting in a carnivale levelling, everyone stripped of status and design. As compensation, the animals carried the people's clothes; there were cats with feather boas around their necks, horses wearing buffalo greatcoats, dogs in t-shirts. Because their hats and tailcoats were essential to their duties, the doormen kept those on, although they discarded shirts and pants and shoes, and were able to yawn just as effectively in semi-uniform. During Rodeo Tip got a job as a necromancer, using her magician's apprenticeship as experience. Curled inside his wooden coffin she had indeed felt herself close to the dead, even wondered if she should try to get closer. She sometimes thought what would happen if she remained stretched flat in the coffin, if she lay with her hands folded across her breast and her eyes lightly closed, with her legs neatly stretched, knee to knee and ankle to ankle under the incipient scrape of the saw, if magic would really happen, if the toothed blade would caress its way through her body without noticeable harm. That recurring idea was what made her decide to run away from the job. Some night she might be tempted to try it and would end up as titillation for the diseased audience.

Necromancy was a good racket down six-gun alley; everyone needed to communicate with their dead, not so much because of the future but because of the present, which was as close as most of them could come to imagining the future. All Tip had to do was persuade them that the voice coming from the ceiling was the voice of their own particular loved one, and with some artificial smoke and red lighting, a heavy and pervasive incense, most people were quite willing to believe that their mother, who had had a soprano voice in real life, would have a raspy contralto in death. The answers to their questions were easy to devise. Falling in love had become unfashionable, and most people's questions had to do with careers and jobs. There was no predictable plot. Tip dressed in an old wedding gown minus veil and train and wrapped a tie-dyed scarf around her curly hair. She put on some half granny glasses for disguise and made sure that she was wearing tennis shoes and that the dress was easily torn off. If the magician stumbled onto her, she wanted to be able to run.

When she wanted to Rodeo dance she went to the Brass Ring. Like everything else in Calgary, you had to know how to get in. You could hear the music, you could see bodies moving through intermittent windows, but you could not find the door; there was no door, you entered through a complicated series of inter-connecting underground passages and back alleys which let out onto a box alley that was always carefully watched. This was no place for hunters or pickups but for real drinkers and dancers, people who wanted to move to the inspiration of alcohol in their bloodstreams and the music—all of it old and hardly heard or remembered by the young. The average age was forty and the bouncer made an attempt to keep everyone under thirty out. Tip slipped him a twenty and got in that way; found herself a table in a dark corner on the lower level and waited for the morning, watching the people thump the brilliantined floor, watching the bodies work their way closer as the night wore on; she danced too, with the lean bandannaed men in wrist and neckline tans, uneasy with the nakedness required by Rodeo. All the music that the headphoned jockey played was from the fifties, Tip's mother's tunes. For Tip, this was a better memory exercise than the machines in the arcades. This was human, noisy, sweaty, the determined bodies writhing or leaning over each other, the broken strobe, the massive bouncer flexing his arm across the door, the table girl's ferocious seating plan, pointing out tables with a six-gun; if you moved without her permission, she'd shoot, hit a hamstring or a funnybone with narrow-eyed deliberance. Everyone was terrified of her pointed bouncing breasts and her choppy walk, her levelled finger. All the bouncer did was watch the door, she didn't need muscle.

The Brass Ring filled you up, satisfied you. When you hit the cool air of the alley at four in the morning, you were high, strung at a pitch that could keep you vibrating for hours. When you went home to sleep the dancing went on and on in your ears. Tip went to the Brass Ring every night after her red-light necromancies, danced and danced until her breasts fell from bouncing, ran all the way home and high-kicked inside the door before she put her earrings in the fridge and fell fast asleep, not even hesitating to dream about the magician she knew was pursuing her.

Every night during Rodeo the hot-air balloons puffed their way south, south-east above the city; a house, an ice-cream cone and a propane tank among the striped and shivering coloured globes. They floated and duffed, rose and fell. Tip watched for them, the slight hiss that they gave to the air, their implacable float. All of Calgary's dogs hated them, perked their ears and twitched sleeping tails and growled, dived under chairs or ran to windows and barked, tore madly after the balloon's wake or burst through screendoors into their human's houses. During Rodeo dogs scanned the sky before going outside, anxiety on their muzzles, their raised and pointed noses. The balloons began to fly longer, all day and all night, glowing teardrops hanging above the city in darkness, the balloonists as a dare beginning to detonate fireworks from their baskets, lighting the sky in unpredictably celebratory purples and greens. The dog population of Calgary went crazy, neurosis and psychosis increasing until they refused to chase cars or cats, refused to water hydrants and instead spent all their time eyeing the transfixed sky. The balloon baskets carried groups of laughing people having champagne breakfasts and cognac lunches, tossing pennies into the sky for luck, renting a feather bed basket in order to become a member of the hot air club, piquancy to lovemaking in the air that did not exist in the hotels and alleys below. Tip fell in love with a balloonist, even though he never removed his leather goggles and aviator's helmet, mainly because she wanted him to teach her his trade. His eyes behind the brown circles were kind, were preoccupied, and when he was on the ground he was always looking up, wanting to hiss his way to the mare's tails of clouds that streamed above the city.

One night in the Brass Ring with her aviator, Tip saw the magician. He was in disguise but she knew it was him, she recognized his mustache. At first she froze, then comforted herself that he would not recognize her. But of course he did and came toward her table, even though the table girl pointed her pearl-handled six-gun at him. He held up his palms, "I know these people," and she spun her gun around her forefinger and walked away.

"I've missed you," he said to Tip.

"Haven't you found a replacement?"

"She's not as good as you were." He smiled.

Tip was starting to sweat. The balloonist looked at the ceiling, he didn't notice. "I've got a new job."

He twitched his mustache and smiled again. "I wouldn't mind," he said reasonably, "if I could get back the pants that I had specially made for you. They were expensive and I think they'd fit the new girl."

"I don't have them anymore."

The magician looked thoughtful and drew at the blue silk bandanna that was knotted around his neck. It came undone and at his gentle tugs grew larger and larger until he held up a new pair of apprentice pants, blue this time, the pockets even more capacious than those of the previous pair. "I'd like you back," he said. "I'd teach you my tricks and you could eventually take over."

Tip shook her head. "There's no future in it. I'd always be your apprentice." The balloonist stood up to go to the can and the magician dared to lay a soft white hand on her knee.

"It's more secure than Calgary. Come now, my dear. Hanging out with balloonists and doormen? Not your style is it?"

"I like it fine. Better than being sawn in half every night." He ignored that. "I've added a couple of trunk escapes to my repertoire. You'd be perfect."

"What do you do? Stick swords through it?"

"See?" he said gently. "You know the trade. Clever girl." His hand vised itself over her knee. "Come on now, without making a scene. You know you were meant for me. Besides, the gate receipts . . ."

Tip had no weapon and the aviator must have encountered a lineup at the urinal. She stood up, the magician's hand squeezing her arm.

"No funny stuff now," he said happily.

Tip shook her head. They climbed the stairs, moved toward the edge of the dance floor which was right by the door. A greying cowboy lurched against them and turned to slur, "Hey sweetie, wanna dance?"

"Yes," said Tip. "Please." The magician had to let go. The cowboy steered her onto the floor of naked bodies and began to jive, spinning Tip around. She could see the magician by the door looking patient. There was only one exit.

"Please," she said to the cowboy, "I'm getting dizzy."

He swung her into a slow, belly-rubbing waltz and as they turned around the light-pinpointed floor, she worked him deeper and deeper into the crowd. At the end of the waltz she kissed his cheek and slithered to the floor, began to crawl towards the dark warren of tables. She knew without looking that the magician was starting to scan the crowd, check heads. She knew that in a few seconds he would act, would invade, if he had to, the whole of the Brass Ring, would either begin to perform or threaten: the tables would start flying through the air, the d-j's record would begin to spin backwards, the wind would begin to blow. Tip peered from under the edge of an askew tablecloth. One of his best tricks was making his apprentice disappear. Maybe, in the storm he was bound to create, in the energy he would have to unleash, she could make herself disappear. She chuckled suddenly. It was the old rule. If you guess how he did it, the apprentice got to saw the magician in half; the apprentice became the magician. Tip knew the story had to come from somewhere, it had to be possible. She held her breath and concentrated.

When does a magician's apprentice know that she has absorbed her master's knowledge? If she knew, there might be more rebellions, more magicians sawn in half for inflamed crowds. When apprentice becomes magician history hesitates. It's a rare occasion; most apprentices never dare to try. Tip squeezed her eyes shut and willed herself to disappear. When she opened them, she was floating above the table she had been hiding under and the Brass Ring was in an uproar. The magician was flinging bolts of lightning from his palms. Half the crowd thought it was part of the floorshow and the other half thought the situation was serious. The bouncer, who was closest to the magician, had grabbed him, only to find himself flat on his back in a corner with a lump on the side of his head and a chair leg bent around his wrist. There were screams, laughter, and Tip saw her pre-occupied balloonist lose both his goggles and his flying helmet to an unseen hand. She almost giggled but caught herself in time. Putting on his knowledge with his power made her see the indifferent strength of his illusion.

She stayed where she was and watched the turntable trail into silence, the confused jumble of the people on the dance floor, the lights going up to expose the stained walls and the empty glasses. The magician scanned the crowd for Tip, and then all his strength waned. He felt he had better sit down. She had escaped. He hadn't expected her to usurp his power, hadn't expected her to have the nerve to revolt so thoroughly. He was angry but he was also impressed. He knew enough to retreat gracefully.

He stood, bowed to the titsy table girl who strode up and levelled her six-gun at him. "You're supposed to stay at the table I give you," she said. "Those are the rules." She cocked the hammer of the gun.

"Would you like a job? I need an apprentice," he said.

She shook her head and pointed her gun toward the door. He looked at her and nodded and as he moved away, from his fingers drifted hundreds of tiny hot-air balloons that bobbed and swung in the draft of the room and its bodies, as though he were wishing Tip well.

The music began again.

The day after Rodeo ended, Tip took her fifty-nine dollars and went downtown to look for an object to add to her U-haul collection. Her necromancing was over and now she planned to become a hot air pilot under the tutelage of her preoccupied balloonist. The dogs had returned to their occupations, the doormen to yawning and the people to clothes. An Indian slept on a bench on the Stephen Avenue Mall and a window washer performed his tenuous ballet high against the side of a golden-mirrored building.

Tip looked up at the chartreuse sky, down at the dusty sidewalk. She had found the blue silk pants with the capacious pockets folded into a neat square in her mailbox. What if the magician returned? She stopped in front of a gun store. Inside were racks of shotguns, velvet cases of pistols, knives in leather sheaths. She went in and fingered a double-bladed throwing knife, then shoved it back across the counter at the clerk. "I don't think I need it," she said. As she pulled the wooden door shut behind her, she saw the half-effaced sign stencilled in gothic script on its glass. ALL STORIES   ND. The rack of twenty-twos in the window winked at her.

She would stay here, live in Calgary and wait for next year's Rodeo.

Aritha van Herk's most recent novel is Restlessness. *She is a winner of the Seal First Novel Award and has been nominated for the Governor General's Award for fiction. She is currently fiction editor for Red Deer Press and teaches creative writing at the University of Calgary.*

BOSS IN THE HOUSE

ARMIN WIEBE

A WOMAN CAN SURE DO LOTS OF THINGS if you only give her a chance. I mean, just look at Oata there driving that 27 John Deere combine like she was born on it. And her father always complained that his fat daughter couldn't do nothing right. For sure Nobah Naze would never have had to hire an oabeida if he had just let Oata do a few things. I mean, I only showed Oata how to drive the combine because she said she almost fainted while she was shovelling off the grain by the auger so I figured things would go faster if Oata could drive the combine a little while I shovelled. At least then we shouldn't have to hold up the thrashing each time the hopper was full. But now I can't get Oata off the combine, she likes it so much. And it's her combine so what can I do? I sit in the truck waiting for her hopper to fill up and I drive the half-ton to the yard and load off the grain with that old auger that has the motor tied together with binder twine.

Yes sir, Oata has come a long way since Nobah Naze died. Who would have thought only two months after her Futtachi went dead that she would be driving the combine all herself and that she would have engaged herself with me, Yasch Siemens the dow-nix, and be going with me every Sunday to church and *me* making a testimony by the Christian Endeavor and everything? But then who would have thought that fat Oata Needarp who we always nerked in school would have gotten a catsup bottle full with chokecherry wine from out of the cellar and made me forget that I was heista kopp in love with skinny Sadie Nickel? Well, such a thing you never really forget all the way, but for sure Oata has made me to see things different, like maybe it's not so bad to do things that other people do, like go to church and get married and be a farmer.

That's the best part, being a farmer. With my own land. Well, Oata's land and her mother's, but her mother is in the mental home and I mean the land will be as good as mine, at least after we've gone to stand the preacher in front in the spring when I have learned the catechism and let the eltesta pour water over my head.

It's pretty good really, watching Oata handle that combine. I sit here in the half-ton with a straw in my teeth and I feel like I'm in a cartoon that I saw in the *Cooperator* once about the olden days when people only had a little bit fur to wear for clothes and this man has these two women pulling the plow for him. Well, in farming you do what you have to to make it all work, and I am thinking that if Oata is so good with driving combine that means we shouldn't ever have to hire a helper to get the work done in the busy seasons.

Still, I wish Oata would let me drive the combine sometimes. Driving a big outfit, like a tractor or combine, now that's farming. A person feels real strong standing on a 4010 John Deere pulling a big CCIL disker or a twenty-foot John Deere deep tillage cultivator. Yes sir, when you turn that rig around at the end of the field and your hands and your feet smoothly move the brakes and the clutch pedal and the hydraulic lever and the throttle and you feel those shovels sink into the ground and the diesel puffs black from the muffler when the shovels are in a little too deep so you pull back to make it just right, well it's almost like it is with Oata when she is feeling her oats and won't let me go home for night. Mind you, Oata's 27 John Deere combine isn't exactly a big rig and her old Fordson Major tractor is no Versatile four-wheel drive. But it's a start and anyways it's the land that's important. I mean, a guy can have a big outfit but if he doesn't have a field to plow, what's the use?

But it bothers me a little bit when I come to Oata's place this morning and she is already with the grease gun by the combine pumping all the zirks full.

"Yasch, you go milk the cows. I have to change oil and clean the air cleaner yet!"

Change oil and clean the air cleaner? What knows a woman about that? And milking cows? Well for sure that is the woman's job, especially at thrashing time when the man should be busy keeping the combine fixed ready and stuff like that. On a farm it's supposed to be fifty-fifty—the woman works in the house and the barn and the man works with the machinery on the field. But what can I do? It's still Oata's place and I guess if she wants to do the man's work she can. I mean if I wasn't engaged with her she would have to do it all herself anyway, or hire somebody. So I milk the cows.

"Fry some eggs for breakfast!" Oata calls when I bring the milk out from the barn. "I'll be in to eat soon." Well, okay, I think to myself, just today, but for sure this isn't the way it's supposed to be.

So I'm picking egg shell out of the eggs in the frying pan when Oata hurries herself into the house and goes straight to the phone.

"A sprocket has some teeth broken out," she says as she cranks the phone for the operator. "I'm phoning John Deere Derksen to see if he has a new one." I put Oata's eggs on her plate and I hear her say, "Good, I'll come pick it up this forenoon."

Oata starts to eat her eggs and I say, "Maybe I can pick up some beer. It would sure taste good after a hot thrashing day."

"Oh you don't have to come with. I can find John Deere Derksen's place easy myself. Somebody has to wash dishes and feed the pigs and chickens yet."

"Wash dishes?" I don't believe what is coming to my ears.

"Yeah, they haven't been washed for two days already. I have to go." Oata hurries herself outside before I can even say anything more.

Well, I start to get dizzy. I mean it seems like something is turning the wrong way here. *I* should be getting the parts and *she* should be washing the dishes. I think maybe we should start having devotions and reading the Bible by breakfast time so that Oata can learn herself that the man is supposed to be the boss in the house.

I feed the pigs and the chickens. Then I look at the combine where Oata has taken the sprocket off. I think maybe I can finish changing oil for her but it is finished already. I go around with the grease gun but every zirk has lots of grease even the one I sometimes forget. The air cleaner has fresh oil and is wiped clean. The gas tank is full.

I look at my watch. I put gas in the auger motor and change the oil. I clean the spark plug. I start the motor up. It runs okay but I play around with the timing screw anyway. In the pasture I see the cows jumping on each other and I think I should maybe call Henry the bull, but Henry will be thrashing, too, and I don't think he would come. I clean out the little bit manure from the gutter in the barn and tickle the calf's ear. I pump full the water trough. Then I sweep out the granary that I swept out already last week. I go back in the barn and check to see if all the lights are working and I change one bulb in the hayloft that was burned out already last summer when I worked for Nobah Naze.

The sun starts to get hot. I see Hingst Heinrichs's truck driving on the mile road and it turns in by Ha Ha Nickel's. And I wish I was there again, working by Ha Ha Nickel's and playing catch with Sadie in the evenings. But that can't never be now. Sadie and Pug Peters are having a hurry up shroutflint wedding next week. So sticks the fork in the handle.

I am starting to get a little bit hungry when I see the dust from the '51 Ford coming down the road.

"Did you make dinner?" Oata calls when she jumps out of the car with the new sprocket in her hand.

"No," I say. "I didn't know when you were coming."

"Well, hurry go make something while I put the sprocket on. The forecast says rain for tonight!"

"No, you go make dinner. I can put the sprocket on." I reach for the sprocket and Oata swings herself away.

"No! I'll put it on and you go make dinner!" I reach for it again and Oata swings the sprocket with her arm and almost cuts my nose off. "Go make dinner!" Then Oata is bending over a little bit, drops the sprocket and holds her stomach with her hands.

"What's loose? Oata, what's loose?"

"Nothing. Just go make dinner." Oata picks the sprocket up and turns to the combine. So I go to the house wondering maybe if there was some egg shell in the breakfast and she swallowed some and has a stomach ache.

Well, making dinner doesn't hurry itself so easy because I have to wash some pots first before I can cook something and that old range takes so long to make the water hot and then I have to figure out something to cook and the potatoes have to be peeled yet and the knife doesn't want to cut the baloney and the water in the pot doesn't want to boil. When Oata comes in the potatoes are still so hard that you can hardly stick the fork in and the baloney is burned black in the pan.

"How come you didn't wash the dishes?"

"Didn't have time."

"Get some buns and jam. We don't have time to wait. You can fry the potatoes for supper."

So goes it then. Oata drives the combine, I load off the grain and make the faspa and cook the supper. We use the last clean dish. The rain holds off till two in the morning and we finish the field. I think tomorrow Oata will have time to wash the dishes.

I stand up a little bit late and when I get to Oata's place the '51 Ford is gone and Oata has put a big sign on the house door: WASH THE DISHES. Well, holem de gruel. What does that woman think this is? I mean Oata should like to be in the house washing dishes and listening to "Back to the Bible" and "Heart to Heart" on the radio. What's loose with that? So I don't even go into the house. Instead I do the barn chores and measure how much grain is in the granary and stuff like that. But by dinner time Oata isn't home yet so I go to Muttachi's to eat. While I'm driving my half-ton down the muddy road it all of a sudden falls me by that maybe I can ask Muttachi to come wash dishes and cook for us during thrashing when we are so busy. I mean everybody needs help at thrashing, so Muttachi could easy come over for a while and work for us and then we wouldn't have to worry about who will wash the dishes and cook.

But Muttachi doesn't think at all that it's a good idea for her to come and wash Oata's dishes. "What you think I am?" Muttachi says from the table where she is sitting with a cup of tea and a carrot and one small bun. "You think I will stick my nose into Oata's business? No way."

"You wouldn't be sticking your nose in her business. We just need some help now while we're so busy with thrashing."

"Who's thrashing today in the rain, huh?"

"Well . . ."

"How come you can't wash your dishes today when you're not thrashing?"

"Well, Oata went to town today and we don't have any . . ."

"So what's loose with you, you're not crippled! Why can't you wash the dishes?"

"But Muttachi, that's the woman's job."

"Who says it's the woman's job?"

"In the Bible it says the man is supposed to be boss in the house."

"Then go be boss in the house and wash your dishes!"

"But Futtachi never had to wash dishes at our place."

"Sure he did. Not very often, but he did. You were just too young to remember."

"Hey, is that all there is for dinner?"

"That's all I need. The doctor said I don't need to eat so much."

"Well, make me something, I'm really hungry."

"Go pull a carrot out of the garden and wash it off for yourself."

"No, I mean cook something!"

"Yasch, let me say you something. Twenty-three years I cooked for you and wiped your narsch. Now you're getting married I quit. I don't need to cook dinner for myself and I won't cook it for you. I will not come your dishes to wash. Besides, Shaftich Shreedas are taking me with to visit some people by New Bothwell so I don't have time to wash dishes for lazy people."

I'm really bedutzed now. My own Muttachi telling me that she won't make me something to eat and that she won't come to help me and Oata. It sounds like it's maybe the second coming or something. Maybe I should go to Preacher Janzen's place and tell him that it must be the end of the world. But my stomach is hanging crooked and it's growling and I know I have to go back to Oata's if I'm not going to die from hunger. I am flat broke so I couldn't even go to town to eat.

Oata isn't home yet and it's raining harder again so there isn't much that a person can do outside. So I go in the house and eat the last baloney with some buns and mustard pickles. I try to reckon out when I ever saw my Futtachi wash dishes or cook something and I'm thinking through when I was young and the things I can remember about my dad and all I can remember is about the time me and him cut pigs together. We had waited till the pigs were too old and five of the little boars died and that was the first time I ever knew that Futtachi hated to cut pigs even if he was doing it for all the neighbours. And I think about one other time when my Futtachi was very important to me, that time when I was nine years old and we were living in town because Futtachi was building the new elevator and the Brunk Tent Crusade came to the fair grounds and everybody went every night to hear the preaching, even Futtachi sometimes, though he was tired from building the elevator all himself, and this one night the preacher preached real loud and long and I was real scared that for sure I was going to go to hell because I was bad all the time and I had to try real hard not to let the tears come when they were singing "Just as I am without one plea" and the song is sure one to grab on to your tears, especially when you don't know what a plea is except that for sure you know you don't have one. When they had hummed it about ten times I just couldn't stand it no more, so I grabbed Futtachi's hand and he squeezed mine and I looked at his rough fingers and the thumbnail that was black from where he had hit himself with the hammer and the hand seemed so strong and big like maybe I could crawl all the way into it and then for sure no devil or satan that a Brunk Tent Crusade talked about would be able to hurt me and I held on to Dad's hand all the way home to that little house by the train tracks. And I wasn't scared one little bit.

My head reckons even farther back to the time when we still lived by Yanzeed. I was still very small when one night Futtachi woke me up and said we had to go to the hospital because Muttachi was going to get a baby. We drove into town and stopped by the hospital where there were lots of lights on and Futtachi said I should stay in the car and he took Muttachi into the hospital. I went to sleep in the car and then Futtachi came back alone and he said that Muttachi was going to stay there for a while and that was when Futtachi washed dishes. He didn't leave them for Muttachi to do when she got home. Even a few days later when Muttachi came home and there was no baby along and Futtachi said the hospital didn't have one fixed ready for us and Muttachi just went to bed and she stayed in bed for a long time, Futtachi was almost all the time cooking and washing dishes and I can't remember that he ever complained that he had to do women's work. When he finished washing dishes he played with me checkers on that old board with checkers sawed off from a broomstick.

So I'm sitting in Oata's house listening to the rain on the windows, smelling the dirty dishes, and I hear again my Muttachi say that for twenty-three years she cooked for me and wiped my narsch and for sure Muttachi is right like Muttachis always are. I feel real small. I look at the cupboard and the dishes. I get up, switch the range on and heat up a pail of water.

So I wash those dishes and it's not easy when the food has dried on for three days already, but I keep rubbing and scratching till I at least can't see no more dirt on them. And it doesn't seem like such a bad thing what with listening to the radio and looking out the window at the rain. Still it is almost time to do the chores when I finish.

I am creamering the milk when Oata comes home. She walks into the house very slowly. She is wearing her pink dress and looks like she's been crying.

"Oata, what is loose?" I ask quietly.

Oata doesn't say nothing, just sits down by the table. She doesn't look at me.

"Oata, where have you been? What's wrong?"

The clock ticks. Oata looks at me, then past me. "You washed the dishes!"

"Well, for sure. Somebody has to be boss in the house around here."

Oata smiles a little bit. "Sit down," she says. I sit down at the table across from her and put my hand on her hand. My hand is clean white from washing dishes and her hand still seems to have some grease from the oil change around the edges of her fingernails.

"Yasch, we will have to get married right after the thrashing is finished."

"Okay, but I thought we would marry ourselves in the spring."

"We can't wait that long."

"Why not?"

"Yasch, I'm going to have a baby."

"What?"

"I'm going to have a baby."

"A baby?"

"Yeah, a baby. So I don't think we should wait till spring to get married."

I don't know what to say. I mean for sure such things will happen when you stay for night, but well you just don't think that, well I mean it's just that how is a person to believe that such a thing could really happen, that that is really the way it's done. Sure a person knows all that but I mean you never know really that that is really cross your heart true. Oh shit, I'm just all mixed up.

"Yasch."

"What?"

"Are you mad at me?"

"Mad at you? What for?"

"Well, uh, well we have to get married early."

"For sure not. I mean we were getting married anyways."

"Will it bother you what the people will say?"

"What people?" I squeeze Oata's hand.

"Well, all the people."

"Oata, the only people that matter is us. If we let other people bother us we will never be happy. That's how we are." Then I remember that I still have to take the blue milk to the pigs. When I get to the door I think of something else. "Uh, Oata, now that you are having a baby does that mean you can't drive combine no more?"

Oata laughs. "Yasch, just because I'm going to have a baby doesn't mean I'm crippled. I can still drive combine. For sure it's easier than washing dishes."

Armin Wiebe's three comic novels—The Salvation of Yasch Siemens, Murder in Gutenthal *and* The Second Coming of Yeeat Shpanst—*have been nominated for awards such as the* Books in Canada *First Novel Award, the Stephen Leacock Award for Humour, and the McNally Robinson Book of the Year. He has served as writer-in-residence at the Saskatoon Public Library and the Parkland Regional Library in Dauphin, Manitoba.*

LIGHT READING

Meeka Walsh

She came from New York, at least that's what she said when asked. "Yes, I'm from New York," she'd say and sometimes she'd say, "Yes, I'm *of* New York," hearing when she said it what the questioner also heard. That is, a slightly pretentious assignment of place as though she were identifying herself as the Rothchilds of Paris so as not to be confused with, say, the Rothchilds of Geneva, when all she was really doing was being precise. She was of New York because she wasn't of any other place and she was of New York because it appeared to her—so far as she knew—that she wasn't the child of Mr. and Mrs. Father and Mother or the sister of Lydia Manhattan or Clive Brooklyn or Aunt Julia Queens. She was without family, had always been, so far as she could say, had no memory outside of this city, suffered no associative memory flashes or sense of dislocation and was, besides, sturdy on her feet and not the least bit lonely. She had just always been there, or here, in New York City.

To say she was never lonely is not to suggest that she was never unhappy. And here's why she was less than happy, though it could also be said that her reasons were insufficient. And one thing should be clear, she was no amnesiac; it was history she lacked, not recollection. She always knew where she lived, where the lettuces were freshest and cheapest, where she could find her papers and colours (because she was an artist) at the best price, and the names of all the artists and galleries and dealers and curators and who said and did and liked what and how they worked and why. Also where.

Her reasons for being unhappy, or less than content, had to do with light. She lived, luckily, in the neighbourhood of SoHo and in SoHo, on one of those nice, squarely intersecting streets in a building with seven floors, in a place which was on the fourth of the seven floors which was one room big enough to hold her bed and books and shelves for paint and paper and boards and the materials she used for her work and a table and two chairs, very nice with rush seats, and two large rocking chairs, each with its own woven woolen throw and plain cotton pillows and a small rug for the chairs' bowed bottoms and the ordinary things which are necessary for living. She lacked nothing, not plants to stand before the windows, nor equipment to provide music, nor fresh flowers or crusty bread, because she sold the things she made and it was sufficient. For light, of course, she had lamps; this is New York. Lamps and tracks and spots and all.

In her fourth floor room one row of windows opened to the street. Across the narrow street was another building, also seven stories. One of her windows on a side wall looked across the roof of a smaller building to a solid brick wall which had been painted to simulate a brick wall which had windows interrupting its surface. These windows were painted in detail with different curtains and window boxes and one had a balcony on which rested a flat, pigment cat. The window on the third wall opened to its adjacent building so near that if someone had held her ankles while she bellied on the sill she could leave crackers for the pigeons on the neighbouring ledge. The fourth wall opened to the hall. A commodious and convenient place to live and work but the sky was invisible, sunlight weakened by its travel through packed and dense New York air sifted briefly on her painted wood floors and then only in the months when it was highest in the sky as it rolled over the earth, lighting longer and more fully, she knew, in places other than here.

Now what, if she had all the convenience of manufactured light and this very nice room, was she wanting? And maybe, more importantly, why? Well, here's why, or maybe why. Since she didn't have a mother or father she could ask and anyway wasn't entirely sure about this question concerning happiness, she came up with an answer or what served for an answer, by herself. It had to do with being formed or set. (She thought in these terms because she was an artist.) What she believed, or felt she needed for happiness was a sense of being fixed, being set. At present, she felt as though she were an image on photographic paper and was just the smallest bit indistinct, not sharply etched, an image not fully emerged from processing. And an unassuming girl—seeing herself as basic and essential—the process she identified with was the photo-printing that even children could do involving light-sensitive paper, an object, and the sun. But here, the problem was access to enough of the sun, to its full light. Not its heat, mind you, just its light. Also, she felt—since so far as she could say, and about this she was fairly sure—she was missing some certain pure truth, some opening out that she believed parents transferred at birth or through raising, directly to their children, as a sustaining and necessary gift. She sought this as well as sufficient, completing light. If she were in a place with enough light this truth might present itself or could be determined.

On Saturdays in SoHo, vendors set up stalls or tables or sometimes only a blanket and offered wonderful things: silk scarves with patterns copied from the best French fashion houses, jewellery from India, New Mexico, Turkey, plastic shoes from Taiwan in colours like fruit jellies, T-shirts with edifying slogans, sticky sugared pecans, soft pretzels, charred chestnuts and, best of all, books—new art books, histories, biographies and the treasures of the world's great museums. Also heavy, old, hard-sided books that cracked and puffed dust when you laid back their covers. These, lacking her own history, interested her most. She picked up an atlas as big as a journey itself and opened the front cover. It had been printed in England in 1923, a year of no particular significance, a good year to consider the world. When she tucked it under her arm it rested on the jut of her hip and bit softly into her underarm. She carried this wall of a book to her building around the corner, up the four flights and laid it out on the wooden floor in the small panel of light stencilled there. She pressed back the cover and lifted the first page. It was stiff and dry, foxed and brown at the edges which crumbled in her fingers. The page lifted from its binding and she set it aside. She was scanning the topographies printed in pale colours, reading the drawn ridges of foothills and small coloured cones representing mountain ranges, looking for a place where nothing would interfere with the sun's light; she wanted no shadows. In New York the Meissen glass and steel verticals, the cast iron building fronts, the engineering advances which had allowed structures to rise and rise so that they swayed with the wind and still remained standing—this architectural forest blocked her light. She wanted no geographical impediments either, if she were to leave this place. Page by page she picked off countries, regions, cities, setting them aside like the sheets of a calendar. Afghanistan, Bolivia, Chile, Japan, Nepal, Peru, Pittsburgh, Rotterdam, Toronto, Uruguay, Victoria, Winnipeg. She paused. Here there was nothing—a single, solid colour denoting flat planes, no marked, zigged ridges of mountains, not even shading suggesting rolling hills. Flat, in the middle of the continent and no mountains below or above. Here she would go. She could feel her breath move free in her chest. Here would be light. Some things change over years; facts concerning population and crops could be outdated but hours of sunlight and levels of rainfall are mostly static. She consulted the book's appendix. Yes, Winnipeg was blessed with sun year round. Temperatures were of no moment, she decided. Just like that—she packed, sold what remained of her work, had her furniture crated and shipped by truck. A few days later she followed it, flying, she felt, under her own power, supported by the light and space she could see increasing as she flew west and then north.

It was February and no one moves to Winnipeg in February but she didn't know this. All she knew was that in New York, without light, she would disappear. The atlas hadn't mentioned that in February the sun would be low in the sky for much of the time on either side of noon. The sky, as noted, was blue, such a blue that she could only open her mouth wide and drink it in in a bubble that hurt her chest with joy and excess. The atlas hadn't said—or maybe she'd neglected to read that everything, everything would be covered in a crust of white and that this white was such a white that even after the sun slid from its high point her eyes—two apertures fixed at open—recorded the dazzle and stored it so that she read without turning on the overhead light, late into the nights. So ready and so sensitive to light was she that she was able to perceive that day by day each one began earlier, and evening by evening each one began later. So the light stretched. In this light, this extraordinary sweet and liquid light she expected to find the city of Winnipeg filled with artists. In time she came to recognize that this was so.

Through habit she located herself at the city's centre in an area which, if the city were more crowded and jammed with commerce, would be as like SoHo as any other. Named for its history as a centre of trade it was called The Exchange District and here, in an old building, she made her home. Now she lived on the fifth floor of a red brick building but there were no floors above hers and no buildings so near that they blocked the light that washed through the high arched windows or ranged along the other two walls of what she knew now was her home.

Close by was a long wide street, so wide she might have thought she was in Paris and that this was the Champs Elysées, so generously did she wish to see, and her eyes still dazzled by light. This was Main Street she was told and it ran north and south on an uninterrupted axis. And here, at its middle was another wide, wide street and this one ran from east to west and it was named Portage Avenue and where they met was a star and when she stood in this star late one night after all the traffic had stopped she felt to be in a magnetic centre, this Portage and Main, which set her very being right, pulling and pushing her awkward misalignments until she was steady as the tumblers in an oiled lock.

The surprise, the almost unnecessary bonus, she felt, was that with the lengthening light came increasing warmth, not that she'd been troubled by the cold. In the warmth the white crust covering everything softened, turned lacy, fell in on itself and washed away. Now, the quality of light changed and she became alarmed. There would be less of it if there were no reflecting surfaces.

"But haven't you seen the rivers?" someone asked her when she mentioned her concern. "There's light there," they offered, and she headed out following a directing finger, down Main Street to the sign indicating The Forks. And here, like the wide intersecting streets were two broad rivers, one flowing from the south and the other co-mingling with it from the west to become a single wide moving band of water heading north. So the Red and the Assiniboine Rivers, wide both, moved along through the city playing with light.

Every day for a week she watched to see what they did with the light they were given and every day they showed her something new. First they were filled with ice, churning, rough-shapen tesserae in a moving mosaic that offered and withheld light as the brief surfaces elided, slipped and washed away. As the ice melted the rivers grew full to the lip and appeared sluggish and smooth. Only close looking revealed the treacherous turning and speed beneath their surfaces. They mirrored the sky and were blue or they flicked their silver and grew opaque. As the volume diminished the rivers relaxed and light laughed from the broken surfaces seemingly benign as shallow lakes. A thousand fractures gave back sun. When the sun set, the rivers were orange and rose then blue, before they went dark to begin again with orange and rose at first light.

Winnipeg pleased her, its very artfulness always present, and late one afternoon she attended an exhibition held in a gallery on the upper level of a fine old building very near where she lived. She paid close attention to the art on the walls, to conversation with other artists and viewers but found herself drawn unavoidably to the gallery's large windows through which the sun was still visible. Looking out she was pleased to note her own building and recognized how much like an Edward Hopper painting it was, dark red brick against an empty sky. It confirmed, as did the light, that she'd found home in this flat city which sat resolutely on the prairies, always showing its face and flanks to the sun.

She walked daily and marked the absence of subterranean places. This was indeed, a city of light. And those few places which had been constructed as "under" places were quiet passages, locations for passing through. For their very briefness she liked them. One on McPhillips Street another on Pembina Highway, one at the north end of Main Street, another very near her river forks. All of them supports for trains, bridging the wide streets that filled the city. She would walk up and back through these substructures enjoying the show and play of light on her closed lids as she passed into and out of darkness. She examined the substance of these locations looking down as well as up, and liked what she found there—the dust and debris, the city's detritus: pigeon feathers, newspaper pages yellowed so as to be suitable for application to an early Braque or Picasso, shards of birds' eggshells, cottonwood cotton, a coloured scatter of confetti and a gather, near the gutters, of elm seeds which she'd put in her mouth and chew slowly. She began to collect these fragments and determined that she would apply them to sheets of stiff paper and reconstruct, in collage, her loved city from its own shed skin.

From her loft it was an easy walk to the boulevard called Broadway, resembling not at all the Broadway she'd known earlier, this one being green and treed. As she walked its length she recognized that she, like this small resolute prairie city, was also becoming more resolute. In the steady light the emulsion she imagined was her surface, was fixing, holding. "I'm coming into focus. I have a clearer form," she told herself, and wrapping her arms around her body she took pleasure from the substance she found there.

Someone had mentioned the Legislative Building. "And don't forget to look up when you get there," she'd been told. So she did and there she saw, situated on the very point of the dome, the Little Prince from Oscar Wilde's story for his son. A perfect golden statue and she imagined she could almost pick out the jewels set into his fine eyes. "Safe there," she thought. "Too high for birds to pluck." Now she felt brief envy. There was this lovely golden boy untroubled by any need for shelter and all around him, a bath of light. She coveted only his uninterrupted access to all that light. "Still," she told herself, "I'm developing nicely."

And what of her earlier sense that she'd failed to receive, or had missed a basic truth? She'd found light, a wonderful full light here in this city but would Winnipeg present her with this missing truth? How magical could the city be?

She was without parents, made from the stuff of a bigger, fuller place, the fabrication of New York. For completion she'd been drawn to light and had found another city. Here she could look into a mirror and see with certainty that she was fully emerged, sharp and distinct. Generous light had shown her that the truth is: you are always, wherever you are, your own manufacture. Knowing this she'd become a true citizen.

Meeka Walsh has published a book of journals, Ordinary Magic: Intervals in a Life, *and a collection of short stories,* The Garden of Earthly Intimacies. *Recently she edited a book of photography,* Diana Thorneycroft: The Body, its Lesson and Camouflage. *Since 1993 she has edited the international arts magazine* Border Crossings. *Her writing has earned Gold Medals at the National and Western Magazine Awards.*

BETWIXT AND BETWEEN

JOAN CRATE

THE CHILDREN, each tucked under an arm, press into his warmth. "A story, Daddy," Sarah pleads, and before he can answer, Zach has slithered off the chair and snatched a book from the shelf. *Peter Pan.* It's their favourite, Khalil's as much as the children's, and the pages are pocked from his big thumbs flipping them over and over again, the children's sticky fingers snatching at magic.

"Peter Pan was a strange creature," Khalil begins, "A betwixt and between, neither one thing nor the other." I look up from the elusive buttons I'm attempting to attach to Zach's denim overalls, the needle poking through the holes of the button, getting lost in faded cloth, and see three pairs of molasses-coloured eyes glistening with anticipation.

They take after Khalil's side of the family, our children, the same dark eyes and hair, though their skin is lighter, like mine. We compromised on their names, chose ones that are acceptable in both Arabic and English, though Zach's name is really Zachariah. Still, they are Canadian children, and sometimes I wonder if they could fit into the scrambled puzzle of their father's homeland.

Khalil refuses even to consider taking them to Lebanon to visit. "Not until the wars are all finished," he says, "and that may be never." Still, I wonder whether or not they would feel any attachment to their grandmother, their aunts, uncles, and cousins whom they resemble, but whose language they cannot understand. A family of strangers. And the physicality of the land. Would they feel at home there? Could the sky and sea unveil hidden dreams; or would it be only a foreign country, an address to send postcards from? "Today I helped Grandma dry *burghal* in the sun. Tomorrow if there are no snipers, we'll go down to the sea. I miss you."

Khalil has told us about the farm he grew up on, the almond and olive trees, pomegranates the size of two fists, figs and dates, the five kinds of apple trees, and fields carved from the side of a mountain and brimming with tomatoes and watermelons, until we could smell the swollen fruit, taste its warm juices, and feel the baked mountain soil and scorched air on our skin. We were there, or at least we imagined we were, but really, each of us was in our own familiar world. We can never totally shed the prejudices imposed on us by our birthplace. This I discovered one day when I asked Khalil how big his family's farm is.

I'm no stranger to farms. I grew up on one southeast of here, near Fleming. Every summer I take the children to visit and often Khalil drives down on the weekends to argue with my father about pesticides and taxes over a beer and one of Dad's machine-cranked cigarettes. The children love their grandparents' farm, the space—land stretching as far as the eye can see. Forever, I thought as a child. Planted with just one crop, an endless golden chorus. Dad always takes Zach and Sarah for rides through the fields on the old John Deere, points out the quarter section that their great-great-grandfather started with, tells them stories of old horses and frostbite, and how in the dirty thirties the farm was almost lost to the bank. Although they've seen it all, have heard each of Dad's stories, they find themselves again immersed in earth and words, mesmerized by the unbroken line of land, sky, and generations.

"We had the equivalent to . . . let's see . . . almost five acres," Khalil replied.

Sarah and I burst into laughter. "Almost five acres? You call that a farm?"

I push at the needle, try to coax it through the uncooperative fabric, the too small button hole, then give up and clamp my teeth around it and yank with my jaws. What the hell, it works. But Sarah has noticed. "Mo-om, that's not very safe," she admonishes, stroking the wrinkles from her corduroy pants with delicate fingers, as if it's a gown she's wearing, silk and lace.

We tease Sarah, tell her she was born into the wrong class, and she solemnly agrees. She has such an aristocratic bearing, has had since she emerged from my womb clearly disdainful, and ten days late. She stared blindly down her perfect nose at Khalil and he kissed her and called her "princess." Sarah means princess.

Of all the places we've visited only one has ever lived up to Sarah's impossible standards: Notre Dame Cathedral in Montreal. We were in the city visiting Khalil's sister, Yasmine, and she took us to the cathedral. Sarah and Zach, who was just a toddler at the time, were holding hands, but once inside the entrance, Sarah gazed up into the dome, felt the height, the distance, saw gold-leaved walls, intricately carved alters, statues of bruise-eyed saints, the holy, flowing fountains, mosaics of angels, of the serpent, of Christ stepping from death to immortality, all dyed by shades of light pouring from stained glass windows, and her hands flew into the air. "Yes," she cried, voice shrill amongst the dull murmurs of tourists, and she twirled, eyes lifted to the highest point in that ceiling, hundreds of yards through space. "Yes," more quietly, her tone approving. She sat down on the front pew and glanced contemptuously at those less full of grace shuffling by.

"As if she owned the place," Yasmine commented later as she served us tiny china cups full of sweet, thick coffee. Khalil and I had to agree. Strange what we think we have a right to. Everyone, not just Sarah.

Would she, would Zach, look pale beside the sun-brown faces of their Lebanese relatives, their clothes—fleece sweatsuits and insulated jackets—so terribly out of place, their voices too low and even their limbs, their movements, expansive, melting away in the raucous heat, the shouting, wailing, the explosions, and dazzling sunlight? Would they disappear like so many in Lebanon have done before, but their demise different, nothing to do with guns and blood, a simple dissipation into the air, a transcendence into the vast, sweeping lines of Canada, the hush of winter, their home.

Sarah, Khalil says, reminds him of his niece. Rima, her name was. She was his sister's oldest, and beautiful too. He teased her when she was young, called her "cow eyes." "But really, her eyes were heart-breaking, so large and soft." She was too young to die, just fifteen.

He kisses Sarah's forehead and her nostrils flare slightly against his scratching whiskers. She points to the picture of Wendy, Michael, and John airborne in the bedroom, their beds small countries below them, the boundaries escaped.

Rima ran off and married a man from the mountains, a Shiite Muslim, and her Christian father was incensed. "He wouldn't accept Rima's marriage, was furious, and my sister finally got fed up with his anger and moved back to my parents' house. She and her six other daughters."

I remembered then that Khalil's parents lived in a tiny cottage, three rooms, he had said before, and I tried to imagine the snarl of bodies and gossip, bed rolls, summer sweat and girls' secrets.

One uncle told Khalil that Rima's father hiked up the mountain one day to find his daughter. He wanted to tell her he forgave her for her marriage, to accept his new Shiite son-in-law into the family, and to finally make peace with his wife and six other daughters, still giggling and quarrelling in their grandparents' shack.

But Rima was shot. Her father shot her, or maybe it wasn't him. She could have been caught in crossfire between her father and her husband. Or her husband's friends. Who knows? There are too many stories, too many theories; every relative has a different one. "So which one is right?" I finally shrieked at Khalil in frustration. "Who killed Rima? What is the truth?"

He shrugged.

She was carrying a basket of pomegranates, and when she fell they splattered over the ground. At first her husband thought she had tripped, that the red stains around her were merely pomegranate juice, and he ran to her, her father ran too. I suppose that's when they stopped trying to kill each other.

When I look at the old photographs Khalil keeps in a dresser drawer: his mother and father old and bent from their years together raising children, some who are still in Lebanon, some in Canada, some dead; his six nieces standing over lumpy bags of their belongings, his sister and brother-in-law staring uneasily into the camera lens, the farm, the old donkey long since left in the hills for the wolves, I feel the weight of heat and dust, of anger and gesture impossible to understand, of overwhelming confusion, and I tuck them away under his pile of winter sweaters.

"Tick-tock, tick-tock," the children chorus joyously. Captain Hook aboard his pirate ship winces. Time is running out.

I re-thread the needle and glance towards the fingerprint-smudged window. Outside there's a chinook. Dark cloud is sliced neatly away by a blade of yellow sky and the trees blow with a west wind that tears the snow to tatters. Tomorrow a fresh snow is expected, or so the weatherman says.

I like snow, the way it insulates everything, keeps Khalil's and my pasts separate, yet pushes us together here and now, seeking the warmth of one another's bodies, drifting us into a future together. "Too many differences," my father said when I told him I was going to marry Khalil so many years ago.

"Nevah-nevah land," Zach squeals, pointing at the book. "Never-never land," Khalil repeats, trying to enunciate, though he's never been able to master the Canadian *r*.

Zach has his grandfather's way of watching, Khalil has said many times, the same expression. Just a few months ago we heard that the old man had disappeared. Khalil called his mother's neighbour, the one with the phone, and she ran to get his mother. It was the morning of the next day in Lebanon, the sun already beginning to bleach colour from the trees, but in Calgary it was the middle of night and the sky was stung with cold, white stars. I counted them from the bedroom window while he talked to her, his voice so familiar, so foreign, speaking words I couldn't understand. They had found no trace of his father.

The afternoon he disappeared he and his wife had finished lunch—feta, black olives, bread, tomatoes, and strong, sweet tea, she told Khalil—and then he kissed her throat the way he had done for years—and left for his daily hike up the rocky path, up into the mountains.

He didn't return. No clothing was found, not the ragged patch of a shirt on a prickly *shummuleh* bush, no shoes thrown down a ravine. No shadow torn away like Peter Pan's and left, a smoky film on the ground.

Khalil is at the part of the story where Peter begs Wendy and her brothers to stay in Never-never land and not go back to the real world where they'll grow up and grow old, develop aches in their joints, cry, and worry too much. This is the part the children don't understand, that as a child I questioned. Why didn't they remain in the ageless circle of fairy light, play at being a mother, at being a hero, battle the evil but ultimately harmless Captain Hook and win, win forever? Suddenly they're back in their bedroom at home with Nana the Newfoundland dog.

"Was it a dream, Daddy?" Sarah wants to know. She's getting older, I realize, beginning to understand the uncertainty of truth, the diverse ways it can be interpreted. Khalil and I exchange glances. He winks. Sometimes it seems as if I've always known him and we're each part of something whole. But once we watched a hostage who was released in Beirut on the news, and he said, "When I was kidnapped. . . ." Then I realized there's so much about his life I don't know. He was afraid then, and his fear seeped into the room, into me, and I was afraid too, of our pasts, the places in each other we can't enter, can't even imagine. These are our own personal stories deplete of magic, that bellow out every now and then, that will not be silent, and each language is foreign to the other, though we try. We each try to understand.

Khalil's at the end of the book now, where Mother and Father kiss Wendy and her brothers. As a kid I thought this was pretty corny. Me, the daredevil on a John Deere charging down country roads, and as a young teenager sneaking out my bedroom window and running off with forbidden friends to forbidden parties, always wanting to get away. Now I'm satisfied with this, find the foggy London air, the cozy parlour soothing after swords, ropes, and cannonballs. Even Zach and Sarah look content. Khalil closes the book.

"Want to go outside and make snowballs?" he asks the children, and they run for their coats. "You coming?"

"In a minute, after I finish Zach's pants." The thread struggles up through the last button, anchors it. I can't sew worth a damn. I'm not much of a cook either, but Khalil doesn't care. We use team work to keep house, raise our children, much to his sisters' chagrin. I'm not the responsible little mother I once thought I wanted to be. I've grown up.

I watch him through the window as I knot the thread clumsily, clip the ends away. Sarah and Zach squeal with delight as he sprays them with a handful of snow. They chase him and he falls, rolls on the ground with them, laughing, all three of them laughing. I grab my coat and head out the door.

I catch Khalil gazing up into the sky where warm chinook wind has burrowed through the cloud. There's a hole there someone could fall through—a terrible accident, one blink and they're gone. Or perhaps it's a tunnel for those who must escape a night too dark, a world too strange, one in which they no longer belong: a young torn wife, a tired old man. John, Michael or Wendy. Even Jesus.

Joan Crate teaches First Nations literature and creative writing at Red Deer College. She has won awards for both her short stories and her poetry. She has published a novel, Burning Water, *and a book of poetry,* Pale As Real Ladies: Poems for Pauline Johnson.

HEY

David Bergen

Sometimes in the evening Lily pitches to me. It is the hour between light and dark so I have to strain to see her face; in fact, the blue of her eyes is not there, so all I see are dark holes that flash occasional light. Her arm, a windmill, is a blur, and suddenly the ball is there spinning out of the dusk into my mitt, stinging my palm. I crouch and give her signals, but mostly she can't see them or ignores me and gives me curves, change-ups and fastballs aimed right at my nose. Then it's too dark to see and she yells, "Hey," and ambles towards me. I hunker down and watch her come, small flower, sweat beading on the nose I can't see and, ah, she's there, her crotch level with my face, her loose jeans dusty from a thwacking glove, and she says, "Good. That was good."

She's good; a small woman with a big accurate arm. She puts her medium-length blonde hair up inside her hat and looks like a child. Initially she fools the batters. They get cocky and she gets impish and actually laughs as they go down swinging. I love to watch her pitch and for a split second as she releases the ball she is airborne. She lands with her head cocked to the left, following the pitch; she is dropping pebbles into a frog's mouth.

She can't hit so I try to teach her. I stand behind her, my belly on her shoulder-blades, and slow-mo a swing. But she shrugs me off and says, "I'm a pitcher. I don't hit." Actually, she thinks it would be sacrilegious to hit off another pitcher. Sometimes, when the ump doesn't show, I take over and then Lily gets angry with me. At the end of an inning I follow her with my eyes from behind my mask and watch her kick a water-bottle or wing her glove at a parked car. In those moments I think of what great breasts she has, small fauns, and how I want to share them with the whole world.

I begin to ump regularly. Two games a week. Sometimes I ump Lily's games, sometimes not. Lily says she's going to lodge a complaint. She says I'm tougher on her than on other pitchers. "Your judgement's way off," she says.

"Lodge away," I say, allowing silently that she may be right. "I call 'em as I see 'em," I add and grin. Actually, the strike zone in fastball is higher than in baseball and a lot of people have a hard time grasping that.

Lily knows exactly where the strike zone is and likes to play the edges. I let her do that a bit but not for a whole game. "You make a good ump," Lily says. "Just like you make a good teacher. You love rules." I shrug. Sometimes I think I like this kind of umping because I'm surrounded by the turning, milling, sliding and sweating of female bodies. But I don't admit that. I'm not even sure if that's right.

Lily is studying religion. She has one degree and now she's going for another. I don't mind this except sometimes I get tired of teaching just so she can fill her head with Eckhardt and Brueggemann. I try to be fair but I keep asking, "And to what end?" I guess what I really want is to move to the suburbs and have a family. Lily says, "No problem, just three more years."

I take her to open-houses on Sundays and we traipse around these showhomes that are vast and carpeted and all look the same. I love their common features, their smell of glue, wood shavings and paint. I pull Lily into the kitchen and show her the European cabinets and their extended hinges. She patronizes me and studies the cutlery drawer. The family room has a fireplace, and I tell her we could install an energy-efficient stove, use the room as a baby room: playpen over there, mobile hanging here. When we leave these places she looks confused. And I am angry. It is in part because of these futile Sundays that quite suddenly one day I decide to leave her.

This day too is a Sunday. My parents are having company, a theologian and his wife, and ask Lily and me if we will join them for lunch. Lily, who has read this theologian and doesn't like him, jumps at the chance. I roll my eyes, bracing for acrimonious table-talk. We arrive and are introduced to Len, a tall, thin, bearded man who bites his nails, and Elsie, who is much younger than Len and has her hair pulled back. She is a tall woman with a stately, young, clean face. During the meal I keep smelling something nice, which I deduce must be Elsie. She strikes me as a woman who wants to be something or somebody she can't. We sit down and my father prays. I watch Elsie, who is staring at her plate.

My mother serves roast beef, baked potatoes and stir-fried vegetables. I am sitting across from Elsie. As usual, my mother is up more than down, running for food. Lily, Len and my father have conquered one end of the table and are talking liberation theology. I remember how Lily, in one of her stages, came to bed with books by Gutiérrez and Echegaray and talked about structures. I pour Elsie some ice-water. She asks, "What do you do, Andy?"

"Teach school," I say. She waits, so I continue. "Junior high math." She nods. I feel small. It's always like that with people like her. I feel I should be a drama prof, a film-maker or even a fisherman for their sakes.

"Do you like it?" she asks.

"I get shit on," I say. I watch her eyes. She doesn't blink. She has big teeth and chews slowly. She wears just a trace of make-up. Len probably doesn't let her use much because that would seem vulgar. I wonder if Elsie notices other men. I wonder if she likes the way I look, is thinking, *God, I love his jaw.*

Len talks about the purification of history and then solidarity. *Solidarity* is a big word these days. It's supposed to mean union, loyalty, respect for others, sharing of wealth, renouncing self, looking after the poor. I once asked Lily who was caring for the rich and she gave me this 'eye of the needle' stuff. I told her, "Right, left, it's all a cesspool of corruption, so don't get your hopes up about changing the world or run off to Central America or something." She called me cynical.

The discussion is heating up at the other end of the table. My father keeps saying "yes . . . but" and getting no further. Lily and Len are talking and no one's listening. I turn to Elsie and ask her what she does. She says she is at home. She smiles. I ogle her teeth and think of riding the bus in high school and the grade twelve girls with their scrubbed faces, their hair pulled back, their widow's peaks, their shine, their blush of expectancy. Elsie looks like that.

I ask "Do you have children?"

"A one-year-old boy. He stayed in Toronto with his grandma." She wants to talk about him, I can tell. So that is what we do. While Lily and Len spit across the table, Elsie talks to my mother and me about Dieter. Her eyes are oily patches, and she begins to raise her voice but catches and hushes herself. Though she does not say it exactly, she is telling everyone that children are the answer to the purification of history. I smell her as she talks. Surrounded by her, I see her as lost. I see her as wandering in a maze of diapers, God, bottles and Martin Buber. For a moment I imagine myself as her saviour. I look over at Len and laugh inside. He doesn't have a clue. I do. Come, Elsie, I'll rescue you from the clutches of this blind theologian. Does he quote Whitehead as he lies on top of you? Come, Elsie, let's talk about demand feeding, cradle-cap, cracked nipples, the colour of crap.

Suddenly Lily raises her voice and asks Len if he thinks language can save us. My mother looks at my father, who raises his wide hands in the air and says that dessert is ready. Len gives *me* a withering look. It is at this point that I decide to leave Lily. I am suddenly and painfully disappointed in our marriage. Lily is an enthusiast. It's as simple as that. She doesn't hear me. I look at her, she is quiet now, almost sullen, and I wonder, if she knew my thoughts, whether they would be more important than the anaemic man across from her, or language. Right now. I mean, right now. Elsie asks if I would like some coffee and her voice is so soft that I think she has asked me to lay my head on her lap. I say, "Yes."

Of course, I do my usual flip-flop and decide not to leave Lily. She's been pretty nice to me lately; little favours here and there, and when I ump these days she doesn't complain. She just swats me on the bum and says, "Good game," even though we both know I made some lousy calls. I'm realizing too that women like Elsie have weak personalities; that's what Lily said when I asked her what she thought of Elsie. "She may have a beautiful forehead, Andrew, but she's a clinger. She's weak." I don't agree with her wholeheartedly, but I admit she has a needy smell—though I keep it secret that I like that smell.

And then into the first game of the play-offs Lily loses her pitch. She hits a few batters, hesitates in her wind-up, forgets to skip through the windmill; everything about her pitch looks bad. She seems diminished. I watch and try to figure out what exactly is *not* happening; so now, when I ump, my head is elsewhere, and I begin to waffle on the calls and that's no good. One evening after we have practised into the dark and are sitting on our back lawn drinking wine coolers, she says, "I find myself concentrating on the steps: where are my fingers on the seams, how close is my elbow to my body, is my left heel angled enough? I've lost the spontaneity. It's no more fun." She is wearing a yellow tank top and her shoulders and neck glow in the dark. I put an arm around her. She says she doesn't really care about baseball, it just pisses her off that it doesn't feel good any more.

Rubbing her shoulder, I say, "Maybe Augustine has affected your pitch. You should stop reading that old sinner." She laughs; she knows I'm only half serious. Still, all that fall/redemption musing might affect her in some way. The mosquitoes are getting bad, so Lily lights a coil. I rub her neck and she rubs my leg and we smell burnt poison and listen to sirens and cats and later trace each other's jaws with our tongues.

ONE DAY I ASK LILY if she thinks language can save us and if so from what and do we want saving anyway? She says in some way we all want another life and maybe language can do that for us. So I say, "Thanks a lot, Lily."

She never does get her pitch back. Not that summer. She shrugs and says maybe the talent moved on to someone else. She believes that kind of stuff. Right around this time she gets flushed and frenetic. She decides we need a new cedar deck. She re-sods the back yard. She studies the kitchen and plans to build a nook. She is constantly grabbing at me, holding me, pinning me up against a wall, grinning madly and asking if now is a good time. She drops out of her summer course and stops reading St. Augustine. She says the world doesn't need more people like my father and me. I wonder what she means.

Everything seems hopeful, but of course I keep checking over my shoulder. To me it all feels precarious. I keep on the lookout for rot. I study the elms for tent caterpillars. When I scrape and paint our old house, I look into cracks and holes for termites or decay. I steer away from women with high foreheads. I press my ear into Lily's tummy, as if by doing this I may detect deformities.

I join a slo-pitch team. First base. The rules are different but I'm learning fast. When I bat, the ball comes high, an arc teasing me, begging me to swing earlier, earlier. But the trick is to wait, and wait, and then *crack, give 'er.* This one time when I hit the ball I just know it's gone it feels so sweet. And as I circle the bases I wave at Lily, who's sitting in a lawnchair, fat and happy by the car, but she doesn't see me. She's talking with Glenda—Glenda's almost full term, Lily's only three months—and I realize that Lily never saw my hit. She's leaning forward in her chair, her back to me, and her hands are flying around her face. She's excited, as if all of this, this miracle, this thing happening to us, was her idea.

David Bergen is the author of a collection of short stories, Sitting Opposite My Brother, *as well as two novels,* See the Child *and* A Year of Lesser, *which won the McNally Robinson Book of the Year Award and was a* New York Times *Notable Book. His short story* "How Can *n* Men Share a Bottle of Vodka?" *won the* Saturday Night–CBC Canadian Literary Award.

IT IS A MATTER OF FACT

CLAIRE HARRIS
From *Drawing Down a Daughter*

IT IS A MATTER OF FACT that the girl waits till the man from the capital begins to dress before she asks diffidently, "Where you leave your car?"

Burri buttons his shirt carefully before he replies, "It on the other side, near the big house. It park round the bend near the temple. Why you ask?"

"We could go for a drive."

"We could go for a drive!" He smiles. "Jocelyn, you ain't see how late it is? What your mother go say, girl?" His smile broadens, he strikes a pose and asks again, "You want she coming after me with a cutlass?"

"Well we have to talk."

"Eh, eh! I thought we was talking. What you have to say you can't say here?" He is laughing as he says this.

"It too late to stay here . . . I can't afford to catch cold!"

With a flourish, "Here, put on my jacket." Then seeing her seriousness, "You see how warm you get." His arm goes around her shoulders. He nibbles on her ear and chuckles.

"Look, I want to talk!"

"SO, talk!" He still nibbles, moving down the column of her neck, his fingers turn her face away from the river to face him.

"I ain't get my menses this month, again."

"What you saying . . ." he begins casually, then suddenly alert he sits up. "You ain't get . . . Look girl, what you trying on me?" His voice is rough. His movements abrupt.

"Nothing! Is true. I pregnant."

"Well, that's great! . . . So, you see a doctor? When?"

"I get the results Monday."

He stares at her, frowning.

"I want you to come and see my mother."

He has decided to be cool, "Me! What I want with your mother!" His eyes are wide. He is smiling. He puts his arm around her. "Is you I want." He pats her stomach. "I'll bet is a boy!"

"How we go marry if you ain't talk?"

"Marry!" He is amazed. "Look girl, I ask you to marry me? Is the man does ask!" He scowls, "I ain't ready to marry nobody."

"But ain't you say you love me? What you think my mother go say? Where I go go?"

He is contemptuous. "Is town you go to school? You never hear about tablet? If is mine, ask your grandmother to give you a tea to drink, because I ain't marrying nobody." He begins to gather his things together. He checks his car keys, his wallet. Draws his Seiko on over his wrist.

"But I can't . . . I ain't never . . . nobody . . ."

Now he is gentle again. He takes her hand and seems to think. "Girl, I sorry. Don't do anything yet. I go think of a way. Don't say nothing if you frighten."

"What you mean?"

"A way to fix everything. What? You think I just go leave you?" He smiles, bends to kiss her, straightens, looks around. "But look how late you keep me here! Is a good thing it have moon. How else to see to go through all that bush?"

"When you coming back?"

"Thursday."

The lie trips from his tongue as smooth as butter, and the girl hears it though she is desperate to believe. She stands on the ledge by the falls watching him bound down the hill towards the river. His jacket slung over one shoulder flaps in his lean surefooted grace. He does not look back until he comes to the clump of bamboo before the bend in the river and sets foot on the path. She knows he has turned, because she can see the trim white shirt tucked neatly back into his pants, and the gleaming silver buckle in his belt. He has come to her straight from his clean civil service job in the intimidating red pile of the Legislature. She does not return his wave. But waits to stop the tears that come of their own volition. When she is no longer shuddering, she wipes her face and begins to plan how to get to her room at the back of the house without coming face to face with her mother. Later she will claim a headache. This at least is true. She begins to climb up to the road to the village. Her fingers stray to the medallion dangling against her sore breasts.

OF ALL THIS: the river valley, the girl Jocelyn, the pregnancy, Burri as snake, the old storyteller will say nothing. She has no truck with this simple form, with its order and its inherent possibility of justice. Though she speaks the language, she knows the real world where men wander is full of unseen presences, of interruptions, of rupture. In such a world, men have only tricks and magic. When she makes her old voice growl, or rise and fall on the gutter and flare of candlelight, her tale is not only a small meeting: chance and the implacable at the crossroads, i.e. in the individual. Her tale is a celebration, and a binding of community. Her theme is survival in the current of river-life. Her eyes scan the gathered children fiercely, "You can learn how to deal with life; you cannot avoid what nests in you." There is something of the ancestral, of Africa in this. The children hear. They are polite. They nod solemnly. But their eyes lust after the story.

She laughs in the disconcerting way of old women, lights the candles, orders the electric lights switched off. Now she is ready.

"*See-ah,*" she growls.

"*See-ah,*" the children growl back.

"*See-ah Burri See-ah.*"

"*See-ah Burri See-ah,*" the children sing hugging their knees and moving closer, almost huddling.

"*It have a man,* Burri, he go see he girl by the river and he stay too late.

They must have had talk or something because usually he leave while it light because he know about forest, riverbank, and La Diablesse. Well, this Burri, he hurry long through the tunnel form by the arching bamboo. All time he watching the forest, looking round and thing. He ain't really 'fraid, but he know in a few minutes darkness be King. Only moon for light. He ain't running, but he walking real fast. He feel he got to get to the car quick. It seem to him he walking and walking but he ain't getting nowhere. He think perhaps he miss the crossing stones. But he can't see how he do that because it ain't got no turn off. Well, this Burri, he decide to stop for a minute and light a cigarette. Well is who tell Burri do that?

"*See-ah Burri See-ah*
See-ah Burri Mammy oh.
See-ah Burri Mammy oh," respond the children.

"Crick-crack," says a small boy who wants to get on with the story.

"First thing he know he can't find his lighter anywhere. He check breast pocket, breast pocket say, 'check shirt pocket.' He check shirt pocket, shirt pocket say, 'check pant pocket.' He check pant pocket, pant pocket say, 'check jacket pocket.' He check jacket pocket, and jacket pocket say, 'ain't my business if you drop it.'

Is now he in big trouble. Pitch black and no way to make a light. He begin to really hurry, and see heself looking straight into old eye of mappipi zanana. Snake straight and flat on the branch. Now he really begin to run. He run like he mad. Like snake chasing him. Branch catch at him, grass like it want to hold him back. A bird fly straight up out of the ground in front of him flapping and screaming. He running so hard that Burri half-way cross the clearing before he realize it.

He slow heself down. He bend over holding his knee like Olympic runner. When he heart return to he chest, he look back to the mouth of the bamboo grove. He ain't see nothing. He walk on now. He thinking how big and bright the moon. And is so it hanging low over the river. Well, is finally he come to the steppin stones and them. The water low in the river and he ain't think it go be slippery. And he standing there, shivering a little, because like is something cold trying to bind him, when he see a flash of something white.

Like it moving in the trees on the other side of the river. Even before she come out in the moonlight he know is a woman. Is so some of those men does be. Anyhow she standing in the open looking frighten, and he see one time she pretty for so. Real pretty-pretty. And she got that high-boned face and full lips like the girl he just leave. Not that he thinking about she. What he thinking is how the moonlight so bright-bright, and how he clothes so mess up with all that running and thing. Instant he begin to fix up he shirt, and he jacket, he even take he tie out he pocket and put it back on.

And all the time he whistling. Like somebody give he something, and he real, real please . . .

"*See-ah Burri See-ah*
Burri cross de river oh
Burri itch he scratch-oh.
Burri itch he scratch-oh," sang the children happily.

"Crick-crack," says the small boy who knows his role.

The old woman turns to the small boy, "You is man, all you don't have no real sense. Is not only what you see that there." She pauses a moment, "And not all what smell sweet does taste sweet." Then she begins again.

"Well, now that he tidy, Burri feel that he is who he is. He walk to the stones and all the whole time he smiling at the girl. He measure the first jump and he start crossing, jumping from stone to stone, and like he showing off a little for the girl. So he look up to see how she taking it, and he see her eyes. They like a lasso. They like a fishline, and Burri hook. He fall. He slip and he fall and feel heself struggling, the water close over he head, he thrash out and kick up, and he know the water ain't deep. But he head butt against sand, he eye open to the green wall of a pool. Current catch him, he toss like twig. His chest heavy and hurting, he see stars, and white light exploding, and red. Sudden he is boy again. This girl, Anita, skin like clay pot, that colour, her hair trailing in the water, her breast buds glistening, she floating on the surface of the river. Fragile and open as if she alone, as if none of the rest of them there. He swim over to her quiet, quiet, then he grab a bud in his mouth. How after the shock she scream and scream, and she grab his head and hold it down in the river bottom. How the thin wiry legs scissor and ride him. How the blood roar in he ears, and the darkness catch him. And then the weight lift and the light break through. How he jump and jerk and fight the line, the hooked finger. And how in the end he flop on the bank. How he lungs burn in the moonlight and water pour from eyes, nose, mouth. Meanwhile the woman just standing there under the cocoa. She ain't say nothing. He land on the riverbank at she feet where the skirt circle her in a frothing green frill.

Well, Burri fright leave as he see the woman kind of smiling, like she just too polite to laugh out loud. So now he start to feel stupid for so! But the girl bend down and give he a hand, and he stand up, and she say real nice, "You ain't careful, you catch cold!"

He just nod he head. Burri no fool, he figure he go let she do the talking and just nod and thing. He know if she start feeling sorry for him, he set. And right away he want to know she real, real well.

"You have far to go?" she voice have this sweet lilt.

Burri say, "It quite town I have to go!" He shiver a little bit then he say, "Is only my chest I 'fraid."

"You could come by me and dry out. Is only my grandmother there." And she smiling real sweet, and her voice like she promising something.

Burri ain't stop to ask heself how come a girl standing out there in the moonlight by sheself. He ain't ask heself how come he feeling so happy all of a sudden. He feeling happy, he just feel happy. And the woman herself, she just looking prettier and prettier. The woman self, she too happy because normally she does have to beg, but this one he just coming with her easy-easy.

"*See-ah Burri See-ah.*" The old woman is drumming on her knees.

"*See-ah Burri See-ah.*" The boy has got a bottle an' spoon.

"*See-ah Burri See-ah*

Burri lock in a box oh

What lock he in, can't open oh."

Knees bent, turning slightly sideways, the old lady does a calypso shuffle, "*What lock he in, can't open oh.*"

Arms waving, pelvis shifting, the children dance around the room.

"*What lock he in, can't open oh*

See-ah Burri See-ah."

The boy gets tired of the bottle an' spoon. He decides to assert control.

"Crick-crack," he says. And again, "Crick-crack!" The old lady sighs, sits. The children collapse at her feet. The old lady eyes the boy. "Your pee ain't froth, you can't be man," she says. The boy's eyes go round with surprise. The girls giggle. The old lady is talking rudeness! For a moment her voice crackles as she picks up the tale.

"Well now, Burri, he going up the hill with the lady. And he noticing how sweet she smelling, like is flowers. And how she turn she head, and walk a little sideways. He thinking how lucky he is. And how he never realize Lopinot have so many pretty girls. His head so full a plans for the girl, he never notice she limping until they get to the car. Is when playing real gentleman he open the car door for she that he see the funny foot. Still his mind ain't tell him nothing. Is so when you talking love you don't see what you don't want to see. Burri get in the car, take out he car keys, and say to the girl, real formal, "So where do you live Miss . . . ?" and he kind of pause like he waiting for she to give he a name, but she ain't say no name. She just give him directions for a road near the ravine. The ravine about a mile and a half up the road. Burri thinking is so she want to play it? If she ain't give me a name, I ain't giving she one neither. He look at she sitting there beside him, and he thinking how smooth she skin, and he wondering what she grandmother going to say, and he hoping she real old. Perhaps is thinking of old that make he think of death. Anyway it suddenly hit him what the scent in the car remind him of. Is how the house smell when they bring all the wreaths for his mother funeral. Burri really love he mother now she dead. Just thinking about her could bring tears to his eye. The girl ain't saying nothing. She just sitting there smiling to she-self private like. Burri car have signal in the engine. But he begin to do show-off drive. He open the car window and begin to make pretty-pretty signal with his whole arm. Then he reach for he cigarettes. As soon as she see the cigarette, she begin to frown. She say "That does make me sick, yes?"

Burri forget all about he wet clothes, which practically dry by now. He thinking this woman bold, yes! She ask me for a lift. Now she telling me I can't smoke in my own car! Is right now to see who is boss.

He say, "The window open, you don't see?" But she smart too. Quick as crazy ants her hand move to the dashboard, and she grab the extra lighter he does keep there. All the time she laughing like is joke. Burri ain't think is joke, but he laugh like he think is joke.

He smiling and he smiling, but he mind working overtime. "God!" he say, "but you stubborn yes! And in my own car too?" Is because he was looking at her that he see she face slip a little when he say "God!" He think, 'I ketch! Now is Lawd help me!' And he see she face. He see it slip. And she put she hand up to hide it, and he grab the lighter from she. The whole car filling up with the scent of dead flowers. And he light the cigarette."

"Ah, Burri!" the children exclaim.

"So what you think happen next?" the old lady asks. She is relaxed, at ease. *"You lucky, eh Burri, You lucky."*

The children vie with each other in their banshee wailing,

"I woulda break you neck fuh you
de devil eat you, Burri."

They try to fill the room with wild laughter.

"Well, then she disappear," the old lady says, *"Is so Burri tell me and now I come here to tell you."*

A SMALL GIRL FINGERS HER FACE. "Ah, Burri," she sighs, eyes busy with the horror of a face slipping. Is it possible to be a La Diablesse and not know it, she wonders, where would you go when they found you out?

"BUT HOW SHE SITTING HERE in the dark like that?"

"Girl, turn on the electricity and throw some light on things."

I'LL TRY. But this isn't easy. For one thing, I doubt the ability of anyone to relate a series of facts accurately. For another, I doubt that it is possible to consider any event a fact except in the simplest use of that word. Take, for instance, the laughable, the incontrovertible idea that I am writing this. True, these are my hands that strike the keys. But I have so little control over what is being written that I know the story is writing me.

I have been brooding over these events since I rediscovered them in 1983. Once I was determined to write a straightforward narrative. A soupçon of horror. A fiction. Yet this has become an autobiography. Of sorts. And this short paragraph a kick against that fate. For we do not know if any of this really happened. Yet I remember the story being told. I remember the old woman. And I am sure the story was told as I have written it because that is how the books say Afro-Caribbean tales are told. Your books, I mean. But this is not really about style. This is about plot. For, a few years later, seven years after the telling, to be precise, I met John Burian Armstrong.

He was dressed all in white except for a navy shirt. Close-cropped greying hair topped what I was later on to learn was called an ageless face. At the time I thought that in spite of the deep crevasses that ran down to the corner of his mouth, he was young. There I was curled up in my father's chair on the verandah, reading, I am sure, though I am not sure what I was reading. He stood there smiling at me, sucking at his lower lip as if I reminded him of food, and in spite of his cane, or perhaps because of it, managing to look Mr. Cool.

"You must be Mr. Williams' daughter!"

It crossed my mind suddenly to say coldly, "Not really, I'm a La Diablesse in waiting."

Well . . . Not really.

I'm trying for fact. A little artistic licence here, a little there, and the next thing you know I'm writing history.

A few minutes later I heard him say to my father, "I'm John Burian Armstrong. People around here say I should talk to you."

I was not very surprised by this opening. "Talking to my father" was something the villagers did regularly. He was the recipient of their dreams and their fears. As the only educated black man who came to the village regularly, he was frequently asked to help when anything 'official' or unusual came into their lives. Sometimes, perhaps often, the villagers simply needed someone to know what life, or 'they who does run everything' had done to them, again. So when Armstrong introduced himself, my father sat back in his dark mahogany easy chair with the cushioned slats and prepared to listen.

"Oh! So what is it you have to tell me, Mr. Armstrong?"

"Everyone calls me 'Burri'."

"Burri, then."

"Sir what I have to say is God's truth! People say I was drunk. But that time I didn't drink. A drink now and then, yes. But drink to get drunk, no! Not even till today."

It was the name, Burri, that did it. *"See-ah Burri See-ah."* I moved a Morris chair as close to the windows looking on the verandah as possible. Very quietly indeed I prepared to eavesdrop.

"Let me start from the beginning. Is true I get a girl pregnant. Is true I had no mind for marriage. We argue a bit and it get late. I leave her there and I start to walk along the river to get to the path what you cut there from the pool. Nothing so strange happen until I reach the steppin stones. Just before I cross to come to this side I see a girl standing on the bank, she just standing there on this side near the big cocoa tree where the steps begin."

"What time would that have been?"

"About what o'clock? About seven for the latest. I kind of wave to her and I start crossing. Half way I slip on the stones, fall into the water, and the current sweep me in to the little cave it have under the bank near the bend. I really thought I was gone. Every which way I turn I coming up water. Anyway the girl bend over and give me a hand."

"Did you see her do that yourself?"

"Well, Mr. Williams, there wasn't anybody else there! I figure it have to be her."

"Reasonable. But it's always better if you tell me exactly what you know for a fact. Not what you think it must have been.

"Well, when I get back my strength, I start talking and she offer to take me home with her to dry off my clothes. She tell me her mother gone to visit her sister in San Fernando, but the rest of the family, home. I ask her her name and she tell me 'Mera,' is short for 'Ramera.' I tell my name, Burri. Is true I never hear that name before, but they have lots of 'pagnol people living up here, so I ain't surprise."

"And she didn't look like anyone you know? Not even a little? You know how moonlight is tricky."

"To tell you the truth she look a lot like the girl I was seeing. I thought they might have been some relation. But she herself I never see before."

"Go on."

"We come to the top of the road, and as I crossing over to the car I see she limping. I figure is a stone or something and I walk over to the other side. I open the car door and I get in. She tell me where she live and I start driving. The car smelling musty so I roll down the car window. I don't want the girl thinking my car nasty. Mosquitos start coming in the car so I reach for a cigarette. She say smoke does bother her. I reach for my lighter and my hand touch the bible with the Christopher medal my mother put there when I first buy the car. As God is my witness, Mr. Williams, I light the cigarette. The next thing I know the car rushing into the bank and I can't do anything. Sametime I look over, put out my hand, and the woman ain't there. Before the car hit the bank I see the whole thing. The car door stay close but the woman gone!

"The car crumple like somebody fold it up. I wait there half an hour before anybody come. Then they couldn't get me out."

"You never saw her again?"

"I'll tell you. While I was waiting for the ambulance and the police, I tell the people there was a woman in the car. I describe her. They say perhaps she fall out. They look all night. Nobody see anything. Two days later the police come, question me. They say nobody reported missing. Nobody dead."

"You sure you didn't lose consciousness? Sometimes it's hard to tell."

"Well, I'll admit. My doctor tell me so too. So I come up here and I question everybody. Nobody ever hear of the family. Is that what convince me."

"You know you ought to write that down. One hears of these things, but no one ever has first-hand experience."

"But if a thing like that could happen what kind of world is this?"

WHAT KIND OF WORLD INDEED! For Mr. Armstrong claimed to have had his amazing experience three years earlier. Four years after the night we had danced wildly around the back verandah chanting:

"de devil eat you, Burri"

FIRST YOU POINT OUT to your sceptical parents that you have never before or since heard the name Burri. Have they? No they haven't. Infected by Newton and the church, they insist on coincidence. You are invited to clean up your imagination, to attend daily Mass. But something lovely has been given to you. A world in which each fact like the legs of runners photographed at slow speeds is an amalgam of variations of itself. Myriad versions of event reaching out of time, out of space, individual to each observer.

It is March, 1954. Though he has friends among the villagers, we never see Mr. Armstrong again. My father, however, has discovered that his cane is merely a matter of fashion. "Just practicing," he says, looking at me quizzically, "just practising."

THE FICTION PERSISTS that autobiography is non-fiction. A matter of fact. The question, of course, is what is fact: what is reality. Though the myth of La Diablesse sticks to convention, the stories themselves are specific to a particular event. Is it possible that that old lady bodying forth a world in that long ago August night gave it flesh?

Or was it Burri himself? The power of his experience/delusion stretching both backwards and forwards into time.

Or did the face of reality slip?

HERE ARE THE NOTES I MADE over thirty years ago for the last half of the story.
- (i) In the darkness he slips and breaks his legs.
- (ii) The villagers hear him calling in delirium but are convinced that a spirit calls them to doom.

(iii) He calls the girl by name: there is a dream sequence.
(iv) He is found four days later by a hunting pack. Barely alive.
(v)   His leg never mends properly. (Serve him right!)

SEQUEL

HE CHANGES. Nice girl meets him and falls in love. He refuses to marry her and blight her life because of his leg. Somebody dies and leaves him a million dollars (US). The girl, who is poor, agrees to marry him because her little sister has nearly died from polio. The money helps them to buy better doctors. End on a kiss.

I could have been a romance novelist.

THESE I KNOW TO BE FACTS: the 'Burri' tale; John Burian Armstrong; the Lopinot river; Jocelyn. By stopping here, I am being a purist. It is possible that the writing of this, this telling, began in 1983, when, on one of my rare trips to the island, I set out to visit the old lady, the storyteller of my childhood. I would have gone to see her anyway, but I also wanted to know if there had been an accident; more than that, I wanted to know where her story had come from. She was then 103 years old, this Great Aunt of mine, and she had the telegrams to prove it.

She looked at me cynically and observed, "All you so, ain't know what true from what ain't true!"

"You know. You tell me."

"You don't tell thing so to strangers."

"Come on! I am not a stranger!"

"Overseas water you blood! Don't know if you going or coming! Youself!"

She wouldn't sell me a plot of land either. She owned thirty acres, "All you had and you throw it away!"

BUT THERE HAD REALLY BEEN AN ACCIDENT. That much I had got from her.

I DISCOVERED THAT A FRIEND, Dr. Harry Wilson-Janes of UWI, could get me into the *Guardian* morgue. I wanted to find out if Mr. Armstrong's accident had been reported. It had been. Strong black lines to give it prominence. But I found it only by the merest fluke and in a paper dated *five* years after Mr. Armstrong's visit to my father:

> AROUCA—The police are interested in interviewing the woman who was riding with Mr. John B. Armstrong when his car crashed near the half mile post on the Lopinot Road at approximately 7:40 P.M. on Thursday, February 18, 1959. A witness saw a young woman get into the car about 7:36 P.M. You are asked to contact Inspector Jarvis at the Arouca police station. (J. Badsee)

AFTER A FEW DAYS OF DITHERING, I called the Arouca police station. Inspector Jarvis had retired. But the desk sergeant cheerfully gave me his number at home. Because I didn't have the nerve to ask a retired Superintendent of Police whether he remembered a traffic accident which had taken place twenty-four years earlier, face to face, I decided to phone him. It took me several tries to contact him, but when I did, his voice was strong and clear.

Mine was hesitant. Did he remember the Armstrong accident? He did. He certainly did. Why was I asking? Armstrong had been a friend of mine . . . I had been away . . . some very funny stories going around. When had the accident taken place? February 1959. He was certain. Had there been another accident in 1954? 1955? No. He was sure of it. Armstrong had had only one accident. God knows he had made it his business to find out everything there was to know about that man. And he went to his funeral in 1980, yes, and made sure to check out the coffin. Did he ever find the woman? That was a funny, funny thing happened there. He remembered it still. Couldn't get it out of his head.

(Here he paused for several minutes to check out my genealogy: Which Williams? Oh, so soandso is your cousin! Which brother was grandfather? Oh, so you relate to soandso!

In some quarters it takes three generations to establish trust. Both sides of the family.)

His next question was direct and much to the point. Did I believe in the old-time things? Convince me. I don't know what I believe. Like everybody else. Silence. W . . . ell, it was a long story, he would cut it short for me. When they got to the crash, Armstrong was conscious. Trapped. His legs twisted up. But his mind was clear. He said he picked up this woman and was taking her home when the car crashed. Asked him where the woman was. Funny look come over his face. Said he didn't know. To tell the truth, Jarvis thought it was going to be one of those gruesome cases. He and Sergeant Dick organized village search parties. Lanterns. Torchlight. Flambeaux. Ten groups of three spread out. Nothing. No woman. Next day, dogs and the police teams. Nothing. House to house; signals to every police station in the island. Signals to Tobago, Grenada. Nothing. He and Dick by themselves talked to every woman in the place. All the little tracks and hillhouses. Nothing.

By then the whole place started to panic. Country people. Taxi-drivers refused to drive after dark. Buses breaking down in the garage, come five-thirty. Visiting nurses sicken-off. Pressure! Pressure! He went to see Armstrong in the hospital, and Armstrong told him a strange, strange story. Went back to the accident reports. First thing, no skid marks. Yet that car, folded up like an accordion. De Silva, what own the plantation, he had called the station. Went back to see him. He wasn't there, he talked to his wife. The lady, English. At that time she was only here eight months. The lady didn't know anything about Trinidad. She swear she was sitting on her verandah having a drink after dinner. She, De Silva, and his brother. The car was parked under the hill, round the bend, after that is straight road. They saw the man come out the trees on the river track. They was watching for him. She know the girl young because she very slim, and though she had a limp she walk real queenly. Also she had on a very long skirt with a frill, like she was going to a ball. She thought it was funny to see that in the country, coming out of the bush. You know how those colonist type does think! She said it was bright moonlight.

Then the husband come in. He had hear all the rumours and he was kind of looking at Jarvis funny. Stressing that his wife English. He said they watch the couple get in the car. He stressed how modern they looked together. His wife laughed and said, "Like an advertisement." But then they get serious, and he said they watch the car drive real slow and kind of erratic as if the driver had only one hand on the wheel. Then the car head for the bank. De Silva gave him a queer look and said (he remembers his exact words), "The car head for the bank like it was going home. Quiet and peaceful. It hardly make any noise. The horn blare once and shut off." They stand on the verandah arguing about going down. His brother didn't believe the car crashed. They sent one of their men down to check and he came running back up the hill, shout up is a bad crash. De Silva said he didn't know why he asked him, but he ask his foreman, "How many people in the car?" The man said, "One."

There was a long silence. After a while I said, "Thank you. It's hard to get the truth of such a thing. The facts, I mean." Superintendent Jarvis wished me well. Then he said, "Nobody knows exactly what happen there that night. But is the kind of thing you think is story . . . You have to think is story."

Claire Harris's most recent book is She, *a novel in verse. Harris won a Commonwealth Award for Poetry for* Fables from the Women's Quarter *and was shortlisted for a Governor General's Award for* Drawing Down a Daughter. *Her* Travelling to Find a Remedy *won the Alberta Culture Award and the Stephan G. Stephansson Award for Poetry.*

A GIRL'S STORY

DAVID ARNASON

YOU'VE WONDERED what it would be like to be a character in a story, to sort of slip out of your ordinary self and into some other character. Well, I'm offering you the opportunity. I've been trying to think of a heroine for this story, and frankly, it hasn't been going too well. A writer's life isn't easy, especially if, like me, he's got a tendency sometimes to drink a little bit too much. Yesterday, I went for a beer with Dennis and Ken (they're real-life friends of mine) and we stayed a little longer than we should have. Then I came home and quickly mixed a drink and starting drinking it so my wife would think the liquor on my breath came from the drink I was drinking and not from the drinks I had had earlier. I wasn't going to tell her about those drinks. Anyway, Wayne dropped over in the evening and I had some more drinks, and this morning my head isn't working very well.

To be absolutely frank about it, I always have trouble getting characters, even when I'm stone cold sober. I can think of plots; plots are really easy. If you can't think of one, you just pick up a book, and sure enough, there's a plot. You just move a few things around and nobody knows you stole the idea. Characters are the problem. It doesn't matter how good the plot is if your characters are dull. You can steal characters too, and put them into different plots. I've done that. I stole Eustacia Vye from Hardy and gave her another name. The problem was that she turned out a lot sulkier than I remembered and the plot I put her in was a light comedy. Now nobody wants to publish the story. I'm still sending it out, though. If you send a story to enough publishers, no matter how bad it is, somebody will ultimately publish it.

For this story I need a beautiful girl. You probably don't think you're beautiful enough, but I can fix that. I can do all kinds of retouching once I've got the basic material, and if I miss anything, Karl (he's my editor) will find it. So I'm going to make you fairly tall, about five-foot eight and a quarter in your stocking feet. I'm going to give you long blonde hair because long blonde hair is sexy and virtuous. Black hair can be sexy too, but it doesn't go with virtue. I've got to deal with a whole literary tradition where black-haired women are basically evil. If I were feeling better I might be able to do it in an ironic way, then black hair would be okay, but I don't think I'm up to it this morning. If you're going to use irony, then you've got to be really careful about tone. I could make you a redhead, but redheads have a way of turning out pixie-ish, and that would wreck my plot.

So you've got long blonde hair and you're this tall slender girl with amazingly blue eyes. Your face is narrow and your nose is straight and thin. I could have turned up the nose a little, but that would have made you cute, and I really need a beautiful girl. I'm going to put a tiny black mole on your cheek. It's traditional. If you want your character to be really beautiful there has to be some minor defect.

Now, I'm going to sit you on the bank of a river. I'm not much for setting. I've read so many things where you get great long descriptions of the setting, and mostly it's just boring. When my last book came out, one of the reviewers suggested that the reason I don't do settings is that I'm not very good at them. That's just silly. I'm writing a different kind of story, not that old realist stuff. If you think I can't do setting, just watch.

There's a curl in the river just below the old dam where the water seems to make a broad sweep. That flatness is deceptive, though. Under the innocent sheen of the mirroring surface, the current is treacherous. The water swirls, stabs, takes sharp angles and dangerous vectors. The trees that lean from the bank shimmer with the multi-hued greenness of elm, oak, maple and aspen. The leaves turn in the gentle breeze, showing their paler green undersides. The undergrowth, too, is thick and green, hiding the poison ivy, the poison sumac and the thorns. On a patch of grass that slopes gently to the water, the only clear part of the bank on that side of the river, a girl sits, a girl with long blonde hair. She has slipped a ring from her finger and seems to be holding it toward the light.

You see? I could do a lot more of that, but you wouldn't like it. I slipped a lot of details in there and provided all those hints about strange and dangerous things under the surface. That's called foreshadowing. I put in the ring at the end there so that you'd wonder what was going to happen. That's to create suspense. You're supposed to ask yourself what the ring means. Obviously it has something to do with love, rings always do, and since she's taken it off, obviously something has gone wrong in the love relationship. Now I just have to hold off answering that question for as long as I can, and I've got my story. I've got a friend who's also a writer who says never tell the buggers anything until they absolutely have to know.

I'm going to have trouble with the feminists about this story. I can see that already. I've got that river that's calm on the surface and boiling underneath, and I've got those trees that are gentle and beautiful with poisonous and dangerous undergrowth. Obviously, the girl is going to be like that, calm on the surface but passionate underneath. The feminists are going to say that I'm perpetuating stereotypes, that by giving the impression the girl is full of hidden passion I'm encouraging rapists. That's crazy. I'm just using a literary convention. Most of the world's great books are about the conflict between reason and passion. If you take that away, what's left to write about?

So I've got you sitting on the riverbank, twirling your ring. I forgot the birds. The trees are full of singing birds. There are meadowlarks and vireos and even Blackburnian warblers. I know a lot about birds but I'm not going to put in too many. You've got to be careful not to overdo things. In a minute I'm going to enter your mind and reveal what you're thinking. I'm going to do this in the third person. Using the first person is sometimes more effective, but I'm always afraid to do a female character in the first person. It seems wrong to me, like putting on a woman's dress.

Your name is Linda. I had to be careful not to give you a biblical name like Judith or Rachel. I don't want any symbolism in this story. Symbolism makes me sick, especially biblical symbolism. You always end up with some crazy moral argument that you don't believe and none of the readers believe. Then you lose control of your characters, because they've got to be like the biblical characters. You've got this terrific episode you'd like to use, but you can't because Rachel or Judith or whoever wouldn't do it. I think of stories with a lot of symbolism in them as sticky.

Here goes.

Linda held the ring up toward the light. The diamond flashed rainbow colours. It was a small diamond, and Linda reflected that it was probably a perfect symbol of her relationship with Gregg. Everything Gregg did was on a small scale. He was careful with his money and just as careful with his emotions. In one week they would have a small wedding and then move into a small apartment. She supposed that she ought to be happy. Gregg was very handsome, and she did love him. Why did it seem that she was walking into a trap?

That sounds kind of distant, but it's supposed to be distant. I'm using indirect quotation because the reader has just met Linda, and we don't want to get too intimate right away. Besides, I've got to get a lot of explaining done quickly, and if you can do it with the character's thoughts, then that's best.

Linda twirled the ring again, then with a suddenness that surprised her, she stood up and threw it into the river. She was immediately struck by a feeling of panic. For a moment she almost decided to dive into the river to try to recover it. Then, suddenly, she felt free. It was now impossible to marry Gregg. He would not forgive her for throwing the ring away. Gregg would say he'd had enough of her theatrics for one lifetime. He always accused her of being a romantic. She'd never had the courage to admit that he was correct, and that she intended to continue being a romantic. She was sitting alone by the river in a long blue dress because it was a romantic pose. Anyway, she thought a little wryly, you're only likely to find romance if you look for it in romantic places and dress for the occasion.

Suddenly, she heard a rustling in the bush, the sound of someone coming down the narrow path from the road above.

I had to do that, you see. I'd used up all the potential in the relationship with Gregg, and the plot would have started to flag if I hadn't introduced a new character. The man who is coming down the path is tall and athletic with wavy brown hair. He has dark brown eyes that crinkle when he smiles, and he looks kind. His skin is tanned, as if he spends a lot of time outdoors, and he moves gracefully. He is smoking a pipe. I don't want to give too many details. I'm not absolutely sure what features women find attractive in men these days, but what I've described seems safe enough. I got all of it from stories written by women, and I assume they must know. I could give him a chiselled jaw, but that's about as far as I'll go.

The man stepped into the clearing. He carried an old-fashioned wicker fishing creel and a telescoped fishing rod. Linda remained sitting on the grass, her blue dress spread out around her. The man noticed her and apologized.

"I'm sorry, I always come here to fish on Saturday afternoons and I've never encountered anyone here before." His voice was low with something of an amused tone in it.

"Don't worry," Linda replied. "I'll only be here for a little while. Go ahead and fish. I won't make any noise." In some way she couldn't understand, the man looked familiar to her. She felt she knew him. She thought she might have seen him on television or in a movie, but of course she knew that movie and television stars do not spend every Saturday afternoon fishing on the banks of small, muddy rivers.

"You can make all the noise you want," he told her. "The fish in this river are almost entirely deaf. Besides, I don't care if I catch any. I only like the act of fishing. If I catch them, then I have to take them home and clean them. Then I've got to cook them and eat them. I don't even like fish that much, and the fish you catch here all taste of mud."

"Why do you bother fishing then?" Linda asked him. "Why don't you just come and sit on the riverbank?"

"It's not that easy," he told her. "A beautiful girl in a blue dress may go and sit on a riverbank any time she wants. But a man can only sit on a riverbank if he has a very good reason. Because I fish, I am a man with a hobby. After a hard week of work, I deserve some relaxation. But if I just came and sat on the riverbank, I would be a romantic fool. People would make fun of me. They would think I was irresponsible, and before long I would be a failure." As he spoke, he attached a lure to his line, untelescoped his fishing pole and cast his line into the water.

You may object that this would not have happened in real life, that the conversation would have been awkward, that Linda would have been a bit frightened by the man. Well, why don't you just run out to the grocery store and buy a bottle of milk and a loaf of bread? The grocer will give you your change without even looking at you. That's what happens in real life, and if that's what you're after, why are you reading a book?

I'm sorry. I shouldn't have got upset. But it's not easy you know. Dialogue is about the hardest stuff to write. You've got all those "he saids" and "she saids" and "he replieds." And you've got to remember the quotation marks and whether the comma is inside or outside the quotation marks. Sometimes you can leave out the "he saids" and the "she saids" but then the reader gets confused and can't figure out who's talking. Hemingway is bad for that. Sometimes you can read an entire chapter without figuring out who is on what side.

Anyway, something must have been in the air that afternoon. Linda felt free and open.

Did I mention that it was warm and the sun was shining?

She chattered away, telling the stranger all about her life, what she had done when she was a little girl, the time her dad had taken the whole family to Hawaii and she got such a bad sunburn that she was peeling in February, how she was a better water skier than Gregg and how mad he got when she beat him at tennis. The man, whose name was Michael (you can use biblical names for men as long as you avoid Joshua or Isaac), told her he was a doctor, but had always wanted to be a cowboy. He told her about the time he skinned his knee when he fell off his bicycle and had to spend two weeks in the hospital because of infection. In short, they did what people who are falling in love always do. They unfolded their brightest and happiest memories and gave them to each other as gifts.

Then Michael took a bottle of wine and a Klik sandwich out of his wicker creel and invited Linda to join him in a picnic. He had forgotten his corkscrew and he had to push the cork down into the bottle with his filletting knife. They drank wine and laughed and spat out little pieces of cork. Michael reeled in his line, and to his amazement discovered a diamond ring on his hook. Linda didn't dare tell him where the ring had come from. Then Michael took Linda's hand, and slipped the ring onto her finger. In a comic-solemn voice, he asked her to marry him. With the same kind of comic solemnity, she agreed. Then they kissed, a first gentle kiss with their lips barely brushing and without touching each other.

Now I've got to bring this to some kind of ending. You think writers know how stories end before they write them, but that's not true. We're wracked with confusion and guilt about how things are going to end. And just as you're playing the role of Linda in this story, Michael is my alter ego. He even looks a little like me and he smokes the same kind of pipe. We all want this to end happily. If I were going to be realistic about this, I suppose I'd have to let them make love. Then, shaken with guilt and horror, Linda would go back and marry Gregg, and the doctor would go back to his practice. But I'm not going to do that. In the story from which I stole the plot, Michael turned out not to be a doctor at all, but a returned soldier who had always been in love with Linda. She recognized him as they kissed, because they had kissed as children, and even though they had grown up and changed, she recognized the flavour of wintergreen on his breath. That's no good. It brings in too many unexplained facts at the last minute.

I'm going to end it right here at the moment of the kiss. You can do what you want with the rest of it, except you can't make him a returned soldier, and you can't have them make love then separate forever. I've eliminated those options. In fact, I think I'll eliminate all options. This is where the story ends, at the moment of the kiss. It goes on and on forever while cities burn, nations rise and fall, galaxies are born and die, and the universe snuffs out the stars one by one. It goes on, the story, the brush of a kiss.

David Arnason is a Winnipeg writer and teacher of creative writing. He has published collections of poetry and short fiction, and has written novels; film, television and radio scripts; and academic articles. His latest works are a short story collection, If Pigs Could Fly, *and a documentary film,* Tied by Blood.

MRS. TURNER CUTTING THE GRASS

CAROL SHIELDS

Oh, Mrs. Turner is a sight cutting the grass on a hot afternoon in June! She climbs into an ancient pair of shorts and ties on her halter top and wedges her feet into crepe-soled sandals and covers her red-gray frizz with Gord's old golf cap—Gord is dead now, ten years ago, a seizure on a Saturday night while winding the mantel clock.

The grass flies up around Mrs. Turner's knees. Why doesn't she use a catcher, the Saschers next door wonder. Everyone knows that leaving the clippings like that is bad for the lawn. Each fallen blade of grass throws a minute shadow which impedes growth and repair. The Saschers themselves use their clippings to make compost which they hope one day will be ripe as the good manure that Sally Sascher's father used to spread on his fields down near Emerson Township.

Mrs. Turner's carelessness over the clippings plucks away at Sally, but her husband Roy is far more concerned about the Killex that Mrs. Turner dumps on her dandelions. It's true that in Winnipeg the dandelion roots go right to the middle of the earth, but Roy is patient and persistent in pulling them out, knowing exactly how to grasp the coarse leaves in his hand and how much pressure to apply. Mostly they come up like corks with their roots intact. And he and Sally are experimenting with new ways to cook dandelion greens, believing as they do that the components of nature are arranged for a specific purpose—if only that purpose can be divined.

In the early summer Mrs. Turner is out every morning by ten with her sprinkling can of chemical killer, and Roy, watching from his front porch, imagines how this poison will enter the ecosystem and move by quick capillary surges into his fenced vegetable plot, newly seeded now with green beans and lettuce. His children, his two little girls aged two and four—that they should be touched by such poison makes him morose and angry. But he and Sally so far have said nothing to Mrs. Turner about her abuse of the planet because they're hoping she'll go into an old-folks home soon or maybe die, and then all will proceed as it should.

High-school girls on their way home in the afternoon see Mrs. Turner cutting her grass and are mildly, momentarily repelled by the lapped, striated flesh on her upper thighs. At her age. Doesn't she realize? Every last one of them is intimate with the vocabulary of skin care and knows that what has claimed Mrs. Turner's thighs is the enemy called cellulite, but they can't understand why she doesn't take the trouble to hide it. It makes them queasy; it makes them fear for the future.

The things Mrs. Turner doesn't know would fill the Saschers' new compost pit, would sink a ship, would set off a tidal wave, would make her want to kill herself. Back and forth, back and forth she goes with the electric lawn mower, the grass flying out sideways like whiskers. Oh, the things she doesn't know! She has never heard, for example, of the folk-rock recording star Neil Young, though the high school just around the corner from her house happens to be the very school Neil Young attended as a lad. His initials can actually be seen carved on one of the desks, and a few of the teachers say they remember him, quiet fellow of neat appearance and always very polite in class. The desk with the initials N.Y. is kept in a corner of Mr. Pring's homeroom, and it's considered lucky—despite the fact that the renowned singer wasn't a great scholar—to touch the incised letters just before an exam. Since it's exam time now, the second week of June, the girls walking past Mrs. Turner's front yard (and shuddering over her display of cellulite) are carrying on their fingertips the spiritual scent, the essence, the fragrance, the aura of Neil Young, but Mrs. Turner is as ignorant of that fact as the girls are that she, Mrs. Turner, possesses a first name—which is Geraldine.

Not that she's ever been called Geraldine. Where she grew up in Boissevain, Manitoba, she was known always—the Lord knows why—as Girlie Fergus, the youngest of the three Fergus girls and the one who got herself in hot water. Her sister Em went to normal school and her sister Muriel went to Brandon to work at Eaton's, but Girlie got caught one night—she was nineteen—in a Boissevain hotel room with a local farmer, married, named Gus MacGregor. It was her father who got wind of where she might be and came banging on the door, shouting and weeping. "Girlie, Girlie, what have you done to me?"

Girlie had been working in the Boissevain Dairy since she'd left school at sixteen and had a bit of money saved up, and so, a week after the humiliation in the local hotel, she wrote a farewell note to the family, crept out of the house at midnight and caught the bus to Winnipeg. From there she got another bus down to Minneapolis, then to Chicago and finally New York City. The journey was endless and wretched, and on the way across Indiana and Ohio and Pennsylvania she saw hundreds and hundreds of towns whose unpaved streets and narrow blinded houses made her fear some conspiratorial, punishing power had carried her back to Boissevain. Her father's soppy-stern voice sang and sang in her ears as the wooden bus rattled its way eastward. It was summer, 1930.

New York was immense and wonderful, dirty, perilous and puzzling. She found herself longing for a sight of real earth which she assumed must lie somewhere beneath the tough pavement. On the other hand, the brown flat-roofed factories with their little windows tilted skyward pumped her full of happiness, as did the dusty trees, when she finally discovered them, lining the long avenues. Every last person in the world seemed to be outside, walking around, filling the streets, and every corner breezed with noise and sunlight. She had to pinch herself to believe this was the same sunlight that filtered its way into the rooms of the house back in Boissevain, fading the curtains but nourishing her mother's ferns. She sent postcards to Em and Muriel that said, "Don't worry about me. I've got a job in the theater business."

It was true. For eight and a half months she was an usherette in the Lamar Movie Palace in Brooklyn. She loved her perky maroon uniform, the way it fit on her shoulders, the way the strips of crinkly gold braid outlined her figure. With a little flashlight in hand she was able to send streams of light across the furry darkness of the theater and onto the plum-colored aisle carpet. The voices from the screen talked on and on. She felt after a time that their resonant declarations and tender replies belonged to her.

She met a man named Kiki her first month in New York and moved in with him. His skin was as black as ebony. *As black as ebony*—that was the phrase that hung like a ribbon on the end of his name, and it's also the phrase she uses, infrequently, when she wants to call up his memory, though she's more than a little doubtful about what *ebony* is. It may be a kind of stone, she thinks, something round and polished that comes out of a deep mine.

Kiki was a good-hearted man, though she didn't like the beer he drank, and he stayed with her, willingly, for several months after she had to stop working because of the baby. It was the baby itself that frightened him off, the way it cried probably. Leaving fifty dollars on the table, he slipped out one July afternoon when Girlie was shopping, and went back to Troy, New York, where he'd been raised.

Her first thought was to take the baby and get on a bus and go find him, but there wasn't enough money, and the thought of the baby crying all the way on the hot bus made her feel tired. She was worried about the rent and about the little red sores in the baby's ears—it was a boy, rather sweetly formed, with wonderful smooth feet and hands. On a murderously hot night, a night when the humidity was especially bad, she wrapped him in a clean piece of sheeting and carried him all the way to Brooklyn Heights where the houses were large and solid and surrounded by grass. There was a house on a corner she particularly liked because it had a wide front porch (like those in Boissevain) with a curved railing—and parked on the porch, its brake on, was a beautiful wicker baby carriage. It was here she placed her baby, giving one last look to his sleeping face, as round and calm as the moon. She walked home, taking her time, swinging her legs. If she had known the word *foundling*—which she didn't—she would have bounded along on its rhythmic back, so airy and wide did the world seem that night.

Most of these secrets she keeps locked away inside her mottled thighs or in the curled pinkness of her genital flesh. She has no idea what happened to Kiki, whether he ever went off to Alaska as he wanted to or whether he fell down a flight of stone steps in the silverware factory in Troy, New York, and died of head injuries before his 30th birthday. Or what happened to her son—whether he was bitten that night in the baby carriage by a rabid neighborhood cat or whether he was discovered the next morning and adopted by the large, loving family who lived in the house. As a rule, Girlie tries not to think about the things she can't even guess at. All she thinks is that she did the best she could under the circumstances.

In a year she saved enough money to take the train home to Boissevain. She took with her all her belongings, and also gifts for Em and Muriel, boxes of hose, bottles of apple-blossom cologne, phonograph records. For her mother she took an embroidered apron and for her father a pipe made of curious gnarled wood. "Girlie, my Girlie," her father said, embracing her at the Boissevain station. Then he said, "Don't ever leave us again," in a way that frightened her and made her resolve to leave as quickly as possible.

But she didn't go so far the second time around. She and Gordon Turner—he was, for all his life, a tongue-tied man, though he did manage a proper proposal—settled down in Winnipeg, first in St. Boniface where the rents were cheap and then Fort Rouge and finally the little house in River Heights just around the corner from the high school. It was her husband, Gord, who planted the grass that Mrs. Turner now shaves in the summertime. It was Gord who trimmed and shaped the caragana hedge and Gord who painted the little shutters with the cut-out hearts. He was a man who loved every inch of his house, the wide wooden steps, the oak door with its glass inset, the radiators and the baseboards and the snug sash windows. And he loved every inch of this wife, Girlie, too, saying to her once and only once that he knew about her past (meaning Gus MacGregor and the incident in the Boissevain Hotel), and that as far as he was concerned the slate had been wiped clean. Once he came home with a little package in his pocket; inside was a diamond ring, delicate and glittering. Once he took Girlie on a picnic all the way up to Steep Rock, and in the woods he took off her dress and underthings and kissed every part of her body.

After he died, Girlie began to travel. She was far from rich, as she liked to say, but with care she could manage one trip every spring.

She has never known such ease. She and Em and Muriel have been to Disneyland as well as Disneyworld. They've been to Europe, taking a sixteen-day trip through seven countries. The three of them have visited the south and seen the famous antebellum houses of Georgia, Alabama and Mississippi, after which they spent a week in the city of New Orleans. They went to Mexico one year and took pictures of Mayan ruins and queer shadowy gods cut squarely from stone. And three years ago they did what they swore they'd never have the nerve to do: they got on an airplane and went to Japan.

The package tour started in Tokyo where Mrs. Turner ate, on her first night there, a chrysanthemum fried in hot oil. She saw a village where everyone earned a living by making dolls and another village where everyone made pottery. Members of the tour group, each holding up a green flag so their tour leader could keep track of them, climbed on a little train, zoomed off to Osaka where they visited an electronics factory, and then went to a restaurant to eat uncooked fish. They visited more temples and shrines than Mrs. Turner could keep track of. Once they stayed the night in a Japanese hotel where she and Em and Muriel bedded down on floor mats and little pillows stuffed with cracked wheat, and woke up, laughing, with backaches and shooting pains in their legs.

That was the same day they visited the Golden Pavilion in Kyoto. The three-storied temple was made of wood and had a roof like a set of wings and was painted a soft old flaky gold. Everybody in the group took pictures—Em took a whole roll—and bought postcards; everybody, that is, except a single tour member, the one they all referred to as the Professor.

The Professor traveled without a camera, but jotted notes almost continuously into a little pocket scribbler. He was bald, had a trim body and wore Bermuda shorts, sandals and black nylon socks. Those who asked him learned that he really was a professor, a teacher of English poetry in a small college in Massachusetts. He was also a poet who, at the time of the Japanese trip, had published two small chapbooks based mainly on the breakdown of his marriage. The poems, sadly, had not caused much stir.

It grieved him to think of that paltry, guarded nut-like thing that was his artistic reputation. His domestic life had been too cluttered; there had been too many professional demands; the political situation in America had drained him of energy—these were the thoughts that buzzed in his skull as he scribbled and scribbled, like a man with a fever, in the back seat of a tour bus traveling through Japan.

Here in this crowded, confused country he discovered simplicity and order and something spiritual, too, which he recognized as being authentic. He felt as though a flower, something like a lily, only smaller and tougher, had unfurled in his hand and was nudging along his fountain pen. He wrote and wrote, shaken by catharsis, but lulled into a new sense of his powers.

Not surprisingly, a solid little book of poems came out of his experience. It was published soon afterwards by a well-thought-of Boston publisher who, as soon as possible, sent him around the United States to give poetry readings.

Mostly the Professor read his poems in universities and colleges where his book was already listed on the Contemporary Poetry course. He read in faculty clubs, student centers, classrooms, gymnasiums and auditoriums, and usually, partway through a reading, someone or other would call from the back of the room, "Give us your Golden Pavilion poem."

He would have preferred to read his Fuji meditation or the tone poem on the Inner Sea, but he was happy to oblige his audiences, though he felt "A Day At The Golden Pavilion" was a somewhat light piece, even what is sometimes known on the circuit as a "crowd pleaser." People (admittedly they were mostly undergraduates) laughed out loud when they heard it; he read it well, too, in a moist, avuncular amateur actor's voice, reminding himself to pause frequently, to look upward and raise an ironic eyebrow.

The poem was not really about the Golden Pavilion at all, but about three midwestern lady tourists who, while viewing the temple and madly snapping photos, had talked incessantly and in loud, flat-bottomed voices about knitting patterns, indigestion, sore feet, breast lumps, the cost of plastic raincoats and a previous trip they'd made together to Mexico. They had wondered, these three—noisily, repeatedly—who back home in Manitoba should receive a postcard, what they'd give for an honest cup of tea, if there was an easy way to remove stains from an electric coffee maker, and where they would go the following year—Hawaii? They were the three furies, the three witches, who for vulgarity and tastelessness formed a shattering counterpoint to the Professor's own state of transcendence. He had been affronted, angered, half-crazed.

One of the sisters, a little pug of a woman, particularly stirred his contempt, she of the pink pantsuit, the red toenails, the grapefruity buttocks, the overly bright souvenirs, the garish Mexican straw bag containing Dentyne chewing gum, aspirin, breath mints, sun goggles, envelopes of saccharine, and photos of her dead husband standing in front of a squat, ugly house in Winnipeg. This defilement she had spread before the ancient and exquisitely proportioned Golden Pavilion of Kyoto, proving—and here the Professor's tone became grave—proving that sublime beauty can be brought to the very doorway of human eyes, ears and lips and remain unperceived.

When he comes to the end of "A Day At The Golden Pavilion" there is generally a thoughtful half second of silence, then laughter and applause. Students turn in their seats and exchange looks with their fellows. They have seen such unspeakable tourists themselves. There was old Auntie Marigold or Auntie Flossie. There was that tacky Mrs. Shannon with her rouge and her jewelry. They know—despite their youth they know—the irreconcilable distance between taste and banality. Or perhaps that's too harsh; perhaps it's only the difference between those who know about the world and those who don't.

It's true Mrs. Turner remembers little about her travels. She's never had much of a head for history or dates; she never did learn, for instance, the difference between a Buddhist temple and a Shinto shrine. She gets on a tour bus and goes and goes, and that's all there is to it. She doesn't know if she's going north or south or east or west. What does it matter? She's having a grand time. And she's reassured, always, by the sameness of the world. She's never heard the word *commonality,* but is nevertheless fused with its sense. In Japan she was made as happy to see carrots and lettuce growing in the fields as she was to see sunlight, years earlier, pouring into the streets of New York City. Everywhere she's been she's seen people eating and sleeping and working and making things with their hands and urging things to grow. There have been cats and dogs, fences and bicycles and telephone poles, and objects to buy and take care of; it is amazing, she thinks, that she can understand so much of the world and that it comes to her as easily as bars of music floating out of a radio.

Her sisters have long forgotten about her wild days. Now the three of them love to sit on tour buses and chatter away about old friends and family members, their stern father and their mother who never once took their part against him. Muriel carries on about her children (a son in California and a daughter in Toronto) and she brings along snaps of her grandchildren to pass round. Em has retired from school teaching and is a volunteer in the Boissevain Local History Museum, to which she has donated several family mementos: her father's old carved pipe and her mother's wedding veil and, in a separate case, for all the world to see, a white cotton garment labeled "Girlie Fergus' Underdrawers, handmade, trimmed with lace, circa 1918." If Mrs. Turner knew the word *irony* she would relish this. Even without knowing the word irony, she relishes it.

The professor from Massachusetts has won an important international award for his book of poems; translation rights have been sold to a number of foreign publishers; and recently his picture appeared in the *New York Times,* along with a lengthy quotation from "A Day At The Golden Pavilion." How providential, some will think, that Mrs. Turner doesn't read the *New York Times* or attend poetry readings, for it might injure her deeply to know how she appears in certain people's eyes, but then there are so many things she doesn't know.

In the summer as she cuts the grass, to and fro, to and fro, she waves to everyone she sees. She waves to the high-school girls who timidly wave back. She hollers hello to Sally and Roy Sascher and asks them how their garden is coming on. She cannot imagine that anyone would wish her harm. All she's done is live her life. The green grass flies up in the air, a buoyant cloud swirling about her head. Oh, what a sight is Mrs. Turner cutting her grass and how, like an ornament, she shines.

Carol Shields is the author of Larry's Party *and* The Stone Diaries, *which won the 1995 Pulitzer Prize for fiction, the National Book Critics' Circle Award and the Governor General's Award. Her most recent book is a short story collection,* Dressing Up for the Carnival.

TEN MEN RESPOND TO AN AIR-BRUSHED PHOTOGRAPH OF A NUDE WOMAN CHAINED TO A BULL

BONNIE BURNARD

THE PHOTOGRAPH WAS ORIGINALLY an eight-by-ten glossy, taken, developed and held for a time in a file with other similar photographs in the expectation that it could be sold.

The woman in the photograph is a toughened twenty-something. Her long hair is platinum blonde with just a slight growth of dark roots at the skull, and deliberately wild; it surrounds a delicate face reminiscent of Tuesday Weld's when she was young and fresh. Her breasts are wide and bulbous but the rest of her body is quite thin, particularly her arms and her neck. She looks healthy except for the few small bruises on the flesh of her upper arms and thighs.

The young woman is standing in a corral with her back partially turned to a full-sized Black Angus bull. Her hands grip the top board of a rail fence. There's a bit of sparse grass outside the fence, and a few weeds, thistles, but the earth in the corral is muddy grey and barren. The bull is about five feet away from her. He is well groomed but glassy-eyed. His thick tongue hangs from his mouth as if it is finally too heavy to hold in, as if he is extremely thirsty.

The woman and the bull are connected by two sturdy chains which extend from her wrists to a leather collar around the bull's neck. She is implicitly but clearly susceptible to any movement the bull might make. If he takes off, if he is spooked, she'll have to try to keep up. If he charges, she's got the rail fence. She'll have to get over it fast, trust its strength. The expression on her face is one of high excitement; anything can happen.

The photograph has been reproduced in a magazine with very good distribution and surprisingly classy ads.

THE PHOTOGRAPHER who captured the image and sold it to the magazine works freelance and lives alone, for the moment, in a medium-sized city. He's been married, once, and has a daughter in another province. The kid's eleven. His ex-wife wanted her and he was easy, one way or the other. He figures it wouldn't be much of a life for a kid living with him. He's away quite a bit.

Recently, he's been attending night classes in computer science. He thinks that's what the future holds. His ex-wife makes noises about money every time he hears from her, she's got stats on how much money it takes to raise a kid and she reads them to him over the phone, long distance. When she says, "Do you hear what I'm saying to you?" he laughs and says, "It's your dime, talk all you want."

The investment in the camera and the darkroom equipment has paid off. He sells photographs whenever and wherever he can. He takes all kinds: city streets, houses, shopping centres, animals, cars, sports, women. The market's there for nearly anything if you can make the connections, although some are easier to move than others. He sends his ex-wife a hundred bucks here and there, when he can, no questions asked. At Christmas, on a whim, he dropped a red fifty-dollar bill into the clear plastic Salvation Army bucket in the mall where he does most of his browsing. He hangs out in malls a

Ten Men Respond to an Air-Brushed Photograph of a Nude Woman Chained to a Bull

lot, studying the walks and stances and faces and overall physical attitudes of spoiled middle-class teenagers.

He didn't know the blonde at the farm. He didn't know the bull either. A friend of a friend set it up. His friend drove him out to this farm in a rented van and they met the blonde there; she'd driven out with another guy, a manager type, who was quite a bit older. The farmer who owned the bull and the local vet were waiting for them at the house, on the porch. Before they started the shoot they each downed a light beer from a case on the porch step. Money was paid and then the guy who owned the bull disappeared somewhere in his truck.

THE PHOTOGRAPHER's response: I'm pretty happy with it, technically. She was an experienced model. There's a nice play, a nice tension between the coarseness of the bull and the dirt, between the roughness of the rails and the bruises, and her obvious delicacy. The light was nearly perfect. You can see how it works differently on everything it hits.

THE PUBLISHER is in late middle age, works as a team with his wife out of their basement in a small New England town. Their daughter works for them as a part-time secretary, takes the calls from their network of photographers and writers around the U.S. and Canada, does the filing and the billing. Their other kids are grown and gone. He didn't know much about publishing when they started, he has his high school certificate and a diploma in drafting, so over the years he and his wife have taken turns attending conferences and seminars for publishers and small-business operators. They have made many useful contacts with people who have been in the business long enough to know the ropes. It's been a long hard climb from nowhere but they feel they have finally established themselves. They know they're not going to get rich by any means, and they've accepted that. All they really want is a half-decent living.

THE PUBLISHER's response: It's staged, of course. Ninety-nine per cent of this stuff is staged, just like most of what you get at the newsstand, only the rest of it's called journalism. The bull is doped to the gills. The bruises are made up. We've never allowed ourselves to get pulled into the kind of stuff where people can get hurt. There's no need, really. And the girls get paid, more than you'd think, likely more than you and I get paid. That particular girl's doing commercials now, we've seen her on television, my wife recognized her holding a garden hose in some chemical thing. Her hair's different, all they have to do is cut it off and let it grow back normally, and she's got her breasts under control. So working this market hasn't done her career any harm. We keep a firm eye on the competition, we have to, but there are choices to make. There's a line we won't cross no matter what the competition's doing. And you can make a living without crossing the line.

HARVEY is fifty-six and has worked most of his life at a small factory which makes artificial turf. He has just enough authority at the plant to give him a feeling of satisfaction, and his retirement looks not half bad thanks to some high-interest rates in the eighties. He's been married to the same woman for twenty-four years, and although he's been a little rough with her a few times he's never meant to, it was only because he was real tired and she wouldn't stop and nothing else would work. And she gives as good as she gets. They've got four kids who are going to do all right. Harvey is a sucker for ceremony. His favourite times of the year are Christmas and Thanksgiving when everyone in the family dresses up, sits down and waits for him to carve the turkey. He always wears his suit jacket to the table but halfway through the meal he takes it off and drapes it over the back of his chair. It's a family joke. He's had no major problems over the years, except once in a while with money, but that was not a big surprise.

He found the magazine during a routine drug check through his seventeen-year-old son's dresser. The kid's no trouble and Harvey wants it to stay that way, so he does an inventory once or twice a month. He dug the magazine out of the bottom drawer and flipped through the pages and stopped at our picture.

HARVEY's response: I'll break his ass. If he thinks his mother and I have worked our butts off all these years to have our home polluted with shit like this, he hasn't been paying attention. This would kill his mother. What's wrong with the talent at his school, for God's sake. They better start putting out before he finds himself thinking black and blue is pretty.

RICHARD is Harvey's son, the one with the dresser. He's a fair student and no trouble to anyone. He plays soccer every chance he gets. In his Dad's day it was hockey, but hockey's mostly for the biggest and the baddest now, and Richard's never had the weight. When he was very small his Dad laid a couple of good ones on his rear end to establish the ground rules but he's never touched him since. Richard makes damn sure he has no reason to. He's dark skinned like his mother and he has most of her facial features, including the overbite which has never been attended to, although she dreamed when he was small of getting that done for him. Still, he turns heads. He hangs out with one girl, the first one to say yes to his awkward interest. They eat together at the mall a lot of the time, chinese, tacos, pizza, hamburgers, and they see most of the movies.

She's a big fan of Arnold Schwarzenegger. She thinks he's a riot. And she watches Richard play soccer, although she's not athletic herself. She's not as flashy as some of the others at school, no leather, no nail polish, no hair spray, no boots, no earrings down to her elbows, but she's considerably smarter. She never talks to him much and she just fumbles around if a teacher asks her anything, but she pulls in the A's every time. She came to the house only once, his mother's idea, and she won't come back. When Richard asked her why, she told him the truth, because she thought it was important. She said, guessing he'd likely drop her, "Your Dad makes me sort of uncomfortable." Richard feels her up a lot but she's got control. He thinks she's afraid to touch him.

He bought the magazine for fun, for laughs.

RICHARD's response: Right. So what. That picture's nothing compared to most of it. I can read between the lines. I know what's normal. I know what the bull means and I know what the chains mean and I know I'm not gonna treat my wife like that. I just like long legs. And I like my privacy.

Besides, you start looking for rules about that kind of stuff, you've got to decide who gets to make the rules. And it won't be you and it won't be me. It'll be some loser with a Bible.

JOHN is thirty-four. He sells cameras at a department store. He graduated from university with a fairly good history degree but the system's all plugged up with old teachers, there won't be any jobs, not any time soon, so he signed up for night classes in engineering at the local university. He takes a holiday once a year in the Caribbean with his wife, who is a legal steno with the biggest law firm in the city. They're lucky, their two young children can stay with his mother during the day while they earn the money. He's only ever been in trouble once in his life. When he was in second year at McGill a guy came on to him in the washroom of a pub. He and a friend pounded the guy to a pulp, a reflex action more or less, and subsequently spent the night in jail. But the guy didn't lay any charges. John believed then and he believes now that everyone should get a shot at whatever it is they want, as long as his own path stays clear. His wife's still got most of what she brought to the marriage; she works out and doesn't eat very much. One of the joys of his marriage is seeing heads turn when he meets her at a restaurant downtown for lunch, or when they line up for a movie. He loves taking her south.

He has a subscription to the magazine.

JOHN's response: That's not one of my favourite pictures by any means. The bull and the chains, that stuff will pass. The bull is all souped up on something anyway, guaranteed. Probably more likely to fall over than take off. It's almost an aesthetic thing with me, you know? Women are beautiful and nothing's going to change that. And who would want to change it? My wife doesn't mind, but then she's confident, which she's got every right to be. Nobody's gettin' hurt here.

FATHER MICHAEL is a semi-retired priest who has worked and taught for most of his life in a small Manitoba town. He had been a gentle, shy boy but he gradually learned, with training, how to reach out to people. He looks harmless and has not once in his life raised his voice in anger. He has thanked God for the small successes he has had with the members of his parish. What he's learned is that people, men and women both, usually just need to talk one-to-one with someone who will let them talk.

He found the photograph taped to the wall inside the confessional. He imagines it was put there by the boys. Not one boy, but a group of boys, one who had the idea, one who taped the picture up, and a few others huddled outside the confessional in the spirit of encouragement. He realizes he'll never know who exactly was involved, and this bothers him. It's the secrecy.

FATHER MICHAEL's response: I've been a teacher you should remember. Very little surprises me. I suppose that's why the boys placed the picture there, because they feel the need to surprise me, or to shock me. Children want reaction. They need it sometimes. Defiance is just another word for growing up, isn't it? Perhaps I should make a big show of anger. I've given it some thought. Of course, they have defiled their church and one day down the road some other priest in some other church will hear their confessions. I have prayed for them, they know enough to expect that. As for the woman, as for the photographer and the magazine from which the picture was ripped, that's a bigger prayer, isn't it?

DON is forty. He works as a broker at the Vancouver stock exchange and wears twelve-hundred-dollar suits. He drives a yellow Mercedes 450 SL. He takes his three children regularly and has taught them to sail and to play tennis. He is seeing two women, the social worker regularly and formally and the university student intermittently. He plans to marry again, the social worker, in about two years. He is adept at making people feel good about themselves. His philosophy is that everyone has something going for them. His assistant, whom he hired himself, works out of her house because she's partially paralyzed and uses a wheelchair. She's a crack typist and one of the most precise thinkers he has ever come across. Before his divorce he suffered, briefly, from a kind of impotence, which he regarded as simply an outward manifestation.

He picks up a men's magazine only occasionally, usually because things are a little too tame in his own bed.

DON's response: It's been going on from the beginning of time. And fifty years from now, count on it, we'll be back to modesty, prudery. That's where we're headed. Some day soon the mere glimpse of a woman's ankle will drive a man mad again. It's like lapels. Narrow, wide, narrow, wide. But right now this threshold is the one we're on and this is where the thrills are. Take it or leave it. Nobody's forcing anything. The bruises are make-up, the bull is doped, and the farmer will have something to remember, likely bought his wife a dishwasher with the money the bull earned. The young lady knows what she's doin' and a lot of people would probably thank her for it. Maybe you've noticed that hookers are fighting in court for the right to hook. And I read in *Harper's* about a prostitute, a free woman in a free country, who will let men spit on her for a quick twenty bucks. What's it to you and me? There are bigger problems. Read the paper, any paper.

DR. FRANCIS ELMERS is an obstetrician. He is fifty. His wife is a dentist. They have a daughter who is just finishing her first degree; she's a sensible, serious kid. She's got an academic record which will allow her to choose from almost anything the world has to offer. For twelve years Dr. Elmers has rented an acre of land at the sunny nonindustrial edge of the city. Each year he plants a garden there and he retreats to this garden when he is overtired. He is extremely good looking and even at fifty is still dealing with the inevitable infatuation of some of his undeniably beautiful pregnant patients. In spite of his long-term professional attendance at open birth canals and at the surgical incisions made necessary by C-Sections in spite of his familiarity with blood and pain and complications, Dr. Elmers regards birth and all things which make it possible, particularly the bodies of women, as miracles. He has never lost either a mother or a baby in childbirth, although there have been failures, deformities, physiological aberrations that would shock outsiders. In these cases, almost always, nature takes its course.

He has consistently refused to sit on the abortion panel at the hospital where he has privileges and, although his daughter occasionally accuses him of hiding his head in the sand, he remains firm. He believes in full state support for young women who must raise their babies alone, and he believes this support should be collected by the state from the young men whose sperm seems recently to be so profuse. He has defended these opinions at many dinner parties. When he was in medical school, his girlfriend, a nursing student, became pregnant.

They couldn't marry and she gave the child up. In moments of weakness he catches himself wishing she'd kept the child because he sees now, in retrospect, that he would have been able to contribute financially without much strain. But usually he takes the attitude, what's done is done. Another of his secrets is that he has been a long-time collector of erotica, not actual photographs or books but carefully selected images to hold in his mind.

Dr. Elmers saw the magazine at counter level in a narrow little convenience store near the hospital, where he'd stopped to buy breath mints. He lifted it out and leafed through it quickly. When he saw the bull he asked to see the store manager. He told the manager to get this material behind the counter or he'd have himself a visit he wouldn't forget.

DR. ELMERS's response: Beneath contempt. It is not worth serious discussion.

RAYMOND is twenty-two. He has almost finished serving a reduced four years of an eight-year sentence in Kingston for break and enter with a weapon. He's tall, he's got a good muscular build from working out and his face, which is almost a ringer for River Phoenix's face, is still softly scored with the scars of adolescent acne. He grew up in the East, in poverty, in a family where nurturing meant there was nearly enough to eat. He doesn't even think his father's name but he writes to his mother and to his youngest sister every week, she's had a baby whose middle name is Raymond. Prison has given him the chance to get his grade twelve and he's also taken some mechanics training; they say he's a natural. He feels pretty sure there'll be a job waiting when he gets out, which will be soon. He knows it was a major error getting involved with the guys who organized the thing. He was just young and stupid. He was only taking a few months to knock around before he signed on with the mine. He's no criminal. They gave him the gun and he held it all right, but to this day he doesn't know how to fire one. Although he'd never share that. He keeps his nose firmly out of other people's business and his mouth shut, a skill which he figures is a whole hell of a lot more valuable than knowing how to use a gun. There are lots of knives and drugs around, but not as many as people think, it's not compulsory. He has been approached a few times in the showers, and once, early on, he didn't get away, but there was just that once, before he started to work out. New guys will sometimes select him and try to buddy him up, looking for protection from the unknown. But it's not available, at least not from him.

A friend threw the magazine at him in the prison library.

RAYMOND's response: I'll tell you how it makes me feel. I'd be delighted. You want all the slimy details? You have time? I'll tell you what they got here to offer the average man is sweet nothin'. There is nothing soft or easy in this place. So we *respond* to pictures. You want to hear about the alternatives? You think we're the guys who hurt women? You're wrong. The last thing I wanna do to a woman when I'm outta here is hurt her. There'll be a woman all right, maybe several dozen, but they won't be gettin' hurt and they sure as hell won't look like this one. A bull, for God's sake. What's that, a stockbroker's wet dream?

RYAN is five years old, and of course he doesn't quite qualify as a man. But he'll get there, faster than he thinks. He lives in an apartment in a decent neighbourhood with his single mother, who receives fair and adequate maintenance payments from his father, who doesn't believe in marriage. She has explained their circumstances to Ryan, using language he can understand, trying to protect his feelings about his usually absent father. She is a thoughtful and careful woman, in every respect. She didn't automatically enrol Ryan in the closest nursery school but first interviewed several teachers in several different schools around the city. Ryan eats every vegetable but cauliflower and brussels sprouts, he can read a bit, he runs hard and flat out whenever he gets the chance, and he considers himself an accomplished kid. His mother has instilled that confidence in him because she considers it his birthright. She wants them to have their own separate house, away from the stink of the apartment halls and the dingy laundry room and the passing of strangers on the stairs. She inherited twenty thousand dollars for a down payment from her father, who died of an aneurysm in the spring, and she thinks she could manage a small house if she works full-time when Ryan goes to school.

She had to leave Ryan with a neighbour friend when she went downtown for a job interview. Ryan and Cody, the neighbour's boy, found the magazine in a bathroom drawer. Cody took it out of the drawer but it slipped from his hands and dropped to the tile floor, fell open to our photograph. They stared down at the woman and the bull for a few seconds, they saw the pubic hair and the bruises and the thick tongue hanging from the bull's mouth, and then Cody jumped on the page, jumped up and down on it and laughed, as little boys do. Neither of them had seen a naked woman before, they couldn't even remember their mothers' breasts, although they'd both been nursed as infants. Caught, they said they were just looking for some more toilet paper.

RYAN's response: When his mother asks him about the magazine, in her careful, thoughtful way, he says nothing, except that he's sorry and that he will never go looking through other people's things again, which is a lie for which he might be excused. She tells him it's okay and the only really important thing he has to remember is that magazines like that have nothing to do with them. He listens, he hears what she says, but he knows he's discovered something, something no one would have told him about if he hadn't found it for himself. Like the snakes that crawl around in the woodpile at the farm, for the shade, his uncle said. Or the slugs he found under the tomato leaves in his other grandmother's garden, trailing what she called mucus but he calls something else. Or the dark round thing that grows under his mother's arm, a mole, she said, it's only an ordinary mole, which he saw by mistake the very last time he charged into her room without knocking.

Bonnie Burnard was the fiction editor for Grain *magazine from 1982–1986. She won the Commonwealth Best First Book Award for her short fiction collection* Women of Influence *and a Giller Prize nomination for* Casino & Other Stories. *In 1999 Burnard won the Giller Prize for her novel* A Good House.

About the Editor

Birk Sproxton writes, edits and teaches in Red Deer, Alberta. Born in Flin Flon, Manitoba, he spent much time chasing hockey pucks before heading off to Winnipeg to earn a string of university degrees. His writing appears in many literary magazines and anthologies. He is the author of a short fiction collection, The Hockey Fan Came Riding, *a long-poem,* Headframe:, *and a novel,* The Red-Headed Woman with the Black Black Heart, *awarded a prize for historical fiction by the Manitoba Historical Society. His work as an editor includes a volume of essays,* Trace: Prairie Writers on Writing *and a special edition of* Prairie Fire *on "Winnipeg in Fiction." In 1999 he launched an online magazine,* Taking Place: Canadian Prairie Writing. *He regularly reviews books for* Border Crossings. *Currently he is writing a book of literary nonfiction in which he continues his ongoing battle against gravity.*